Number 21

R. B. CARIAD

Disclaimer

This book contains strong language and scenes that may offend sensitive readers. This is not a sweet romance book. It contains graphic sex and dubious consent scenes, scenes of a disturbing and violent nature and references to mental health issues.

Recommended for readers over 18 years of age.

This book is the work of fiction. Characters, names, places, and incidents are products of the author's imagination or used factiously. Any resemblance to actual events, location, buildings, events, institutions, or persons living or dead is purely coincidental.

Published by R. B. Cariad

Copyright © 2022 R. B. Cariad

To request permissions, contact rbcariadauthor@gmail.com
Website: http://rbcariad.com
First paperback edition

Edited by Katherine Tate
Cover art by Virtualrover

Join R. B. Cariad and The Cascade of Lies by signing up for her newsletter and giveaways at

Home – R.B. CARIAD author (rbcariadauthor.com)

Follow RB

facebook.com/R.B.Cariad

instagram.com/rbcariadauthor

tiktok.com/@rbcariadauthor

CHAPTER ONE
Mom's Dead!

PORTLAND OREGON

"Shit!" Ari gasped, checking the cold, dead woman's wrist for a pulse. She had found Nancy's body just moments before when she came to check on her. Nancy was lying there, pupils fixed and dilated, with a needle hanging out of her arm and using Junior's old school tie as a tourniquet. It appeared to be a heroin overdose and just as Nancy was making progress!

Tears fled down Ari's tanned cheeks. "How the hell am I supposed to tell Junior that his mother's dead? This will destroy him." His mom had been a volatile creature, despite being clean of late. Ari struggled to understand how Nancy had put the child through so much, and now she had done the unthinkable and committed suicide.

"I mean, why have him in the first place?" Ari said to herself.

Ari had paid for multiple trips to rehab to help Nancy get clean—for Junior's sake—and although she had safeguarded him from finding his mother's corpse, she now had the terrible task of breaking his heart all over again by telling him that his mother was dead.

Ari, now grateful she had made Junior wait in the car, as she always did, ensuring it was safe for him to enter his mom's apartment, trembled as she retrieved her phone from her back pocket and contacted the local sheriff. After she reported the incident, the sheriff instructed her to wait by her car until he arrived.

Ari headed outside, inhaling a deep breath, grateful for the fresh air that flooded her lungs and the warmth of the sun shining down on her face. But it provided her with no comfort, as she headed to the car, wiping her tears on her sleeve so Junior didn't see her cry. She opened the car door where a gangly teenage boy with bright blond hair was sitting with his headphones stuck inside his ears and bopping his head to something upbeat until she caught his attention with her gaunt expression. There he was, looking up at her, smiling innocently as she was about to break his heart.

"Junior, we need to talk, buddy," she said.

His smile vanished. "What's up, Ari? Oh, man! Has she gone off the rails again? It was inevitable I suppose," he said exasperated and running his hand through his hair. "I don't want to live like this anymore; I'm going to ask her to just sign the papers. I want to live with you and Remy forever. You're more of a mom to me than she'll ever be, Ari. Please don't make me come back here anymore."

Ari knelt on the floor next to the car before taking a deep breath. Her tear-filled eyes, glistening in the low hanging son as she took his hand in hers. "Junior, I'm not sure how to tell you this, but..."

"Is she..."

Ari nodded. "I'm so sorry son!" she said as tears streamed down her face.

"Wh... what do you mean? We just came to check on her. She was getting clean."

"I'm so sorry," Ari cried.

"Well, where is she? I need to see her," he cried as he tried to get out of the car.

Ari took hold of him. Struggling, he was like a slippery snake as

2

she held him tight to stop him from getting out of the car and entering the building, he had once called home.

"Junior, no, buddy! It's best you don't see her like that! I'm sorry, son, but she's gone!"

"No, she was getting better!" he cried as Ari continued to hold him close while he sobbed! Despite all of what that woman had done to this sweet, sweet boy, she was his mom and, deep down, he loved her.

Ari held him close, allowing him to cry out as he gripped her. He was so strong for such a gangly teen; he was crushing the air out of her lungs. Ari raked in slow and controlled breaths rather than ask anything of him right now. He needed to grieve, so she put her head against the side of the car and blinked away the tears that fell from her eyes as she waited for the sheriff to arrive.

By the time the sheriff arrived with his deputy, Ari was feeling much older than she had before entering Nancy's apartment just a short while ago. The sheriff approached the car offering his condolences, before asking Ari to accompany him back into the apartment building.

"Will you be okay here, while I talk to the sheriff, bud?" she asked Junior.

He nodded as he began wiping his nose with the back of his hand.

"I'll look after him, Ari," the deputy said as he sat on the ground next to the car to talk to Junior.

Ari walked to the apartment building with the sheriff, where he jotted down a statement and called the coroner. He headed inside alone, before shortly returning, shaking his head in disarray.

"Looks like an overdose," the sheriff said as he came out of the apartment where Ari was standing. "Had she been acting differently lately?"

Ari shook her head. "No. She finished her rehab, and she has been home since Christmas."

Still shaken up by what she had seen, she wrapped her arms

around herself, rubbing her scrawny triceps for comfort before continuing. "She has been really trying with Junior, too. I'm so sorry, I should have checked on her last night, but we were so busy with Junior's game and Remy's coding project...."

The sheriff took her hand. "Ari, she has been dead at least twenty-four hours, if not longer. When did you see her last?"

"The night before last, she asked to come over for dinner!"

"Was that normal for her to ask to come over?" the sheriff asked. "I mean, it's not that long ago you had to beg her to come and see Junior."

"Uh, no, actually this was a first."

"Did she say or do anything unusual? It's clear she was using again?"

"No, nothing. She said that she had beaten the drugs. She helped me with dinner, thanked me again for helping her with Junior and even expressed to Junior how proud she was of him. We had a coffee and then I dropped her home," Ari explained. Then, "Oh Shit! Shit. Oh, God."

"What is it Ari?" the sheriff asked, eyes now wide and eager.

"She told me that Junior was lucky to have a mom like me in his life. Shit! Do you reckon she planned to...?"

"Ari, I believe she was a very troubled woman, and you did your best to help her," the sheriff interrupted. "I mean, I hate to speak ill of the dead and all that, but you gave her far more than she deserved for what she put that boy through!" Putting a hand on her shoulder to comfort her, he continued, "Is there anyone you'd like me to call? What about the boy's dad?"

Ari, who was still numb from seeing Nancy's dead body, replied, "No, there is no one else besides Adam and Joe. Junior hasn't seen his dad since he was little and there's no name on his birth certificate."

"I'll have to inform social services."

"Hang on a minute! I have temporary custody. They're not taking him away. He's been with me for two years! My son has been through enough!"

The sheriff looked at her sympathetically. "Ari, what you have done with that lad is a miracle. I mean, he has gone from street rat to a model young man in such a short time with you. Social services will see that, I'm sure. Understand, there are procedures to follow, okay?"

Ari nodded as her brow furrowed into an angry frown, as her hands gripped her hips. "Okay."

"Now let's get you both home," he advised, acknowledging her frustration, before continuing. "No child should ever see their mom taken away in a body bag," shaking his head in disbelief as he led Ari back to the car.

As they returned to the car, the sun was going down and the night sky was drawing in, leaving subtle blue and pink colors all around them. An exhausted Ari tried to shake the images of Nancy's corpse from her mind as the sheriff instructed Deputy Daniels to drive Ari and Junior home in her car. She was in no fit state to drive this evening. The sheriff would follow closely behind, allowing him to pick up the deputy once they reached their destination.

While they sat in the back of the car, Ari held Junior close. Her heart was breaking for him. A quick trip to check in on Nancy had turned out to be their worst nightmare. Ari shuddered in fear of what was going to happen to Junior, the boy she loved as her son and the best friend of her biological son, Remy. They were inseparable, apart from when Remy went to visit his dad and Junior visited his half-brother, Joe, on the weekends. Joe, who lived with his dad, Adam, lived just a few blocks from Nancy's. Lost in the sea of traffic outside her window, she sat in silence for several minutes.

But a sudden thought had her asking, "Do I tell Adam or leave it to the sheriff? Joe is only six, and he's her son too. He's never met her, as Adam took custody of Joe as soon as he was born, but Adam needs to be informed."

"The sheriff will handle it, Ari. Let's just get you home, okay?"

"Right, yeah. But he will tell him?" she pressed. "See, Junior spends every weekend with him to bond with Joe, and I don't want him getting mad at us for not telling him," she explained as she continued to gaze into the night sky.

Joe was Junior's brother, and he adored him. Adam, a builder and one of Nancy's former clients, knew that Nancy was an unfit mother and demanded custody of his child upon the baby's birth. Nancy never wanted contact with Joe. However, Adam had always allowed Junior to be a part of Joe's life. He didn't beat Junior like Nancy's other clients often did, and Junior was always grateful to him for that. Nancy had wanted Adam to take Junior too, as he was an inconvenience to her job as a hooker. Her other clients hadn't taken too well to a young boy interrupting their paid time with Nancy, and Junior's scars proved that.

Stroking Junior's head, Ari feared the worst, now having to face the possibility of losing her son to social services.

"I'm sorry, Junior. Everything is such a mess right now and just as you are making so much progress," she said.

She had welcomed the boy into her life just a couple of years before. Fixed him up, clothed him. Held him through the night terrors that haunted him because of his horrific ordeal. And he was now at the peril of social services and risked being placed in the system, if Ari did not meet the criteria required to adopt him. Ari and Remy had spent a lot of time getting Junior to open up about what had happened to him. When she took him in on the day of the fight, she saw a scraggly haired, malnourished, and scarred boy with brown teeth and ripped jeans. Two years on and that scraggly haired boy had turned into a handsome thirteen-year-old, no longer had bad teeth or ripped clothes and had filled out to be a healthy looking teen thanks to Ari's loving care. She had held him through his night terrors when he woke up screaming about being beaten because he tried to intervene when drunk clients got violent with Nancy. This kid had been through so much, and Ari and Remy had helped him heal these past two years. There was no way Ari was letting him go anywhere without a fight. He was her son, and Ari was prepared to fight to the death to keep him!

"Ari," Junior said, glancing up at her as he lay with his head in her lap, "what's going to happen to me now? They only granted you temporary custody, so will they take me away?"

"Hey! I will never let that happen to you. You have been my son for two years; you have a home and a family, and I will let no one take that away from you, okay?"

"Promise!"

"Promise, buddy! Now Listen, social services are going to pop by at some point, but I don't want you to worry! We'll straighten this out, okay?" Ari said.

"Okay! I love you Ari."

"I love you too, son!"

CHAPTER TWO
Who is Mack Senior?

After the funeral, Ari, Remy, and Junior went to Nancy's apartment and sorted through her things. Junior needed to decide what items of his mother's he wanted to keep. Ari was a little nervous as she went through Nancy's property. She dreaded what she might find and, of course, she made sure that she and the boys wore gloves. The apartment was rancid, and she didn't want her boys picking up any germs. Ari made sure that she took care of Nancy's more personal items, such as underwear and her array of dirty sex toys that she'd kept in a shoebox under the bed. Fearing the boys might discover something dangerous or disgusting, she left Junior and Remy to go through some old boxes that she had found in Nancy's closet.

"Hey, who's Mack Senior?" Remy asked, handing Junior a brown shoebox with the name written on it in black marker pen.

"My dad. My mom moved us away when I was seven, and I never saw him again," Junior said.

"Why? Was he a bad guy?"

"No, not that I recall. My dad was my best friend in the entire world, and he used to take me to the park and carry me on his shoulders. He was part of an MC, and he was so cool; he even had a cut with a scary dog on the patch."

"He rode a motorcycle?"

"Yeah! I used to always climb up onto it and pretend that I was racing down the highway."

"Whoa! That's so cool! So why did your mom take you away?"

Ari, who had caught the conversation as she entered the room, sat next to Junior, waiting for his response.

"I have no idea. She just put me and Mr. Jelly Legs in the car one day and never explained why. She always got mad if I asked, so I stopped asking," Junior said, face strained and looking confused.

"Mr. Jelly Legs?" Remy asked in amusement.

"Yeah, it was a character from my favorite TV show, and I had the teddy until my mom took it off me shortly after we left my dad because she hated me singing the show's theme song. She said it reminded her of when my dad used to sing it to me, so she took it away," Junior said with a look of disappointment on his face.

"Sorry dude, I didn't mean to—"

"It's fine. I had forgotten about my dad until today, to be honest, and it's obvious he's not a good dad, because he hasn't bothered to find me."

"Junior, for all you know, he's out there searching for you now," Ari said as she rummaged through the brown box. Inside there were a load of old photos, what looked like a hand-drawn portrait of Junior as a toddler, and a dirty old looking stuffed octopus. It had what looked like a little boy's body with an octopus's legs.

"Junior, this isn't Mr. Jelly Legs by any chance, is it?" Ari asked, pulling the filthy plush toy out of the box suppressing a shudder of revulsion.

"Oh, my God! It is Mr. Jelly Legs!" he shrieked, snatching it from Ari and embracing it.

"There are also photos in this box son, come see."

Junior sat beside Ari, rummaging through the photographs.

"I remember this one! My dad had just bought a new bike and he let me sit on it," he said, pointing at himself in the picture sat on a

9

motorbike with a man with blue eyes, messy blond hair and a big beard sat behind him.

Junior's eyes lit up, sparkling like stars in the night sky. Ari had never seen him this excited before. Staring at the image then back at Junior, she said, "You are the image of your father, and he's quite handsome with his striking blue eyes and prominent cheekbones." Ari liked a man with character, and the man sat in the photograph with Junior had plenty of it.

"Yeah, well, if he ever turns up, I'll put in a good word for you," he said, smiling.

"Thank you!" Ari laughed. "Junior, you've never mentioned your dad. Why is that?"

"I forgot about him, just like he forgot about me, I guess."

She studied Junior, a lump forming in her throat at the image of him feeling like he was a forgotten boy.

"Darling boy, he may not have forgotten about you. He may have been trying to find you. We don't know why your mother ran away with you."

Junior, looking down at the photograph, shrugged. "Maybe."

"Look, there're more pictures," Remy said, changing the subject and rifling through the box. He picked out another one with Junior on a man's shoulders who had curly blond hair. He looked shorter than Junior's dad as he stood next to him in the picture, along with a tall, pot-bellied man with big teeth and brown hair and a big, muscular man with short black hair and a long goatee beard. Junior took the photograph, and, on the back, it read 'Irish Mack Senior, Noah, Zander, and Jimmy at the park in 2011.'

"Ah, I always dream of this, where they toss me up in the air at the park and catch me. The big guy is my Uncle Zander, the blond man is my uncle Noah, and the tall guy with the enormous belly is Uncle Jimmy. They always teased my dad about his Irish accent, which is funny, as I recall, Uncle Zander having a funny accent too."

"Your dad is Irish?" Ari asked, trying to show him how enthusiastic she was about learning about his family.

"Yeah, I'm sure of it! Everything is still fuzzy, though, and to be honest, I always believed it was a dream that I made up in my head to pretend that I had a dad!" he said as a small chuckle escaped his lips.

"What else is in there?" he asked, taking the box from Remy and retrieving a picture of himself as a baby.

"This is me! My dad drew this. I remember he was always drawing. He let me use his special pencils to draw too. It's why I love drawing so much now."

Ari stared at Junior as he reminisced about his past. She imagined the cogs in his head working overtime as he attempted to regain his forgotten memories.

Staring at him, she asked, "Junior, do you know where these pictures were taken?"

"Nah, I remember very little about my life before."

"What about your dad? Do you remember where he is from or his second name or anything else about him?"

"All I remember is that he was Irish, and he was in a motorcycle club with a dog on the patch, not that I remember the logo or anything. It's hard to know what's real and what's dreams sometimes."

Ari didn't want to push it anymore, so she left it there. "Come on boys, we're done here. Let's get Mr. Jelly Legs home and in the wash. I'll even order pizza."

That night Junior started having terrible night terrors again, but this time they weren't just about Nancy's horrible clients, they were about his dad too. He dreamt about the trip to the park with his dad and uncles Jimmy, Noah, and Zander. However, instead of tossing him up in the air and catching him or even playing with him, they left him there for Nancy's clients to attack him. He woke up screaming and soaked in sweat, clutching a now clean Mr. Jelly Legs.

Ari and Remy ran to his side and Ari held him, soothing him until he got back to sleep. She never imagined soothing her thirteen-year-old following night terrors, but in the last two years, she had spent countless times soothing this terrified teenager from his awful past. She believed the night terrors were behind them. They had stopped a few months before Nancy had passed. He didn't get them after she died, and it was since finding the box of his father's things they had started again.

****

A few months had passed when Remy brought the mail into where Ari and Junior were eating breakfast.

"It's here! It's here!" he shouted as he ran into the room and tossed Ari the brown envelope.

Smiling, Ari opened it up to reveal the official certification that Junior was now hers and handed it to Junior. "It's official! You are now my son by law!"

Junior looked at the document and saw his name in bold black capital letters 'JUNIOR BARRINGTON' and burst into tears!

"That's it? I'm yours?"

"You have always been mine, my boy," Ari said as she wiped away his tears.

Junior hugged her tight. "Thank you, Ari, I love you so much! Am I allowed to call you Mom now?" he asked.

"Of course," Ari said, choking back tears of her own.

Remy, smiling from ear to ear, chipped in, "Yeah and I'm your brother, your big brother and just you remember that."

"You're like five months older than me!"

"Yeah, so that means I'm your older brother," Remy teased.

Junior sat at the dining table with a huge grin on his face, staring at the paperwork, but a few minutes later, Ari noticed something else was bothering him as he continued studying the paper, but had gone pale and developed a guilty expression.

"That face. It's about your dad, isn't it, bud?" she asked.

"How did you guess?"

"Because I can see how it's plagued you since we found that old box of his."

"Are you mad?"

"No, Junior," she said, smiling. "You have every right to be curious about him."

Junior sat forward in his chair. He looked at Ari and released a deep and long sigh.

"I just want answers! I need to know if he's alive or if he has ever come looking for me, or if he even cares about me. I just want to find him, so I can understand once and for all why we had to leave him behind when my mom took me away that night," he explained, dropping his head in his hands. "I need an answer to why he was asleep on the sofa when me and my mom left so late at night."

"Junior..." Ari said removing his hands from his face to take hold of them.

"I'm sorry Ari. I mean Mom. I don't want to upset you. You've given me everything and now I feel like I'm punching you in the gut for wanting answers about my dad."

"It's understandable that you want answers Junior. Any normal person would,"

"But I don't want to make you mad or upset because you're the best mom in the world. I just hate not knowing. I would do anything to find out what happened that night,"

"Well, you better come into my study. I have something to show you," she said quietly.

Junior's curious mind led him to follow her down the hall and into her study to be confronted with a big pin board with pins pointing to specific areas on a map of America. Remy followed too and Ari studied the boys and explained.

"Take a look." Ari said, gesturing to the pin board. "We're here on the West Coast and I have found twenty-one motorcycle clubs across the states with dogs on their patches. We don't have a lot to go on, but we have a starting point. Do you recognize any of the patches?" Ari asked.

Junior shook his head as he studied the pin board. "You did all of this for me?"

"Well, it's going to tear you apart until we put it to bed, so yes, I am! And I'm not saying that I will find anything, so you better not get your hopes up. But Junior, you are my son, and I will do anything to make you happy."

A single tear ran down Junior's pale cheek. "Thank you, thank you," he cried as he embraced her.

"Listen, I have rules though," she said. "If we are going to do this, we do this my way. I won't have this tearing up our lives, okay? So, school comes first, and I check these places out by myself when you are staying with Adam and Joe, agreed?"

He gave a tentative nod.

"Oh, and if things get too much, we all agree to step away from this, okay?" she said.

"Agreed, Mom!"

"Great! Well, I better get some supplies and create a plan of action!" she said as she took his hand and skipped back to the kitchen.

CHAPTER THREE
Mack, B & Everything In Between

Mack was a handsome Irishman, standing in all six-foot, two inches in stature. As a thirty-nine-year-old wide chested man from County Cork, Ireland, he was proud of his heritage and strong Celtic virtues. Mack digested the world in all its colors, taking the good when it was good and the bad, when it was bad, just like anybody else did. See, Mack had a past and while there were a lot of things that he made peace with, there was one thing that haunted him and that was the day his drug addict girlfriend skipped town with their seven-year-old son. No warning, just gone! Vanished without a trace and never to be found, even six years later.

It was a Friday night when Nancy had executed her vile plan. Mack had just finished another criminal act for his MC President, which Mack didn't mind. In his world it was dog eat dog. He did what he needed to do to survive in what was, to him, a tough but wonderful world. Mack did anything to earn a living; even if that meant jacking cars, selling guns, or handling stolen goods. Earning enough to provide for his family and buy his son a treat every now and again was all that mattered to him.

Mack had enjoyed the simple life when he was younger. As a member of the Red Pitbull MC, he was always eager to please his ruthless Prez. No job was too big or too small for him. He just got on and did it and if it earned him brownie points with the Prez, even better. However, his priorities changed a few years in, after he had a one-night stand with a local girl who liked to entertain the bikers at his MC. Having been one of the few men not to have had his way with the girl, a lot of the older heads had egged him on to take his turn with the town bike. Nancy, who had a drug addiction, was often off her face on blow by the time she reached the bar and did anything requested of her for another hit.

One night, under the influence of a lot of drugs and alcohol and combined with peer pressure, he offered the young woman to come back to his room at the club. She turned up to see Mack every week from that night on, and he kept her level every time she needed a fix. Nancy didn't have anywhere else to be. She didn't have anyone, no family or friends. She was a loner, and Mack sympathized with her having no one to call family and enjoyed the sexual payment that he received for keeping her high. It was a transaction: drugs for sex, and both parties enjoyed the arrangement, becoming inseparable in the weeks that followed.

Six weeks into their little arrangement, their lives were turned upside down as Mack took Nancy to hospital after she collapsed in the bar one night. Placing Nancy on a gurney, Mack believed she had taken too much blow, until the doctor revealed she was pregnant with his baby. A frantic Nancy demanded an abortion on the spot. However, Mack didn't believe in that kind of thing, so he offered to pay her all his savings of $7500 to keep clean and sober until the baby was born. Mack was happy to raise the baby alone if she carried it to term, and she needed not have anything to do with them after it was born. Nancy, tempted by the money, agreed, explaining it was too big of a deal to decline.

During the pregnancy, Mack kept her close, moving her into his apartment. He was like a lion protecting his lioness and as Nancy became clean, their relationship blossomed. Mack had hoped that Nancy's maternal instincts would kick in following the birth of

Junior, and they did. Even after the baby was born, they began to make a go of it. That was, until Junior was five. Truth be told, Nancy had no interest in being a mother. This was all nothing but another transaction to her, and a month after Junior's fifth birthday, she was back on the drugs and alcohol. It was as if she was living a lie, trying to be a mother, and Mack tried so hard to help her see what a wonderful child Junior was, but she wasn't interested.

When Junior turned seven, Nancy, after a long seven years of trying to play happy family, demanded the money that Mack had promised her at the start of her pregnancy. Mack being Mack, he gave it to her, believing she needed to let off steam and would return to being a mom again. Nancy had other ideas, as she dwindled the money away on drugs, disappearing for days and sometimes weeks at a time, leaving Junior in tears when Mack arrived home from work, scared that his mother had left him. Then, after she had blown all her money from Mack; Nancy demanded more, suggesting that Junior was worth at least twice what Mack had paid for him, and it was then that Mack understood she required professional help. After trying for so long, he learned Nancy didn't want help. She enjoyed her life and did not want the life that he wanted with their son. It was then Mack told her he was filing for sole custody of Junior and asked her to leave by the end of the week. However, he never expected the events that followed.

One Friday night, after a heated discussion regarding custody, Nancy committed the cruelest act: To teach Mack a lesson for not giving her more money, she disappeared in the cold dead of night, intending to take Junior away from him for good. After waiting for him to fall asleep, she bundled Junior into her car and left without a trace. When Mack woke the next morning feeling groggy, he realized Nancy must have slipped something into his drink that night, because he passed out right after settling Junior down after one bottle of beer. He searched everywhere for them that day, fearing the worst. He called the police, something a biker like him should never do. But it was all to no avail. They were gone. Junior was gone!

The night after Nancy and Junior's disappearance, and just when Mack believed it was impossible for things to get any worse, he found himself entangled with the Prez's wife. She had entered his room at the club, explaining that she was checking in on him, but clearly, she had intended to seduce him. She'd always been way too forward with him and on that night, despite being married to the most dangerous man in town, she attempted to take advantage of the broken soul by straddling him, a man who needed a shoulder to cry on that night and did so as the Prez came into his room. The acts that followed saw Mack barely escaping with his life after his close friends aided him in secret, in fear of their best friend losing his life to the sadistic Prez. Mack then headed out of town to save his own life. He had lost his family, his home, and his job, all in one day, and was now on the run from a murderous MC President. Weeks went by as Mack rode from town to town, looking for work and a place to stay. All he had was the clothes on his back, his rickety old bike, and he slept in store doorways when the frosty nights hit.

"Why didn't I buy a fecking car? I'd be warm now," he cursed.

It was two weeks before Christmas, when Mack found himself in the little town of Uskiville, Oregon, a quaint little place with plenty of forested areas, where Mack pitched up a tent to live a life of solitude. Mack had been through so much by then, he had shut himself off from the world. He'd lost everything, even having to sell his beloved motorcycle so he could purchase food, a fishing rod, and a tent for shelter. Mack loved that bike so much. He had saved for months to earn all the money doing extra jobs for his Prez, to scrape enough together to buy his bike from his best friend, Zander.

Zander was one of the club members who had helped Mack escape in secret on that frightful evening, and Mack owed him and his other friend Noah a debt that he vowed to pay back one day. The Prez would have killed him had he'd not dove out of the window to escape the man's wrath. But escaping that night wasn't any comfort to Mack when he had lost everything, anyway. It was a living nightmare for the hurt and traumatized Irishman, who now lived in a tent in a forest, a stone's throw away from a big woodland cabin, complete with a jacuzzi and swimming pool. It disgusted him that he had to sneak into the garden once a week, when the owner was out, just to bathe and wash his clothes in the outdoor swimming pool. The pool was always left full of bubbles, and the pool boy always wore a flabbergasted expression the next day, tearing his hair out as he hunted for the cause of this phenomenon, cursing as he cleaned the filthy pool water. Mack hated he had to wash in a pool, but despite being homeless, he still had standards of cleanliness.

One chilly evening, Mack was bathing in the swimming pool again, when the owner arrived home earlier than expected to find a naked Mack in her pool, washing himself and his socks. Mack turned to discover her staring at him, with a confused expression on her face. She was the most beautiful woman he had ever seen. B was like an angel as the sun shone down on her, magnifying her piercing blue eyes and long blond hair that draped over her shoulders. But just when Mack believed the woman would scream, she threw him a towel and offered him the use of a hot shower and a cup of tea in her broad Welsh accent.

Sweet Jesus! She's a stunner! But what's a gorgeous Dragon doing so far from home?

She was a Celt just like him. In all his time in the states, Mack had met one other Celt; his best friend Zander. Yet amazingly, standing there, looking down at his freezing, naked body was a beautiful Welsh dragon!

Mack, dropping his socks in shock as he covered his manhood, accepted her offer with a nod of his head. He stepped out of the pool, wrapped the towel around his freezing, stiff body and followed her, noticing the natural curves of her body, as she directed him to one of her many spare rooms. As he followed her into the Jack and Jill bathroom, he stared at her toned backside as she retrieved and handed him another clean towel, a dressing gown, and some spare clothes that she told him a friend had left behind the week before. It had been so long since he had been with a woman; he fixated on her beautiful features, making him want her. Desperate for her touch, her kiss, and her body entwined with his. In that moment, Mack convinced himself he had found his person.

Mack hurried through his shower, despite the luxurious feeling of the hot water soothing his skin. Convinced the local law enforcement was waiting for him, he got dressed and rushed into the kitchen, hoping he might explain to his hostess that he wasn't a threat to her. Maybe then she might let him stay in the warmth for a little while. It was freezing in the forest when the sun went down, and Mack had nightmares and panic attacks as the frosty nights drew in.

Mack entered the kitchen, and to his surprise he found no officer lying in wait, only the woman, who had just finished placing his dirty laundry into her washing machine. Mack tucked his hands into his pockets, trying to stop himself from shaking, trying to calm himself and stop his heart from escaping out of his mouth. He had never experienced fear until recent times, when he found being alone too much to handle, forcing himself into the depths of despair as he shook and cried out at night.

He stared at her, unable to speak, fearing the worst as the different, conceivable outcomes raced through his mind. *Is she stalling me until the cops arrive? Well, at least I'll be warmer in the slammer.*

"Don't be frightened, lovely boy. I won't hurt you," she interrupted, placing a mug of tea in front of him. "I'm B. What's your name, my lovely?"

"Er, thanks. I'm Mack," he said, clenching his fists to stop them shaking so he could pick up his tea.

"So, what's a handsome Irish fella doing on the other side of the pond and bathing in my pool? My pool boy has been doing his nut in because of you," she said, smiling, as she bent over the countertop, with her V-neck T-shirt revealing her cleavage as she cradled her mug of tea.

"Er, sorry, I, er, I'm homeless. I've got a tent pitched up in the woods behind your cabin. Please don't call the cops," he asked.

B's lips curled into a grin, dimples highlighting her gorgeous face.

"Do I need to call the cops? Are you dangerous, Mackie boy?"

"No, I'm just a sad and desperate ex-con with nothing left to live for."

B's eyes grew wide as Mack dropped his head in despair. "Everyone has something to live for, Mackie boy, even when they are at their worst."

"Nah, not me! Maybe God is punishing me for being a nasty son of a bitch for so long. I got nothing to live for now."

"I don't believe that lovely boy! Here, have a Welsh cake and go sit by the fire. I'm going to grab a bottle of the good stuff and you are going to offload your troubles." She handed him a plate full of what looked like a cross between a cake and a biscuit.

"The good stuff?" he asked as he tucked into the Welsh cakes. He was starving. He had spent his last few dollars on bread the day before, which he'd polished off later that night.

"Welsh whisky, lovely boy! It slips down your throat like warm silk and there's nothing like it," she explained, ushering him to the sofa by the fire in her enormous, open plan woodland cabin. She collected a bottle of amber liquid from a bar cart and set it on the coffee table in front of him. "Here, you sit by the fire and pour us a glass while I fetch us some real food. You look like you've not eaten in forever, and I've just made my favorite for tea; pulled pork loaded fries."

Mack's mouth watered as he poured the whisky into their glasses. He hadn't had a meal in weeks. Knocking back the shot and pouring another, he waited for B to return as the smoky aromas engulfed his palate. Waiting made him feel anxious, and his hand shook again as fear flooded his soul once more.

Why isn't she scared of me? I'm a down and out, a thug,

B interrupted his thoughts, sitting on the sofa as Mack tossed his second whisky back in one.

It was like liquid heaven as it warmed the back of his throat. "That's beautiful stuff. How did you find it over here?" he asked.

"I order a case from Wales every month. I'm not a fan of the crap in the shops around here," she said, giving him a wink and handing over an enormous plate of pulled pork and loaded fries.

"Thank you, I appreciate this, B. I haven't had a meal in a while."

"Well, eat up and if you want to stay out of the cold, explain what you're about. If you convince me you're not a psychopath, I'll do my best to help a fellow Celt. See, us Celts need to stick together across the pond, Mackie boy. There aren't many of us about. But, if you turn out to be a psychopath, my fiery dragon eyes will appear, and I will snap you like a twig," she said in a calm but take no bullshit attitude.

Mack, now choking on his fries, gazed at her in disbelief. This gorgeous, leggy blonde was as fiery as they came. He had heard that the Welsh were fearless and passionate people, but this woman was a real dragon, and he loved that she had the guts to tell him straight.

"Geez, you are a fiery dragon, aren't you?" he choked. "I'm not a psychopath, although I'm an ex-con. I was a dangerous one-percenter in an MC in Sunnyville, California, but now I'm nothing, a nobody,"

As B listened to his story and plied him with food and copious amount of the good stuff, Mack opened up about his entire ordeal, pouring his heart out to a woman he had just met. B listened until he cracked. He sat sobbing in her arms like a baby, with relief washing over him, as he unburdened himself. Just having her warm arms around him and having her stroke his head, made him feel safe for the first time in a long time. His troubles had been crushing him since the night he left Sunnyville, leaving him feeling isolated, until now. Tonight was the night his life changed forever. The night he fell in love, the night he was no longer scared, alone and homeless, the night he found his best friend, his savior and, as he called her, his Dragon.

CHAPTER FOUR

Junior, Remy, & Ari

WHERE IT ALL BEGAN

Ari had stumbled across Junior after her son Remy had gotten himself into a fight at school. Remy was a quiet boy, so it surprised Ari to get a call from the school office that day explaining that Remy had been fighting. Ari refused to believe it when the call came into her office. Remy went to the same school where she taught at and had never been in trouble in his life. He was a studious boy with a brilliant future ahead of him, so Ari was more than shocked to discover that her son had been fighting at school.

"Are you sure that you're talking about my son, Remy Barrington?" she asked the school receptionist.

"Ari! I am surprised as you are! But it's true, I'm afraid. He is in with Pickersgill now and it's becoming quite heated in there. So, you'd better get up here!" she advised.

"Something's very wrong!" she said, beside herself as she raced to the principal's office.

As Ari stood at the principal's door, echoes of angry voices erupted into the corridor, her son, Remy, arguing with the principal.

"You are discriminating against him with your white-collar attitude," Remy shouted in anger.

"How dare you! Your mother will hear of this!" the principal said.

Ari knocked on the door and entered, confused by her son's rage. Inside, Remy was sitting next to a scruffy-looking boy who appeared gaunt and dirty. His shoes were falling off his feet, his T-shirt was full of holes as he sat rocking in his seat.

"Ms. Barrington, come on in. You will want to hear about this!" the principal said in a cocky manner, as if Remy was in for it now.

"What's going on?" Ari asked.

"Your son thinks fighting is acceptable in my school and has had the audacity to accuse me of discriminating against another student."

Ari glanced at Remy and noted the venom in his eyes! He glared at her as if to say, *don't you dare believe him over me!*

So, Ari turned to the principal and said, "Well, I'm sure Remy and his friend will explain. My son has never been in a fight in his life."

"I believe your son is being led astray by Mr. Marks here!" The principal gestured toward the scruffy-looking boy who fidgeted in his seat.

"What do you mean?" Ari asked as she noticed his black eye, split lip and grazes up his arm.

"Your son needs to stop being encouraged by this delinquent and concentrate on his own education before he lands himself in some serious hot water! Now I will allow you to discipline him at home on this occasion, if he agrees to stay away from Mr. Marks here!" he stated, looking at Ari as if to say he was doing her a favor.

Ari regarded the now trembling boy, and then studied Remy, who was hanging onto his seat, gripping the arms of the chair tight, displaying his anger. Something was off for her son to act like this, and she wasn't about to discipline him until she found out what the hell was going on.

"With all due respect, Mr. Pickersgill, I'm going to have to listen to the entire story before I discipline my son. Now, Remy, what's happened here today?" she asked. "And son, I want no stone left unturned."

He released a sigh as relief flashed across his face before he explained. "Well, I was in the cafeteria when I saw Kyle and his gang pushing Junior around for no reason! Junior was just trying to get his lunch when the boys whacked the tray out of his hand, sending it flying." He explained. "Then when Junior tried to pick his tray up, Kyle punched him to the ground with three of his douchebag friends joining in. They all started hitting him, Mom. It was four on one, and I wasn't going to sit there and let them beat him up. So, I went to pull them off him and that's when they started hitting me!"

"It's okay, son, just take a deep breath," she advised.

Ari glowered at Pickersgill as Remy inhaled deeply through his nose and then blew out to expel the carbon dioxide.

Remy continued, "I just tried to defend myself and stop them from hurting Junior, and that's when the principal came in and dragged Junior and me away!"

"Is this true?" Ari asked Junior, looking at him for confirmation.

"Y-yes ma'am! I've never met your son before today and he was the only one in the whole canteen to help me. Those boys bully me every day because I don't have the right clothes or the latest phone and nobody has ever battered an eye until today. Today Remy helped me, and I don't want to get him into trouble ma'am, I promise. I just want to come to school and learn without getting beat up all the time."

"This is horse pucky!" the principal blurted, sneering at the young man as if he was ready to throttle him.

"With all due respect, Mr. Pickersgill, I know my son, and if he said this happened, then I believe him," Ari snapped, putting the principal back in his place. "Good grief, he's never been in a fight in his life, and I'm well aware of Kyle and the boys from my English class. I've warned him many times for bullying! So, I suggest we look at the security footage to see what happened." She stared at the principal feeling like a lioness protecting her cubs.

"Ms. Barrington, I saw these boys with my own eyes. They are the culprits here."

"Then you won't mind showing me the footage!" she insisted as she walked out of the principal's office and into the security office next door, leaving the principal staring in utter shock, before regaining his composure and rushing after her.

Upon reaching the security office, Ari asked Ray, the school's security officer, to show her the footage from the cafeteria. As they replayed the footage, the principal gulped, almost choking on his Adam's apple as it revealed Remy was telling the truth.

"You liar!" Ari snapped, turning to him with her eyes narrowed as she foamed at the mouth in temper.

"Now Ms. Barrington, I must have been mistaken, that's all," the principal said, loosening his tie.

"Or did you see what you wanted to see? Seriously, what in God's name went through your head? Oh, let's pin it on the scruffy kid. He must be the one in the wrong. It's never the privileged children. Mommy and Daddy donate too much money to the school, so it's best to pin it on the less fortunate. Is that it?" she asked.

"How dare you!"

"No! How dare you!" she screamed. "You accuse my son and that poor boy, when it's clear as day that you stood by and allowed this to happen, then continued to lie, when Kyle and his gang were the ones causing trouble."

Ari tore strips off the principal.

"You, sir, have forgotten your moral fiber and selected these two boys as an easy target. After all, stereotyping is far easier than dealing with the truth. All those privileged parents being dragged into the principal's office, threatening to stop those not-so-chari- table checks. No, it's far easier for you to pin it all on the scruffy kid and your head of the English Department's son."

The principal stood looking like a wide-mouthed frog as Ari lost herself in a fit of rage. "Look what those monsters did to that poor boy because his face doesn't fit. And because his mommy and daddy don't donate to the school like Kyle's parents, you throw him under the bus! Shame on you! This footage needs to go to the police if you're not going to do anything. They have assaulted that boy on school property and not for the first time, by the looks of it. I bet if we were to pull all the footage, then you will discover multiple assaults on this boy."

The principal, now white as a sheet and sweating profusely through his shirt, tried to rectify the situation. "Now, now, the police don't need to be involved in this! Let's sort this in school, shall we?"

"Why? Scared it will reveal you as the snake that you are? You were quite happy for me to discipline my son for defending a helpless boy who you called a delinquent a minute ago," she said, throwing his words back in his face.

The principal snapped back, "Well, he is! Just look at him. He turns up for school looking like a vagrant. I have had many complaints about his hygiene, and his mother looked like she was high as a kite the last time I called her in. Mr. Marks does not belong in Purebody High. He won't add up to anything. He will be like his mother, a junkie!"

"With that discriminative attitude, he certainly will," she spat. "How dare you! You have a duty to safeguard all the children in this school, not just the wealthy ones! This is outrageous!" she bellowed, trembling with fury. "How is this boy supposed to get anywhere in life when nobody will help him?"

Ari saw red. She had been such a quiet and smiley woman until today, and now she was furious. Furious at the boys who had struck the young boy and her son. Furious at the principal for turning a blind eye and treating the boy with such contempt and furious at society for allowing this behavior to become acceptable.

She went on, "Here's an idea. Rather than look the other way when this boy is getting bullied and treating him like a criminal, do your job and discipline the students who have been beating him on the daily. And if you're incapable of doing that, then you will have to find yourself another head of the English Department and face the police and my lawyers when I take this case all the way. I am sure the Department of Education will be interested in learning how one of its principals discriminates against low-income families."

The principal slumped against the wall looking as deflated as a lead balloon. "Okay, you're right! I'm sorry! I will make this right!"

"Good! Then I want those boys expelled!" Ari demanded.

"But Ms. Barrington, do you have any idea how much money Kyle's parents donate to the school each year?"

Ari's eyes widened again. "I don't care how deep their parents' pockets are. Deal with it or I promise you I will unleash my wrath! Oh, and make sure you apologize and explain to that poor boy how sorry you are for letting him down and how you are going to make it up to him for being so wrong."

The principal agreed. He couldn't afford to lose his reputation or his head of the English Department over this, no matter how much money Kyle's parents donated to the school.

After their exchange of words, which left the security officer looking stunned, they headed back to the office where Junior and Remy waited.

"Hey, listen! My mom will fix this, I promise!" Remy explained, trying to reassure Junior, who was shaking like a leaf.

"No offense! But the principal hates me because I don't come from a rich family. He's going to do anything to kick me out of this school and he won't be satisfied until he does."

"Well, where I come from, the only time you look down on someone is when you are helping them up!" Remy said to Junior with a smile. "My mother taught me that, and I promise you, she will fix this!"

"You're lucky. My mother has never taught me anything or done anything for me. That's why I'm in this mess!" Junior said.

"What about your dad? Does he teach you stuff?"

And just as Junior was just about to answer, both the principal and Ari, came back into the office. Junior gulped as he awaited his fate.

"Uh boys, I owe you an apology," said the principal as he adjusted his collar, staring at the stunned expression on their faces.

Shifting himself in his seat, the principal continued, "After reviewing the security footage, I see that have made a terrible mistake, and it's clear that Remy was defending you from those bullies, Mr. Marks. There will be a thorough investigation into your treatment here at Purebody High. Oh, and I will deal with all individuals involved in your misfortune, to the fullest extent of the school rules." He continued as he regarded Ari, who was looking at him, ensuring that he didn't skip a beat.

"Oh, and please accept my sincerest apologies for the mistake boys, and to you, Mr. Marks, for calling you a delinquent, which you are not, of course. I will also call your mother to explain the incident too," he said as he fumbled with his USB stick.

"No, no, that's okay, thank you! My mother works nights, and I don't want to disturb her. I just want to go back to class. Please, sir?" Junior asked.

"Very well," he agreed. "But I will send a letter home and you have your mother call me when she wakes, please?"

"Yes, sir."

"And to you, Remy." The principal turned. "I apologize! You showed great courage standing up to those boys and I am sorry I didn't believe you."

"Thank you, sir. May I go back to class now too? We are missing a chemistry test!" Remy informed him.

"Oh, yes, of course! And tell Mr. Stevens that it's my fault that you boys are late. Now off you go." he said, pointing to the door.

Once outside the office, Junior punched the sky in victory.

"Oh, my God! Thanks, man. Your mom was amazing in there! Nobody has ever stood up for me before. They just judge me because I come from nothing. Will you thank her for me?" he asked as he beamed, feeling high on adrenaline, and elated that for the first time in his life, someone had stood up for him.

"Yeah. no problem! And my mom, she gets it. She had a rough upbringing too!"

"For real?" Junior asked.

"Yeah! She got knocked around a lot by her dad and she left home as soon as she was old enough. Every time she got beat down, she got back up until she got where she wanted to be!"

"Wow! That's what I want to do! Prove everyone wrong, but it's hard when you have no one there for you," Junior sighed.

"What about your parents?"

Junior cast his eyes at the ground, kicking the air. "My mom always gets wasted and is never there for me, and I haven't seen my dad since I was seven."

"That sucks, dude! But you're wrong. You have people who care, people like me and my mom. We'll help you!"

Junior angled his head and studied Remy. He wasn't used to anyone being nice to him or offering him help. The single person who was nice to him was one of his mom's clients from her hooker business. "Remy, I appreciate everything that you and your mom just did for me, but we've just met and I'm bad news. Bad things are just meant to happen to me and if you try to help me, bad things will happen to you too. I-I'm cursed."

"I don't believe that! I believe things happen for a reason. I think we were meant to meet today." Remy said.

Junior blinked. "You're willing to help a complete stranger?"

Remy smiled at Junior. "You're not a stranger anymore, dude. I just got into a fight for you. So, that makes you, my friend."

"I've never had a friend my age," Junior said, feeling a little embarrassed.

Remy put his arm around him, smiling and making him feel a little uneasy.

"Well, you do now!"

CHAPTER FIVE
The Pin Board

It excited Ari to start her search for Junior's father. To Ari, this was a quest to find answers, much like the characters in her school textbooks who searched for answers of their own. Ari, now ready to search for Mack, began by searching for all motorcycle clubs with dogs on their patch. At first, finding a few, she wrote the name and location of each one on a sticky tab. After a while, Ari discovered she was drifting off to sleep.

"This is like searching for a needle in a haystack," she mumbled. She turned to social media to discover a few more. She even messaged them but received no replies. Feeling like she was trudging through quicksand, she wrote all the names and addresses of the clubs that she found on sticky tabs.

When Ari had originally started her search, she had no idea where Junior was from or where he had grown up, other than his disjointed memories and after eight solid hours of searching, she found sixty-three MCs across the country that had dog patches. She had to narrow it down somehow, so she searched clubs with locations in colder regions, narrowing it down to twenty-one clubs. Ari then printed out a map of the country and placed it onto the pin board before placing each address on the map by attaching each one to a white pin. Upon finishing it, she stood back to admire her handiwork, feeling extremely pleased with herself. With each destination pinned safely on the map, she had a plan, and she was eager to get started!

After revealing the pin board to her boys earlier on in the week, Ari waited patiently for Friday to arrive, and the boys went to their respective family members for the weekend, leaving Ari free for the to investigate each MC. For her first jaunt, Ari selected the clubs farthest away from where she lived, to get them out of the way and because they were in the coldest climate regions. After placing her suitcase in the trunk of her car, she set off on her four-hour journey to Centrum City, Washington. Ari had never been to Centrum City before; she was really excited about taking a trip there. It was like an adventure to her. The only adventures she had embarked on before now happened when she became lost in fantasies while reading books. Ari loved the drive up. The scenery was simply breathtaking, so much so that she stopped for coffee at a rest stop to take in the natural beauty that surrounded her.

By the time she got to Centrum, it was late evening, with Ari deciding to check into her hotel before heading out to the club. The dark night sky didn't bother her much as she left the hotel that night, although it was much colder than her hometown. Ari zipped up her fleece lined hoodie and headed for the first MC, which was a fifteen-minute drive from the hotel.

Pulling into the parking lot of the bright and vibrant looking club, Ari inhaled through her nose, taking a deep breath before heading inside. She gave herself a quick pep talk.

I have to do this for Junior's sake.

As she made her way inside, she received some strange looks. Determined not to be deterred, she waltzed through the crowds of burly bikers in her pretty little floral skirt. Glancing around the bar, it was now clear that she stood out like a sore thumb in her classy hippie chick outfit and three-hundred-dollar boots, a gift from a wealthy ex-boyfriend a few years ago.

When she finally reached the bar, she came face to face with a bartender, looking at her with a glint of humor in his eyes.

"Beer or whisky?" he asked.

"Oh, hi, I'm Ari, pleased to meet you!" she said, holding out her hand to shake his and ignoring his offer of a drink.

The bartender laughed, shaking her hand.

Ari continued, "I was wondering if you have an Irishman by the name of Mack here, please? He may be a member of your club."

"No Irish Mack here. But the guys at the pool table might help you as they have been here longer than anyone," he said, gesturing to a handful of men playing pool adjacent to the bar.

Ari glanced over her shoulder to see a gang of menacing looking bikers. "Thank you," she said, gulping the beer-soaked air before strolling the bar again and attracting more attention to herself.

She approached the man closest to her, posing the same question regarding Mack.

"Fuck off, princess!" he snarled.

Ari stopped in her tracks, taken back a little by his tone. "Please answer my question," she squeaked.

"Look, lady, no one has heard of or seen this Irish guy of yours, so go back home and play house like a good little girl! Little girls shouldn't be out this late at night!" said a creepy-looking man with greasy black hair that hung around his face like curtains and a mouth absent of teeth.

Ari, feeling a little despondent now, turned on her heels to leave as another man took her by the waist, pinning her against the wall, laughing.

"But if you need a new man, doll face, I'm more than happy to oblige" he said to her as he leaned in attempting to kiss her, reeking of cheap whisky, and sweat.

"No, no thank you!" she said politely as she pushed him off her with all her strength and barely budging him enough to slip out from his grasp. It was then that she panicked and headed for the door. As Ari made haste for the exit, the crowded bar slurred at her, teasing her about her appearance and making suggestive remarks. So, she quickened her pace and headed outside, gasping for air as her chest rose and fell at rapid speed. Panicking, she stumbled to her car, feeling nauseous. She climbed in the front seat and locked the door, taking a moment to calm herself.

"Just breathe, Ari," she told herself over and over until she stopped trembling, and just as she did, a loud crashing sound rattled off the rear-view window. Beer washed down the glass as the plastic cup bounced onto the ground. Lowering her driver side window and peering out, she witnessed a middle-aged woman wearing a very short red dress pick up another cup of beer, as if she was ready to launch a second cup. Ari rolled her eyes at the woman, closed her window again and sped off. She'd had enough for one evening!

Later that night, Ari struggled to sleep. Still high and full of adrenaline as it coursed through her body like a sea of molten lava burning everything in its path. The closest she'd come to experiencing anything like this was when she cheered on Junior at soccer on a Friday night, where she'd get excited every time he'd kick a ball. But this was different. This was exhilarating. This was the first club Ari had checked off her list, which made her one step closer to finding Mack. Ari chalked up ruling out her first club in her quest to find Mack as a success tonight and told herself she would try again tomorrow.

The next morning, Ari had a spring in her step and a smile on her face despite how rude the men in the first MC were to her the night before. Ari, now more determined than ever, told herself today was going to be better as she headed a farther fifty minutes north to the second club on her list: Bulldog Reaper MC. It was here, an extremely naïve Ari came to learn that the world wasn't full of fluffy bunnies and beautiful green meadows and, in fact, sometimes the world was very cruel and not beautiful at all.

CHAPTER SIX
Best Friends

B became Mack's best friend. She was his guiding light, his shooting star, and his voice of reason. They had been inseparable since the day B took him in off the streets six years earlier. They worked together, had lunch together, grappled together, drank together, and even parented B's boys together when B needed support. They did this along with the support of their closest friend, Frankie who Mack insisted on bringing into the fold a year after they met. Frankie, an ex-marine had come to the retreat searching for work and after one conversation with him, Mack knew he'd be an asset to his workforce and the MC he was building. Mack showed him the ropes but found himself learning from Frankie too. Frankie brought a lot of wisdom to Uskiville, teaching Mack how to become a better fighter and educating him on things he learned in the marines. Despite being Mack's employee and Vice President in the newly formed MC, he taught Mack how to see the forest through the trees, rather than continue with his bull in a china shop approach to life. Mack was a volatile person, a melting pot of emotion, and it was as if Frankie was trying to teach him to be calmer and more worldly, to be a better man. Mack had but one criticism of Frankie and that was his problem with authority. As a former high-ranking officer, Frankie wasn't scared to tell people when he thought they were wrong or out of line, even vocally expressing his concerns to B and Mack, if he thought it was warranted. Initially Mack didn't appreciate this as he was the bigshot in Uskiville; he was his boss and MC president after all. So, a mutual agreement was made where Frankie could express his concerns if they were regarding B's safety or if he believed his Prez was incompetent thus affecting his ability to lead the Gray Wolves MC. Mack warned him that he could never question him in any other capacity, and he needed to respect his role in Uskiville. B however, recognized Frankie's qualities, despite not being keen on him initially. B thought Frankie was too regimental for her following his time in the marines, but she knew he was struggling somehow. She couldn't put her finger on why and he never opened up about it. Nevertheless, she trusted Mack with her life and reluctantly agreed to employ Frankie as head of her security. Over the years, Frankie and B became close after he asked to grapple with her a few months after working on the retreat. B was so impressed by his grappling skills, she decided to invest more time getting to know the man who kept her safe and asked him to join her and her family for dinner. Mack was thrilled with this as he respected his MC brother, and it was clear from the get-go that Frankie was no threat to his relationship with B. B and Frankie had a different kind of relationship and with Frankie being a good few year her senior, he adopted a big brother attitude towards her. B welcomed this, especially after he helped her when she was having trouble with her ex-husband over custody of her boys. He was always threatening her with a custody battle if he didn't get his way and after seeing B so down one night, Frankie took it upon himself to talk to the guy, making it clear his behavior wouldn't be tolerated. B didn't ever ask for help but with Frankie, she welcomed it knowing she had somebody other than a hot-headed Mack in her corner. Welcoming him into her home and her private life, Frankie then guarded her and the boys with his life. Mack also took comfort knowing B would never date another man as he had fallen in love with her; in fact, he worshipped her. The only problem was that B didn't love him in the same way. Mack had fallen in love with her from the moment he saw her, but B loved him more like a brother. She looked after him like she would a sibling. She just didn't see him as anything else. She didn't look at any man like that. Not since before her divorce seven years earlier. B had been married for almost twenty years to her sons' dad until she came home from work early one day to find him in bed with a young woman. Discovering they had been having an affair for months, B demanded he leave. Her husband begged her to let him stay, and she was about to give him a second chance until she found out the young woman was pregnant with his baby. This devastated B. She had begged her husband for ten years for another child, only for it to fall on deaf ears, crushing B's soul, leaving her feeling empty. B put her feelings aside and stayed true to her marriage, despite wanting another child, and he repaid her by cheating. B instantly divorced him and sold the family home, and the day she called time on her marriage was the day B broke, just as Mack had the day Nancy had taken his son away. She no longer saw the world in color, simply seeing it as good and bad, black, and white. She didn't date and refused to get close to or trust anyone again. B had locked her heart and soul away, leaving nothing but an empty vessel and a fearless dragon.

Since the divorce, she had put everything into her business, her job as a successful soccer coach, and her children. Mack absolutely loved that about her, perhaps because she was so different from Nancy. One night, after a few too many drinks, Mack drummed up the courage to confess his love for her, hoping to be with her. Only to witness her face crumple as she told him how sorry she was for not feeling the same way about him. Panicking, B suggested they go their separate ways, leaving Mack devastated at the thought! Quickly, he informed her that he respected her feelings. He explained he valued their friendship too much to leave and vowed to never mention his feelings again, rather than losing her. So, the pair agreed to forget the conversation ever happened and move forward with their friendship.

Mack found it hard at first, as his heart continued to beat to her drum. His stomach would flutter with increasing intensity every time she walked into the room. Falling in love with his dragon was hard, and he continued to put her on a pedestal, despite the way she looked at him and the rest of the world. He loved her for all her quirks and crazy. To him, she was his savior, and he loved her more than anything in the world. They had a unique bond, like it tethered them to one another, and they would do anything for each other. They were a formidable team as they searched for Junior together over the years, and there was nothing or no one capable of breaking their unbreakable bond. Few had tried and failed, but together they were unstoppable.

Mack and B spent all their time together, and they often loved to escape to Gen Lake City, Montana, for a booze and sex-filled weekend. Once a month, they stayed at the Sultry Slalom Hotel to release their frustrations from a hard month of busting their asses. They didn't sleep with each other, of course, much to the dislike of Mack who wanted nothing more than to be inside B, as opposed to a seedy waitress or woman at a bar. But he respected her decision not to be with him, and that it was final.

B had been going to the Sultry Slalom Hotel long before she had met Mack. It was owned by her friend, whom B had bailed out after he'd hit money trouble when he first opened. So, B naturally had a two-bedroom, penthouse suite for her troubles. The hotel was a classy, discreet, and a very up-market venue where high end businesspeople relaxed and indulged in all things a little less vanilla. All guests had to sign a non-disclosure form, and there was strictly no photography allowed as it wasn't unnatural for clientele such as the mayor or chief of police to be getting up close and personal with women, unbeknown to their wives.

The Sultry Slalom was the only place that B could dabble freely with her male counterparts, without having her face over the local papers. See, B was a local celebrity as a successful high school soccer coach. She was high profile and had taken her team to at least half a dozen state championship victories over the years. Coaching soccer and being a female coach in a man's world like soccer, was no simple task, and what made B good at her job was that she was affable and intuitive. She was quick-witted and had a rare talent of making people bend to her will, turning them into putty in her hands. This wasn't because of her good looks, but because she was so down to earth, she also didn't judge anyone by class, especially as she had come from nothing herself. Mack was her business partner, and he helped her run her other business and home, the Uskiville Woodland Biker Retreat. But the biggest reason for keeping everything discreet was that B was also a mother, and she didn't want her teenage boys to find out that she hooked up with random high-end businessmen once a month to relieve some tension from her busy lifestyle as a mom, businesswoman and coach.

It was a lovely and warm sunny evening when Mack and B set off on their usual trip to Gen Lake City. It had been so crazy this past month with the business that the two best friends needed some release. Mack sensed B needed it, as she had become a little more grouchy than usual and beat the crap out of him when they grappled. This was an enormous sign that B had to get laid.

As B drove them through the beautiful country lanes, heading for the freeway that day, Mack wrestled with his thoughts. Running his fingers through his beard, he became lost in translation as the thought of B, his precious dragon, never wanting to settle down, was unnerving to him. Sex would be on tap if she had someone, and it troubled Mack that B didn't want that. To Mack, she was perfect, beautiful inside and out, and not understanding why she had cut herself off from love plagued his thoughts and dreams. Mack sensed it was the divorce that hurt B previously. He wasn't privy to the details of it as B didn't discuss it, leaving him to believe that it may be the reason behind her incapability of loving anyone other than her children. B discussed nothing that involved feelings, and whenever he sensed something was wrong, he tried to make her feel better. He had originally tried to talk to her, as he wanted her to confide in him, but B just shut him down with a joke, calling him a sissy boy, telling him that if he wanted a better BFF, then to talk to Frankie, their other best friend. But tonight, Mack wanted answers and as B sang along to her favorite love song on the radio, he just blurted it out.

"Tell me something, Dragon," he said, using his pet name for her.

"How is it you love all things romantic, like listening to these mushy songs and you make us sit through all those movies where the girl always gets the guy, yet here we are heading to the Sultry Slalom for a weekend of shameless sex with strangers?"

"You said you loved shameless sex," she joked, trying to deflect from what he was really asking her.

"Oh, I do! Yes! But that's me. You clearly are an old romantic, so why don't you ever indulge yourself?"

"Who are you calling old you cheeky..."

"You know what I fecking mean, Dragon. Stop changing the subject and answer the question."

B huffed, shook her head and looked at him, "Okay, fine! I'm a fan, so what?"

"So, why are we not going to a nice little bar in Uskiville, setting you up with someone to create your happily ever after with?" Mack asked.

"What? Are you okay or what? Did you bump your head, or did I choke you for a little longer than usual when we grappled today? I mean, where the fuck is this coming from?"

"I'm just saying that I'd like to see you happy and settled down with someone," he said, hoping that someone, would be him one day.

B looked at him while also trying to keep her eye on the road.

"Mackie, I am happy. Now what's got into you? If you don't want to go, I'll take you home. It's no trouble."

"No, are you kidding? I want to get laid tonight. I want to bury my face in some strange and sexy woman's boobs. No way! I'm coming."

"Okay, then why are you banging on about all of this sissy shit? I don't like it."

"I just don't want my best friend to grow old alone. That's all."

B let out a wry smile. "I won't, I have you. Unless you are the one that wants to settle down?"

He looked at her, unsure of what to say next. "Umm, well, er. I do eventually, but not yet. I'm not done sowing my oats."

"Sowing your oats! For fuck's sake, Mackie boy. Sometimes you sound like an eighty-two-year-old woman. Who the fuck says, 'sowing your oats' these days?"

Mack chuckled. "I fecking do!"

"Well, you definitely won't settle down using phrases like that!" B teased.

"For your information, Dragon, a woman has not turned me down, ever!"

"Oh, really?" she said, staring at him with amusement.

"Oh, you had to bring that up, didn't you?" he joked. "Oh, okay Dragon, you are and will always be the one who turned me down. God, the one time I get all messed up in the head and say stupid shit and you'll never let me live it down." He cussed, while inside he was trying not to let his heart break anymore.

B laughed. "I didn't bring it up, you did!"

"Fine, whatever! Let's just change the subject, shall we?"

"Fine by me," she said. After a few seconds, she opened her mouth again. "Mackie, if you wanted to settle down, I'm happy for you. I don't want you to keep coming away with me if you don't want to."

Mack looked at her. "And who's gone soft now?"

"Fine, fuck you. I try to be nice, and you throw it back at me," she snapped with ill humor.

"Dragon, I'm happy and I'm always going to be happy in Uskiville with you. So, why don't we just hurry the fuck up and get to the hotel? This built-up tension is making us both crazy."

B and Mack were just about to leave for the hotel room when

Mack demanded they go over the rules of engagement. Just as he did every time they came here.

"Right, Dragon, let me hear it."

B rolled her eyes like a fed-up teenager. "No guys bigger than you," she huffed.

"Look, I'm aware of your skillset. You could destroy every man and woman in here, but we have to be careful. That's why we made these rules," Mack said.

B nodded. "Okay, now you?"

"No bunny boilers and no giving out our address so that crazy women turn up and frighten the boys again."

B, now grinning like a Cheshire cat, stared at him. "Promise me, Mackie. You have a tendency to pick complete psychos, and we don't need that negativity in our lives."

"Feck off!" he joked

"Okay, well I'll just find a big guy to throw me around the room if you don't."

"Dragon, you may rule the roost. Hell, you may even kick my ass, but I promise you if you pick up a big guy tonight, then I will murder him and throw you around the room. And I promise you, you won't like it."

"Uh, leave black and sinister Mack in the hotel room, please? You're ruining my sex vibe."

They both laughed at each other; However, they understood the importance of keeping their family safe.

"Right, we have the rules down, so let's get out of here, shall we?" Mack said, ushering her out the door.

They headed down to the basement of the hotel's nightclub where B bought a round of drinks. Giving Mack her most devious grin, she asked him: "Say the words and let me go?"

Mack met her gaze then pressed his forehead to hers and said what she needed to hear.

"Best friends never quit!" he said before planting a kiss on her cheek.

"Right back at you," she said and headed off to the dancefloor.

Mack never understood what she meant when she asked him to say those words. It was as if he had to remind her that he would never quit on her, never leave her while she went to find herself a companion for the night.

He fixated on her as she waltzed onto the dancefloor without a care in the world, flowing to the beat of the music. B was not vain; she didn't love herself. She just knew she was free to mingle here without judgment, and within seconds; she had a flock of men wanting to bask in her beauty. Still fixated on her, undressing her with his eyes, Mack gazed upon her as she waited for her perfect mate to come along. Mack's gaze turned into a glare when she found her plaything for the night. Peering over to him, she indicated she was off to the Hotel, not to make him aware of her exit, but to inform him of her alone time in the penthouse with her fancy man. Mack tipped his glass to her, giving her a nod of acknowledgement, and B lured the man to her suite. It drove Mack mad, as he tried to shake the image of another man with his precious dragon and he knew that if he ever confessed his love to her again, she would relieve him of his duties as her best friend, business partner and maybe his life. B had rules. She liked nothing that made her feel uncomfortable and Mack being in love with her, violated them.

Feeling discontent with the whole situation, Mack approached the nearest woman to him, taking her by the arm. He never even looked at her when he whispered into her ear.

"Hey honey, how about you let me take you upstairs and make you scream with pleasure?"

The woman, all too happy to oblige, followed Mack to his hotel room. Mack didn't care about B's private time; he was angry and frustrated as he wanted to be the one inside her, not some random guy, who didn't give a crap about her. He led the woman into the penthouse suite to be met with the pleasurable cries of a man.

"Geez, again? What are you doing to me? You're out of this world!" the stranger's voice cried from the bedroom.

Mack grimaced, grinding his teeth so hard, his jaw hurt, as the woman looked at him for an explanation.

"My best friend," he said through gritted teeth. "Don't worry about them," he said, before taking his mouth to her breasts, making her gasp as he sunk his teeth into her.

"Are you ready for me to bend you over and make you scream?" he growled.

"Yes!" The woman moaned in compliance as Mack lifted her skirt and tore off her underwear. He bent her over the couch before plunging himself inside her. No foreplay, no whispering sweet nothings into her ear. He just penetrated her with all his glory, listening to her scream in pleasure as he relieved himself of the anguish he suffered from not having the woman he loved. As he filled the stranger with his long thrusts, he fantasized about being inside his precious Dragon. Imagining how it felt to make her his, and in his mind, he was no longer taking some stranger in the middle of the penthouse suite sitting room. He was making love to the woman he loved. He was making love to his Dragon.

CHAPTER SEVEN
Two, Three and Four

Bulldog Reaper MC was eerily quiet when Ari pulled into the parking lot. The frost glistened on the cars that hadn't quite thawed by the morning sun. There was a bitter cold chill in the air as Ari stepped out of the car. She could see her breath as she exhaled deeply as she approached the big bar door. The door was heavy, forcing her to utilize the strength from all five feet, four inches of her as she struggled to open it. Placing two hands on the thick cast iron handle, she pulled it open, trying not to cut herself on the small blade like icicles hanging from it.

Ari strolled inside to discover bikers sprawled out on the floor and across the tables, completely passed out. A sea of half-naked women entwined with half-naked men were strung across the sofas. Ari heaved at the disgusting stench invading her nasal cavity, a mixture of body odor, stale perfume, and vomit. She turned for the door, to take a moment to get some air and compose herself, when she was confronted by a skinny middle-aged woman looking worse for wear.

"What the hell are you doing in my man's bar, missy?" the woman spat. "Did he send for another one of those pretty schoolgirl types again? I've had enough of little hussies trying to steal my man. The Prez is mine!" She pushed Ari, sending her hurdling across the bar.

Ari, still trying hard not to retch, which was becoming increasingly difficult given that the woman's body odor was now adding to the musky stench of the disgusting bar, rose to her feet and tried to explain to the woman who she was.

"No, I don't know what you are talking about. Please," Ari pleaded! "I'm looking for someone!"

"Well, not here you're not, missy! Now get the hell out of here!"

"If you could please just stop pushing me for a moment, I could explain!" Ari persevered.

"I don't need your lies! Now get outta here before I rip those pretty little earrings out of your ears! Go on, make tracks!"

Distracted by heavy footsteps approaching them from the bar, Ari's eyes widened at the presence of a beastly biker with greasy, thick, black hair, invading her personal space.

"Well, what do we have here?" he asked with a salacious undertone.

"This little missy is just leaving, Jasper," the woman forcefully exclaimed.

"Is that a fact, Barbara?" he said looking at her in contempt. "I'm the fucking Prez and I want this pretty little ray of sunshine to stay awhile!" he chirped as he undressed Ari with his eyes, making her retch in fear.

Barbara backed away, cowering from the look Jasper gave her as Ari gulped the manky air, as the hairs on the back of her neck stood tall. Staring at her, he licked his dry and shriveled lips as if she was a prime rib, "What's your name, darling?" he asked in a slippery tone, hovering his filthy, dirty hand over Ari's head as if he was going to stroke her hair.

Terror stabbed Ari's heart with fear as she stared into his sadistic eyes. "My name... my name is Ari and I'm looking for an Irishman by the name of Mack. D-do you have someone in your club that goes by that name, please?"

Flashing her a sinister looking smile, Jasper shook his head. "I'm afraid not, no Irish, no Mack, but don't let that stop you from staying a while!"

"Um, thank you, but my children are waiting for me!" Ari said as she slowly backed away from him, afraid to make any sudden movements.

The man's face turned into a huge psychotic grin.

"Wow, we have a real woman here, Barbara. She may be a pint-sized little thing, but at least she can bear children," he said, sneering at the cowering Barbara, who didn't dare reply.

Ari turned to leave in haste now and that's when she felt his slippery, greasy hand take hold of her wrist. Ari tried desperately to pull it away, but despite his slug-like appearances, he was too strong for her.

"Let go of me!" she shouted in fear.

"I said, stay a while!" Jasper demanded, as he licked the side of her face.

Ari screamed, repulsed, as she fought to free herself from his tight grasp, waking up half of the bar in the process. A stir of echoes christened the bar as Ari screamed for help once more, hoping someone might wake up and assist her. Until Jasper back handed her, gliding his old sovereign rings across her cheek, sending her crashing to the ground.

"This ain't the movies, darling! Nobody here is gonna rescue you!" He grinned as Ari scrambled away from him, making her way to the door. Jasper stomped toward her, fisting her hair and lifting her off the ground with one hand, sniggering in satisfaction when Ari screamed in pain as he dragged her around like a rag doll.

"Take your hands off me, please," she begged as the pain of every hair strand being ripped out of her head tortured every fiber of her being.

"No chance, butterfly. You're mine now, and you'll never flutter away now that I have you in my grasp," he teased as he proceeded to drag her toward the door behind the bar.

Ari kicked and screamed, clawing at him with everything she had to break free, earning herself nothing more than a punch to the stomach. She choked, gasping for air as his blow knocked the wind out of her, leaving her fearing she wouldn't take another breath ever again.

Just when Ari thought she was done for, she heard a loud smashing noise and felt his grasp loosen. Trying to drag in oxygen again, Ari gazed up to discover Barbara with a broken optic bottle in her hand and Jasper crashed out on the floor covered in whisky.

"Go!" she shouted. "Go before he wakes up and kills us both and don't ever come back here!"

Ari, dazed and confused, scrambled to her feet. Turning to Barbara, she asked; "What about you?"

Barbara inhaled the putrid air. "This ain't my first rodeo, missy! I've been doing this for years. Now get!" she demanded, as the murmurs stirring behind her became louder.

Ari didn't hesitate and ran for the door. Using the last of her strength, she fled to her car, started the engine, and sped out of the parking lot as quick as she could. Crying hysterically, she drove at high speed, still terrified, trying to put as much distance between her and the Bulldog Reaper MC as she could. Thinking of Barbara, it dawned on Ari how depraved the world was, and how the people she approached were dishonest and sinister. Ari had just wanted a little information, and it hadn't occurred to her that information would come at a price!

Ari arrived home late on Saturday evening; she was exhausted after her two-day ordeal. Her head hurt from where that vile human grabbed at her hair, almost ripping it out! She hadn't foreseen getting attacked. In Ari's world, everything was beautiful, and violence stayed in the movies.

Upon opening her red front door, she dropped her case and

strolled into the kitchen to make a cup of tea. Sitting at her breakfast bar, she inhaled the calming and soft smell of chamomile. A far cry from the repulsive smells that invaded her nasal cavity at the Bulldog Reaper MC this morning. Ari sat in her chair sighing long and hard, before cradling her cup in both hands and shaking her head as she wandered down the hallway and into the study. Heading straight to the pin board, she pulled out the white pin where Number 1 was located and replaced it with a green pin: "One wasn't too bad, I suppose!" she said to herself and put a cross on the sticky tab to indicate her lack of success. "Two, well, he was vile," she said, as she replaced the white with a yellow pin.

Of the twenty-one pins on the board, nineteen remained white. However, she now had one green and one yellow and that was a start! Ari started to rank the color-coded pins in order of how the MCs treated her. Green, non-violent, yellow for violent and red, for downright evil. Yellow was bad enough for her, and Ari now understood her adventure might get worse before it got better. Ari reserved the red pins for incidents far worse than yellow, saved for the unthinkable acts, and Ari hoped that she would never have to use them.

"Two down, nineteen to go! You can't give up now!" she said to herself as she stood staring at the board.

Ari then spent the rest of the day wondering if she'd made a mistake taking on the huge task of finding Mack; it hadn't occurred to her that it might be dangerous. She had no idea that these people could be so evil. However, she remembered how this was affecting Junior and she hated to see him so broken and incomplete. Dead or alive, his father had to be out there somewhere and not knowing where, troubled him. His nightmares had increased tenfold since the discovery of the box at Nancy's, and a small part of Ari wished that they had never found those old photographs or Mr. Jelly Legs, who Junior clenched tightly each night. Ari, now determined not to falter, wanted to make things better for him, so she dragged her tired body back to her laptop, searching for information on Numbers 3 and 4 ahead of next weekend.

The boys arrived home on Sunday around midday with Junior hurdling into the house to find out if his mom had found any new information regarding his father.

"So, how'd it go?" he asked her.

"We struck out on the first two, but don't be disheartened. There are plenty of MCs left to search," she explained.

Ari watched as Junior's inquisitive smile turned into a frown.

"Hey, hey!" she said, putting an arm around his shoulder. "This is just the beginning! You can't expect to find him on the first try!"

Junior dragged his hands down his face in despair.

"Junior, we will find him, but you need to promise me, you won't get your hopes up every week. It's not healthy. We have to follow the breadcrumbs, okay?" she said with sheer enthusiasm and giving him a gentle squeeze.

Junior let out a wry smile. His mom made him feel better whenever he was down and she wasn't a quitter and always remained positive, no matter the odds.

"Okay!" He smiled.

Ari regarded her son, biting her bottom lip. "There's something else I'd like you to be aware of," she said as Junior looked at her, puzzled. "When we find him, your dad I mean, I want you to understand that he might not be the dad you expect!"

Junior looked confused. "What do you mean?"

"What I mean is, we don't know anything about him, and we have to tread carefully, that's all, okay?"

"Do you think he'll be a bad guy?"

"I'm sure that he won't be, but I just don't want you putting him on a pedestal until we get to meet him and get to know him properly. Either way, soon we'll have answers about him, and you'll have peace of mind!" she said, kissing the top of his head.

Junior nodded in compliance; however, Ari could see the look in his troubled eyes, and she hated it. It hurt her knowing that her son was so unfulfilled. She had to find Mack and find him soon!

The following weekend, Ari attempted to fit Numbers 3, 4, and 5 into her weekend search. All three MCs were situated within two hours of one another, and Ari was determined to finish her list as soon as possible. She wanted her life back to normal with her weekly trips to Boulder Street Coffee House, where she would sit and read her latest novel as well as chatting up the barista, who shared her love of books. Ari hoped to put a real smile back on Junior's face. She had missed his devilish smile and hadn't seen him smile since before Nancy had passed away. At the same time, she didn't want the search for Mack affecting Remy, her biological son. He had been so great with the adoption and sharing his house and mother with his best friend, but she didn't want this to damage their relationship. Ari and Remy had always been close. It had always just been the two of them against the world until Junior came into their lives and Ari didn't want their bond to break under the pressures of searching for Mack.

Ari approached the following weekend like a new woman. It was a new start, and she was going to be more prepared! Armed with her fresh attitude, Ari did her best to blend in with the crowd at the bar. She laughed at herself, thinking of how she waltzed around last week. "So naïve," she said. No, this time she adopted a more subtle approach, dressing appropriately and parking her car close to the bar in case a quick getaway was required. Ari also decided that she wouldn't stroll into quiet and eerie looking bars if it didn't look safe and looked for fire escapes just in case, she found herself in trouble again.

Number 3 was surprisingly pleasant. It didn't have the MC vibe, as it was a retirees' club by rights. The kind folk at the bar welcomed Ari and weren't the least bit frightening. Despite their age, they still rode their motorcycle or trikes, and their wives made the most delicious sweet potato pies, ready for their return. Ari even had the pleasure of sampling them, as she chatted to the club members, who were all disappointed that they couldn't help her. Although disappointed at another dead end, Ari was ecstatic to be putting another green pin on her pin board, not yellow or red, green.

Number 4 was very different from Number 3. It had the same aggressive undertones as Number 2, and once again Ari found herself tossed around as the president of the club shouted, "You're a cop!"

"NO! I am just looking for some information!" Ari pleaded

The Prez clearly didn't believe her as he slapped her across the face, splitting her lip in the process. A disorientated Ari, shivering in shock as blood seeped from the side of her mouth, tried to stop the tears falling from her eyes as the Prez rained down his next blow, this time landing a boot to her chest. The hard blow knocked the wind out of her once again, and she struggled for breath. He kicked her again and again, and on his third attempt, she managed to protect her ribs with her arms. She knew that she couldn't take another blow to the chest. Ari had already felt something crack in her ribs, experiencing the searing pain that followed, as he kicked her repeatedly. She then experienced the same searing pain in her wrist after yet another vicious boot. The unbearable pain paralyzing her like snake's venom as Ari lay on the beer-soaked floor trembling, praying it would stop.

"I'm not a cop! Please! I'm looking for my son's father! Just let me go, please?" she cried once more in what she thought was her last attempt to convince him otherwise.

"Well, let's have a look if you're telling the truth, shall we?" He grimaced as he ripped her handbag away from her blood-soaked body. Taking out her purse, he retrieved her driver's license before sifting through her bag for a badge or a gun. When he came up empty, he threw her things at her in anger.

Eyes wide and angry, he peered down at her. "You picked the wrong bar tonight, sweetheart!"

Ari glanced up at him as he turned, shaking his head, and running his hand through his hair. He hadn't expected her to be honest with him.

"Get the hell out of my bar! You shouldn't have come here!" he bellowed awkwardly.

A grateful Ari tried to scramble to her feet, only to find his firm grasp manhandling her out of the door and throwing her to the ground.

"Oh, and I have your license details, so if you go to the police, I'll find you and kill you and everyone you love!" he said calmly and bluntly, before heading back inside and slamming the door behind him.

"A yellow for you, you psychopath," she muttered to herself, thinking how worse things would have to get before she awarded a Prez with a red. She cradled her arm and stumbled slowly to her car with careful movement to minimize the pain. Ari was hurt, and she was quite sure that she had broken at least one bone in her body. With blood-stained lips, she slowly clambered into her car, wincing, and crying with pain! She'd never felt pain like it before. Even child-birth wasn't this bad.

She managed to start the engine with her good hand before searching for the nearest ER or urgent care center on her Sat Nav system. Ari seethed, clenching her teeth together in pain. A trip to the hospital was imperative to Ari as she clutched her ribs, leaving MC Number 4 in her rearview mirror.

At the hospital, the nurse on the desk instantly placed Ari on a gurney and took her to triage, where Ari was treated for multiple fractures in her hand, wrist, and ribs. She was instructed to stay the night by the doctor on call, who advised her very strongly to report the incident to the police. However, this wasn't an option for Ari. Her family would be at risk, and she didn't want that. She just wanted to forget the whole thing. She would have to come back for Number 5 another day, as she just wasn't up for another MC after tonight. Ari realized that she had been lulled into a false sense of hope with Number 3 and here she was hospitalized by Number 4. She didn't know whether she could continue through to Number 21 anymore. This was only Number 4, and she had already sustained multiple fractures and a split lip. What state would she be in by Number 21? Would she even make it? she asked herself as she stared at the ceiling on the hospital ward. Ari was once again exhausted, but this time, she felt utterly broken. How would she be able to explain this to her boys? They would be so worried about her, and Junior would feel terrible, she thought to herself, before closing her eyes and drifting off to sleep.

CHAPTER EIGHT
Number 5

"Argh!" Ari cried as another rib cracked from the blow from a Prez from yet another MC! One and two had been manageable, just slapping or punching her. That was small stuff in comparison, and Number 3 had been lovely. It was a shame that all the MCs couldn't be kind like three, Ari thought. The Prez from Number 4 was horrible and the first to do serious damage to Ari. His skill set ensured Ari took a few weeks off from her search due to the extensive damage he'd caused, all because he thought that she was a cop. But this guy, Number 5, well, he was a vicious son of a bitch! He made Number 4 look like a dream.

The crunching noise, like a potato chip being stomped on, echoed in her ears as agony soared through her fingers in her left hand. The Prez snapping them like a twig as he rained down on her ribs with another three blows. He didn't just slap or kick, he stomped down on her as if he was trying to squash her like a spider. She had been trying to protect her ribs with her hands to stop them from fracturing any further or breaking. But now, between her fingers and her ribs, she couldn't breathe as the torment rippled through her body.

Now all too familiar with her own cries, "Please stop!" she

begged.

The Prez at Number 5 picked her up by her hair as one other before him had and threw her against her little black car. Scrambling and struggling to breathe, Ari tried in vain to reach for the door, only to receive a crushing blow from his knee as it collided with her stomach, knocking the air out of her lungs. Gasping for breath and just a fingertip away from the handle, she told herself to get the car door open no matter what, as he held her against her car.

The tall and scrawny Prez laughed in her face as he swept his raggedy long blond hair from his face. As he got close to her, the beer on his smelly drunken breath made her feel queasy as his gray eyes feasted upon her.

"Please let me go!" she pleaded, to no avail.

"Oh, you can go, but not until I'm finished with you!" he teased as he unbuckled his belt!

"Shit! No! Please?" she begged.

"Shut up, bitch!"

Ari pressed up against the door, fingers clasped around the handle as she waited for the Prez to reach for his zipper. Just as he did, she kneed him hard between the legs and watched him drop to the ground.

"You bitch!" he cried cradling himself but making no move to stand.

Ari dived into her car, locking the door behind her. The Prez went ballistic as he tried to compose himself, and Ari knew there wasn't much time to escape. She turned the key in the ignition, and the car roared to life. Ari sped off, frantic and desperate to be free of the sadistic asshole that had beat her and attempted to take advantage of her. Tears raced from her distressed eyes as she raced onto the highway to get as far away from him as possible, searching for yet another emergency room. Ari was in trouble, bleeding and hurting after another round with a fearless Prez, just as she was a few weeks ago with Number 4. Finding it hard to breathe as her lungs crashed against her ribcage, she said to herself, "Shit! Another dead end."

The nurse on the reception desk gasped at the sight of a blood-soaked Ari as she clambered through the hospital doors. Rushing to her aid, the nurse caught her before she collapsed in pain. They raced her up to x-ray to discover she had four cracked ribs, one old and three new, two broken fingers, and a broken nose. They offered to call someone, but Ari refused. The nice nurse attempted to extract Ari's version of events that night, but Ari stared at her broken body and said nothing. She had learned from Number 4 that it was too risky. The trauma doctors gave her a pep talk about domestic violence as they patched her up, assuming that her wounds had been inflicted by an aggressive significant other. Smirking to herself in disbelief and thinking how they had no idea, she winced as the doctor put her back together again. Ari had no choice but to remain in the hospital overnight for observation and, once again, the doctor advised Ari to go to the police, advice that fell on deaf ears. Ari thanked the doctor and waited until morning to leave for home.

On the journey home, Ari wondered how she was going to explain herself to her boys and what would she say to her students and her boss. She had been able to hide the cuts and bruises from Numbers 1, 2, and 4, as they were mostly under her clothes or easily hidden with makeup. After suffering at the hands of Number 5, Ari had to change the narrative. She couldn't continue on this road of destruction. Her boys would arrive home tomorrow, and they couldn't see her like this, so she stopped to get some high-end, durable makeup. The expensive makeup could cover anything. It cost a fortune, but if it hid her horrific black eyes, she didn't care.

The girl serving Ari stared, asking with a patronizing rather than an endearing tone, "Do you need help, honey?"

Ari explained what she wanted, and the woman came back with an array of makeup for her. Proceeding to put the items through the register, she said, "Listen honey, I know you think you love him, but he doesn't love you, so get yourself out of there before he kills you."

Ari couldn't help but laugh. *This Barbie Doll has no fucking idea, casting aspersions and commenting on something that she knows nothing about, and her judgmental tones are making my blood boil.*

Ari was close to losing it for the first time, not with a Prez, but with a shop girl offering her advice.

She quickly found her composure, reminding herself that it wasn't the woman's fault she was in this mess, before politely thanking the woman and heading home.

"Five down and sixteen more to go," she murmured as she scurried through the traffic, desperate to get home.

As she opened her front door and stepped inside, all Ari wanted was to have a bath and curl up in bed. So, she ran a bath while looking at Number 6's location ahead of next weekend's trip. Despite her injuries and setbacks, she was invested now and in too deep, she would continue even if she died trying to help her son.

The boys came home the following day, and Ari did everything she could to hide her injuries. The makeup worked well enough. The staff in school thought Ari looked great with extra color on her cheeks. They had no idea what was hiding underneath the bronzer and eye shadow. She even managed to stop herself from wincing when the boys gave her a hug.

Over the next month, Ari became exceptionally good at hiding cuts and bruises from everyone she knew and loved. She became an English teacher quoting Romeo and Juliet and soccer mom on the weekdays, and a daddy hunter getting smacked around over the weekend, with each MC being worse than the rest. In MC's six through to thirteen, she suffered two more broken ribs, a fractured wrist and seven stitches in her head and eight in her shin of all places. She lied to her boys, explaining how she slipped and banged her head in the shower after Number 13's handiwork accounted for most of her recent injuries.

Ari had painfully discovered that MCs didn't take kindly to strangers. Most presidents assumed Ari was a cop and others just smacked her around for a bit of fun, and not one had provided a fraction of a clue to reveal the location of Junior's dad.

Ari was also getting tired of keeping secrets from her boys and began living off beers and pain killers to get her through the pain she endured week in week out. She even joined a roller derby team as a cover once her wrist had healed, to try to account for her injuries.

She was so surprised that people in the town believed her. They would say, "Are you sure you want to keep playing that game? It's dangerous."

And Ari would lie to them. "Yeah, I love it!"

Even the boys believed her and kept nagging to watch her play. She hated herself for the lies, but she couldn't tell them the truth. She couldn't tell anyone. She kept it all to herself, and it made her feel lonely. Ari longed for someone to hold her and tell her everything was going to be okay, but her body now started to look like a train wreck, and she just didn't trust anyone anymore.

Number 14 was another harrowing and terrifying experience for Ari and, just like the others. It had stolen a piece of her soul. This soul-destroying mission that she once called an adventure started to take its toll on a tired and weary Ari.

She had gone out to Moonlight Cove, to the Moonlight Rottweilers Cavern, home of the Rottweilers MC. Sitting at the bar, drinking a beer, Ari glanced around, checking if she recognized anyone from Junior's photographs, but she didn't spot anyone.

It wasn't long before a short dumpy fellow approached her with his grease ball pick-up line: "I like your shirt, darlin'. It would look great on my bedroom floor" he said, looking at her as if she was a piece of meat.

"Sorry, but I'm hoping to find someone here," Ari said.

"Well, maybe I can help. I'm the bar manager. But you gotta let me buy you a drink before I help you find who you are looking for?"

"Okay, fine," Ari agreed.

He was the nicest fella she had met yet, besides the oldies at Number 3, and at least he offered to buy her a drink. The man then proceeded behind the bar to fix a shot before he returned and sat at the bar next to her, looking at her with a big smile on his face. He was short like Ari, had red curly hair, piercing blue eyes and a boat load of freckles, which made him look like a teenager when he smiled. The only things that gave away his age were the wrinkles on his forehead and a slight tinge of gray on his stubble ridden chin.

"Cheers!" he said, handing her a shot, and they both knocked it back in one. "Who are you waiting for?" he asked.

"An Irish man named Mack; is there anyone who goes by that name here?"

"Oh, you don't mean Big Mack, do you? Because he's upstairs. I can introduce you if you like."

Ari jumped to her feet like an excited teenage girl who had just discovered her crush liked her back.

"Oh my God, yes please, if you don't mind?" Ari beamed, almost dancing on the spot. Please let it be him, she thought, getting ahead of herself.

"Not at all, Pumpkin, but only if you have another drink with me after."

"If this is my guy, I will buy you all your drinks," she said, embracing him with glee.

"I'll hold you to that. Come on, let's go." He laughed, taking Ari by the hand, and yanking her out of her seat.

Ari followed him behind the bar, tingling with anticipation and feeling a little overwhelmed at the possibility of finding Mack at last. They climbed the stairs together and, as Ari reached the top step, she felt a little light-headed. Everything started to spin.

"I don't feel so good," she muttered before collapsing with the fella, scooping her up as she did.

Ari came around to find the short stumpy fella on top of her. Her shirt was unbuttoned as she felt his lips on her neck.

She tried to talk, but her throat was too dry. He looked at her as he stood to take his pants down. "You just lay there like a good girl, and this will be over soon, okay?" he said to her as he ran his grubby finger over her chest.

Oh my God! This guy is trying to rape me.

Ari began to panic, making her attacker more excited.

"Now, hold on little miss, I'm not going to hurt you," he teased as she began to wrestle him as he attempted to unbutton her jeans.

"No!" she screamed, finding her voice.

"Hold still, you little bitch," he shouted as he tried to pin her down.

She noticed he wasn't that strong. Maybe that's why he needed to drug his prey so they couldn't fight back. He obviously hadn't planned on Ari waking up so soon.

Ari, now regaining her strength, pushed him off her and tried to make a run for the door.

"Oh no, you don't," he growled as he grabbed her by the neck, making her scream. He threw her back down on the bed and climbed on top of her again.

Ari, scanning the room for anything that might aid her in her escape, spotted an ashtray on the side of the bed. She waited for him to grope her again, pretending to act compliant.

"That's it! Now you're getting it." He chuckled with a devilish look in his eyes. "And if you lie still while I fuck you, I'll let you go afterwards. I promise."

Ari nodded as he looked at her and he released his erect penis from his ripped boxer shorts. He peered down, reaching for her jeans' buttons once more, and when she was convinced, he was distracted, she smashed him over the head hard with the ashtray.

He was out cold as he slumped onto Ari, so she pushed him off, hunting for her belongings. Discovering her coat on the chair by the door, she grabbed it and quickly checked that her car keys were still inside the pocket. When they jingled, a rush of relief washed over her, but she still had to get out.

She headed to the door without thinking before stopping herself suddenly. What if someone was waiting outside or if the bartender saw her leave? They could stop her. Ari decided to leave via the window instead. Checking over her shoulder, making sure that her attacker was still incapacitated, she climbed out of the window and onto the fire escape. Peering out the side of the building, Ari could see her car just a short distance away, but as she went to make a run for it, another bartender appeared out front for a cigarette. She waited patiently for him to finish, praying she would still have enough time to escape.

Once she climbed down the ladder, she rushed to her car, ducking down to creep inside, making sure that nobody saw her leave. After locking the door, Ari didn't hang around and sped off into the night. The adrenaline coursing through her body after fight or flight had kicked in was another feeling that had become familiar to Ari, and it wasn't until she was an hour down the road that she realized her shirt and the top button of her jeans were still undone. Gazing down at herself, Ari burst into tears. She couldn't carry on like this and would need to change her tactics if she were to continue looking for Mack.

The drive home provided Ari with an opportunity to brainstorm her future directions, and she came up with a new plan. She would only visit the MCs in daylight now, as there was more chance the vicious bikers at the MCs would think twice about attacking an innocent woman in the cold light of day.

Junior asked for updates every Sunday when Ari arrived to pick him up from Adam and Joe's house, and she hated seeing his face every time she told him that she had once again came up empty. Adam poured her a coffee as she sat down at his table, disappointed again.

"Don't worry, Mom, you will find a clue soon. I just know it!" Junior said with his eyes still full of hope.

Ari's heart had held that hope once...until fourteen different men from fourteen different MCs made her feel otherwise.

"Junior, can you go and play with Joe for five minutes? I just need to talk to your mom for a second, please."

"Yeah, of course!" Junior said and left the room.

Ari knew what was coming next. Adam had said the same to her every Sunday since she had started her search for Mack.

"Any more cuts and bruises this week?" he asked.

Ari just stared at him.

"Come on, Ari, this can't go on. Every week I see another piece of you destroyed by this madness. How long are you going to keep doing this to yourself? Everyone else may fall for that roller derby shit, but you're not fooling me. I've known you too long."

"I'm fine!" she snapped.

"You're not fine. You're a mess, and I hate seeing you like that. You are my friend and the mother of my son's brother. Please, can you stop this now? Junior will understand. You have tried so hard. Maybe this guy doesn't want to be found."

"No! I made a promise to Junior, and I'm keeping it!"

"Yeah, and it will cost you your life at this rate. And that will destroy him and Remy. Have you thought about that?"

"It won't come to that."

"Ari, you're lucky to be alive, so for the love of God, will you please stop?"

"Six more clubs, Adam, six, and then I will stop."

He drew a deep breath, blew it out. "That's six too many, Ari!"

"Please Adam, I really appreciate you having Junior so I could do this for him."

"What, get yourself killed, you mean? Listen, I'll give you the last six, but I won't have Junior overnight after that if I find that you're going to carry on with this charade. I won't have a part in your death. You are an amazing woman, and I can't stand seeing you get hurt."

Just then, Joe and Junior entered the room to play a video game. Adam stood to help, kissing Ari on the cheek before he went to assist them.

As they left to go home, Adam hugged Ari. "Please be careful," he whispered to her.

Ari took his hand. "Thank you for everything! You are pretty awesome yourself, you know!"

Adam blushed as they said their goodbyes, and then Ari and Junior headed off home.

CHAPTER NINE

The Cabin in the Woods

Mack sat on B's driveway, fixing up his bike. Strangely enough, he preferred to sit cross-legged on the ground as he worked on his bike. He found it comfortable as he got lost in a world of tinkering. He was getting ready for a short road trip with his best friend, Frankie, as they both loved to ride. Riding on his Harley Davidson with the wind in his face was like therapy to him. He loved to ride, and he loved to fish. Both could be done in solitude, which he enjoyed as the peace and quiet gave him a chance to practice some mindfulness, gather his thoughts and be at one with himself. B had taught him that when she hired him.

B approached from her cabin, sitting next to him, handing him a mug of coffee. "Now make sure you put that back together properly, my lovely. I don't want you getting hurt on this death trip of yours."

"B, it's an hour up the road in a bloody cabin in the woods. We're going on a hunting and fishing trip, not going to a bike fest or anything," he teased.

B sat sulking as she watched him play with his lights.

He released a sigh. "You could always come along. Frankie and I would love to teach you how to shoot."

She looked at him in disgust, "Uh. No bloody thank you. You know I hate guns!"

Mack shook his head in frustration. "Why do you hate them so much? You can choke me and Frankie unconscious when we grapple, yet you won't learn how to defend yourself with a gun."

"Yes, but I am in control of my arms, and guns are just bloody dangerous!"

"You're bloody dangerous!" he scoffed. "If there was a guy holding a gun on you at point blank range and just one of you could survive, then my fecking money would be on you, Dragon."

He changed the subject to more serious matters, matters B had hoped that she might have avoided for now. But no. Mack stared at his wrench, voice low. He asked her the question. "Any luck this week with the PI?"

Staring at him in with the same disappointed expression she gave him every time he asked.

"Sorry Mackie, He's asking for more information again."

Mack launched his wrench, sending it hurdling down the drive.

"He has all the fecking information," he said, running his hands through his hair frantically. "All the money you are paying this guy and I'm still no closer to finding Jelly Legs. It's been nearly six years, for fuck's sake."

B usually challenged people who lashed out like that. But this was her only exception. Seeing the devastation in Mack's eyes after she came up empty again destroyed her insides, making them tie in knots. Despite spending thousands of dollars on private investigators, they still didn't have Junior's location. Mack provided them with information, but Nancy and Junior were untraceable, as there wasn't enough information for investigators to conduct a thorough search with each investigator suggesting that Nancy changed their identities upon leaving Sunnyville.

B rose to leave, making her way up the steps to her cabin as the lump in her throat threatened to choke her. She didn't want to upset her best friend anymore today, and she desperately wanted to find Junior to end his suffering.

Mack chased after her and grabbed her hand. "Wait! Dragon, please. I'm sorry!"

B couldn't even look at him. B only displayed emotion when she thought she had failed him.

Mack lifted her chin to face him, but she looked away again. "Hey, look at me, please!" he said softly, taking her chin between his thumb and index finger and turning her head to his. "I'm sorry. I didn't mean to lash out. I know that you are doing everything you can to find Junior."

"Yeah, but it's not good enough, is it? I should have a location on him, Mackie, I'm paying them enough, and I can see it's destroying you, and I hate not being able to fix this for you."

Mack put his forehead on hers, taking hold of the back of her head with his hand. It was their act of endearment toward one another. "You've already fixed me, Dragon. You've given me everything I've ever dreamed of. Without you, I would have been dead years ago, and I know, if anyone is going to find Jelly Legs, it's you!"

Staring into his glacier-like eyes, with all the love and determination she could muster for her best friend, she said; "I'll never give up, Mackie. Best friends never quit! You know that, right?"

"I know, Dragon, and that's why I love you," he said as he embraced her and kissed her cheek. "Oh, and thanks for not unleashing the fiery dragon on me for being a dick."

"You get a free pass, Boyoh, but you better return from the cabin in one piece, or the fiery dragon will come back."

Mack furrowed his brow and pursed his lips. "Dragon, you know I'd never leave you, don't you?"

B nodded in silence as Mack continued. "Look, I know you're stressing about Frankie and me leaving and going to play with guns for the weekend and I know you hate them, but I promise you that we won't kill ourselves. We're not stupid."

"I know it's just that we're a team and if..."

"Nothing is going to happen to us! Best friends never quit, remember?" he repeated to her. "And what kind of friend would I be if I did something stupid and got myself killed?" he joked, making B laugh.

"Just promise me that you'll both come back in one piece," she said.

"Promise," he said, nudging her chin with his fist. "But you have to promise me something, too."

B looked at him with a confused expression on her face. "Okay?" She waited for him to clarify.

"You need to promise me that you won't go to the Sultry Slalom without me this weekend."

B's face was an absolute picture, like a bulldog chewing a wasp. "No way! That's not fair! Just cause you're not getting any this weekend, doesn't mean I shouldn't."

"Please, Dragon, I don't want you going there when I'm not there. I know you can handle yourself, but at least when I'm with you, I know that you're okay."

"Mackie, I can kick your ass, and you're the biggest and toughest son of a bitch I know, so stop being a worry wart and let me enjoy my weekend. It's been a bitch of a week, and I deserve to get laid."

Mack smirked. "Oh, so I'm the worry wart? You're the one who's been skulking all week because you're worried that your best pals are going to shoot themselves."

"No, I'm not! I don't worry! I just hate the thought of being lumbered with the business if you shoot yourself," she lied. B was worried, but she would never admit it to him, or anyone, for that matter.

"You're full of shite!" he said to her, teasing her again.

B pouted her way up the steps to her cabin. "Whatever, you silly Irish prick. At least I'm not a bloody fun sponge."

"Uh, Dragon...are you forgetting something?"

She looked at him and then rolled her eyes and shouted at him in frustration. "Argh... God, I bloody hate you! Fine, I promise I will stay here and be miserable instead of having some deliciously hot and sexy stranger between my legs! Happy?"

An ear-to-ear grin spread over Mack's face. "Ecstatic... Oh, and I promise to make it up to you next weekend."

"You better!"

"I will. Next weekend I'll be there with bells on, and we'll have you swimming in dick. Just as long as you return the favor and pick out some beautiful pussy for me," he said, smiling and giving her a wink.

B nodded. "Fine, but you're not getting the food hamper that I made for you boys to take. I'm eating all that myself now. So, no homemade steak pies, Welsh cakes, or muffins and certainly none of the good stuff; You deprive me, and I deprive you! That's the way the cookie crumbles, Mackie boy."

"Oh, come on! You know I can't go five minutes without your baked goods and Welsh whisky," he stated, but B had already headed inside. Mack shook his head and headed in after her. "I'm getting those fecking Welsh cakes," he muttered under his breath.

CHAPTER TEN
All Roads Lead to Sunnyville

"Crunch!" There went another three fingers broke as she cried out in agony. "Whack!" Yet another blow to the face! The echoes of Ari's broken bones rattled around her brain, her synapses demanding that she put an end to the torture as her nerve endings and receptors screamed in agony.

"For God's sake, what is it with you bikers and cops! I am not a cop, okay? So please just stop!" she begged as the sixty-something-year-old brute laid into her.

"Yeah, then why are you sniffing around for an Irishman?" the Prez seethed, slapping her in broad daylight and not giving a damn who saw.

"I'm looking for my son's father," she choked as blood poured down the back of her throat.

"Looking for a baby daddy, hey? I'll be a baby daddy for you, sweetheart," he said as he grabbed her hair and ground up against her.

She felt physically sick as the pot-bellied pig of a man attempted to grope her.

Surely to God he isn't going to try anything here, what is it with bikers thinking they can take what they want? she thought, until he forced his hands into her pants.

"No!" she cried. Then, "Somebody, please help!" she screamed, hoping someone would rescue her while the MC members mocked her and laughed. "There's nobody coming to rescue you here! They know better than to call the cops on me in my town," he said as he licked her face.

Ari fought hard to push him off with what little strength she could muster. She wished that she had at least taken self-defense classes before embarking on this journey through hell. Ari, never in a million years, had thought she would get attacked by anyone; she had just been naïve enough to believe she could ask some questions and return home. See, Ari always saw the good in people, assuming people would do for her what she did for them, and she was beginning to regret it, following recent events. Pinned against her car once more with some violent and dirty pervert about to rape her, she cried out again, hoping, praying someone would do the right thing and rescue her.

Number 17 was the worst Prez yet and not for the beating he gave her, but because he was more sadistic than the other MC presidents. His sinister laugh made her toes curl as he enjoyed watching her scream and squirm, thinking he was invincible in broad daylight. He didn't give a damn about the townspeople walking past as he tormented her. They all appeared to be too scared to intervene.

Just when she thought that all hope was lost, a blue flashing light pulled slowly into the side street, causing the bikers to scramble.

"This is your lucky day, sweet pea," Number 17 growled as he clawed his way out of her pants, digging into her skin as he removed his hands in disappointment, leaving Ari to drop to the ground, sobbing once again.

The officer pulled up in front of the car and stepped out of his vehicle before making a call on his radio. He saw the battered Ari on the cement and immediately called for an ambulance. From there, she was taken to a nearby hospital for treatment.

"Fractured left hand, hair line fracture of the jaw, fractured ribs and sutures running down to her pubic bone" The doctor revealed to the officer outside Ari's room.

"Jesus," the officer gasped!

"There's more! She has clearly been through hell. Her ribs have at least seven old fractures. There are multiple old fractures covering her entire body, and her right wrist has barely healed from a fracture about four weeks old. I believe she's been tortured.

"You're kidding! Did she say what happened?"

"No, she just said thank you and that's it," the doctor explained.

"Alright, well, thank you. I'll take it from here," the officer said before entering Ari's room.

"Hey! I'm Officer James. How are you feeling?" he asked.

"A little sore," Ari murmured

"The doctor said you've been in some battles, so, tell me, why there's an English teacher from Portland out here, tangled up with a load of bikers."

Ari took a deep breath and began to explain to the officer about her quest to find Junior's father, leaving out any information that would incriminate the bikers who threatened her life.

"So, you mean to tell me that you have been roaming around the country, going into dangerous bars in search of your adopted son's father?"

"Uh, yes," she replied. Glaring at him as if he was stupid.

"Well, maybe I can help. What's this person's name?"

"Mack."

"Mack who?"

"I'm not sure!"

The officer sighed as he rubbed the back of his neck with his hand. "So, you're looking for a guy whose last name you don't know? Jesus, lady!"

"No, I mean yes, but it's not as straight cut as that. I adopted a boy, and I am looking for his dad. I know his name is Mack. He's Irish, and he was in a motorcycle club with a dog on the patch."

"What, so you just started going around MC's and politely asking if they knew Irish Mack?

Ari couldn't help but laugh. "Pretty much!"

"Are you crazy? Do you know how dangerous MCs are? They house some of the most notorious criminals in America."

"Yeah, I have learned that the hard way." She sighed, wincing on exhalation.

"Look lady, you are going to get yourself killed and frankly, I am surprised that you haven't been already. How many clubs have you been to?"

"A few..."

"Yeah, looking at the state of you, I'd say you are lucky to be alive. Now stop before your son loses his mom."

"I can't do that. I have five clubs left to search until I complete my list."

"For crying out loud, you are not listening to me. These guys don't play nice. They will kill you and no offense, but if he wanted to be a father, you wouldn't be searching for him, and being a dangerous biker, he's probably dead," the officer said.

"Either way, I have to know!"

"Look," he said exhaustedly. "You have to stay overnight anyway. So, give me the list of MCs, and I'll search the database."

"You'll help me?"

"Yeah, I'll have to, just to stop you from getting yourself killed."

"Really!" she said, getting so excited that she nearly split her stitches.

"Yeah, but only if you stay put. No more going out to crazy clubs. You got it!" He said sternly.

"Oh my God! Yes! Thank you!"

The officer pursed his lips and nodded. "Now, is there anyone that I can call for you?" he asked.

Ari shook her head.

"Well, you rest up and I'll be back in the morning, okay?"

Ari nodded, and the officer headed for the exit. "Officer James," she called, waiting while he turned on his heels, then, "Thank you."

The officer nodded and departed, leaving Ari to get some sleep.

The next morning Ari woke to officer James clearing his throat. "Morning! Did you get some rest?" he asked.

"A little."

"Well, I have some information for you.... the next four clubs are duds. Not one club has a guy called Mack, so cross them off your list. The last MC on your list had a Macintyre Ryan of Irish decent, but the rap sheet is over six years old, and if it was him, he's not there now. There are no other records of a Macintyre Ryan anywhere else in the system, Ari, dead or alive."

"What do you think happened to him?"

"My guess, he's either changed his name, or he's dead. So, don't go there, as you will probably end up in a grave next to him."

Ari glared at the officer. "But there's bound to be somebody there who knows what has happened to him."

"You are not listening to me. If he was there, he's not now and nobody will tell you shit. You are a white woman driving around in nice car and expensive clothes, so they are going to think you're a cop or a high-end PI and probably shoot you!" he explained.

"That makes sense, seen as half of the club's Presidents thought I was a cop."

"Classy looking white female with designer clothes, pricey car. What did you expect? Oh, and just in case you were thinking of going there, I have flagged your car, so the minute you enter that town you will be arrested for impeding an investigation, and I've done that for your own safety. So, for the love of God, listen to me okay."

"What investigation?"

"My investigation into what the hell has happened to you."

"Please, officer, I don't want to press charges. If you arrest them, they will come after my family," she pleaded.

"Then promise me you'll get in your car, go home, and stay

there." he said, handing her the information that he had found on the police database.

Ari nodded and thanked the officer for his help before he left. He had explained that her car had been transported to the hospital parking lot by the local police department, so Ari headed home once again. But this time, she was excited. At last, she finally had a clue. Suddenly all the beat downs seemed worth it and, of course, she wasn't going to listen to the officer when he had provided her with the key to Mack's whereabouts. She would just borrow another car to get to Sunnyville. The last thing she needed was to lose her job by getting arrested.

After arriving back in Portland, Ari headed to Adam's house to pick up Junior, and although she looked and felt battered, she had a spring in her step due to the huge clue Officer James had provided her. She rang the doorbell, and Adam opened the door.

"Shit! Ari honey, are you okay?" Adam asked as he touched her bruised and swollen cheek. It was so dark; her makeup didn't hide it.

"I'm fine! Is Junior ready? I have to get home for Remy. His dad is dropping him off early."

"Junior, your mom is here," he yelled and turned back to Ari.

"Tell me that you are going to stop this madness. I can't take seeing you like this anymore."

"Last one next week, and guess what! A police officer checked the last five MCs left on my list and the last one used to have a guy called Mack there."

Adam looked a little puzzled. "What do you mean, used to have?"

"Well, it was five years ago and...."

"Damn it Ari, you have to stop this," he said as he ruffled his hair. "Enough is enough. You are going to get yourself killed!"

With that, Junior entered the room. "What's going on? Who is going to get killed?" he asked before gasping at the state of his mother. "What happened and before you tell me it was another roller derby game; I know it wasn't. Remy and I know that you're getting hurt at these MCs, Mom."

Ari studied her son, who looked concerned. "Okay," she said. "So last night I did get knocked about a bit, but I found a massive clue, Junior, and next week I may finally have some answers about your dad."

Junior looked at his mother and took her hand, "But Mom, if I have to lose you to find my dad then I'm not interested. Remy and I have talked about it, and we don't want to see you get hurt anymore."

"Darling, I'm fine, and next week—"

"Mom, you are not fine!" Junior shouted. "You don't eat, you hardly ever sleep, and every week there's a new bruise. I think you should stop."

"Junior, I am so close to finding your dad. I know it, son, and I promise you, if next week is a bust then I will stop, okay?"

Junior glared at her.

"Look, Number 21 is the last on the list, I promise."

He looked at his mother and saw how desperate she was, with her face all black and blue. He could see it was important to her. Stamping his feet and throwing his head back in frustration, he glared at her. "Last one and we put it to bed, Mom. We had an agreement, remember?"

Ari nodded in agreement as she cast her mind back to the day she had informed Junior of her plan to search for his dad. It seemed forever ago. Ari was happy then, with not a care in the world, and now nearly five months on, she was a battered wreck with an increasing drink problem to calm her nerves and ease her pain.

She hugged her son and told him that she loved him. Turning to Adam, she asked him a question. "Hey, can I borrow your truck on Friday and you take my car, please? I'll have it back to you by Saturday lunch."

"Yeah, but what's wrong with your car? It's brand new."

"Nothing, it's just— I'll blend in better if I take your truck."

"Fine, but if you wreck it, I'm keeping your car."

"Great, we'll swap on Friday when I drop Junior off," she informed him as she headed out of the door.

Ari spent all week thinking about Number 21 and the new lead she had. She was adamant someone at the MC would have the answers that she required, and she found herself counting down the days until Friday.

She tried to focus on teaching but found herself daydreaming about how MC Number 21 could hold all the answers to finding Mack, until one of her students would interrupt her thoughts by asking questions about Shakespeare. Ari even tried to spend some time with the boys watching movies, rather than locking herself in her study searching for MCs and looking at the pin board with gratitude because there weren't any red pins on the board as her search was coming to an end, and she exhaled in relief that her quest might soon be over.

Friday came, and Ari couldn't wait for the school bell to ring, to visit Number 21 and hopefully put an end to her and Junior's pain once and for all. Her stomach churned as something was telling her that the answers, she sought lay there. The bell finally went off, and she waited for Junior in her car as Remy was going straight to his dad's for the weekend.

They arrived at Adam's house just after four, which meant Ari could switch cars and still arrive in Sunnyville about six. The sun still shone in the sky still at six, which made her feel better than if she arrived at night.

She was about to leave the car when Junior grabbed her hand. She looked at him as he said, "Remember Mom, you promised."

"I know, last one," she said, smiling sweetly, before hugging him goodbye and heading off in Adam's battered truck.

CHAPTER ELEVEN

Sunnyville & the Mauler

Sunnyville was a small town in a picturesque valley where local law enforcement was controlled by the local MC: The Red Pitbulls. The Red Pitbulls were one-percenters, notorious for murder, drug smuggling, theft and robbery and were run by a sadistic president who had recently become known to everyone as "the Mauler." The Mauler, an evil and downright sadistic Prez, rained terror upon his enemies and the townspeople. In recent years, he had developed a fetish for wearing a claw-like glove to maul his prey. He was notorious for being the nastiest, most vicious bastard around, and even the local law enforcement worked for him and feared him. Everyone knew about the Red Pitbull's and their shenanigans, but they dared to say anything and only club members dared go anywhere near the MC after dark.

The Mauler would sit and get drunk every day, getting nasty and bullying his club members. The club wasn't huge, but it was fearsome and dangerous. It consisted of the Mauler's nephew Noah, who was his Vice President, and Zander, his Sergeant-at-Arms, who had saved Noah's life years ago as he was passing through Sunnyville. Zander had intercepted an attack on Noah, killing a rival gang member in the process and the Mauler was so impressed by his murdering skill set that he patched him in.

The other members were Jimmy, the club's secretary, who had been patched in ten years ago after his parents passed away. Tiny, the club's tail gunner, who was the opposite of his namesake, and Tyr the club's roadie, who looked like a Viking with his prominent cheekbones, bright blond hair, and crystal-like blue eyes. He was currently accompanying Tiny on a trip to Washington state. Tiny was taking a few months' sabbatical to help his mother on her ranch after his father had passed away, and he was grateful for Tyr's help. They weren't needed at the MC at present, as the Mauler was always too intoxicated to go on ride outs or take excursions, and lost their last weapons contract to a more efficient and reliable, one-percenter MC. The arms dealer decided The Red Pitbull's were a liability due to the Mauler bringing too much heat to his well-oiled business with his claw fetish. Grunts, known as youngsters, made up the rest of the MC, uneducated idiots the Mauler made do his dirty work, younger than the rest of the members and not very bright.

The MC members were terrified of their leader. Nobody would ever dare to cross him, especially after the Mack incident. Mack had been a member of the club for years, when the Mauler believed he betrayed him. Going berserk, he attempted to kill him. Fortunately, the Irishman was too quick for the huge Mauler and managed to escape on his bike thanks to two MC members helping him in secret. The Mauler never recovered from his brother's betrayal, and five years later, he still went crazy at the mention of Mack's name. It made the Mauler's blood boil that the Irishman was the only person to escape his fate, and he vowed that if he ever saw him again, he would tear him limb from limb.

The other members weren't as vicious. They were a lot smarter than the Mauler, with his nephew Noah dreaming he would take over the family business eventually and make a lot of changes with Zander and Jimmy by his side. Noah had always wanted to be a businessperson. He would spend hours reading borrowed library books that he had kept hidden from his uncle, even as a grown adult. However, his uncle was a bully and laughed at Noah the day he came home and asked to go to business school, and instead led him down a road of murder, guns, and violence. Noah had always hated him for that.

Noah, Zander, and Jimmy wanted more for the MC, fed up with living off the Maulers' scraps. They had grown tired of risking their lives for dimes. Noah devised a plan to create an MC worth being a part of, where members didn't despise themselves and worked for a profitable living. Zander was the worst affected by his life as a one-percenter, desperate for work when the Mauler patched him in. He went from hero veteran to a vicious and merciless one-percenter. Forced to become someone he despised, and just like Noah and Jimmy, they hated their lives of crime and pillaging. But they swore an oath, bound until death, or exiled to Alaska and no matter how much they hated their leader, they would have to follow and obey him until the end of his reign.

CHAPTER TWELVE
Number 21

"Revenge is a dish, best served cold"

Ari hit Sunnyville just after six, as planned. The valley was beautiful as the sun was shining in the picture-perfect blue sky. Ari smiled as the wind blew her luscious locks of brown hair behind her as she drove through the town. Encapsulating the breath-taking scenery, Ari's mind cut to Number 21, thinking, just maybe, the town's beauty was a good sign for things to come and the MC would provide her with everything she needed to find Mack. Ari, hoped to put an end to her search and the brutality that was unleashed upon her by the twenty clubs before it. She was hoping that Number 21 would be her salvation and a happy ending for both her and Junior.

Pulling into the club parking lot, Ari caught the bewildered expressions of three men sitting outside drinking beer. Smirking as she climbed out of the driver's seat, they stood awaiting her approach.

"My name's Noah. This is Zander and that's Jimmy," the man introduced. "Can I help you with something, doll face?" he asked.

Ari nervously answered, "Yeah, I was wondering if you could

help me. I'm looking for someone who may have been part of your club years back. His name was Mack."

The man glared at his friends in disbelief. "Nah, sorry doll face, never heard of him, so off you trot, it's dangerous here when the sun goes down."

"Please! I desperately need to find him," she explained as the guys tried to usher her back to the truck.

"Well, who's this pretty little thing?" slurred a big fella, appearing from behind them unexpectedly.

"Aye, no one boss, just a lassie who's a bit lost, I think!" Zander said nervously, obviously trying to move Ari swiftly along.

"I'm not lost. I am looking for a man named Mack," she shouted. "I've been to twenty clubs before this one, and I'm not leaving until I get some answers."

At this point, she'd had enough. She knew she was close to finding Junior's father. She could feel it, and something told her that Prez Number 21 knew something. So now she was demanding answers.

The color drained from all three men's faces as the big fella beamed with delight.

"Are you talking about Irish Mack by any chance?" he asked, dangerously curious.

"Yes, he had a son thirteen years ago with—"

"Nancy?" the big fella finished, unable to hide the grin that was growing wide across his face.

"Yes, do you know where he is? I'm desperate to find him."

The three men gawked in apparent horror as the drunken big fella pushed past them to embrace her.

"Darlin', you have come to the right place," he said, smirking deviously. "I have his forwarding address inside if you want it. I'll even make a coffee and give him a ring if you want."

"Oh, really?" she cried, unable to contain her excitement. To Ari, this was the closest that she had genuinely been to finding answers to Junior's past and answers to Mack's location.

"Yeah, and just ignore these three," he explained casually, glaring at his brothers. "Mack moved owing them money and they're still upset with him." The man's arm coiled around Ari's waist as he grinned from ear to ear and peered down at her tiny frame. "Let's head to my office and call my favorite Irishman."

The three men froze in place as he led Ari inside.

Ari followed the big fellow, so excited she didn't see the warning signs. Walking down the corridor to an office next to the bar, she smiled, amused that the MC Prez looked a bit like a muscular version of Santa Claus. He looked to be in his early sixties, with white hair, although it was shaved at the sides and spikey on the top. He had a thick beard that had been squared off, as opposed to Santa's shaggier beard, and he looked muscular around his chest, arms, and shoulders. But below his muscular upper extremities sat a huge round protruding belly, just like Santa Claus. The only difference being that Santa's belly was filled with mince pies and not whisky.

"I'm Ari," she introduced herself. "What's your name?"

"Folks around here call me the Mauler." He gestured to a nearby chair. "Take a seat, sugar. I'm just putting the kettle on," he said, filling a tea kettle with water from the cold tap.

Ari naively took a seat with her back to him. Then, without a moment's notice, he slammed her head hard onto the desk, splitting her forehead open and knocking her unconscious.

Ari woke up a short while later, feeling disorientated as she lay face-down on the desk with nothing on her top half. The Mauler was tugging at her jeans, pulling them down around her ankles.

"No!" she cried as she tried to get her bearings, to get up off the desk. But the Mauler had other ideas, gripping her head, and pushing her back down onto the desk as he tried to control her. She tried to resist, so he punched her hard across the side of her face, busting Ari's already swollen nose wide open. He sneered as he hovered over as he teased and taunted her by explaining what was coming next.

"This is going to hurt in ways beyond your comprehension,

sugar, and when I'm done with you, you can go and tell that Irish prick what I've done to you! Tell him that revenge is a dish that's best served cold and I'm coming for him and everyone he's ever loved." He spoke in a menacing tone that shook Ari to her core.

Meanwhile, outside, Zander started to rage, "I swear to God, Noah, if he hurts that innocent lassie then I'm oot. Drug dealers, gangbangers, criminals I don't mind, but I draw the fucking line at innocent lassies," he wailed in his broad Scottish accent.

Noah, pacing up and down, growled. "I know, just let me think."

"We have to get her out of there," Jimmy whispered with urgency, as if the Mauler might hear them.

They sat quietly, as they attempted to figure out how to save the woman from her fate, until the sound of her screams deafened them.

Zander threw his hands through his perfect mane, snarling, "What's the fucking plan Noah? God knows what he is fucking doing to her!"

Back in the Mauler's office, the Mauler held Ari down with one hand, laughing as he took his manky bear claw and ripped through the flesh on her back, like a knife through butter as Ari screamed in agony. She almost passed out in pain as he did it again and again, shredding her skin as if it was pulled pork. She lost consciousness briefly, but he kept slapping her to wake her up. He wanted her conscious for all of it and rained blows down onto her ribs as she felt each one crack worse than ever before.

Finally, Ari couldn't take any more. She was in so much pain she wanted to die. The Mauler flipped her over like a rag doll as she bled onto the desk with blood pouring from her torn flesh. Apparently, he wanted to stare into her soul as he ripped off her underwear, wanting her to know what was coming next. Ari's crying eyes couldn't help but stare back into his; they were black like his soul as he grinned sadistically, while trying to gain access to a petrified Ari. Number 21 was worse than the devil himself. A Prez more nefarious than Ari had crossed paths with previously. The bilious expression on his face haunted her as he reveled in her torture.

What did Mack do to him to make him react like this?

She screamed and fought to keep him from entering her. Ari's body, exhausted with pain and under the weight of the demonic Mauler as she tried in vain to stop him from raping her, and just when she was losing her fight, she caught a glimpse of the three men from outside creeping into the room. Signaling to a desperate Ari to be quiet, Noah, the one who had spoken to her first, crept up behind the distracted Prez and smashed him over the head with a wrench, knocking him unconscious onto a traumatized Ari. Zander retrieved a blanket from the sofa, while Noah and Jimmy pulled the Prez off her and watched as he slumped to the floor in one big heap.

Wrapping Ari carefully in the blanket, Zander rushed to her truck with Jimmy grabbing all her belongings. It was agreed that Noah would stay behind just in case his uncle woke, while Zander and Jimmy took Ari to the hospital.

They put Ari in the back of the truck, and Zander desperately tried to pack her wounds with bandages from the first aid kit they found in the truck.

Ari screamed in agony.

"I know darlin', hang on in there. We're nearly there," Zander said, shaking his head in disgust as he finished dressing her wounds.

"Please, I can't take the pain."

Zander held her tight, allowing her to cry out in pain until they arrived at the hospital. Carrying a now pale Ari inside the accident and emergency room, he shouted for help, explaining to the medical staff they found her on the roadside and brought her into hospital, being good Samaritans. Zander placed a note in her jacket pocket and left her keys and jacket at the front desk, making sure he left before the police arrived.

On their return to the club, Jimmy asked Zander a question. "What did you put in her jacket?"

"Mack's address."

Jimmy's jaw dropped, eyes wide in disbelief. "What? You know where he is?"

"Noah and I helped him get out of Sunnyville. We've always known where he is. Mack asked us to keep in touch and inform him if Junior ever turned up. We put him in touch with someone to get him fake papers, so he goes by Mack Kelly as opposed to Ryan now. But Jimmy, that stays between you, me, and Noah. That sick bastard can never find out!"

"Are you going to inform Mack? He wanted to hear of anything regarding the boy."

"Let's let Noah decide. We have no idea who this woman is or what she wants with him."

"Zand, we are dead when the boss finds out that we helped her."

"Not with Noah's plan, we're not. He's smarter than Prez," Zander said, taking a step back from the sidewalk as two the youngsters pulled up alongside them.

"Right, he's conscious and thinks you are in pursuit of four men," the first youngster began to explain.

"Noah told him they held us at gunpoint, smashing the boss on the head and hauling the woman off in her truck," the second youngster said. "Oh, and Noah told him they had AR-15s so, you waited for them to leave before grabbing your weapons and bravely giving chase. Return to the club and tell Prez you lost them. Oh, and boys, get rid of ya blood-stained shirts."

Zander and Jimmy did exactly what Noah had instructed, returning a few hours later to the angry and groggy Mauler thanking them for pursuing the truck. Noah had relied on his uncle's drunkenness and an apparent lack of brain cells to believe the story that the club had fed him, and fortunately, he did. Sobering up, the Mauler seethed at the thought of his prey escaping and instructed everyone to hunt down the culprits who allegedly stormed the club. Noah, Jimmy, and Zander were in the clear for now.

CHAPTER THIRTEEN
This is all my fault

Ari screamed in agony as the trauma doctors tried to tend to her wounds. Number 21 had maimed and tortured her worse than the devil himself might have done. She would need surgery immediately to correct the damage that the Mauler had done to her. Following all the tests and x-rays, Ari underwent surgery to repair her damaged and broken body. The surgeons had to take skin from her thigh to repair the areas of her back that were torn up too badly to stitch back together, causing Ari more trauma. Her muscles were torn to shreds and Ari required physical therapy to get her back on her feet again. Ari's ribs were once again broken, and she was fortunate there was no internal bleeding from being beaten to within an inch of her life. Ari had seven stitches across her eyebrow, along with a broken nose and one hundred and eleven sutures in her back, including the dissolvable ones placed to knit her muscles back together.

While she was unconscious, police officers appeared; evidence was collected from Ari's body and her clothes were bagged as evidence too. Her family was called, and Adam rushed to the hospital with a distraught Junior and Remy to be by their mother's side.

Ari woke the next day screaming in pain. The doctors gave her morphine to help, but it barely took the edge off. Her boys wept with joy as she woke up, and Ari was relieved to see them, to be alive, and grateful to the three men who had rescued her.

Shortly after waking, a police officer arrived to ask Ari some questions, so Adam took Junior and Remy to the cafeteria, leaving the officer to talk to Ari.

"You, my dear, are incredibly lucky to be alive. Can you tell me what happened?" the officer said to Ari.

"No, thank you, I don't want to talk about it, and I won't be pressing charges, officer!" Ari said as she gritted her teeth through the pain and thinking what Number 21 would do to her if she said a word.

The officer looked down at her sympathetically. "I know you're scared, but please help us bring the monster who did this to you to justice."

Tears filled Ari's black eyes as the officer continued, "Could you tell us about the men who brought you in?"

"It wasn't their fault. They had nothing to do with it!"

"Please, let me get the bastard who did this. Put him behind bars so he can't do this to anyone else."

Ari stared down the officer. "I made a stupid mistake, that's all! Please stop asking me questions. My mind is made up, so leave."

The officer nodded, making his way to the door. Turning to Ari, he said to her: "Officer James sent his regards and wishes you a speedy recovery. He also advised that you walk away from this death ride of yours."

Ari scowled at the officer. "Don't worry, I'm done!"

"Good," he said, leaving the room.

Ari burst into tears and sobbed uncontrollably, struggling to cope with all she had endured. "I've failed my son!" she screamed in devastation.

Adam and the boys found her hysterical, so Adam slid onto the bed next to her to hold her gently while she wept. The boys sobbed as they looked on at their beaten mother, who reached out for them when she had stopped crying.

"I am so sorry boys, I never wanted you to see me like this. I am so sorry that I failed you, Junior!" Ari said.

"Mom, you never failed me. You put yourself through hell to help me. This is all my fault! I should have never mentioned my dad. It was stupid, and now you're hurt because of me. I am so sorry," he sobbed.

"No! Don't you dare blame yourself. This is on me! You asked me to stop, and I didn't because I thought I could find him for you!"

"Well, I don't want you to find him anymore, Mom. I don't need him. I just want you, Remy Adam, and Joe, okay. Please, Mom, promise me no more. I can't take seeing you beaten up anymore," Junior cried.

"Junior's right. You have to stop, Mom!" Remy pleaded as he wiped his tears.

"I know, boys, and I am so sorry. This is my fault, and I'll make it up to you both. No more, I promise!"

***

A month had passed since Ari had left the hospital, and she was now almost able to move without pain. She had spent over a week in hospital before she was allowed home with antibiotics, pain pills, and clean dressings. The hospital advised Ari to have counseling for her suffered trauma, as she would wake up in cold sweats screaming after reliving the events of that night.

Number 21 had stripped everything from her that evening when all she'd hoped for was some answers. He had stolen her mind, her body, and her soul with the sordid and sadistic abuse he had inflicted upon her. Living with her broken body was bad enough, but he had invaded her mind too, with his sinister grin and his evil tone. She would never forget the words he had spoken before tearing into her flesh like he did. There was nothing humane about the way he'd ripped her body apart, taunting her, and Ari relived it every night. She found it exhausting and dreaded closing her eyes at night. Ari could never talk to anyone about what had happened that evening.

She wanted to forget everything, not relive it. It was bad enough doing so in her dreams.

Ari tried everything to stop the nightmares, sleeping pills, meditation, alcohol to make her so drunk that surely, she would have to sleep soundly, she thought. But nothing seemed to work. So, Ari placed her energy into making up for lost time with Junior and Remy, and as soon as she was up to it, she took a trip to the store to get plenty of junk food for movie nights and showered them with gifts. Deep down, Ari knew she was trying to relieve her guilt from letting Junior down and putting her boys through so much.

The news of Ari spread like wildfire, shocking the town to its core. The house was still flooded with cards and homemade food from well-wishers wanting to help their friend. Her students made handmade cards, and she received a card and a huge bouquet from the principal. Ari appreciated the lovely gestures, but she was ready to take control of her life again. She went for walks and chatted to the neighbors, reintegrating herself back into society after being cooped up for a month, and the office door remained shut. Ari didn't go near it; she couldn't bring herself to. She just kept the door closed and pretended like it wasn't there. She was doing well again, building her confidence up by going to the coffee shop and eating healthy foods. She even returned to work to bring some normality back into her life.

Almost six weeks after her brutal attack, Ari was just returning from her walk when Adam pulled into her drive.

"Hey! What are you doing here?" she asked as he rolled down his window.

"Just dropping this off," he said, handing her blood-stained leather jacket.

"Thanks!"

Backing out of the drive, he shouted to her, "You may want to get it dry cleaned, though as it's been in my car a while and God knows what germs it's collect in there. I'll see you on Friday when you drop Junior off."

Ari waved him off and headed into her house with her trusty leather jacket, popping it on the counter to empty the pockets. She must have pulled out at least ten candy wrappers before she found a folded, blood-stained piece of paper. Ari, shaking as the flashbacks of that dreaded night etched into her brain, stared down at the note. Her eyebrows narrowed as she unfolded the paper and found herself feeling nauseous as she read the handwritten words.

"I'm sorry for what that monster did to you. Sorry we didn't help you sooner! Mack is living at the Gray Wolves Woodland Retreat in Uskiville. Good luck and feel better soon."

Ari gasped and dropped the note on the counter. "Where had the note come from? Was this a twisted game Number 21 was playing to entice her back for round two? Was that what he did to his victims?"

Ari reached to get a glass of water, but she couldn't steady her hand enough to pick up the glass, so she splashed her face instead and slid down against the cabinet, wrapping her hands around her knees, hugging them tight. Tears falling from her eyes as she rocked back and forth on the cold tiled floor to comfort herself.

An hour had passed, and Ari was still sitting and staring up at the note.

"Ari, this is fucking stupid! Pull yourself together, it's just a note," she told herself as she pushed herself to her feet, picking up the note and headed to her office. She unlocked the door, took a deep breath, and headed inside in search of her laptop. She turned on her laptop and waited for it to fire up. Looking at her pin board, seeing a sea of yellow and a couple of green pins, she picked up a red pin and attached it to the board as she had with the twenty pins before it. She had been on such a journey to find Mack and she wasn't sure if she had the strength in her to search for him anymore, not to mention that she had promised the boys she would stop looking for Junior's dad.

Once the computer screen was ready, Ari searched for the Gray Wolves Woodland Retreat in Uskiville. "Oh, you have got to be fucking kidding me! It's only fifty-minutes away," she blasted in frustration.

She had been driving for anything up to ten hours to the twenty-one clubs that she had visited over these past ten months and Mack was living fifty minutes away! Slamming the laptop closed as she stood to leave the room, but her feet dragged her onto the pin board as if they had a mind of their own. Glaring at the twenty-one numbers and their violent color-coded ratings attached to them, she shuddered. They made her feel dirty, so she went to take a shower.

Ari studied her scarred body and sighed. "Nobody will ever love me again! I'm a beast!" she said aloud as the hot water drenched her skin. The heat of the shower helped soothed her scars and torn muscles as even six weeks on, they still tried to heal. Ari would get paralyzed with pain when her back muscles spasmed in the cold and her boys would rush to her aid with Remy rubbing her back and Junior warming her lavender heating pad in the microwave as he held back tears of guilt. Junior hated seeing her in pain and blamed himself for what had happened to her.

Two days after finding the note, Ari was beside herself, as the nightmares decimated her sleep. She couldn't stop thinking about whether Mack was at the retreat. The Woodland Retreat looked nothing like an MC. It wasn't a run down, violent base for thieves and criminals and it didn't look like the air there smelt of lusty sweat and whisky. It looked like a haven, somewhere to escape, losing oneself, in the beauty of the forestry. It certainly didn't look like it housed a one-percenter.

"What is Mack doing there? Is he hiding from Number 21 or is he every bit as sadistic as Number 21 himself?" she murmured to herself as she sipped her coffee, staring at her laptop.

Ari couldn't stand the not knowing anymore. She knew this was a risk and broke her promise to her boys, but she was determined to find out once and for all if Mack was there.

"This time will be different," she said to herself. It would be different because Ari was going to arm herself. Ari was buying a gun.

Ari went to the local hunting shop to purchase a gun and gun license, undertaking all the necessary checks with the vendor. She took a block of lessons at the gun range and, to her surprise, found that she was quite good with her aim, making her feel confident for the first time in a long time. She was ready this time. She wasn't the same naïve woman that strolled to the bar at Number 1 anymore. There were no more rose-tinted glasses, rainbows, butterflies, or blue skies for Ari. She had been hardened. These past months had subjected her to violence, pain, suffering, and lies and there was no way that she wasn't going to defend herself and she would demand answers this time.

CHAPTER FOURTEEN
The Woodland Retreat

Ari set off on Friday morning to head for the small town of Uskiville, arranging with Adam to collect Junior from school. Lies were all Ari knew these days. She had spent months being lied to and lured into dangerous places; she had told a ton herself, and today was no different. Ari couldn't believe Mack may only be an hour away and it wasn't long before she would be there herself.

Uskiville was a small town that experienced all the seasons due to its location. In the summer, it was boiling hot, and you could see the sunrise over the big grassy hills. In the autumn it was beautiful with all the warm colors of taking hold of the trees and when the leaves fell, they would cover the beautiful landscape in a sea of orange, red, brown, and yellow: It was simply picturesque. Winter was cold as the snow covered the hillsides in beautiful white sheets, but today it was spring. Spring was fresh and spritely with flowers everywhere and the trees stood tall within the forestry that footed the hills. The town was simply sublime, idyllic, and Ari could see herself sat on a red checkered picnic blanket reading a book on the brow of the hill.

Ari saw the local townspeople going about their business. Some were buying groceries, some sat on park benches, indulging in delicious looking ice creams, while others mingled at the local park to talk to the gardeners who were planting some beautiful marigolds.

Ari continued to follow the sat nav system as it guided her through beautiful country lanes that came out near the foot of the hill. She had to make a sharp right, turn onto another dusty country road which had signs for the Woodland Retreat. Ari thought how beautiful it would be to stay in a luxurious log cabin with a big old fireplace so she could cozy up and read a book: all her fantasies involved her sitting comfortably with a book. Although, she did find her mind wandering as she wondered if they had a hot tub and a bar. Ari's imagination continued to wander, thinking she might stay the night if the retreat didn't turn out to be another sadistic MC.

Ari had been in a position of optimism before, only to find it being clawed out of her, and now she started to panic. The thought of being brutalized again severed the vocal cords of her optimistic voice inside, instead it now screamed in fear of her getting hurt again. Her head raged at her, saying how this last encounter was irresponsible and to turn the car around. She'd barely healed from the Mauler's almighty wrath, and she knew that she shouldn't really be driving yet, as she still got headaches from when he knocked her unconscious. She shook her head, shoeing away the sensible voice in her head and telling herself.

"I HAVE TO DO THIS!

Straight up ahead, Ari saw cabins in the distance. "Please don't say I came out here for nothing," she muttered to herself as she pulled up at the retreat's reception. She hadn't called ahead to check if Mack was there. She couldn't take any more lies or deceit and, although risky, she wanted to check for herself.

Ari got out of the car and headed inside. Even the reception area was beautiful. It had a huge oak countertop with glorious woodland colors in the center of the room, and a grand log fire heating the room, beckoning the guests to sit and enjoy it's warmth. Above the fireplace sat a large, hand-drawn landscape of unfamiliar hills in a white oak picture frame. Ari approached the picture, intrigued about where it was from, and read the little plaque that said, "Brecon Beacons — The Welsh Valleys by McIntyre Kelly.

Ari gasped. "This has to be him!"

Just then, another voice entering the room interrupted her thoughts. "Can I help you?" The woman spoke in a stern Welsh accent.

Ari turned toward the voice. A tall and curvy woman in her late thirties stood before her. As the newcomer tilted her head in query, blond hair swished over her shoulder.

"Oh, hi!" Ari said, smiling but feeling intimidated by the woman, who stood glaring at Ari, as her T-shirt pulled tight across her well-defined abdominal muscles.

"I'm sorry to bother you, but I was wondering if you could help me find someone?"

The woman raised an eyebrow at her.

"Sorry, what I mean is. I am looking for Mack. Do you know if he lives here?" she asked, hoping this woman would not murder her as her jaw stiffened and her eyes narrowed. Ari thought she looked intense, uptight almost, as she approached Ari with her mug of tea in hand.

"And who exactly wants to know?" she asked as she sat in the leather armchair by the fire, sipping her tea.

"Excuse me! And who are *you* exactly?"

"I'll be your worst bloody nightmare if you don't tell me who you are and why you have had the audacity to bring a gun onto my land," the woman said, eyes calm, sipping on her tea.

"I doubt that very much!" Ari said as she pulled her shirt down, trying to conceal her weapon.

"Pointless, trying to hide it now. Besides, I guarantee you I could snap your wrist long before you could pull it from your waistband."

This woman is a certified nut job. Ari believed the woman was taunting her to reach for her gun, just so she could show her power and control over the situation.

"So, is that your plan, my lovely? To stroll onto my land and attempt to shoot my family? Because you won't get far, I promise you that!" she said, as subtle as ever, and with fire in her eyes, watching Ari's every move.

"What? No!" Ari said, shaking her head. "I'm the adoptive mother of Mack's son, Junior, and I've been trying to find him to reconnect. I've spent months looking all over the country, going to bar after bar, getting knocked about, beaten and..." Ari went silent as she shook her head, blinking back tears. "Please, just tell me if he's here."

The woman now sat up straight in her chair, eyes wide, giving Ari her undivided attention.

Ari wiped her tears. "Shit, sorry!"

"How many MCs have you visited? How many Presidents have you met?" the woman asked.

"Twenty-one before this. Please tell me this is the last."

"Do you want a cup of tea?" the crazy woman asked, getting up from her chair. "You look as though you need a cup of tea. I only have the best here. None of that fruity rubbish that you Americans like to drink, real British tea."

Ari stared at her, raising her eyebrows.

"Tea makes everything feel better where I come from. When you sit enjoying a nice cuppa, it allows you to think, puts things into perspective," the woman explained. "You sit tight, and I'll fetch you some. But before I do, can you please pop your gun into the lockbox? I hate guns, and there are kids around here." She handed Ari a small black metal box.

Ari, now very confused, retrieved the gun from her waistband. She set it in the box and watched as the woman locked it and placed it under the counter.

"You'll get it back when you leave, I promise." She nodded and headed out back to make the tea.

Ari sat, scared and afraid. This woman was a psychopath, and rather than offer up any information regarding Mack, she went to make tea. Ari had been lured under false pretenses previously, and she wasn't going to let it happen again. No, Ari was going to make this scary woman tell her where Mack was if it took her last breath to do it.

A short while later, the woman returned with a tray, complete with everything required to make tea, as well as a plate of cookies. "There we are. Now, how would you like it?"

Ari stared at her, confused, "Uh, I'm not sure. I've never had tea like this before," she said quietly.

The woman raised an eyebrow, smiling as she poured the tea into the cups arranged onto their saucers. "Well, I prefer just milk, but you could have it without. But you look like a milk and sugar kind of girl, so we'll go with that," she stated, before adding milk, a cube of sugar and stirring it all delicately before handing it to Ari.

Ari took the tea, still feeling confused about the whole situation.

"Biscuit," the woman offered, holding a plate of what looked like cookies, in her hand.

"It's a cookie?"

"Not where I'm from and I made them, so that makes them biscuits to me," she said, smiling at Ari in amusement.

"Thank you," Ari said, taking what looked like a ginger snap from the plate.

She watched as the woman placed the plate onto the table before taking one for herself and dunking it right into her tea then quickly popping it into her mouth. "The best way to have a biscuit is to dunk them in your tea. Try it."

Ari did exactly that and discovered a taste sensation, much to her surprise. She found the warming ginger flavors and the sweetness of the tea delicious as it soaked her palate.

"Wow! This is good."

The woman chuckled. "See? I told you! Tea and biscuits put everything into perspective."

Ari let out a laugh before sipping on her tea. "I never knew that tea could taste so good," she said as she helped herself to another biscuit and dunked it in her tea.

"You've never had a Welsh woman make you a real cup of tea. I'm B by the way."

"Ari."

B nodded, sitting back in her chair, slack-jawed, as Ari devoured one biscuit after another.

Ari plucked up the courage to ask B a question: "Are you Mack's wife? Because I'm not here to cause trouble, I promise you. See, my son is desperate to find his dad and I've been on a hell of a journey to get here and..." Ari blurted out, getting upset again.

"Ha-ha!" B mocked. "God, no!" She burst into a fit of laughter, leaving Ari looking at her and feeling strange. B composed herself, clearing her throat. "We are best friends! We have been for years. We look out for each other. I have his back, and he has mine."

Ari stared at her, waiting for her to continue.

"When I met Mack, he had lost everything: his son, his family, his home, and his friends. He was homeless when I met him. In fact, I caught him having a bath in my swimming pool out back one evening." She shook her head in amusement.

"My pool boy searched for weeks for a problem with my pool. I'd come home from work on a Friday evening and my pool would be full of bubbles. Little did I know that Mack had been bathing and washing his bloody clothes in it while I was out, before heading back to his tent in the woods behind my cabin."

Ari stared, incredulous. "He was homeless?"

"Yeah! You should have seen his face when I came home early that day. He was naked in my pool, washing his dirty socks! I invited him in, made him a cuppa and listened to his story, and after that I gave him a job and a cabin to live in. Now, he helps me run this place. My kids see him as an uncle, and we wouldn't be without him. He's... our family!"

"So, you just gave him a home, job, and everything?"

"After hearing his story, I knew that he just needed a break. Mackie boy needed to know the world wasn't against him. It is something everyone needs at some point in their life. Besides, he's a Celt and us Celts look after one another."

"What exactly happened to Mack, B?"

"That's his story to tell, I'm afraid. I will kill anyone who hurts him, and I won't allow him to be destroyed again. I know you've been through a lot, but before I consider allowing you to have contact with him, I have to know that you are legit and mean well."

"Meaning?" Ari asked crossly.

"Meaning that you're not full of shit. A weirdo sent here to fuck up his life. Meaning that I want to see proof, meaning you understand that we have been searching for Junior for five bloody years and there's no way in hell that you are going to stop my Mackie from seeing Junior if you get cold feet after they make contact."

Ari stared at her and could see her eyes widening, as if fire was burning in her eyes. This woman was clearly willing to protect Mack at all costs.

"There's not a day that's gone by that Mack hasn't thought of Jelly Legs, and he's never given up on him. Not to mention the thousands of dollars that I've spent trying to locate him. Mackie needs his boy back in his life. He will never feel complete until he is. So, I'm asking you to allow that to happen. If you're not lying to me, that is." B said and not asking at all.

Ari sensed B really would die for Mack. She also knew that she didn't want to make an enemy of her. She thought B was intense and crazy, but she resonated with her as they both would do anything for the ones they love.

Ari retrieved her phone from her pocket, showing B a recent picture of Junior.

B grinned with delight, her eyes glowing like embers. "He's the image of Mackie."

"You said you have kids?" Ari asked.

B nodded. "Yeah, boys. Why do you ask?"

"Well, imagine that you adopted a kid that your son befriended one day, to find his mother didn't want him and told him so repeatedly, allowing her Johns to beat him. Imagine he'd been neglected, beaten, and subjected to so much trauma that you had to hold him while he screamed at night."

B's unblinking eyes fixed on Ari, her jaw clenched shut with veins popping out of her forehead as she listened to Ari explain about Junior's life over the years, the years without Mack to guide him, hold him, and tell him everything was going to be all right.

Ari was aware that it angered B. She was a mother too, and Ari had no doubt that she would protect them with everything she had if required. She continued, wanting B to understand a few things.

"Imagine one day having to tell him that his mother passed away after you found her dead with a needle in her arm, while he sat in the car waiting for you to tell him it was safe to check on her, because despite everything, he still loved her. Then, after the funeral and you officially adopt him as your own after two and a half years of temporary foster care, you find he's still unfulfilled and broken because he found old pictures of his missing father. Imagine staring into his eyes and seeing so much hurt, because he doesn't understand what happened to his dad or why he hasn't seen him in six years. You would do anything to find the father, right?" she asked.

"Of course," B answered in a serious tone.

"Well, that's just what I've done, anything and everything to get here today and I have the scars to prove it," she said as she removed her T-shirt, revealing the scars left by most of the twenty-one MC's.

B circled Ari, taking in the full extent of her scars, pursing her lips. Ari watched her clench her fist until her knuckles went white. B was raging.

"Ari, I'm sorry this happened to you, and I want to thank you for looking after Junior the way you have. Those scars tell a story and tell me that we have an understanding. So, I will set you up in one of my cabins while I get Mack. He's fishing up at a creek about an hour away. I will talk to him and bring him back to your room, okay?"

Ari caught her breath, confused. "Why can't I come with you?"

"Trust me, he needs to hear this from me first. I must prepare him for this, and I'm not sure what it will do to him. Mackie has always carried the world on his shoulders, and this will bring him both joy and sadness. You have to let me handle this, and I promise you I will bring him back with me."

Ari nodded. "Okay!"

B retrieved a key from the key cupboard and booked out the corresponding cabin for the weekend and the two women headed to cabin number thirty-five after Ari retrieved her suitcase from her car. B took it from her as Ari struggled to lift it and carried it without even breaking a sweat. B then opened the cabin door and placed the case next to the bed. She gave Ari the run-down of the little cabin that came complete with a fireplace, reading chair, double bed, bedside cabinets, and a small dining table situated at the window. The bathroom had a beautiful walk-in shower and Ari liked the quaint and cozy vibe it gave off.

"What's this?" Ari asked, taking hold of what looked like an overly thick blanket that covered the bed.

"That's a duvet!" B pointed out. "In the UK, winters can be cold, so we have thick and cozy bedspreads filled with duck feathers or stuffing if you like. It feels like you are having a cwtch with one of them wrapped around you," she explained.

"A cwtch?" Ari asked

"A cuddle or snuggle, but better! Us Welsh are very passionate people, so when we cwtch, it has so much more meaning, and cwtch deserves its own name," she explained.

Ari looked amused. "I see!"

"Oh, here, I almost forgot," B said, handing Ari a tube of cream.

"It will help with the old bruising and scarring. Now, I'll be a couple of hours, so please rest up until I get back." And that said, B headed out.

Ari was exhausted as she sat on the soft bed. She couldn't believe how nice it was there, and, although terrifying, how nice B had been to her. Ari liked B's honesty and didn't feel the need to worry about her or Mack tricking or luring her into a trap of any kind, especially as they had been searching for Junior too. Junior would be ecstatic when she told him the news. But now, she wanted to rest while she waited for B to bring Mack back. She had so many emotions running through her head that she welcomed the chance to lie down, so she slipped off her jeans and climbed into the soft bed with the duvet that did in fact feel like she was having a cuddle, and within moments, she was asleep.

CHAPTER FIFTEEN
Relief and Release

B parked her Humvee outside the cabin to discover Mack and Frankie fishing at the small creek out front. The rest of the cabin was surrounded by an endless primeval forest that stretched for miles, with seas of green and brown ebbing and flowing across the landscape.

Mack saw B's truck approach the cabin and instantly dropped his fishing rod; he knew that something was wrong. B would never drive up to the cabin, especially as she knew that they were practicing their shooting during their stay.

"Something's wrong," he said, panicking and racing over to B. He could feel in every fiber of his being. "What's happened?" he said.

B stood and stared at him, wondering how she should break the news.

He glanced at Frankie in despair, who had raced to B too. "Dragon, you're scaring me."

"Hey, B," Frankie said to her. "You look like you've seen a ghost!"

B's fiery stare shot back at Mack. "You have a visitor back home."

Mack stepped closer to her, trembling, "What do you mean? Who is it? I've never seen you like this," he said, embracing her and putting his forehead to hers.

B placed her hands to his cheeks and stared into his frantic eyes. "It's Junior's adopted mom, Mackie, and she's been to hell and back to find you."

Mack froze, staring back at her and trying to comprehend what she said. With his voice hoarse, palms sweaty and heart beating so violently it felt like it was trying to escape his chest, Mack tried to gather everything he could to push three simple and important words out of the depths of his soul.

"Is he alive?"

B looked at him, smiling. "Yes Mackie, he's very much alive my lovely."

Mack dropped to his knees and sobbed uncontrollably as the torment of the past six years ripped through him then leaving his body and being replaced by relief that washed over him like a wave washing over warm sand. His body shook violently as warm, salty tears flooded him and seeped into his mouth that was wide open as he howled with happiness. He felt B's strong and warm arms wrap around him as she too dropped to her knees to comfort him, holding him tight, just as she did when they had first met.

B continued to hold Mack until he calmed down, just as she did a thousand times before, and Frankie, who was an ex-marine and Mack's other best friend, went into the cabin to fetch their Welsh whisky and three glasses.

"Get this down you Mackie boy. I think you need it," he said, handing Mack a double shot of the good stuff.

Mack looked up and took the glass from the six foot, six inches muscular beast of a man who offered his best friend a drink. Frankie was good like that. Just like B, he always knew what to do in the moment.

After handing B a glass too, he left the two of them to talk. Frankie, a quiet guy, didn't say much and very rarely offered advice, but when he did, people listened.

B's cwtch along with the whisky provided Mack with a sense of calm. Taking a deep breath, he glanced at B.

"Tell me everything, Dragon, I need to hear it!"

B explained everything that Ari had told her, leaving Mack devastated that he hadn't been there for Junior when he'd needed him and, despite her death, he remained angry with Nancy for taking him away. B explained about the twenty-one MCs that left their mark on Ari, infuriating Mack who hated that she endured so much to find him. However, his mind was fixated on Junior, so relieved that he was alive.

After a long chat and plenty more tears, Mack collected his things and waited in the car for B to take him home to meet Ari, the woman responsible for saving his son and bringing them back together.

B closed the trunk and leaned against it as she drew in a long and hard breath. It had been an eventful day, and she wanted to collect herself for a moment.

Frankie, who liked to keep a watchful eye on B, approached her. "Hey,"

She tilted her head toward him. "Hey."

"You handled that well for an emotional cripple," he teased

"Thanks."

"Is he...okay?"

"I hope so, Frankie, because I have a bad bloody feeling about all this."

"Hold on, you're nervous? You're never nervous," he said, taking her by the arm, urging her to explain further.

B pressed her lips together and glanced behind her to make sure that Mack was out of earshot. "My gut tells me that trouble is headed our way, and I hope for all of our sakes that I'm wrong."

"How so?" he asked.

B shook her head, kicking the dirt in frustration. "Ari...she seems lovely, but the scars on her body tell a story, and I can't shake the feeling that something black is coming, something so dark that it could destroy us."

Frankie knew better than to think that B was dramatizing things;

despite being void of emotion, seeing the world in shades of black and white, B's instincts were always spot on.

"B you're like a little sister to me and you know I mean well when I ask this. You sure you aren't just nervous about Mack having them enter his life?"

"No, honestly. I'm happy for him, but that poor woman waiting in number thirty-five is a fucking mess, and I'm not talking about her scars."

"Shit!" Frankie accepted. "Look, let's just get Mackie boy through today and we'll figure the rest out together tomorrow."

"Okay, bring it in so I can get down the road," she said, embracing her other best friend.

"I'm here for you B, always and forever, don't you forget it and whatever it is that's making those fiery dragon embers ignite in your belly, we'll handle it," he said to her as he hugged her back.

Frankie opened the Humvee door for B to climb in. "See you soon Mackie Boy, just holler if you need me."

Mack nodded and headed back home so he could talk to Ari.

***

Ari was still sleeping when B returned with Mack, so B made Mack take his shoes off and wait in the open doorway while she woke Ari gently.

"Hey!" she said as Ari stirred awake. "I have someone who wants to talk to you," she said with a big smile on her face, peering over at Mack.

Ari's eyes widened as she saw the big, handsome Irishman stood in the doorway. "Hey!" she said softly, "Come in please, sit down," she requested, gesturing to the bed.

"I'll be at reception if any of you need me," B explained, kissing Mack on the cheek on her way out.

"She's intense, that one!" Ari said jokingly, to break the ice.

Mack chuckled as he approached nervously and slowly sitting

himself on the bed next to her. "You're okay, though. She doesn't hit women."

"I don't know. I'm pretty sure that she was ready to kill me earlier."

"She's very protective, that's all. Look, I'm so sorry for what happened to you and grateful that you found me. I have been tormented every day since my little Jelly Legs was taken."

Ari felt a huge lump in her throat as she edged closer to him to wipe his tears. She looked into his eyes and could see how much he was hurting, and she began to cry, too. "I can't believe I actually found you. It's been hell trying to find you."

"Ari, thank you so much for taking care of my boy." Overcome by emotion, Mack broke down in tears. "I am so sorry. B told me what you've been through, and I'll never forgive myself for what's happened to you. If I had just kept an eye on Nancy when she went downhill, I could have prevented this from happening to you."

Ari pulled him in close and held him, but he was twice her size. So, she wrapped her arms around him as best she could. The pair sobbed in Union as they began stroking each other in sympathy for one another. Then, out of nowhere, Ari found herself stroking him a little firmer, only to feel Mack reciprocating her touch, stroking her more forcefully, too.

Mack's eyes met hers and she could see the raw emotion staring back at her, like she could see inside his soul. She found herself moving her lips closer to his as she became lost in his big, blue, glacier-like eyes. Mack watched her every move, scared to move, and before Ari realized what she was doing, she found her lips on his. They were so soft, like silk, as she slipped her tongue inside his warm mouth, tasting his divine flavor as she pulled him closer with her hand firmly gripping the back of his head. Ari was turned on as she forcefully explored his mouth with her tongue, with Mack massaging her tongue with his, making her moan with pleasure. Ari had forgotten what it felt like to be entwined with a man and she never thought she could let a man explore her again, especially after what Number 21 had done to her. Yet here she was in an emotionally raw riptide, thrashing about furiously, tearing off Mack's clothes. She got the vibe that Mack was caught up in the same emotional riptide too, as he frantically ripped off her T-shirt and removed her bra. They had an urgency about them, like they were searching for relief from all the pain and suffering that they had each endured up until now.

Mack lowered a moaning Ari down onto the bed as she unzipped his jeans. Freeing him from his pants, she felt his wet lips sink into the nape of her neck. Ari's eyes rolled back into her head as he kissed her passionately, as he reached down and pulled her lace thong to one side. Stood to attention, he teased her entrance with his sex, forcing a loud moan from Ari's delicate mouth. Her damaged and shattered body convulsed as he entered her, stretching her sex with his erection, and gasping as he slipped seamlessly inside of her. Mack's eyes glazed over as he penetrated her with slow and steady thrusts, and Ari could feel the raw emotion ripple through her fragile body. He glided in and out effortlessly, causing her to cry out as she become lost in immense pleasure. She could feel his gratitude as he stared deep into her eyes as they lost themselves in the passionate entanglement that now had them writhing with deep animalistic tendencies.

Soft cries and moans echoed throughout the cabin as they continued to please each other. Ari loved the feeling of him deep inside of her, taking her with such sincerity as she watched him tremble as he hardened. Pursing his lips, he drove into her sex, thrusting at a steady pace, allowing Ari to experience his lusty pleasure. Ari, now brimming with her impending orgasm, felt an urgency for him to take her hard and fast. Grabbing his firm backside, she attempted to pull him in deeper as she thrusted her hips harder and faster, indicating to him to take her with ferocious intensity. Mack moaned loudly, gritting his teeth as he tried so hard to reciprocate. Ari screamed as her body cried out into an immense orgasm, her body trembling and struggling to cope with her orgasmic release.

Mack gasped as he climaxed shortly after, allowing him to release every ounce of himself inside of her. Bodies entwined, they continued to kiss passionately until they fulfilled their bodies' natural release, leaving Mack collapsing on top of her.

"Oh, my days sweetheart, what the feck just happened?" he asked in his sweet Irish accent as he came to.

"I don't know. I guess all the emotion and relief of finding you just came together."

"Well, it was fecking amazing, sweetheart." He joked as he removed a stray hair from her face. "And I believe, you were meant to find me so I can reconnect with my son."

"I think you're right. Everything happens for a reason!" she said as she kissed him again. "Geez, Mack, you're incredible!"

Mack smiled as he kissed her back before pulling away again.

"You're gorgeous, sweetheart! You really are, but I think it's best we talk first, don't you!" he said, studying her and stroking her cheek.

"Oh, yes right! Of course."

Mack nodded and kissed her on the cheek as they sat up in bed together. "Well, I assume you want to get to know me before allowing me to see my son again, so what would you like to know?"

"Everything!" she said.

Ari and Mack talked for hours, agreeing that Ari would stay in the cabin tonight and they would head to Ari's, ready for Junior's arrival the following afternoon.

"Thank you, Ari, you have made me the happiest man in the world."

"You've made me happy too, Mack," she said, smiling at him, and as they gazed into each other's eyes, and Ari felt it again. The same raw emotion that engulfed her not ten minutes after she met him. She could feel it in the pit of her stomach. She wanted him, needed him. Desperate for his touch, she leaned in to kiss him once again, hovering her lips over his, but this time he stopped her in her tracks.

"Ari, I'm sorry, but I don't think this is a good idea," he said, trying not to upset her.

"Oh, right! I'm sorry, you're absolutely right!" she said, deflated, turning away in embarrassment.

He took hold of her hand. "Ari, what happened earlier was amazing. But I don't want to complicate things for Junior. He needs to know that he is the most important person in my life. B and I have spent years looking for him, and he needs to know that I didn't give up on him. I don't want him to think I'm getting to know him just so I can bang his mom. Especially when—" He stopped short, looking at Ari sympathetically.

"What is it, Mack?"

"What I mean is, I don't want to confuse him, seeing me with his new mom, when I'm in love with somebody else."

"Oh, shit, you're with someone!" she said, jumping out of the bed, panicking. "God, you must think I'm a slut for coming on to you like that."

Mack stood, taking hold of her waist, "No, no sweetheart. I'm not. Look, will you please sit down for a minute so I can explain?"

Ari sat on the bed, with Mack sitting beside her and resting his elbows on his knees. He looked nervous as he dropped his head in his hands.

"I've been in love with B, or Dragon, as I call her since I arrived in town. My heart bleeds for her, Ari, but she's not interested in me, never has been. I can't be with anyone else because my heart belongs to her."

"Oh! I'm sorry! That must be so hard for you."

"Yeah, it sucks! B and I are like two peas in a pod. We do everything together, everything except being intimate with each other. We're best friends, and while I know I can never be with her, the alternative is unthinkable, because I need her in my life, and I can't live without her!"

"Mack, that is heartbreaking! Does she know?"

Mack let out a sigh and nodded. "I told her not long after we met, but B has her own painful story, too. She doesn't see the world like most people do. She sees people as either good or bad, or black and white, as she puts it. She's a control freak who doesn't make emotional connections with people and she never dates. She sees everything as a business transaction, even sex, and when I confessed how I felt about her, she panicked and asked me to leave."

"Yikes!" Ari said.

Mack, shaking his head in frustration, continued. "She's the most emotionally crippled, dysfunctional, yet brilliant fiery dragon that I have ever met, and I would rather have her as a best friend than nothing at all. I just do not work without her, Ari! We have this connection like we're tethered to one another, and she is my person. She lifted my spirit and breathed life back into my soul when I had nothing left to live for. My Dragon gave me a life that I could only have dreamed of before I met her, and I'll be forever grateful to her for that."

"Wow, you have it bad for her," Ari said, nudging him and smiling.

Mack laughed. "I do! Geez, I even feel guilty about sleeping with you, and don't get me wrong, it was beyond amazing, but it wasn't fair to you. I should have stopped myself somehow."

Ari stood up, taking his head in her hands. "Mack, you have done nothing wrong. Don't feel guilty about what happened between us. It was incredible. And if B can't see how amazing you are, then it's her loss. It's admirable that you're loyal to her, but life is just too short to waste your heart on someone who doesn't see your worth."

"Ari, you don't understand. I haven't loved anyone like I love my dragon!"

"Mack, look at me," she said, as she stood showing off her naked, scar-filled body. "I thought nobody would want me again, but you gave me hope today. You didn't see me as a scarred and broken woman. You made love to me, made me feel attractive, and I want to thank you for that."

Mack stood up to meet her gaze, eyes widening, he stroked her back seductively. Ari could see that he was conflicted. "Sweetheart, I don't see your scars. I see you as a gorgeous and amazing woman who has given me my son back, and I am so fecking grateful."

"Do you want me again?" she whispered.

Mack closed his eyes and bit down on his bottom lip in frustration. "I do sweetheart! I want to taste you on my lips again, but I can't give you my heart. Ari, sex is a transaction to me too these days and nothing more. I can help you release your tension as I release mine, but that's all it will be. I'm sorry. A beautiful woman like you deserves more!"

Peering up at him, she told him, "Mack, I'm not asking you for your heart, I'm asking you to treat me like a woman once more, to give me hope that one day someone else might look at me like you do at B. Treat it like a transaction if you want to, release some tension, I don't care. But please take me again."

Mack pulled out of her grasp and turned away, putting his hands on his hips as Ari dropped her head in disappointment and stared out the window. She turned to retrieve her T-shirt from the floor when Mack took hold of her wrist. His back still turned away from her, he growled through gritted teeth. "Aww, feck it!" he snapped, before turning to her and pulling her into him, slamming her chest into hers, catching Ari's breath. Grabbing her head with both hands, he delivered sharp, hard and fast blows into her mouth with his tongue. He was like a man possessed, picking her up and sitting himself on the bed, with his hard and erect penis pressing against her.

Coming up for air, breaths shallow, he gazed upon her. "Are you sure you want this, sweetheart? Because once we start, I can't stop?"

"God! Yes! I want you inside me, Mack. Let me ride you. I want to thank you for making me feel like a woman again."

Mack covered her mouth with his, tasting all, she had to offer. He ripped off her thong, tearing it off her body in one hard snap as he gorged himself on her huge breasts, tugging at her hard nipples with his lips. A panting Ari lifted her hips and lowered herself directly onto his hard cock with Mack grabbing her ass, pulling her down onto him, encouraging her to accept all his length. Ari gasped as he filled her. He felt much bigger to her this time around, stretching her sex to his will.

Mack's grunts paired rhythmically with his thrusts as Ari rode him. Starting slow and even, she got comfortable with his length and girth tantalizing her G spot as vibrant sparks pulsated through her body.

"God Ari, yes!" Mack growled through jagged breaths as he cupped her bouncing breasts and Ari increased her pace, riding him with the intensity of a blistering sun. Struggling to cope, he brought her mouth to his, covering it, as Ari felt him stiffen. Unable to cope with his stiff and twitching member, Ari screamed, her eyes rolling back into her head as she unraveled, clenching herself around Mack's cock.

"Oh, Ari!" he gasped, looking up at her, her hair flowing freely around her breasts, back arched and her body convulsing in ecstasy as she gave in to her orgasm.

Trembling, Mack let out a loud growl of his own as he exploded deep inside of her, as a screaming Ari continued to ride him. Ari was defenseless as he pulled her down onto him, rolling her over, and driving her into the mattress, so he could finish. Pumping her hard and fast, he let out a rugged and manly cry as Ari felt his body tense on top of her.

Trying to catch his breath, he whispered in her ear. "Ari, I really don't know what's happening to me right now. I don't know how you make my cock want you so bad, but it does, and I can't control it."

Ari, still convulsing from the remnants of her orgasm, gazed at Mack. "Then don't try to control it! Let it want me."

Kissing her soft lips, Mack wiped the sweat from her forehead. "Thank you for everything sweetheart, I'm so glad you found me."

Ari ran her fingers through his sweat-soaked hair, cupping the back of his head as she nibbled on his ear. "Me too. You were definitely worth waiting for."

CHAPTER SIXTEEN
Afterglow

It was nightfall when an exhausted Mack left Ari's cabin. Mack could see B out on the lake with Frankie as they both laughed and chugged beer together. Mack walked along the small pier and sat next to B.

"Do you mind if I talk to B alone a second, please Frankie?" he asked

"Sure, pal." Frankie said, getting up and walking toward the bar.

"Are you alright my lovely?" B asked as she handed him a beer.

"To be honest, I have no fecking idea! I am filled with all these emotions and it's fecking with my head," he said as he ran his fingers through his hair.

"Deep breaths and baby steps Mackie boy!" She said as she clinked his beer bottle, gulped her beer, and looked out onto the lake.

"I'm going to find and kill those bastards for what they've done to her, Dragon."

B looked at him as she downed the rest of her beer. Reaching for another, she spoke to him. "Slow your roll, tough guy! What's happened to her is disgusting. But you are on the verge of seeing your son for the first time in six years, don't jeopardize that by trying to play a hero."

"Dragon, see her body. They fecking mauled her!"

"I have! And as honorable as it is, you hardly know Ari, and how would Junior feel if you ended up inside? How would the boys feel, losing you and how would I function?"

Mack studied her stern expression, eyes glowing like embers as she continued... "You're my best friend. We are a team, a brilliant bloody team and nobody has ever come between us, so please don't let this damsel in distress destroy our bond."

He nodded in agreement. Tapping his fingers on his beer bottle, he looked up at her. "Dragon, there's something else."

B's eyed flashed with curiosity and before she could comment, the words fell out of his mouth

"I had sex with her."

B looked at him in shock. He'd slept with women before. He'd had plenty of meaningless sexual encounters. They both had. It was a monthly game they'd play. Who could land the biggest hottie? But this was different. She could see it in his eyes as he tried to hide it from her, ashamed of what he'd done. This was a passion fueled, love making session with relentless emotion. It wasn't just a random pick up at the bar.

Mack gritted his teeth, disgusted with his behavior. "Did you hear me? I had sex with her. I didn't mean to. It just fecking happened. TWICE! One minute we were pouring our hearts out and the next, we were ripping each other's clothes off, entangled in a lust driven moment of escapism. I'm so sorry, I feel like I've betrayed you." He said as his voice trembled.

Grabbing his head with both hands, B placed her forehead to his. "Bloody hell, Mackie, you haven't betrayed me my lovely. Why would you even think that?"

Mack cried, his tears soaking her chest as they rolled off his cheeks onto her perfect skin. "I'm sorry, Dragon!"

"Look, I can't imagine how hard this must be for you, lovely boy. Having Junior back is all you've dreamed of since I met you, and I would never impede that. But Ari has been through hell too Mackie. Listening to her story and staring at her broken body, I realized she is more damaged than any of us. I mean, look what she went through to find you. Just looking at her, it's obvious she's head fucked. She needs therapy to help her process that shit, and I don't think fucking her is going to help her right now."

"I know, you're right as usual."

"Look, we don't know much about her, how her brain works, what she wants from you. But what I know is that she has the keys to your castle Mackie and one wrong move could see that fragile head of hers crack wide open like an egg, seeing her lock the castle doors and you could lose Junior forever. Tell me you understand that lovely boy!"

Mack wiped his eyes and looked up at her. "You're right. I know! I'll get me shite together."

B staring at him with fire burning in her eyes, lifted his chin to gaze upon her, "No more fucking her until you establish a relation-ship with Junior and find out what she expects from you, okay? Oh, and let me tell you something... If she turns out to be a bloody fruit loop, a bunny boiler, I don't care what she's been through, I will bloody end her!"

Mack caught her grimace, feeling a little worried as he cleared his tear-soaked throat. Looking sullen, he exhaled. "Dragon, she's not a fruit loop."

B's eyebrows drew together forming an angry V, and the veins in her forehead pulsed as she flicked a switch and launched her beer bottle. "Oh, and your analysis came from what, exactly? Five minutes of 'hey, how are you doing?' and ten minutes of riding her? Don't be so naïve lovely boy."

"Dragon, that's unfair!" he said, as if he was sulking.

B closed her eyes, trying to calm herself by inhaling deep into her chest. "Now, I like her. I feel sorry for her, especially with what she's been through to find you. Mackie, I will always be grateful for what she's done for you, but you are my family, my priority, and I'm just saying that if she hurts you, it'll be the last thing she ever does."

It was now obvious to Mack that B's fiery inner dragon had

woken. He'd seen it a hundred times before in the bar whenever trouble had loomed. See as much as B saw herself as white and law abiding. If the people she loved were threatened, her inner Dragon would be released, and she would tear apart anyone in her way. It was one of the many reasons Mack loved her, seeing her in a fit of rage, losing herself to black for just long enough to save them was beautiful to him. It was then that he got to see her for who she really was, stripped bare and desperate for destruction. He'd seen her tear blokes three times her size apart when they had tried to hurt an innocent, or cause trouble in the bar, and she was always careful not to throw the first punch. B knew the law. Her friend was the best lawyer in the country and versed her on the intricacies of self-defense and the law. It was as if she laid in wait, as she sat with her bottle of Welsh whisky, sipping it, waiting patiently for trouble to loom.

It didn't happen often, but when it did, B was ready for it. Mack and Frankie would join B, fighting side by side to defend their own, like superheroes defending the earth. Afterwards, B insisted on calling the police to wrap things up and they'd arrive just as B calmed herself, reverting to the gentle mommy figure who tried to defend her family business. The police would become putty in her hands and cart off the injured troublemakers. Despite the violence from the fire-breathing Dragon, B still saw herself as white, because in her eyes she was doing the right thing by protecting her friends, family, and livelihood. She didn't see it as dirtying the waters or mixing the colors. They were black and would always be black, and she was still very much white.

"So, you're not mad about me sleeping with her?" He asked, as if he was a naughty schoolboy.

B wrapped her arms around him tight and put her head to his forehead. "No lovely boy, I'm not, but if you don't keep it in your pants for a little while, then I'm going to chop it off."

Mack laughed as he held onto her as if he never wanted to release her again. "I love you, Dragon."

Glowering at him and wearing a devilish grin, she teased him. "Shut the fuck up, you sissy! Now, let's get you home so you can clean yourself up. Junior doesn't want a dad who stinks of fish. Geez, why didn't you shower after fishing? God is that what Ari's into because that's just gross!"

"Feck off!" He retorted through his laughter, pushing her. B grabbed his shirt as the pair grappled like playful siblings.

Ari, who looked on from her cabin window, could see the magical bond between them and, despite just meeting Mack, found herself a little jealous of B, after what Mack had told her. But once again, she had to put her feelings aside for Junior's sake and stepped away from the window. She couldn't watch them anymore.

The next morning, Ari decided to go for a walk around the retreat, as she needed to clear her head. The entire experience had become quite surreal to her. She had gone from MC to MC, getting beaten and thrown around and been through the worst kind of torture where Number 21 still haunted her dreams. To finding Mack, who as far as first impressions go, turned out to be a kind, handsome and passionate soul who just needed his son back in his life.

As she wandered around the quiet woodland retreat, she couldn't stop thinking about their entanglement. His powerful body on top of hers, displaying his strength as he made love to her, making her scream as the chemistry and passion roared between them. Ari had experienced nothing like it before. Casting her mind back to the urges she experienced as Mack made love to her, the electrical energy that coursed through her veins as she released made her come over unnecessary. Ari didn't think she would ever indulge in a steamy romp again after her ordeal, but Mack's body told her otherwise. Ari tried so hard not to read too much into what had happened between them, pushing the thoughts of his chiseled torso out of her mind's eye until they engulfed her memory with every intimate caption of the night before.

"Oh, get over yourself Ari, he wants B. So, be the mom you're supposed to and deliver Mack to Junior," she told herself as she tried to rid her mind of lusty sex with Mack.

On her walk, friendly faces greeted Ari saying, 'good morning', to which she acknowledged. The cool and beautiful air blew in her face as she inhaled the sweet smell of spring. She ran her fingers over the soft and colorful flowers that had been planted along the edge of each cabin. She enjoyed absorbing all the beauty the grounds offered. She could see children playing as they clambered along the adventure trail, an old couple hand in hand as they sat and ate ice cream while bikers tinkered with bikes in a home-built bike garage. The retreat housed its own little community, and it was a far cry from the twenty-one dark and dangerous MCs Ari had visited. The Gray Wolves Retreat was a hidden gem, cultivated by both Mack and B as a calm and quaint resort that attempted to abolish the stereotypes regarding motorcycle clubs. Ari headed along to the gym as Mack had told her about the night before, stating that he would be there this morning.

The gym was small and rustic looking. It was nothing special, but it had everything required to get a session done, but nothing more. Ari wandered around, looking for Mack. She was excited to see him again and couldn't wait to get on the road back to Portland to surprise Junior. As she searched for Mack, she got lost in her thoughts again, thinking about how attractive he was, leading her once again to trail off into flash backs of the night before, when Mack had made her feel like a woman again. She became flustered, thinking of how his body glistened with sweat as he made passionate love to her. However, her thoughts were interrupted by a series of loud grunts and growls coming from behind a door in the south corridor. Ari stepped closer as the sounds of rugged breathing and moaning became louder and louder. She had recognized the sounds from the night before, the low growls through gritted teeth. It was Mack!

"No way! Was he fucking another woman?" she thought.

It wasn't as if they were together, but he had sex with her twice yesterday. "Surely, that meant a little something to him." She cursed.

Another growl interrupted her cussing. This time, Mack snarled in a low and strained voice.

"Geez, Dragon, what are you doing to me?"

Ari's heart rate skyrocketed. Had he lied to her already?

Liar! He said they weren't together, she thought as she heard B's voice, also strained and panting.

"Take it like a man, Mackie boy."

Ari's stomach churned, and her blood boiled. She was going to tell Mack what she thought of him as she burst through the doors, to be confronted with Mack and B entwined in a Jiu Jitsu grapple. They were training together! B had her arm around his throat, choking him as Mack tried to break free, when they both stopped with a confused expression after she burst in on them, interrupting their training session.

"Morning," B hissed, not appreciating the intrusion.

Mack stood up to approach her. He was shirtless and dripping with sweat. B had been helping him relieve his frustrations by putting him through his paces. Ari regarded him, speechless, as she watched a single droplet of sweat travel from his chest to his navel, forcing her to catch her breath making her catch her breath.

"Hey, is everything okay? You steamed in here pretty quick," Mack asked, panting, and looking concerned.

"Oh yeah, fine." She giggled. "Sorry, I thought I'd slept in, so I raced over to check if you were still here."

Mack raised an eyebrow at her. "Uh, right then, well, why don't you take a seat? I have one more round to complete and then we can head back to the cabin so I can get sorted and we can get going."

Ari agreed and found a seat to wait in, staring as a half-naked Mack grappled with a half-naked B, who was wearing nothing but a cropped sports vest and gym shorts. She was green with envy as she watched B control Mack as their bodies entwined and she couldn't believe how strong B was, with her tattoos and perfect six pack. Ari thought whether she would have been able to defend herself against Number 21 better if she was as strong as B. She also couldn't understand why B didn't fancy Mack when she herself found him drop dead gorgeous. Her mind continued to wander as she waited, and she realized that she didn't care for B that much.

Anyone who relishes in control must be a megalomaniac, she thought to herself as she watched B annihilate Mack with a smile on her face.

Once they finished, Mack collected his belongings, chucked on his hoodie, and led Ari outside, giving B a kiss on the cheek goodbye as they left.

"Hey, maybe we should talk about last night," Mack suggested as they headed outside into the morning sun.

"Uh, sure!" Ari said.

She had a feeling that she knew what was coming from Mack. He'd already confessed his love for B, and she didn't want to hear any more about how perfect his precious dragon was. Ari wanted more of yesterday and she wanted Mack to tell her he wanted more too. More of the moments that they'd shared, the lusty passion that engulfed her heart and soul, leaving her incapable of thinking about anything else, even if his heart did belong to someone else. Ari was desperate for his body on hers, desperate to be intoxicated by him and wanted to feel under the influence of him again.

He sat her down on the bench outside the gym. The sun was shining, and they were surrounded by the beautiful colors of the flowers that were situated in the raised flower beds around them.

"Look, about last night. What happened between us was incredible and what we both needed at that moment. I had just discovered Junior was alive, and it caught me up in all these emotions, but..."

"It was a mistake because you're in love with B."

A guilty expression flitted across Mack's face, and he hung his head in shame. "Yeah."

"Hey, it's fine, I get it!" she said, feeling like someone had kicked her in the stomach as she cleared her throat.

"I didn't mean to upset you. I think you're amazing, but B is my person, and I can't help how I feel about her. Please don't let this come between Junior and I."

"Mack, I would never do that. I have been through hell to find you. Twenty-one presidents, twenty-one MCs and I finally found you! Here at this beautiful wonderland."

"It's an MC too, newly formed, and I'm the Prez here. In fact, I'm the founder, but don't worry, it's not like any of the MCs you've been to before and I'm not a Prez that beats innocent women."

Ari smiled. "Glad to hear it!"

Mack's face softened as he took her hand. "Ari, I'm sorry. About B I mean."

"Mack, I get it! B's formidable, sexy, clever, and a little scary, and most men would give anything to have her. Hell, I even fancy her a little."

Mack smiled. "So, we're, okay?"

Ari curled her lips into a bashful smile. "Yes! and listen. If she ever changes her mind, consider me for a threesome, would you?"

Mack burst out laughing, "one hundred percent. But I have more chance of winning the lottery than that happening."

"But you have found your son, and I bet you never thought that would happen, so don't give up hope," she said, still feeling disheartened.

"You know, I was losing hope and with every year that passed, I lost a little more faith, thinking I'd never find him. Ari, you brought him back to me, and I want to repay you for that."

"Just be the dad that Junior needs you to be. He's been through so much, Mack. The things that boy has seen and lived through have left him scarred. I don't mean to speak ill of the dead, but what Nancy put him through..." She shuddered just thinking about it.

"Nancy was a very troubled woman, Ari, and believe me, I tried my very best with her. She wasn't maternal, and she took Junior just to spite me. She would disappear for days on end and come back demanding more money for drugs. So, I told her I was filing for sole custody of Junior. That night, I'm positive she drugged me, and when I woke up the next morning, they were gone."

Ari placed her hand on Mack's muscular thigh. "Shit. Mack, I'm so sorry."

"I'll never forgive myself for losing him and I know he probably hates me." Mack said, his voice shaking.

"No, Mack. When he found those old pictures and Mr. Jelly Legs, everything came flooding back to him. I think he'd blocked everything painful out of his mind as a coping mechanism until he laid eyes on the photos of you. In that moment, I knew he needed you and I couldn't give up until I found you."

"Ari, you are incredible, and I'm glad that Junior has had you to take care of him. I can't wait to see him and I'm glad you reunited him with Mr. Jelly Legs."

"Well, make sure that you pack enough clothes for a few days. Spend some time getting to know Junior again. One day isn't enough to catch up on six years."

"For real?"

"Well, I didn't go through hell for you just to say hi," she joked.

He planted a big kiss on her cheek before running off to get ready. Ari sat there for a while, basking in the sun, and enjoying the tranquility. She had dreamed of living in a place like Uskiville, in a house with a white picket fence, with the man of her dreams. It was the American dream to her, and she hoped one day she could experience it. Ari let her mind wander as she imagined walking hand in hand with Mack around this beautiful woodland hideaway. Something had happened to her last night. She had connected with Mack, and she was grateful that he'd treated her as a beautiful woman as opposed to the hideous monster, she thought she had become.

As Ari became lost in her fantasy, B interrupted her thoughts as she left the gym. She even looked beautiful, with her hair all ragged and her body covered in sweat, Ari thought to herself.

"Morning," B said as she locked the gym doors.

"Morning," Ari replied, then, as B headed down the path to leave, "You know he adores you!"

B turned to Ari, raising an eyebrow. "Excuse me?"

"Mack. He worships the ground you walk on!"

"As I do with him, Ari. We're family and that's what family does, love."

"And what if he wants more!" Ari asked

"What are you talking about?"

"B, have you ever considered Mack might like you more than what he's letting on?" She treaded as lightly as she could, not to anger the woman.

B laughed, shaking her head, and turning to walk away. "Um, no! Because he doesn't! We're best friends Ari, Geez!"

"I think he likes you!" Ari shouted and regretting what came out of her mouth.

B turned, glaring at Ari. The amusement had now vanished from her face. "Listen, you crazy bitch and listen good. Mackie and I are best friends, that's it! I don't know what you're playing at, but trust me, you don't want to dance with me. Now I appreciate everything you've done for Mackie and Junior, but don't come to my home and start meddling in stuff that you know nothing about."

Ari found herself angry. She rose to her feet and spat, "You know, it's just plain cruel to string him along like a lost puppy. If you don't want to hurt him, cut him loose and let him move on so he can be happy with someone else."

B stopped dead in the street, dropped her bag and started back up the road toward Ari in haste. Ari gulped; she couldn't believe the words that had come out of her mouth. How jealous she was that B had someone who loved her and, in Ari's eyes, someone she continued to control despite not wanting him.

B's sadistic. Only a weirdo would do something so awful.

B approached Ari, stopping a mere breath away from her face. Her eyes, bold and burning with anger, glaring at her. "You think, because he fucked you last night, you can meddle with his family?

Because let me tell you something, sweetheart, Mackie has a new skirt every weekend. There's plenty of women he has in the club on the regular, so don't go thinking you're special, because you're not. He is all fucked up with emotion right now, and you're taking advantage of that. I don't know what games you're trying to play my lovely, but this won't wash with me. So do the right thing and take him to his son, with no hidden agendas."

"I have no hidden agendas. I had to find him for Junior and FYI, what happened between us last night was beautiful, like a flower blooming in spring."

B pursed her lips together. "You keep telling yourself that lovely girl."

"Y-you don't scare me! You're just a woman with a hero complex, jealous that I've brought Junior back into Mack's life and not you. Well, I'm sorry, but you don't get to be the hero in this story, Dragon."

B laughed. "What the hell are you on, lady? You're bloody cuckoo. I'm happy Mack will see Junior again. It's all he's ever wanted. And I know you two had an emotional connection last night, but Junior should be your priority, not Mack. Trust me, making things difficult before Mack and Junior have bonded is a terrible move. It's not fair to either of them."

"My son is none of your business, and if you're not interested in Mack, stand aside and let him decide what he wants."

B looked at Ari as if she had lost the plot.

"You really are as messed up as I thought, aren't you?" she said with a concerned tone. "Ari, Mackie is a grown man! He can do what he wants. I am just trying to make you see the bigger picture. Let them get reacquainted first and if you both want each other after the dust has settled, then move forward from there. Right now, you are both fucked up and emotional. You can't see the grass from the field, and people could get hurt by this. Junior could get hurt.

"Don't bring Junior into this. I wouldn't do anything to hurt him. I have been threatened, beaten, and mauled to get here. Number 21 ruined my body, and I never thought a man would look at me again, but Mack did, and he wants to look again. I know he does, even if he can't see it yet, but you're stopping him! It's like you have a spell over him, controlling his thoughts and feelings. It's sick!"

B's jaw stiffened, and her face became red with anger. She had grown impatient with Ari as she stood a whisker away from her, clenching her fists until her knuckles went white. Her signature tell.

"Listen to me, you absolute bloody psychopath, as I'll only say this once. If you fuck with my family, fuck with my best friend, I will end you! Now, I think you need help and I'll be quite happy to help you with that. I have a lovely number for a mental health professional. The same one Mackie used. And I know that you've been through hell, so that's why I am going to let this one slide. But if you test me again, I promise you I'll be your worst bloody nightmare.

Ari couldn't help but snort. B was scary, but Ari wasn't scared of a woman after what she had been through.

B's eyes raged like the midday sun. "Oh, believe me when I tell you, I can create scars far worse than you have ever endured. So, get some help, lovely girl, and stop fucking with my family," she hissed, snatching her bag off the floor then storming down the road.

Ari breathed a sigh of relief as B marched off. She didn't know what had come over her as she sat feeling breathless. She had just met Mack; they weren't together, and Mack was clear about his feelings. Yet she'd felt it was necessary to confront B. *Why?* She hadn't come here to cause trouble. She had become lost in a jealous moment. B had done nothing to her, and Ari was just speculating with B and Mack's relationship because Mack hadn't told her much about them. She painted B as a bad person, judging her, despite what Mack had told her about B. He had put B on a pedestal and what would he say when he found out that Ari had tried to come between them mere hours after meeting them?

CHAPTER SEVENTEEN
The Red Pin

Ari packed her things and placed them into the trunk of her car as she waited for Mack to arrive. She sat in the driver's seat, tapping her feet and fidgeting, she was adamant B had told Mack about their confrontation.

"Why did I open my mouth? He is going to be pissed at me!" she mumbled to herself as Mack approached her car.

Resting one hand on the car roof and peering in through the window, he smiled at her.

"Hey sweetheart, is it okay if I follow you down on my bike? I don't enjoy going anywhere without my Harley and as it's new, B suggested I give it a run out to your place."

"I bet she did, meddling cow!" Ari muttered.

Mack looked confused. "Sorry, I didn't catch that."

"I said, of course, it is. Ready to head out?"

"Yeah, I can't wait to see Junior Ari. Let's go!"

When they arrived at Ari's house, Mack was a little surprised. He expected something ostentatious. However, the house was quaint and simplistic looking from the outside. On the inside, the house was full of character, as Ari's love for literature shone throughout with framed poetry, Shakespeare memorabilia and a library of books in a cupboard under the stairs just off the hallway. Everything looked perfect and had its place, until they reached the kitchen, which was full of takeout boxes.

"Er, sorry," she said with embarrassment coloring her cheeks. "I'm not much of a chef, I'm afraid. I'm a TV dinner or takeout kind of gal."

"That's okay sweetheart, here. Let me help you with that," he said as he picked up what looked like a week's worth of empty takeout cartons and followed Ari to the trash bins.

"You know, I could cook something for Junior coming home later," he offered, feeling a little sorry for Ari's lack of cooking skills.

"You don't have to do that, you're our guest," she said, as the color in her cheeks deepened.

"I'd like to, to say thank you for everything. I'm no chef, but Dragon has taught me how to cook."

Ari turned her head away to roll her eyes. She was growing tired of Mack putting her on a pedestal but remained polite.

"That would be lovely."

"Okay, what's Junior's favorite meal?" he asked.

"Junior loves Spaghetti Bolognese. He orders it whenever we eat out."

"Great! I can do that!"

"Okay, well, I'll go to the store when Junior arrives, if you write the ingredients down for me and you and Junior can get reacquainted while I'm gone." Ari said.

"Great!"

Ari gave Mack a tour of the house, allowing him to place his bag in the spare room where he would stay and showing him Junior's room. Mack loved getting a snapshot of Junior's life but didn't like the stabbing pain that pierced his heart as he thought of how much he had missed him. Picking up Junior's artwork, Mack could see that the apple hadn't fallen far from the tree. He couldn't wait for Junior's return to make up for lost time.

Ari studied Mack as he handled a recent picture of Junior. She could see the discomfort he felt as he ran his finger over the picture and pursed his lips. The guilt was written all over his face, so Ari decided to take his mind off Junior and explain how she found him.

She led him into her study and stopped in front of her pin board, studying Mack as he studied the pin board before asking her some questions.

"You visited all these clubs? Ari, sweetheart, I'm glad you found me, but what were you thinking? Most of these clubs are one-percenters, dangerous, murderous criminals, no place for a gorgeous woman like yourself."

"I did! It was horrible yet worth it now that I see you standing here." She tried to shake the sea of her attack images of out of her head.

Mack put his arm around her and kissed her forehead. "Thank you! What are the color-coded pins for though?"

"Green is for non-violent, yellow is for breaks, fractures, bruises and the red…" She paused, looking away.

"Oh, sweetheart, I'm sorry! I didn't mean to upset you."

"No, it's fine. I'm glad you asked. I want you to know everything I went through, so you know you can trust me to never come between you and Junior."

Mack turned her head to face him, caressing her cheek with the pad of his thumb, tracing it over her lips. "I do trust you, and I want to know about each Prez that hurt you. I will make them pay for what they did to you!"

"Okay," she said, slipping out of his grasp.

Mack followed her movements as she removed her clothes and stood naked before him. She wanted to take him on her journey to finding him so he would see what had happened to her.

Mack stared at her broken body as Ari took his hand and directed it to a scar on the bottom of her ribs. "Let me show you Mack," she said.

Mack's eyes grew wide, and Ari could hear his breathing quicken at her touch.

"This one was the first scar that I picked up. Number 4. He was a mean son of a bitch; he was the first to crack my ribs."

Mack studied it, running his fingers over the small, worm-like scar.

"Ari, you don't have to do this," he whispered.

"I want to."

Mack nodded and followed her trail with his hand. Stroking and caressing each scar. Placing his index finger on a scar on her collarbone, Ari continued her journey.

"This one was Number 14. He was vile as he drugged and tried to rape me, but I came to just in time and I hit him over the head with an ashtray I didn't even know I was hurt until I arrived home."

Mack's eyes glazed over as Ari took him on a journey of her body and he continued to follow each scar until things became a little too much for her.

Ari, now unable to stop the sea of tears fleeing from her eyes as she told her story, tried to continue.

"This one and a fractured hand were from Number 17. He was the second worst out of the lot of them. I felt my bones break and he too, would have raped me if it wasn't for a police officer driving by. He made me feel violated."

Mack's eyes narrowed, and his jaw clenched at the sight of her grief.

"Hey, hey, come here!" he said, pulling her into him and holding her close. "Ari, I promise you I will nail these bastards for you, sweetheart!"

Ari calmed in his arms as she met his gaze. "Mack, I don't want you to get into trouble for me. All that is important is moving forward now. I don't want you going to prison, just as Junior has found you. Just as I've found you."

Mack's face softened, eyes doughy and full of admiration as he looked at her. "I'm not going anywhere, sweetheart."

Ari's heart melted as she became lost in his words, and as she gazed into his big brown eyes, she could tell he meant every word.

Locked in their passionate gaze, neither one of them wanted to look away. Ari who was desperate to kiss him again, remained frozen in time. She couldn't take his rejection again, not after knowing he loved his dragon. But to her surprise, he kissed her lips and whispered in her ear; "I want to make you feel better, Ari. Please let me kiss your scars better."

Ari nodded as her heart pounded in her chest. She ran her fingers through his hair and Mack began by kissing the scar on her neck, laying a soft and subtle kiss across the length of the three-inch scar.

Ari let out a slight moan; she hadn't expected this, especially after how he felt about B. But she didn't care, she just closed her eyes as he made his way to the huge scars on her back, showering them with gentle kisses. Mack moved onto the next scar and the next, until he had covered her whole back, showering it with long and soft kisses with his tender lips as he clung to her small frame. Ari panted as she couldn't contain her arousal, she was, struggling to breathe as every synapse, every nerve in her body, felt like it had electricity running through it. Each tender kiss felt electrifying to Ari, as he followed her trail of scars, leaving Ari wanting more.

Mack made his way to the front of her body as he kissed all the tiny scars on her breasts, moaning as he did so. He then covered her ribs and moved down to her navel where the trail ended. Ari expected it to end there, but to her surprise, Mack took his lips to her bikini line, then further, delivering soft blows to her clitoris. Ari had expected him to stop, come to his senses, and pull away from her. But Mack seemed lost in the moment, caressing her entrance with his tongue. Ari moaned, running her fingers through his hair, inviting him into her. Her heart now racing as he massaged her sex.

"Oh, Mack," she moaned.

Mack panted. "Oh, Ari, you're so wet. I need to be inside you sweetheart. Tell me you want me, so I can make you feel better."

Ari, almost undone by the vibrant strokes of his tongue, cried out. "Please Mack, take me. I want you now!"

Mack rose to his feet, pulling her into him, forcing his tongue down her throat as he growled into her mouth.

"Are you ready to feel better sweetheart? To feel me inside you?"

"Yes, yes," she cried as his moist lips sank into her neck and Ari realized then, he was trying to change the narrative, make her see she wasn't just a bundle of scars, and he wanted to make her feel better.

Ari wasn't sure what the driving force behind his attempt to make her feel better was, whether it was guilt or because he felt sorry for her, or plain old primal instinct at the sight of her naked body. But she didn't care and ripped off his shirt with urgency. She pulled at his belt buckle as he continued to seduce her with his plump lips, releasing his erect penis from his boxer shorts. Taking a firm grip of his shaft, she massaged his length, making Mack grit his teeth, unable to compose himself.

Covering his mouth with hers, he sucked her tongue and pinned her against the wall, wrapping her legs around his body. As he lowered her down onto him, Ari welcomed him with her moistness, allowing Mack to enter her, filling her with every inch of himself. Ari howled as he soaked her, synchronizing his growls with powerful thrusts, and slipped her tongue into his mouth, wanting to taste him as he took her. She was so close to coming undone as she writhed with pleasure. His rugged chest pressed up against her breasts as he pinned her hard against the wall and Mack increased the pace, desperate to make her feel, as Ari allowed him to lose himself inside her.

Mack thrusted hard and fast, sending the pin board crashing to the floor, forcing Ari to become lost in her emotions, as she screamed into an intense orgasm. Her body tensed as it ripped through her, releasing so much pleasure that she could feel it from head to toe.

"Oh Mack, what have you done to me?" she cried as he continued to take her, controlling her with his strength.

"God, Ari, I'm going to explode," he barked before letting out an almighty cry as Ari watched relief wash over him and he left everything inside her.

They slowed down to a stop as Mack kissed her soft lips.

"Thank you for letting me help you feel better, sweetheart."

Ari looked up at him. "Thank you. You make me feel like a woman again instead of a monster. I don't deserve to feel like this, looking the way I do."

Mack's jaw dropped. "Sweetheart, you are beautiful, and these scars tell a story that has given me my son back. Not only do I love them, but I am also grateful that each one led me to this moment with you! I don't understand what you're doing to me, Ari, or why my body screams for you. It's mind-blowing and I love it!"

"But what about B?"

Mack paused for a moment before looking into her eyes. "Ari, you are making me realize that life is too short to be hurting every day. I love my dragon and always will. But I want to be happy, and she won't allow me to be happy with her. Besides, looking at you now, seeing you in all your glory, with your soft hair sitting across your breasts and those gorgeous brown eyes, filled with so much passion and sadness..."

"Aww, Mack."

"Ari, what I'm trying to say is, when you bared your soul to me, I thought you were the most beautiful woman I've ever seen, and truth be told, I haven't been able to stop thinking about what happened between us yesterday."

Ari's face glowed in a deep shade of red. She couldn't help but grin as her insides fluttered with joy. She knew yesterday was special but thought that it was all in her head. Especially as Mack told her it shouldn't happen again. Ari looked up at Mack wearing a devilish smile and glowering at her. She reached up to kiss him and this time she wasn't afraid as she wrapped her arms around his neck, coiling them around him to draw him in. As their tongues entwined, Mack pulled her in closer, with his firm hands displaced along the length of her back.

Coming up for air and panting, Mack moaned. "This is crazy!

How on earth can you make me feel like this? I just met you yesterday."

Ari smiled. "Maybe the heart wants what the heart wants."

Mack laughed. "Maybe! But, Ari, whatever is happening between us, we need to keep it from Junior for now. I don't want to confuse him. Not when I'm just getting him back."

Ari gasped. "Shit! Junior! Mack, he'll be here any minute. He can't find us like this."

Mack released her from his grasp in a panic. "You get sorted, and I'll straighten up everything here," he suggested with urgency.

Ari grabbed her clothes and ran for the stairs. Mack pulled up his jeans and buckled his belt then shrugged his shirt on before picking up the pin board they had sent crashing to the floor. Placing it back on the wall, Mack studied the board and took a picture on his phone. He had always had a photographic memory, but this time he wanted an image, just in case. He noticed that all the pins were still attached to the board, and it was only the red pin that had become dislodged. Searching for the red pin, he scoured the floor until he found it tucked under her desk. After retrieving it, he looked at the little tag attached to it, which read Number 21. He then looked at the map, searching for a pin sized hole to find the location.

"Texas, no. New York, no. Washington, no. Sunnyville?" he gasped!

"Christ on a bike!" he shouted as he saw a tiny hole situated where Sunnyville sat on the map. Panic, fear and grief washed over him, trembling as the color drained from his face.

"It can't be? No, no, no. Please, God no!" he prayed, before calling out to Ari. He had to know the truth. Had Ari stumbled into the lion's den? Had she gone to Sunnyville looking for him? Were her scars from the man of Mack's nightmares? So many questions raced through his mind as he waited for Ari to come and join him in her study. He felt liked he'd been waiting for her forever until the door opened. Only it wasn't Ari that appeared in the doorway. It was Junior!

CHAPTER EIGHTEEN
Junior

"Jelly Legs?" Mack murmured as he gawked at the tall, gangly, strawberry-blond headed teenager in the doorway. Already trembling, he could tell it was him from his big blue eyes that used to gaze up at him when Junior was small. Mack stared, waiting for Junior to make a move, and not wanting to scare him.

"Dad, is it really you?" Junior asked, voice wobbling in shock.

Mack nodded as tears of joy streamed down his face.

Junior's face hardened. "What took you so long?" he asked, holding his father's gaze with a hard stare, before breaking out into a huge grin and rushing in to embrace his father.

Long, hard sobs echoed throughout the house, as Ari made her way downstairs again. Mack held onto his son, gripping him hard. He never wanted to let go again. He had waited years for this day and Junior was so small the last time they had hugged. However, he stood in his embrace now, a strong teenager, clinging on to his father, grateful for his return. Junior had grown beyond Mack's expectations, and Mack looked on as the realization hit him, that he had missed so much of Junior's life. He loosened his grasp around him so he could look at him, wiping the tears from his eyes.

"I'm so deeply sorry for everything that you've been through, my boy. I have been searching for you since your mother snatched you away, and I am so grateful to Ari for all that she went through to find me! I promise you I will never let you down again. Please forgive me," he cried as he planted a kiss on the boy's head and embraced him again.

Junior, who was still in shock, sobbed in his father's arms. "Thank you, Dad! Thank you for not giving up on me! I've missed you so much!" he cried as Mack held onto him, soaking his lilac T-shirt with his tears.

Ari, now standing in the doorway, witnessed their embrace, shedding tears of joy herself. Her expression reflected so much happiness as Mack glanced up to catch her gaze.

"Come here!" he said, ushering her to join them.

Ari raced over, embracing them as Mack put his arm around her, sandwiching Junior between them. They held onto one another a little while longer until Junior piped up.

"Wait, I have a gift for you." He looked up at his dad.

Guilt tracked across Mack's face. "Oh, son, I'm so sorry. I didn't even think to bring you anything. I was just so desperate to get here, I didn't even think."

A loving and innocent expression crossed Junior's face, and he smiled. "Dad, you're the best present that I could ever have hoped for. Wait here and I'll be right back," he said as he shot out of the study and ran up the stairs to his bedroom.

Mack stood, overwhelmed by it all. He was rocking but so happy that he had his son back.

"Are you okay?" Ari asked.

Mack glanced at her, pulling her close to him and brushing a stray hair behind her ear with his fingers. "You made all of this happen, Ari. You. A pint-sized, fragile, and beautiful woman made all of this happen. You went through so much pain to make this day possible for myself and Junior. You made everything right again."

Ari gazed up at him, her eyes becoming cloudy with the emotion that filled the air. "I'm glad I got to reunite you and Junior."

"Ari, you made the impossible possible. You brought my son back to me. You are an amazing, beautiful, fecking irresistible woman," he beamed as he lifted her up and twirled her around the room, in his arms.

Ari's tears of joy fell onto his chest. She had no words, shocked that despite so many setbacks, she refused to give up. She was just so grateful to the Scot who had placed the blood-stained note in her jacket for her to find him.

"I'm so happy for you both." She beamed.

Mack placed his fingers on her chin. "But are you happy, sweetheart? You've been through so much."

"Yes!" she gushed as she burst into tears again, sobbing with both joy and relief.

Mack held her tight. "Oh, Ari, sweet, gorgeous Ari. You will never know what you did for me today, but I do, and I promise I will never forget it."

Ari settled down as she wiped her last tears on her sleeve and straightened out her shirt. Scanning the room, she said to him: "You straightened everything up before Junior arrived."

"Yeah!" he said smirking, "I did! But Ari, I have to ask you something. What's the name of the club with the red pin?" he asked in a quiet tone, treading carefully.

Ari's face dropped as the color faded from her skin. The words of Number 21, slammed into her brain again, flooding back into her short-term memory and tormenting her soul. She looked at Mack and gasped as she remembered the words the Mauler had told her, as he ripped through her skin. She had almost allowed herself to forget the words that haunted her as they repeated in her head:

"And when I'm done with you, you can tell that Irish prick what I've done to you! Tell him that revenge is a dish that's best served cold and I'm coming for him and everyone he's ever loved."

"Ari, what's wrong?" Mack asked in a concerned tone as he watched the fear burn in her eyes.

Ari tried to speak, but the words wouldn't come out, then Junior entered the room, interrupting her thoughts.

"Found it!" he declared, beaming with excitement, as he handed Mack a hand drawn portrait of Mack, himself, and his uncles from when he was younger, along with the original photograph to match.

Mack stared at the portrait before looking at Ari, who shook her head, pleading with him not to mention the red pin in front of Junior, and Mack's expression softened in acknowledgement as he looked at his son.

"Wow! Is this for me? Did you draw this? Where did you get the photo?"

"Yeah. we found it in my mom's things when we were clearing the apartment after she died. I saw this picture and I started remembering everything, and I knew I had to find you."

"You take after your old man with this," he said, referring to Junior's artistic flair. "Yeah. I found one of your portraits of me. I have it by my bed."

"Yeah? I'd love to see it and draw with you sometime if you'd like that, that is?"

"Really, Dad? I'd love that too!"

Mack smiled at Junior, completely in awe of him. He was so proud of how strong he had become. Ari had told him that Junior had been through a lot. Yet, his son stood before him a strong, talented, and well-turned-out young man. Mack also felt terrible that Junior had to endure the death of his mother without Mack being there to support him.

Placing his hand on Junior's shoulder and grabbing his attention, Mack opened up to his son. "I am sorry about your mother, Jelly Legs. You know, there was a time when I loved your mother very much and a part of me will always love her because, despite her troubles, she gave me you, son."

Tears filled Junior's eyes. "It's okay, Dad. I know how troubled she was, and I tried to help her, but she kept pushing me away. She never wanted me, and the only thing I don't understand is why you didn't take me away from her? Why did I have to live with her and not you?"

Mack's heart broke for the boy, seeing him wrestle with confusion. He put his arms around Junior, holding him tight as he rested his head on Junior's temple. "Listen, there's something I need to be honest with you about," he said as he ushered him to the brown leather sofa that sat beside the bookshelf in the room's corner.

Kneeling before Junior, looking him straight in the eye, he told Junior the truth about his mother drugging him and whisking Junior off in the dead of night. Mack didn't tell him about having to pay for Junior to be born. He didn't want Junior to live with the ramifications of their arrangements. He had already suffered enough. But he explained that the reason Nancy ran away with him that night was, in his opinion, to spite Mack and stop him from taking custody of him. Junior looked shocked as he listened to every word that came out of his father's mouth.

"So, you see, son, it's my fault. I should have been smarter, handled it better. I never dreamed your mom would take you away from me, and I just hope that you can forgive me. I promise you, me and your aunt B have never stopped looking for you."

Junior dropped his head, sucking in a long breath through his sobs. "It's not your fault, Dad, it never was! These past few months I've been remembering so much. You were always so kind to me, you played games with me, took me to the park with Uncle Zander, Uncle Noah, and Uncle Jimmy. You read me bedtime stories and bought me Mr. Jelly Legs." He beamed. "My mom didn't know how to be like that with me," he whispered as he bowed his head and sighed. "I wanted her to, but I don't think she knew how."

Mack put his hand on Junior's head as his son clung to his shirt.

"Junior, your mom was a troubled woman, and I tried to help her. But in the end, I don't think anyone could help her and it's not your fault that she couldn't see you were the most perfect gift in the world. She was incapable of seeing it son, but I am! You're my world, you always have been, and you always will be! I'm here to right all the wrongs I can, my boy, and if you'll have me, I'll never lose you again. I promise."

"Thank you, Dad! I love you and I missed you so much!"

"I love you too, my boy!" he said as he kissed the top of his head, still shaking with the adrenaline of the day coursing through his veins.

After another long embrace, Mack straightened out Junior's T-shirt and helped him to his feet.

"Hey, go fetch your art set so your old man can teach you a thing or two about drawing. Hell, who am I kidding? You can teach me," he joked as they wandered out of the study, leaving Ari to close the door behind them.

Ari stood at the pin board staring at the awful red pin. She knew she had to tell Mack about the man who mauled her that night and deliver the message. Number 21 wanted Mack to hear his words and Mack's life might depend on it one day, all their lives might depend on it. But not today, she decided. Today was their day, and she would let them have it!

Mack and Junior spent the day laughing, drawing, and getting to know each other. There was a buzz about the house, which was amplified when Remy returned from his dad's. It excited him to meet Mack too and Mack embraced him as if he was his own.

Ari stepped out to enjoy some much-needed fresh air and pick up the ingredients for Mack to cook Dinner.

It enthralled Junior watching his dad cook and listened to stories about how his Aunt B took his dad in off the streets, teaching him most of what he now knew. Junior was so excited about having an aunt and cousins. He knew they weren't biological, but if they were family to his dad, then they were family to him. After dinner and a million questions later, Junior asked his dad to join him in the sitting room to help him. He had been trying to complete a portrait of Ari, much to her embarrassment, and he couldn't quite get the shape of her face correct. So, he asked his dad to show him how.

"Okay, let's have a look, shall we?" Mack took the note pad off Junior and sitting next to him on the sofa.

Ari sat on the opposite sofa, parallel to where the two of them sat, and Mack flashed her a smile. He had discovered so much about her today, about her sacrifices, how she was bringing the boys up, and how she handled everything all on her own. He even learned about her lack of cooking skills as the boys explained how lethal she was in the kitchen. But Mack didn't care about that. He sat there mesmerized by her, in awe of her. As he became acquainted with her, he saw her in a different light. She was no longer a woman he shared a lusty and emotional riptide with but a woman he wanted to get to know better. A woman he believed he might want to be with, and as he gazed upon her, he became enthralled by her beauty.

Making gentle strokes across the paper with his pencil, he sculpted her perfect cheekbones, capturing her essence in his art. Mack was elegant as he put pencil to paper, shading in all the areas to create the perfect portrait. Ari watched in fascination as he studied her, glancing up to capture her, before looking down at the paper again, making even more light and elegant strokes as he went.

Junior gawked at the finished work of art, taking it from Mack and handing it to Ari to look at. "Whoa! Dad, that is amazing! Can you teach me how to do that, please?"

"I'll try, but it's more about practice than anything."

Ari studied the portrait, her eyes wide in awe of Mack's work. It was picture perfect, even down to the stray freckle situated to the right of her chin.

"This is incredible Mack. You are extremely talented!" she said in shock and watching in amusement as she witnessed Mack blush in embarrassment.

He wasn't used to receiving compliments. He always dished them out to get women into bed, but with Ari, he was receiving them, and he liked it. It made him feel good about himself for a change, rather than feeling useless and helpless in all the failed attempts to locate his son.

The day ended with everyone feeling exhausted. Ari returned from the kitchen with a beer for Mack, only to find him and Junior crashed out on the sofa together. Remy had already taken himself off to bed, to allow Junior and Mack some much needed father and son time. He understood how important that was as he looked forward to the weekends with his dad. Ari looked on at them as Mack had his arm around his son, almost cuddling him into him. Taking a blanket from the cupboard, she covered them up and took a picture on her phone to capture the perfect moment before heading to bed herself. Ari slept soundly that night and for the first time in a long time, her nightmares didn't torment her.

Ari's alarm went off at six a.m., ensuring she got herself and the boys ready for school. Jumping out of bed and looking chipper, Ari donned her bathrobe and headed downstairs to see if Mack and Junior were awake.

As she headed into the kitchen, rich aromas of coffee and cinnamon made her mouth water. Standing in the kitchen doorway, her heart skipped a beat as she observed Mack teaching the boys how to make pancakes. She had failed so many times herself to master them over the years that she always reverted to store-bought ones.

"Morning!" she said as she greeted them with her presence.

The three males turned to greet her, with Mack planting a kiss on her cheek, much to the boy's embarrassment.

Giving her a smile and a wink, he said, "Morning sweetheart, we made pancakes!"

"So, I see! I could get used to this!" she said as he poured her a coffee and placed a stack of cinnamon pancakes in front of her.

"You deserve it! Besides, I wanted to thank you for letting me stay and get to know Junior and, well, all of you better, I suppose," he said, taking a seat and sipping on his coffee.

Ari studied him for a second. There was something different about him today. He didn't look disheveled like he had the world on his shoulders. He looked well rested and happy. Ari ogled him, unable to take her eyes off him. She didn't want to. She could see more sparkle in his glacier-like eyes today, finding him irresistible. Mack's lips curved into a wry smile as he caught her looking at him, giving her a cheeky wink when the boys weren't looking, making her flush with embarrassment.

"I think I need some more maple syrup," she said as she rose from her seat to hide her awkwardness, leaving Mack grinning into his coffee.

Once her natural glow had returned to her face, she ushered her boys to get ready for school with Junior panicking that his dad would leave again, and after Mack calmed him down and promised he would be there when he returned home from school, Ari bundled the boys into the car.

"Mack, are you sure that you'll be okay here on your own?"

Mack regarded her with amusement. "I'll be fine! I am a grown man; in case you haven't noticed."

"Okay, smart Alec! The spare house keys are hanging by the front door, if you fancy going for a walk."

"I may head to the shops to pick up something to make for dinner, if that's okay?"

"Great!" she said, backing down the drive, leaving Mack to his own devices for the whole day.

Mack watched them leave and once they were out of sight, he raced inside and headed for Ari's study. He looked for the nearest MC on the list. The Red Mist Scoundrels, 1642 Garland Cross and Number 12 on the pin board. It was a yellow, meaning that they had knocked Ari about. "That'll do nicely!" he said to himself before grabbing his jacket and spare keys and diving onto his bike.

Mack sped up the highway, knowing he had to make good time if he was going to get there and back again, as well as picking up something for dinner. He stopped at a gas station about thirty minutes from his destination to pick up fuel, a pack of gum and a snood that was on a sale rack near the cashier's counter. Mack needed to conceal his identity to protect the ones he loved, especially B, to whom he had promised he would stay out of trouble, stay white like an angel, and keep trouble away from their door. Parking his slick-looking Harley outside the club, he removed his handgun from his bike seat, placing it in his waistband. Mack hoped he wouldn't have to use it, but he took it just in case. Donning his padded gloves, ensuring not to mark his hands, Mack also had to ensure his prey didn't land a punch or mark his face, understanding it was an enormous risk, but a necessary one in his eyes. Everyone who ever hurt Ari would now pay the price. He was determined to make them pay for every mark made to Ari's body, to let them know to never mess with her again. He approached the front door and pulled it open. For all he knew, there could be twenty men inside. He didn't care. He was baying for blood, their blood, and he would have it.

The bar was empty when he stepped inside. He could feel the adrenaline pumping through his blood already in anticipation of meeting the Prez, who had hurt Ari. Out of nowhere, a middle-aged, gray-haired man appeared in a doorway behind the bar.

"Can I help you, friend?" a scrawny-looking man asked as he eyeballed Mack.

"Ah, yeah, I'm looking for a woman, pint-sized little thing, brown hair, nice rack, late thirties. She might have come in looking for me a while back."

The scrawny man appeared curious as he glared at Mack's poker face. Mack gave nothing away. He'd played these games before and could spin any story and make anyone believe anything he said. Mack had crafted his skills years ago and now everything was coming back to him.

"I'm not sure. Why? What has she done to have a guy like you coming after her?" the scrawny man asked.

Mack tapped his fingers on the bar. "She has something that belongs to me. I want it back! Now I don't give a damn about her. I don't care if you all had your turn with her, it's just information that I'm looking for."

"Hmm. There was a stuck-up broad that came in here a while

ago, spouting about an Irishman, super naïve. I told her to leave, but she wasn't having any of it and disrespected my position as club Prez. I put her in her place, you know, Prez style," he said, winking.

"Yeah, I get it man. Did you see where she headed after? Assuming she headed anywhere after you showed her who's boss, that is." He joked even as he filled with rage, while confirming he had his man.

"Well, after I ragged her round a bit, she took her sorry ass back to that fancy little convertible of hers," he said boastfully, with his arrogance infuriating Mack as he stood there wearing his poker face.

"I got you man!" He laughed, while inside he was dancing with rage.

"Hey, can I buy you a drink?" he asked as he pulled a huge wad of cash out of his pocket, knowing that the Prez's eyes would light up at the sight of cash.

"Sure," the Prez said, grinning, making his way around the bar to retrieve a bottle of cheap whisky from the bottom shelf and placing it on the bar with two glasses next to Mack.

Cheapskate, Mack thought to himself, as he watched the man pour him a whisky. Knocking it back in one, he then placed fifty bucks down on the bar.

"Thanks, man. Here, this is for your troubles," he said.

As the man looked down to retrieve it, Mack grabbed the back of his head and smashed him face-first into the bar. The man dropped to the floor in one big slump, legs buckling beneath him. Mack picked up his cash, strolled behind the bar and kicked the man in the ribs. He was furious this Prez had the gall to boast about hurting Ari, relishing in her pain. It disgusted him and he wanted the guy to pay for what he had done to her. He finished kicking the unconscious man, then leaned down to check that he was still breathing. He had a yellow-colored pin after all and didn't deserve to die in Mack's opinion. But he deserved to be beaten like he'd beaten Ari, an eye for an eye so to speak. Mack searched for the security cameras and fortunately, there weren't any. Breathing a sigh of relief after forgetting to wear his snood. Mack proceeded to the exit, placing his glass in his pocket. He wasn't stupid enough to leave any evidence behind. Waltzing out of the MC without being seen and adrenaline stoking the fire in his belly, he sped off on his bike, heading back to Ari's.

The ride home was glorious for Mack, with the adrenaline still coursing through his veins as he sped back down the highway. He had forgotten what it felt like to make a man bleed, as he had spent so long behaving himself for B's sake. After all, she had taken him in and it was her business, her home at stake if he misbehaved. He wouldn't ever jeopardize that for anything. He still loved her. But he loved the rush, the thrill from avenging Ari, and he felt like a hero. He wanted to be Ari's hero, her knight in shining armor, someone that she could rely on no matter what. He felt like he owed her that, for everything that she had done for him and his son. Mack relished in his exhilarating experience, bellowing up the highway. He had crossed off the first MC on his list and no one would mess with Ari again by the time he had finished with them.

Ari and the boys arrived home to find the table set, displaying Mack's homemade curry with an array of side dishes. They all complimented him on the aroma that engulfed their senses as they went about their afternoon routine before sitting at the table. Ari watched as Mack served their meal after he declined her help, telling her to relax after a hard day's work. He then poured her a glass of very expensive red wine; she knew it was expensive because she had picked it up to purchase it once before but returned it to the shelf with haste when she checked the price.

"Wow, expensive wines taste better than the cheap stuff," she said as she took a sip, allowing it to tantalize her palate.

Mack smiled at her as he poured his own, before sitting at the table next to her to join everyone. "Well, I thought it might be nice to celebrate tonight."

"Oh, and what are we celebrating?" she teased.

Mack glanced at her with a huge smile across his face, almost making Ari tremble with excitement. She loved seeing him so happy as she drooled over his prominent jaw line and come-to-bed eyes.

"To making up for lost time and to new beginnings," he toasted, raising his glass to Ari's. Everyone joined in with the toast before wolfing down another home cooked meal.

After everyone had stuffed their faces, Ari instructed the boys to wash up and fill the dishwasher, leaving her alone with Mack at the table, desperate to steal a moment with him. Feeling tipsy, Ari whispered into Mack's ear. "Wine on a school night? If I didn't know better, I would think you're trying to get me drunk Macintyre Kelly."

"Maybe I am?"

Ari leaned into him, but first checking over her shoulder to make sure that the boys were out of earshot. "You don't need to get me drunk, Mack. You already know that I'm like putty in your hands."

Mack, eyes forward, sipped his wine, and stole a glance at her from the corner of his eye. Slipping his hand under the table, he stroked her thigh. Ari's eyes went wide, and she purred at his touch, making her bite down on her bottom lip. She wanted him, but it was impossible with the boys around. Mack was like a forbidden fruit, seducing her with how he looked. Ari sipped her wine, trying to think of a way to get Mack alone, but came up empty. She didn't want to disrupt things with everything going so well between him and Junior. Ari knew she needed to put Junior's feelings first, but it didn't stop her from wanting him. The smell of his expensive aftershave with undertones of citrus and leather mixed with his own distinct smell of masculinity beckoned her to him, enticing her and making her body scream for him. Her lust filled desire fueled her from her toes to the pit of her stomach, knowing he wanted her too.

Ari wanted to combust as she met his gaze, his eyes were bright, as if they were burning into her soul as she leaned in to talk to him.

"Thank you! For everything you've done, for me, for Junior, for our family."

"It's me that should thank you, sweetheart. I have never been happier than I am right now," he explained.

"But what about when you're with B?"

Mack took her hand. "Let's not talk about B tonight, and no, I've never been this happy before," he said, answering the question and rubbing the top of her hand with his thumb. "But Ari, you need to understand that things have to stay casual for now. I like you! But I don't want to mess this up for Junior, you, Remy, or B and her boys, and I can't change how my heart feels right now. I'm so conflicted. I need time to digest."

Ari placed her glass on the table and placed her hand on his. "Agreed! And Mack, I appreciate your honesty about everything."

Mack squeezed her thigh and glanced up at Junior, beaming with pride. Glancing back at Ari, "Understand, it doesn't mean I don't want you, Ari, and I will take you every chance I get. You're like a drug to me, but no pressure, okay?"

Ari's cheeks flushed scarlet. Just as they did whenever he turned her on. "No pressure Mack. I promise!"

Mack smiled. "On a different note, I was wondering if you and the boys wanted to come and stay at my cabin this weekend?"

Ari, almost choking on her wine, responded, "In your cabin, with you?"

Mack laughed. "Yes, with me!"

"Wow, Mack. It's beautiful up there, and I think Junior would love it. But Remy wouldn't be able to join us as he spends the weekends with his dad."

"You and Junior then?"

Ari gazed at Mack. She was glowing with excitement. "I'd love to, but why don't you ask Junior first?"

Mack turned to Junior, calling out to him, "Junior, my boy."

Junior turned to his dad before propping up the breakfast bar to face him.

"Would you and your mother like to stay at my cabin this weekend?"

Junior looked at Mack, then looked at Ari as he struggled to contain his excitement.

"For real?" he asked.

"Of course. I'd like to show you around and introduce you to the rest of your family, if that's okay with you?"

Junior looked at him, grinning from ear to ear.

"Will I get to meet my new Aunt B?" he asked. He had been excited to find he had an aunt and cousins the night before, and when he discovered his aunt was a huge soccer coach, he bombarded Mack with at least a dozen questions about her. Junior loved soccer, and Mack always loved to gush about his successful best friend.

"Sure. She has a big game ahead of her, but we can meet up with her after the game, and I'm sure that she'd even let you on the field if I ask her."

"Oh, yes! This is off the hook! Can we go, Mom, please?"

Ari couldn't believe how excited Junior was, and yet she also couldn't help but feel a little jealous as she thought B had another Kelly man wrapped around her little finger and he hadn't even met her yet.

Snapping herself out of her brief pity party, she agreed. "Of course, but as long as you get all of your homework done before Friday and speak to Adam to let him know you won't be seeing Joe this weekend, okay?"

Junior was bouncing with excitement.

"Yes, thanks Mom, you're the best!" he bellowed as he headed off to ring Joe.

Mack laughed, enjoying seeing his son so happy.

Ari smiled at Mack. "Happy?"

"Ecstatic," he answered, pulling her in close to kiss her lips.

Ari panted, "Mack, we can't! The boys!"

"Did you not hear the stampede as Junior ran upstairs?"

Ari laughed. "You're terrible! Getting me tipsy and trying to seduce me. Shame on you."

"Oh, sweetheart. As conflicted as I am, I have to have you! I want to show you how happy you've made me today," he whispered as he kissed her again.

Ari couldn't contain herself. She wanted him too, so she took his hand and led him to her study again, locking the door behind them.

The next few days saw Mack building his relationships with both Junior and Ari, spending as much time as he could with Junior by day and creeping down the corridor into Ari's room at night. They were like lovesick teenagers, sneaking around in the dark, stealing moments whenever they could. Slipping off to Ari's study while the boys were upstairs doing their homework every chance they got, and Ari even came home for lunch to take advantage of Mack while the boys were at school. They couldn't keep their hands off each other.

Mack was supposed to go home two days later, but he couldn't bear to leave Junior, Ari, and Remy. He was building a relationship with all of them, but he felt he should at least talk to B first and make sure she didn't mind him inviting unfamiliar faces into her home. B was funny like that. There were frequent, fresh faces at the retreat, but that was different. This was B's life, and her home was her haven. He had phoned B several times to keep her updated on his whereabouts, as he knew how much she worried about him.

B seemed happy for Mack and was excited to meet Junior, although Mack had an inclination that she wasn't as keen on seeing Ari again. Mack understood she was worried about him, but he was a grown man who could look after himself. Sometimes he thought he might not need his dragon as much anymore, although he still loved her. That feeling would never leave him, but he could sense that something special was happening with Ari too. Mack didn't feel the way about Ari as he did with B yet; it was different and he had only known her a few days, whereas he had loved B for years. Mack was positive he would feel the same about Ari in time if their relationship blossomed how he had hoped it would.

The next morning, Mack said his goodbyes, explaining to Junior that it would only be two days apart and he would ring him as soon as he got home. He gave Ari a sly kiss goodbye and headed out on his bike. He still hadn't received an explanation about the red pin from Ari. The timing wasn't right, what with being reunited with Junior again. Besides, the look on Ari's face spoke volumes as he watched her beautiful face shatter at its very mention. So, traveling to 8432 Lachlan way would have to suffice. Another yellow on Ari's list. The Prez there, was another who smacked Ari about, so it would at the very least make Mack feel better if he took his frustration out on Number 7.

Mack was raging at the possibility of Number 21 being the one to inflict the most damage on Ari. It made things more personal, given their history, but Mack didn't know for sure. Mack had been away from there for so long, there could be another MC in Sunnyville now. So, he would have to wait for confirmation from Ari before he allowed his thoughts to send him down that rabbit hole. Ari was fast becoming the woman he wanted to be with and in Mack's eyes, scores needed to be settled, and wrongs needed to be put right, and he would be the one to make everything right again.

But what about B? He had promised her he'd stay white, and he hadn't by any means. He had also promised her he wouldn't sleep with Ari again and he'd struck out on that too. She wouldn't under-stand, he thought to himself. She would see him as black now; dark and dangerous. Too dangerous to be around her and her boys. He knew his dragon enough to know that she would think otherwise. But for now, he couldn't think about the ramifications and his dragon. He had a job to do. A mission to complete and that is all that mattered.

Friday came and Ari and Junior arrived in Uskiville just in time to watch B's game. B embraced him after a successful 3-0 win, showing him around, just like Mack said she would. Later, she cooked for them, and invited Frankie to join them too. Frankie also embraced Junior, but seemed uninterested in Ari, much to Ari's disappoint-ment, since she was looking forward to meeting and getting to know Mack's other best friend, thinking she could get at least one of his friends on her side after her temper tantrum with B. Junior listened as B told him stories of her coaching and Mack thanked B as they left that evening, planting a kiss on her cheek before taking Ari and

Junior home. It was only next door, as he insisted on staying close to her.

Junior fell asleep as soon as his head hit the pillow, leaving Ari and Mack alone. Mack tried to kiss her, excited to have her alone again, but Ari pulled away, pouting.

"What is it?" he asked

"Why does Dragon have so much control over you? I mean, you act different around her."

Mack blinked at Ari, confused. "She doesn't control me. I do what I want and believe me sweetheart, if she controlled me then I wouldn't be trying to seduce you right now because she doesn't approve of me sleeping with you."

"Why not? Is she jealous or something? Or is it she doesn't want you, but nobody else can have you?"

Mack chuckled. "No, she's not like that. She's just concerned that Junior will get hurt, that's all."

Ari bolted upright. "My son is none of her business! I'm his mom and I always put my children first, and I can't believe she has the audacity to suggest otherwise."

Mack stared in shock, and a wry smile flashed across his face. "Whoa! Easy, tiger! That's not what she's about. Look, she's divorced, and she's been there, done it and got the T-shirt with children and dysfunctional families. She just wants what's best for us."

"Pfft! For her, more like!"

Running his fingers through his hair, Mack's temper started to flair. "Now stop it, Ari! Jealousy isn't a good look for you, sweetheart, and although B may be a little protective over her family, she's done absolutely nothing but help and welcome you. So please let's just leave it," he said, exhausted by it already.

The pair sat in silence for a while until Ari spoke first. "I'm sorry Mack! This must be difficult for you too. I'll be nice, I promise!"

"Thank you," Mack said, inhaling deeply.

"She doesn't approve of us?" Ari asked him.

"No, she suggested I keep it in my pants until I build some new, solid connections with Junior."

Ari moved closer to Mack, stroking his chest.

"Well, maybe we should start thinking what's best for us too," she said as she undid his belt buckle and freed him from his pants.

A flabbergasted Mack looked on at her, eyes wide and numb in shock, as she slipped off her thong, lifted her dress and straddled him. Mack, now breathless, with eyes burning in desire, moaned with pleasure as Ari took every inch of him inside of her. It paralyzed him with pleasure as she rode rhythmically on top of him.

"Oh, Ari. You're such a bad girl!" he moaned.

Ari bit his earlobe, before whispering, "What B doesn't know doesn't hurt her!"

CHAPTER NINETEEN
Death, Lies, and Truth

Mack spent the next few months yo-yoing back and forth between his home and Ari's. He hadn't bothered with B and the boys since meeting Ari but kept them close to his heart. It wasn't something he did intentionally; it was more like a gravitational pull, pulling him toward his son and pulling him toward Ari. They spent the odd weekend up at his home where B would cook and make Ari and the boys feel welcome, watching as all the children became best friends, and Mack and Ari pretended, they weren't sleeping together. But B could tell a mile off. It didn't bother her they were together. What bothered her was that Mack was lying to her about it.

Mack would spend most of his week with Ari and her boys. His routine became his new way of life. He would leave his home to head for Ari's, only he would spend a day or two crossing a couple of MCs off Ari's list. Most of them were yellow pins, which Mack hated. But he used that hate as a driving force to terrorize the presidents on his list, determined to dish out punishment for every Prez who'd laid a finger on Ari, and he was clinical in doing so. Mack got roughed up on his road to vengeance, but he always managed to carry out his mission and managed to hide his scrapes and bruises well and sticking to his plan, telling Ari he got his wounds from grappling with B and B that he was playing with Junior. It wasn't like he saw B, other than a quick hello when he came home to pick up something and they hadn't grappled together in a while. Mack also knew he didn't have to worry about Ari and B talking to each other either, as they said very few words to one another.

Mack had crossed most of the names off his list within those couple of months and with every name he crossed off, he would cross that corresponding scar off on Ari's body when he snuck into her room in the black of night. Ari had told him which Prez had created each scar or scars, depending on their brutality. So, Mack would beat the living daylights out of them in line with what they did to her, then kiss each scar on Ari's body better before making love to her and crossing it off his list. In a dysfunctional way, Mack saw it as a way of apologizing and making things up to her for what she had been through. All unbeknownst to Ari, too, who thought he found her irresistible and believed he had begun to fall for her like she was falling for him. Mack was, in fact, falling for Ari and wanted to be with her, but vengeance was at the forefront of his mind as the guilt consumed him. Mack blamed himself for every scratch and scar on her body and beating Presidents eased that guilt. Deep down, Mack knew it questioned his moral fiber, but he was in too deep now and had to finish what he'd started.

Just hours after he had broken Number 15's ribs, hearing and feeling them crack under his boots, he was once again sneaking around with Ari. He had just finished taking her in the kitchen on her lunch break after removing her work trousers and kissing the four-inch scar that hovered over her left hip bone.

Ari loved the way he would select a scar to fixate on before seducing her. As naïve as she was, she thought it was sweet that he kissed her better and believed that he was being spontaneous when he took her whenever the opportunity presented itself. She didn't give much thought to why he chose a different scar every time he took her hard upon his arrival from his cabin.

They spent any other time they managed to steal a moment

together, making passionate love to one another. But this was different. Whenever Mack arrived at Ari's after being away, he had to have
her as soon as he came through the door. They would have rampant,
hard, lusty, and sometimes downright dirty sex, and Ari loved it. She
looked forward to it and loved that he wanted her, desperate to have
her there and then. Ari would wait for the door to open and run to
embrace him, and they rarely made it past the hallway. In fact, most
of their shenanigans took place in her study, as Mack couldn't wait
to have his way with her. Ari had become besotted with him. Ari was
in love with a man that she thought could see past her scars, but
consumed by guilt, it was all Mack could see. He was desperate to
complete his list and get his life back again.

Mack was becoming increasingly besotted with Ari and less
conflicted about his feelings for B. But, of course, they were still
there. They always would be. He sometimes found it difficult, as he
knew he was falling for Ari, but he hated the thought of betraying B,
the woman he had fallen hard for first. Some nights it would even
keep him up all night as he wrestled with his conscience. He now
found himself in love with two women and lying to them both.

One afternoon, after losing himself inside Ari again and easing
his conscience once more, he sensed that Ari wanted more from him.

How can I give her more than I am? Mack had made himself a criminal again for avenging Ari—unknown to her, of course. He tried to
make her feel better by making her feel she was the only woman in
the world, despite spreading himself so thin, trying his best to juggle
everything to meet her and Junior's needs. The guilt of not seeing B
and his family back home was also becoming too much for him. He
was supposed to be the manager of the retreat and President of the
Gray Wolves, yet he hadn't really seen them in months. Mack wanted
to make that right before he gave Ari another piece of himself. So, le
laid there with eyes closed, pretending to be asleep.

"Mack, you're not going to sleep on the cold kitchen floor, are
you?" she asked.

"Just resting my eyes, sweetheart."

"Mack, open your eyes a minute. I just want to say something."

Shit! He opened his eyes to find Ari staring into them with the heat of a thousand suns.

"Mack, these past couple of months have been amazing, mind-blowing, in fact, and I wanted to thank you and say I'm glad it was you I found and not another sadistic Prez. I also want you to know that I love you!" she gushed.

Mack stared at her. He thought she was beautiful, amazing, kind, and felt honored that she had chosen him to love. He loved her, too. He had fallen for her in ways that he had never imagined, but he still loved B and accepting Ari's love meant moving on from B. As much as he had fallen for Ari and didn't want to hurt her, he just wasn't sure that he was ready for that. B had been all he'd known until Ari walked into his life. He wanted to tell her he loved her, and how he loved the way she made him feel. But he couldn't! It would only make things worse.

He sat up to look at her. He knew the words that were about to come out of his mouth would cut her like a knife through butter, but he owed her honesty.

"Ari, I am honored that you love me, sweetheart, and I want to say it back. But a big part of my heart will always belong to B. I care about you, princess, and I love being with you, but you knew from the start that I couldn't commit and as much as I want to, I'm conflicted, and I can't change the way I feel."

Ari looked like her heart had just shattered into a thousand pieces. Her eyes became like glaciers as they filled with tears.

"Mack, you've been here with me and the boys for months. You haven't mentioned her. She doesn't even want you, Mack, and I don't think she ever will!" Ari said, sniffing and taking deep breaths to fight back the tears that threatened to flood her face. She continued, "I am right here! I'm in love with you more and I know you feel something for me. So please, give us a chance."

Mack hated upsetting her. Gritting his teeth, he wiped the tears from her eyes and planted a soft kiss on her forehead.

"I'm sorry, sweetheart, I just can't do that. It's not fair to you and Junior. You deserve so much better than me, and I hate hurting you."

Ari, now sobbing, tried to plead with him. "Mack, I am giving you my heart and I'm not asking for all of yours. Just enough for us to be together. Just enough to keep feeling what I feel for you! It would break my heart if someone as amazing as you were to grow old alone and never be happy again, because your love isn't reciprocated."

Tears now leaped from Mack's eyes. He hated the fact that he was breaking Ari's heart. It was hurting him just as much as it was hurting her. He pulled her in close, holding her tight as he pleaded with her now.

"Ari please! I am trying to be a better man than a guy who sleeps with someone he can't give his whole heart and soul. We had a casual arrangement and now it is hurting us. Hurting you and I can't stand it, sweetheart!"

"But I don't need your whole heart. I just need a little. Surely you can give me that?"

"Ari, why would you want a little when someone better could give you their whole heart?"

Ari pushed away from his grasp, glaring at him. "You don't get it, do you Mack?"

"How you feel about B is how I feel about you, and if B offered you a fraction of hers, would you take it?"

Mack looked down at the floor. "Yes!"

"Then please accept mine! Jesus, Mack, all I'm asking is you try, for your sake and mine, and if it doesn't work, at least you can say that you tried to mend that shattered heart of yours."

Mack sat there in silence, still naked from crossing another number off his list. He didn't know what to say. He despised himself for upsetting Ari and he hated how torn he felt. Deep down he knew he could never have B, and he wasn't sure if he still wanted her in that way since meeting Ari. He wondered if he had conditioned himself into thinking loved her over the last five years and his love for B was just a masquerade. Maybe he loved someone who would always be emotionally unavailable to him and maybe he couldn't be with anyone after what Nancy did to him. When he met B, they'd trusted only each other. Yes, they would get laid at the Sultry Slalom, but neither of them needed to trust their sexual encounters. Sex was a means to an end, a release of tension and frustration after a hard week's work, and they always knew where each other was. Just in case one of them needed rescued.

Mack needed time to digest, to think things through and decide what he really wanted. Whether it was to live a life of pain, pining after B who didn't love him, or to live a happy life with Ari and feel guilty for loving her. It wasn't an easy decision for Mack; he knew he could be happy with Ari. She was available and loved him back and he could have none of that with B. But B was his best friend, his person and fiery dragon and he didn't want to be in a world without her in it.

"I need some air," he said as he stood up to get dressed. He could not even look at Ari, he was ashamed of himself. Ashamed of letting things get this far, knowing it would hurt Ari. "Can you tell Junior that something came up at work and I'll be back in a few days? I need to clear my head, Ari, and I can't do it here with you, sweetheart, please?"

Ari, sat numb with shock, nodded, and pulled her sweater in to comfort her, grasping it with two hands and clenching it to her chest. Mack, now dressed, looked down at her and planted a kiss on her head before walking for the front door. Holding the door handle to leave, he hesitated and banged his head against the door. He was so frustrated and confused, a big part of him wanted to scoop her up into his arms and tell her just how much he loved her. But there was a small niggle inside telling him to walk away and stop betraying his dragon.

Glancing over his shoulder at Ari now, hugging her knees as tears poured from her eyes, he knew he had ruined everything. He wiped a single tear from his eye and heading out of the door, racing to his bike, revving his engine, he sped out of town. Mack didn't know where he was going or what he was going to do. He just headed for the highway to clear his head until he found himself an hour and a half up the road with no idea where he was. It looked like he was in the middle of nowhere as he searched for road signs to establish where he was and that is where he saw it, a road sign stating, "Shepton 15 miles." Mack had a lightbulb moment. Remembering a yellow pin from Shepton, a horrible yellow pin, Mack thought Number 14 should have been red for what he had attempted to do to Ari. Retrieving his phone from his jacket pocket, he checked the address from the picture he had taken on his phone before revving the accelerator and heading to Shepton.

Mack arrived, pulling into the desolate and pathetic excuse of an MC and he could see a short and stumpy looking bald fella taking out the trash. He got off his bike and headed toward him, as the chilly wind caught his breath. His new jacket that he had bought for his secret excursions wasn't keeping him warm, it wasn't as warm as his Prez cut. He couldn't risk wearing that. It could lead and reprisals back to Uskiville and back to B. He had to keep her protected, give her plausible deniability if he got arrested. It was better this way! Besides, if she ever found out, he would be finished, cast out, and would lose his best friend forever.

As he got closer to the man sorting the trash, he noticed a fresh-looking scar above his right eye that traveled to his right temple. Ari had described her attacker, and he already fitted the bill, but she had also explained that she had struck him with an ashtray to free herself from his grasp. The scar convinced Mack that he had his guy, but he would have to confirm it first.

"Say, fella," he said with his typical Irish charm. "I was wondering if you could help me. I've come from Tele's Creek, and I'm trying to get to the city, but I'm a little lost."

"Well, you've definitely taken a wrong turn somewhere, bud. You are as far away from the city as you could get out here," the man said without even looking at Mack.

"Well, shit! You couldn't point me back in the right direction, could you?"

The man dropped the trash and turned to Mack, only to find he stopped short of Mack's huge chest muscles.

"Geez, you're one hell of a size! No offence, in fact, you are the biggest man I have ever seen. What are you pressing, man? Like, three hundred pounds or something?"

Mack smiled and winked. "Three hundred and thirty."

Shaking his head in disbelief, the man joked, "Well, you must have one heck of a trainer."

"Oh, I do! She's a right dragon! She busts my balls and shows me no mercy if I show any signs of weakness," he joked, casting his dangerous fishing line, hoping the man would bite.

"Geez, you let a woman keep you in shape?"

"Don't they always? But don't you worry fella, I keep her in her place." Mack raised a hand. "See, the secret is to allow them just enough control to aid you, while using a firm hand to keep them in line, and I have my dragon on a tight leash. She's my plaything, as all women should be. She serves me and when she steps out of line, I put her back in her place. You know the old saying, 'treat them mean, keep them keen'?" he said with all the bravado of a narcissistic womanizer, while deep down feeling disgusted with himself for even talking about his dragon like that. Even if he was lying.

"She your old lady?"

"No, I like to dabble when I can," Mack said as he had the guy eating out of the palm of his hand. He knew the game he had to play to get the answers he needed, despite already being convinced he had his man.

"I'm right with you there, bud! A woman's purpose is to serve her man. They're good for three things, brother. Cooking, cleaning, and fucking!" He bragged before continuing. "Listen, why don't I fix you one for the road, while I write some directions for you?"

"That's kind of you fella, but I don't wanna get you into trouble with your boss," Mack said, still working the guy, fishing for information.

"Nah, it's just me here, bud. The club went out on a run this morning. They won't be back until the bar opens later. See, I'm just the bar manager. I run things...well, they get the spoils of the club."

"That's a raw deal," Mack said to make it sound like he was sympathizing with the man, to get him onside.

"Don't worry about me, bud. I get all the action I want running this place. Now come on in and I'll fix you that drink."

Mack followed the man into the club. *What a dive.* He made a face at the filthy club with old wallpaper coming off the walls. "So, is this place busy?"

"In the evenings, yeah! It doesn't look much but being the only bar around here is great because we get all the women we want. I mean, I can pull two women a night!"

"Then you need to tell me your secret, because I have my eye on one woman but she's the only one I can't snare. I normally take what I want, but with her is different. Playing hard to get is her game. It's the thrill of the chase for her. If I could just get her into bed, I'm know she'll be hooked."

"No way! A handsome guy like you should be entitled to whomever he wants."

"Yeah, it's just I can't seem to get her into my bed, and I can't be bothered with that flirting bullshit. I should be able to just take what I want, like I always do"

"Hell yeah, you should!" he said as he removed the beer cap from the bottle of beer in his hand and handed it to Mack.

Mack took a large gulp. "Cheers! So, how do you do it? Because if I don't have her soon, brother, I'll go mad."

The man looked at Mack and pursed his lips.

Retrieving a small bag of white pills from his pocket, the man glanced around the empty bar and handed Mack the bag. "Oh, all right! I'm taking a risk by giving you this, and the Prez would kill me if he even knew I had you in here, let alone giving you these.

But I can't let a brother suffer. Oh, and you didn't get them here, okay?"

Mack took the bag, and studying them he said, "Thanks brother, but my problem isn't in the bedroom, it's getting her into the bedroom in the first place."

"Well, that's just it, bud. You slip one of these babies in her drink and she'll be out cold. As compliant as you want, won't remember a thing in the morning. What they don't know can't hurt them, right?"

"And this works?"

"Yeah, but be sure to give only one dose and don't bother splitting the tablet in half. I gave a tiny woman a half dose a few months back, because she looked so small, but the bitch woke up and cracked me across the head with an ashtray," he said, pointing to his scar.

"Ouch" Mack said in sympathy, while inside he was dancing: *Bingo! I've got you now, you sick son of a bitch.* Mack played a bit more, continuing to converse with the stumpy man.

After Mack finished his drink, he thanked the man for his hospitality and got ready to leave. "Hey, listen, let me give you my club details. Contact me if you ever want to get out from behind the bar and join us real bikers."

"Yeah?"

"Yeah! We could use a man like you in the fold. Here, take my card," he said as he reached into his back pocket but retrieving his gun from his waist band instead. Pulling out his Beretta, complete with the silencer attached, he pointed it at the man. Mack didn't give him a chance to explain. He'd heard enough, and shot the man right between the eyes, watching as he dropped to the floor. Mack raced behind the bar with adrenaline coursing through his veins and headed into the office to wipe the security footage, knowing exactly where to look and what to do. He had done it time and time before with his brothers back in Sunnyville. It was a frequent thing when rival gangs tried to set up shop near their town. He would always use an unregistered gun and while the others were creating chaos, it was his job to wipe the security footage and switch off the cameras. Making his way to the exit, he picked up his beer bottle. He left, not even giving the dead man a second look.

On the road again, Mack basked in the glory. "Another one down," he thought to himself. Mack knew Ari classified the stumpy man as yellow, but he thought Ari had been too easy on him and had reclassified him as a red. In Mack's eyes, the man didn't deserve to live. He thought about how frightened Ari must have been that night, and it sickened him. Killing him in cold blood made Mack feel like justice had been served and he would sleep easier tonight knowing that there was one less predator on the streets.

Mack drove onto the highway. He was desperate to go back to Ari's. His body called out to her. He had to cross Number 14 off the list, and he experienced a burning desire to be inside Ari. Even after what had happened between them, he had to go to her as his body, mind, and soul craved her scent, taste, and touch. He didn't give B a moment's thought; it was Ari he needed right now, but he couldn't figure out whether it was the need to complete his list or because he genuinely missed her, and he was going to make things right with her.

Mack pulled up at Ari's. It was late. He let himself in with the spare key she had given him after the last time he stayed. Junior had thought that was amazing, telling his dad that they were like a proper family now. And they were.

Mack couldn't wait to strip off and take full advantage of Ari. Only this time, he needed to apologize and convince her to give him another chance. All he could think about was being inside her and placing his lips over the scar on her collarbone. Mack became hard, just thinking about how he wanted to take her as he entered her bedroom and closed the door behind him.

Mack expected her to be asleep, hoping to slip in bed beside her, but she sat up in the bed as soon as she saw him, flicking on the lamp to look at him.

"Hey sweetheart, he whispered as he undressed.

"What are you doing here?" she questioned in a thick voice. "I thought you needed space. It's only been a few hours."

Mack climbed into bed next to her, pulling her into him with Ari conforming to him. He realized he had missed her so much and was glad he had gone back to her.

Taking her head in his hands, he kissed her top lip. "I thought I did too, sweetheart, but a few hours away from you and I was going crazy. I know I messed things up, but I had to come back. I had to be with you. Ari, I am so sorry for breaking your heart."

Ari whimpered. "Oh, Mack!"

"Are you sure that you're all right with me being here? I was desperate to come back to you, but if you want me to go, just say the word and I'll leave," he explained as he kissed her collarbone as if to show to himself that was another one crossed off the list.

Ari's eyes filled relief with relief. "I'm fine! And of course, I want you here, but only if you want to be here, Mack."

Fighting the urge to ravish her there and then, he whispered in her ear. "Oh sweetheart, I am desperate to be here with you, be inside you. I want to right all the wrongs and make you feel better."

"You always make me feel better," she explained as she reached up to the back of his head and pulled him into her to kiss his moist lips.

Mack let out his all too familiar pleasurable moan as he ran his hands through her hair, before climbing on top of her. Devouring her mouth with his as he looked into her eyes. "Ari, I want you, sweetheart, now and forever! I'm ready to be with you. Please forgive me, and I promise I'll be the man you need."

Ari, eyes wide, stared back at him. He could feel her body trembling as his big, muscular body hovered over her. Her body convulsed as he pressed himself up against her inner thigh, riding up toward her entrance. Driving closer to her as he felt her hips beckon him, he wanted to show her he now belonged to her.

Ari, now looking desperate for him, begged him to enter her. "Make love to me Mackie, show me how much you want me."

Mack felt his body tremble as his cock hardened upon entering her. Her seductive sex clambering around him, making him twitch inside her. "Oh Ari, sweetheart, I am going to show you all night long. I'll never leave you again!" he said through gritted teeth. Mack had never felt so strained as his body took over, penetrating her with his shaft stretched inside her.

Mack struggled to contain himself as the pressure roared through his raging erection. His long, slow, and hard thrusts massaging Ari's G spot as he sucked on her neck. He locked eyes with her as he filled her, making her cry out with immense pleasure with every thrust.

"Ari, I want you to feel my love for you, sweetheart. Feel how hard you make me. Take all of me please?" he begged, desperate for her to feel what he felt.

They moaned together as one, and Mack became relentless as Ari's warmth flooded him.

"Oh, yeah, sweetheart! I love to watch your eyes glaze over as you feel me inside you," he cried. Struggling to cope with his impending release, he became thicker and harder than ever before as he indulged in her, trying to take her beyond any expectations she had of him. Ari cried out, and Mack lost control, his jaw clenched shut, as he thrusted hard and fast, delivering sharp and beautiful blows to her G spot. He felt her body tense as he pinned her arms down, ripping through her and making her take him. Growling in fury, Mack became lost in his emotions as he drove her into the mattress, making her explode in an instant. Ari screamed over and over as she came undone, her body shaking as she pulled him in for more. Mack didn't want it to end as he felt him deliver his final blows before bursting into a climax of his own. He didn't stop there though, he couldn't. He didn't even come up for air as he began kissing her all over her body. He stared at her breasts, almost gorging himself with them, breathing heavily as he did so. Her skin tasted divine as he continued to ravish her body with his teeth and lips until he turned her over and pulled her up onto her knees.

"Oh Mackie, take me again!" she cried as he entered her once more.

Mack was determined to give her everything, determined to make her feel every hard and forceful thrust as he took hold of her hips, wanting to make her feel incandescent for him. He slammed into her, growling as he did so, taking her so hard that the headboard rattled against the wall. Ari screamed in delight as she twitched beneath him, asking him for more and telling him how she loved how he took her.

Ari writhed in pleasure as Mack let out all kinds of moans and cries as he finally felt free as he gave himself to her. He could tell Ari's arms were tiring despite feeling that they were both so close to exploding again, and he didn't want to stop now. So, he shifted back, taking hold of her hips, to take some of his weight off her and held her while he thrusted. He watched as Ari dug into the sheets with her nails, gripping them as he plowed through her relentlessly, demanding her orgasm. Ari convulsed as her release washed over her, screaming at the top of her voice in pleasure as she attempted to control her body. Mack could no longer compose himself, gripping down onto her small waist as he vanquished her until he growled into his climax. Continuing to pump her, he couldn't release her until he'd given her everything he had and just hoped that it was enough for her to believe his love for her. Shattered and exhausted, he removed himself from her trembling body and laid down beside her.

"I love you, Ari!" he said as he looked into her eyes and in that moment, he wasn't thinking about her or the list, he was thinking about her and the beautiful moment that they'd shared.

Ari gazed upon him, full of emotion. "I love you too, Mackie!"

"I could tell things were different as soon as you entered my room, and I don't know what's changed your mind and I don't care. All I care about is that you love me now and forever."

CHAPTER TWENTY

From Melting Pot to Breaking Point

A few more weeks had passed since Mack had confessed his love for Ari and he'd still not been back to Uskiville. He hadn't even called or texted B, who had since stopped messaging him too. Mack was content with Ari and his new family in Portland, but he missed B, the boys, and fishing trips with Frankie. He missed his family and the calm of Uskiville, but he was on a mission and had to see it through. His thoughts were occupied by Number 21 and the red pin again, and that night, after the boys went to bed, Mack disappeared into Ari's room.

Ari, lying in bed wearing nothing but a smile, was ready and waiting for him to please her. She dived on Mack as soon as he entered the room, and Mack would oblige by making love to her all night long, but this time he stopped her in her tracks.

"What's wrong?" she asked as he removed her hands from his waistband and sat on the bed next to her.

"Ari, we need to talk, sweetheart."

Concern flashed over Ari's face. "Oh."

Mack met her gaze and whispered, "I've opened up my heart to you. Now you need to do the same. We need to talk about Number 21 and the red pin."

Ari darted upright in her bed and pulled away from him.

Taking her hand and rubbing the top of it with his thumb as he always did when she looked stressed, he began. "Ari, I have to know the name of the club, sweetheart. I left things a while so we could get to know each other, so you would feel more comfortable with me, but now I have to know. I love you, Ari, but the only way this works is if we can be honest with each other. So, tell me the name of the club."

Ari regarded him with trepidation. "Mack, I can't."

Mack studied her, narrowing his eyes. "If you love me, then you'll be honest with me and tell me."

Ari grabbed his hand. "You already know the name of the club, you always have."

Mack already felt queasy, but he forced himself to say the name. "The Red Pitbulls?"

Ari nodded in agreement, and strain etched itself over Mack's face.

Clenching his jaw, he spat through gritted teeth. "Tell me everything... Please?"

Ari sighed. She grabbed her nightgown and slipped it over her head then drew Mack to sit beside her on the bed and tried to explain. "It's bad, Mack, terrible even and you need to promise me you won't get mad when I tell you everything."

Mack glared into Ari's eyes. She was scared and hurting, and truth be told, he was too. He gave a curt nod. "Okay."

Ari told him about the events that had unfolded that night, explaining how Number 21 had lured her inside his club under false pretenses, despite his friends' best efforts to send her packing. She explained how he had attempted to rape her. Mack watched the tears fall from her eyes, drowning her nightgown as the story unfolded. His heartbeat at an uncontrollable pace, and anger fueled the fire in his belly as Ari detailed how Number 21's Prez had mauled her with his rancid bear claw. Mack was so grateful to Noah, Zander, and Jimmy for coming to her rescue. His friends had proved their loyalty to him once again by saving the woman he loved. Noah and Zander had saved his life before, when the Mauler tried to kill him, and Mack owed them a debt for that too.

He held Ari close as she provided an in-depth account of her hospital treatment, grueling recovery, and how the kind Scotsman had slipped a note into her jacket pocket so she could find him. It absolutely devastated him to learn what she had been through. He knew in his heart that any details she had left out must have been even worse than what she told him.

He tried to console a sobbing Ari. "Sweetheart, I'm so sorry that you had to endure that, and that I made you relive it tonight. You never have to speak about it again, baby, I promise," he declared as he held her tight.

Ari wiped her tears. "Mackie, there's more!" she declared, watching Mack's face drop again in disappointment.

He nodded and drew a deep breath. "Tell me."

"When I came to, after he had initially knocked me unconscious," she began in a shaky voice, "he gave me a message for you!" She pursed her lips, looking terrified.

Mack's mouth dropped open as he stared at Ari in in shock. "What did he say Ari?" he asked, shuddering at the thought.

She took a deep breath and quoted the Mauler. "He said, 'And when I'm done with you, you can tell that Irish prick what I've done to you! Tell him that revenge is a dish that's best served cold and I'm coming for him and everyone he's ever loved.'"

She broke down again as she finished, clinging onto him. Only this time, he didn't hold her back. He was numb. The Mauler had taken so much from him already, but now his old Prez had made *Mack* responsible for Ari's horrific wounds. He wanted revenge, craved it, had to have it.

Mack stood up away from Ari, shaking his head. Every emotion ran through him, crippling him. What would B think of this? He had already lied to her about being with Ari but avenging her...and now this. What if he had already found Mack's address? B was as innocent as Ari and although she could hold her own and could probably kill the Mauler, he was a psychopath and could hurt her. It was all too much for Mack. His blood pressure soared, making his head want to explode. Mack needed to release some of the pressure. He needed to leave.

"I need to get out of here!" he said, rushing to his room to get dressed, with Ari in tow.

"Mack, please? Don't leave. Not like this!" she begged. Mack said nothing, but continued to get ready to leave, pulling his hoodie over his head. Ari watched as his eyes narrowed. They looked black like coal, his face stern and jaw clenched as he gritted his teeth. She stood in front of him, placing her hands on his chest.

"Mack, please?" she pleaded again as she clasped his head to make him look at her.

"Ari, I have to go!" he said through gritted teeth.

"No! We need to talk."

A furious Mack threw his hands up in the air in frustration and paced back and for his bedroom. "Ari, that bastard has taken everything from me and now you're telling me he mauled you to get to me. How can I even live with that? You went through a lot to find me, and I felt guilty looking at your body. I know it was your choice, but knowing that your worst attack, your red pin, was from *him* and because of *me*. That's just too much to bear."

"Mack."

"No, Ari! I've tried to get past the guilt I feel. I really have! I've tried to make things right! But I can't get past this!"

Ari's bottom lip trembled. "What are you saying?"

"That B was right. This was never going to work. I love you so much, sweetheart, but now when I look at you now, I'm reminded of him. Reminded of the man who tried to kill me, gave me years of nightmares so terrifying that B had to hold me so I could sleep. Yeah, it's not just Junior who's haunted by his past, Ari, it's me too! I'm sorry, but I just can't do this anymore!" he said as he walked out the bedroom door and put his boots on.

That broke Ari, and she chased after him, grabbing his shoulder. "For crying out loud, Mack, we all have nightmares. Only mine stopped when you came into my life and took me in your arms. Mack, as much as he terrifies me, I moved on because of you, so let me be that person for you and let's move on from this. Please?"

"That's not the same, Ari, and you God damn well know it."

"And what about me? Did you not think that I had gone through the same thing? When I first laid eyes on you? Looking at the man Number 21 attacked me for?"

Mack kept his eyes down as he responded to her. "Well, you kissed me first, sweetheart. In fact, you kept kissing me, luring me into you, despite me telling you I was in love with another and now that other could be in danger too because you kept this from me for so long!"

Ari saw red. "Does everything have to be about B? I fucking hate her, and I can't breathe without someone mentioning her. God, you put her on a fucking pedestal, and what has she done for you besides fucking control you?"

Mack was taken aback. He hadn't heard her swear before. Her face screwed up tight as she seethed at him, but Mack knew that if he'd stayed, he would end up resenting her. The only thing that could make him better was crossing another name off his list, and he had one in mind. Momentarily snapping himself out of his rage, Mack turned his attention back to Ari, who was still ranting about B. Her jealousy of B would always rear its ugly head when Ari became angry or had a bad day. Grown tired of her blaming his best friend for everything that went wrong in her own life and sick of her jealousy, Mack snapped.

"Ari, stop! You're beautiful, sweetheart, but I've told you before, jealousy will never be a good look on you," he said as he started his Harley. "Oh, and tell Junior I'll call him," he added as he revved the engine.

"So that's it, then? You tell me you love me and minutes later, we're done."

Mack turned to her. "Ari, I do love you, but right now I need to process and digest what you've just told me. Now please go inside. It's cold out here!"

"No! Mack, if you leave now, then that's it. We're done!"

"Sorry, sweetheart, it's over!" he said as he revved his bike once more and roared off into the night, leaving Ari devastated.

Mack sped back down the highway; he knew the address of Number 2. Number 2 was last but two on his list, and Mack needed his blood on his hands. That prick was going to pay tonight; he thought to himself as he rode like the wind, desperate to get there. He glanced at his watch; it was only 10:37 p.m. If he pushed it, he could hit the club before closing time. Mack was usually meticulous with his planning. His planning was the reason he remained unscathed until this point, but there was no plan for tonight. Mack was going to waltz right through the front doors. It was suicide, he understood, but he no longer cared. He needed to feel the bones of his prey shatter, to see his face as he tore him apart. Mack needed them to hurt like he did.

An angry and desperate Mack pulled up outside the MC. He had missed last orders as he had to remove his plates just in case he had to escape in a hurry. The club members were still inside when the bartender locked the outside door.

"Hey, I'm looking for the Prez," he said.

"We're closed, pal. Come back tomorrow and he'll sort out whatever you're after then."

Mack pulled out his gun, pressing it to the guy's head. "Take me too him now or die," he said through gritted teeth.

The bartender's voice trembled. "Have you got a death wish or something? There are five bikers in there. Do you believe you can take on all of them?"

"Let's find out, shall we?" Mack sneered, jamming the gun harder into his temple. "Lead the fecking way."

Mack was like a man possessed as he followed the guy into the bar. He was so angry; hurting and wanted to ease his pain. Back home with B, they would grapple their pain away, no matter what time of day it was. They were always there for one another. But not tonight. Tonight, he would have to deal with his pain alone. He had kept B at a distance since he had met Ari, to keep her from finding out the truth about him, to keep her from finding out that he'd gone back to black for Ari. If he told B any of this now, she wouldn't understand. She would cast him out of her life, and he needed her. Mack needed his dragon now more than ever and, to make her understand, he had no choice but to avenge Ari. He loved her and couldn't let the monsters who hurt her roam free and unpunished. He would have to make B see that without releasing her inner dragon and sending her into a fit of rage, where she cast him out of her life, out of his family, and out of his home.

As he walked inside, the five men, including the fat slob of a Prez, were sitting at the bar. They all stopped short of their drinks and glared at Mack. One man attempted to reach for a shotgun that was situated under the bar.

Mack glared at them. "I wouldn't do that if I were you. I don't miss! Now slide all your weapons over to me and let's not forget the ones in your boots, ay fellas?"

"Well, you're stupid or one sandwich short of a picnic, asshole. Coming in here, picking a fight with five of us." The Prez laughed.

"Maybe, I'm both, or maybe I'm in perfect frame of mind and want some fecking answers," he snarled as he held onto the bartender, while still pointing the gun at his head.

"Well, what the fuck do you want?"

"A few months back, a pint-sized brunette looking for an Irishman visited you."

The Prez's eyes went wide.

"Yeah, you remember, don't you, you worthless piece of shite."

The Prez's lips grew wide as he grinned devilishly at the Irishman. "Oh, the little rag doll, you mean. Yeah, I enjoyed playing with her. Feisty, that one! I figured it best to take her down a peg or two, put her in her place."

"So, you admit laying a hand on her!" Mack bellowed in anger.

"Why wouldn't I? The little bitch came into my club looking for answers, but she wasn't willing to stay and service me. She had to learn her lesson, and I would have taken that ass and finished her, but my hag of a wife went rogue. Tired of me putting my cock everywhere but inside her. So, I put her in her place too!"

"Don't worry! I'm gonna put you in your place, fella!" Mack said with a wry smile. He was seething beyond his expectations now, adrenaline coursing through his veins as if he was high on something; and he was high, high on vengeance and he wanted his next fix.

The Prez and his pack laughed wearily as Mack was an unknown quantity to them. They couldn't fathom whether he was nuts or just stupid. Either way, they wanted him dead.

The Prez's eyes turned devious. "Well now, paddy, I think you've had your fun tonight. Why don't you let my guy go and we can have a chat?"

"Do you think I'm fecking stupid?" Mack raged.

"Yes, actually I do! See, you've stepped into my club now, boy, and nobody leaves here alive unless I say so."

"Oh, really?" Mack said sarcastically. Before pointing his gun at the Prez and shooting him in the arm. Mack watched him scream like a girl as blood poured from the gunshot wound. Panic spread as the men stood there, silent, and Mack grinned with satisfaction. "Do I have your attention now?"

"What the fuck do you want exactly?" the Prez roared as he tried to apply pressure to his wound.

"You! I'm going to fecking throw you around like a rag doll, like you did to the woman I love and when I'm done, I might let you live, or I might not. It depends on how I feel while I'm smashing your teeth in."

"And you think my guys are going to let you anywhere near me, do you?"

Mack, now completely lost to adrenaline and anger, smiled

psychotically. "No! I don't." he said and with that, Mack shot two men in the legs then shot the third guy that tried to run at him. The fourth wasn't so stupid, so Mack shot him in the shoulder and did this so gracefully and all while using the terrified bartender as a human shield. Just in case someone had a concealed weapon.

Groans and cries rattled around the bar as Mack looked at the horror scene that he'd created. He didn't care anymore; he was hurting, so why shouldn't everyone else? Besides, these guys were bad guys with souls as black as coal.

"You're fucking dead, paddy! You think you can walk him here and hurt my guys? I'll kill you!"

Mack threw the bartender into the corner of the room. "Move and I'll end you fella," he snarled, leaving the man paralyzed with fear. There was no danger of him even twitching. He clearly valued his life.

Mack walked over to the Prez, kicking the pile of guns farther from reach of the injured bikers who were writhing in pain on the floor. Gun in one hand, he gripped the alpha by the back of the head and threw him to the ground, watching him stumble and trip with his excess fat wobbling like jelly. Placing his gun in the back of his waistband, he kicked the Prez in the face while he was down, listening with satisfaction to the sound of his nose breaking across his instep.

The man squealed in pain and Mack enjoyed it, so he rained down on the Prez, stamping on his chest repeatedly, before weighing in with his fists. The man beneath him screamed in agony, coughing up his teeth just as Mack had promised him. Mack stood to retrieve his gun, but before he realized, he was tackled to the ground while the Prez and the other injured bikers tried to collect themselves. Getting the advantage over Mack, his assailant landed a punch on Mack's face and attempted to choke him as he placed himself in a favorable position.

Mack was no stranger to this position after being on the receiving end of B's moves when they grappled. He swept the unsteady guy using his Jiu jitsu skills, placing himself on top of the man this time. As they wrestled, Mack dug his thumb into the guy's shoulder wound, making him release Mack from his grip so that Mack could punch him in the face, knocking him out. Mack then stumbled to his feet, blood dripping down his face and ribs screaming in agony from his scuffle. He looked around while catching his breath and could see the destruction that he had caused. Reaching down to pick up his gun, which had become dislodged while fighting, he put a bullet in the Prez's belly.

"Now we're even, you fat prick," he spat before turning around and glimpsing at the bartender, cowering in the corner. Mack could see how terrified he was; he had wet himself in fear and Mack wondered why he was in toe with these vile animals. "You, security footage. Where can I find it?"

"We—we don't have any," the man managed, trembling.

"If you're fecking lying to me fella...."

"I'm not, please, please, I beg you. I have a kid. Please?"

Mack dragged him up, dragging him outside. "Move!"

"Please, please," the frightened bartender pleaded.

"Where's your bike?"

"I—I... don't have one. I have a family car over there. The red rust bucket."

Mack dragged the man to his vehicle. "Open it now!"

The man fumbled in his urine-stained trouser pockets for his keys, almost dropping them as he unlocked the car. Mack threw him in the driver's seat, took out his wallet and handed him a wad of notes.

"You saw nothing tonight, you understand me? You tell a soul, and I will come for you and everyone you love! Now go home, get your family, and fucking leave town." He ordered before explaining; "These guys have just watched you bring me into the club. They will think that you colluded with me. Trust me, I know how they think. They will look to blame someone and that someone will be you. So, out of town and don't bother going to the cops. You hear me?"

"Yes, yes, okay, okay," he cried as he started his car and sped out of the parking lot. Mack then stumbled to his bike and sped off.

As he rode along the highway, he felt sick, dizzy, and in pain, his injured body crying out to him. He knew he wouldn't make it back home. Besides, he couldn't let B see him like this. He had no choice but to return to Ari's again. The only other alternative was to stop somewhere and risk being reported to the cops for being covered in blood. So, he took the next exit off the highway to cut through the quiet country lanes to Ari's house. Those roads were dead quiet, so there was less chance of being seen by anyone, he thought to himself as he swerved in and out of traffic, struggled to stay awake.

A couple of hours later and after a long and arduous ride, Mack pulled onto Ari's drive. He glanced up and spotted Ari looking out her bedroom window, probably after recognizing the sound of his bike. Mack gingerly eased himself off his bike and stumbled toward the back door. A terrified Ari met him there.

CHAPTER TWENTY-ONE
Broken

Opening the back door, Ari found Mack covered in blood, propping up the door frame, his eyes swollen as blood dripped from a cut just above his right eyebrow and his nose was bloodied. Mack winced as she grabbed him, and Ari gasped at the state of his black and blue knuckles.

"Oh, God, Mack, what have you done?" she said, gasping in horror as she helped him inside.

"Study," he managed through gritted teeth. "The boys cannot see me like this."

Agony reflected in his eyes and his body shook in anguish as she helped him along the hallway and into the study. After lowering him onto the brown leather sofa, Ari ran to fetch her first aid kit from the kitchen and upon her return, she locked the door behind her just in case the boys woke from the noise. Kneeling, she cleaned Mack up, starting with the cut above his eyebrow. Mack winced as she moved from one injury to the next. Blood visibly seeped through his T-shirt and as she attempted to lift it over his head to remove it, he let out a huge moan of anguish.

"Geez, Ari!" he growled

"I'm sorry, I'm sorry. I'll just cut it off using the scissors," she said as she took them out of her kit and began snipping at his shirt. When she removed his blood-stained shirt, she gasped at the sight of his body. It was all kinds of black, blue, and purple colors. His left side over his ribs oozed with blood, with a small piece of glass embedded in the wound.

"I'm calling 911! You need to see a doctor!" she cried.

"No, no doctors. You need to do this for me, Ari, please?"

Ari tried to hold back her tears. It pained her to see Mack hurting like a bear caught in a trap, desperate for help. Taking a deep breath to calm herself, she left the study and returned minutes later with a bottle of Mack's whiskey. She kneeled beside him again, opened the bottle of whisky and took a huge gulp.

"Shit!" she said, shaking. She hated whisky but needed it for the wound and to calm her nerves. She had grown used to seeing her own body bloodied, battered, and bruised, but this was the man she had fallen in love with, and it broke her. Ari didn't know what had happened to Mack tonight, where he'd been or how he'd gotten himself into such a state. But right now, she didn't care. He needed her help and there would be time for questions later, she thought to herself.

"Here, drink some of this," she said, handing him the bottle of whisky. "It's supposed to help. I saw it in the movies, so it better blinking well, help," she stated.

"Mack guzzled a third of the bottle to help with the pain, before giving it back to her.

Picking up the tweezers to remove the glass, Ari handed him a cushion from the end of the sofa. "Here, bite down on this if you need to. It will muffle any noise."

Biting her top lip to calm her nerves, she asked. "Are you ready?"

Mack pursed his lips and nodded as Ari poured whisky over his wound to clean it, mopping up the excess with his torn shirt. Mack growled into the cushion, panting through gritted teeth.

"Right Ari, pull on your big girl pants, you can do this." She said out loud, giving herself a much-needed pep talk. She took the tweezers and latched onto the chunk of glass, tugging on it to remove it and as she did, she watched blood pour from the wound. Taking the whisky once more, she cleaned it again, hoping Mack didn't pass out from the pain.

"Nearly there Mack, I'm just checking to see if there's any more glass." She said with confidence this time.

Having checked the wound for anymore debris, she closed it as best she could. It wasn't a large wound and nor was it deep, but the bruising surrounding it was horrific. It concerned Ari that he might have broken a rib or punctured a lung, but she knew taking him to the emergency room was not an option. Ari then applied some temporary sutures from the first aid kit and covered them with a sterile self-adhesive antiseptic dressing, hoping that it would be enough to prevent an infection. After dealing with his wounds, she double checked she had missed no other wounds before taking a warm flannel to him to clean him up and towel drying him as he laid there looking numb. She then retrieved some pajama bottoms and a dressing gown from his room and by the time she had returned, Mack had fallen asleep with exhaustion. Checking his pulse and listening to his breathing reassured her he was okay for the moment and needed a lot of rest. Trying not to disturb him, Ari removed his jeans as she realized not all the blood on them was Mack's.

"I need to destroy the evidence," she told herself.

The details of that night remained unclear to her as she protected the man she loved as she removed his boots and socks and unbuckled his jeans. Sliding them down along with his pants with them and being careful not to wake him, Ari then slid his favorite pajama bottoms up and around his waist. Thinking to herself that it was easier than she thought it would be. She didn't move him any further than she had to, so instead of trying to put his dressing gown on him, she placed it over the top of him, covering him like a blanket. She let out a sigh of relief as she watched him sleep, all bandaged up. It was so hard for her to see him like that. He had always looked so strong and in control until tonight. But tonight, she saw an angry, broken, and terrified man and it scared her.

"Have I driven him to this?" she asked herself as she loaded his bloody clothes into the washing machine and placing them on a hot wash.

Ari didn't know what she was doing as she washed the blood stains from his boots in the sink, removing any evidence of where he had been or what he had done tonight. The only knowledge she had to help her was from tv programs and movies, and they weren't real. It was her way of helping him for a change. Her way of protecting him as he had looked after her for months now. Helping her heal and grow. She knew she was breaking the law by disposing the potential evidence and she didn't care that they had had a terrible fight earlier on in the evening because she loved him.

After dealing with Mack's belongings, she had a shower, feeling dirty after cleaning up so much blood. She allowed the hot water and soap to nourish her skin, cleansing her from her ordeal tonight and after drying herself off and putting on her cozy onesie, she headed back down to the study to check on Mack. After checking on him, she retrieved a blanket from the sitting room. She sat on the floor, leaning up against the sofa. Wrapping herself up, she rested her weary head on the sofa before drifting off to sleep.

The next morning, Ari woke to the sound of the boys making breakfast. She got up and headed to the kitchen, closing the study door behind her.

"Mom, there're droplets of blood on the floor here," Junior informed her, looking concerned.

"Shit!" she thought to herself. She had been so frantic and exhausted last night; she had forgotten to check for blood droplets after she had cleaned up last night.

"Oh! That was from your silly father last night, Junior. He was a little tipsy when he put some music on to have a bit of a dance in the kitchen last night and slipped and banged his head on the table," she said, faking laughter.

"What, is he okay?" Junior panicked.

"Oh, yes! He's fine. I checked him over myself and patched him up. But he will have a bit of a headache today, so it's best to leave him asleep, okay? Besides, I'm taking the day off to make sure, so you boys don't have to worry, okay?"

"Okay, Mom," Junior said.

Ari hated lying to them, but she had to tell them something to explain the cuts and bruises on his face and she didn't know what the truth was yet. She would have to extract that from Mack when he woke up this morning.

Ensuring that the boys had eaten, she ferried them off to school, after arranging for the neighbor to drop them off, then she headed to the study to check on Mack.

Upon entering the room, she saw Mack sitting with his head in his hands.

"Hey, how are you feeling?" she asked, placing a hand on his back to comfort him.

"I'm okay. Thank you for what you did for me last night, baby. I'm so sorry for how I reacted last night."

"Mack, I love you! I need to know what's going on. First you tell me you love me, then you break up with me, leaving me heartbroken and then you turn up in the early hours beaten, bruised and covered in blood. I need to know what's happened."

Mack raised his bruised face to glance up at Ari. "I had a run in with Number 2."

Ari, confused, asked, "What? What do you mean?"

"After you told me what the Mauler did to you, I lost control. I could handle everything until then. I was trying to make up for the bad things that happened to you. You know, an eye for an eye, and it helped me deal with it all."

"Mack, I don't understand."

"Looking at your broken body, I knew I was responsible for everything that happened to you, and I wanted to make them pay, Ari, all of them. They hurt you, and I wanted to hurt them, so I paid each one a visit and gave them the same treatment that they gave you. I broke their ribs, fractured their hands, faces, ribs. They regretted the day they met you, and it felt good. I would cross one off my list and come home to you and kiss another one of those beautiful scars better, making love to you as I did so. See, I couldn't live with myself for what had happened to you, and I knew that if I wiped the slate clean by avenging you, then I could live with myself again, live with you, be happy with you." He swallowed and drew a deep breath. "But Number 21 got to me, Ari. That message he gave you for me tore through every fiber of my being. It made me feel sick, scared even. I mean the thought of losing everything again, being alone again. Just like I was when I was on the streets before B saved me." He shook his head. "Ari, I used to cry myself to sleep at night, grieving for all that I'd lost, and I was still doing it long after B took me in and gave me a new life. B used to listen to my sobs, and she would hold me until I fell asleep with exhaustion. That's how bad I suffered, Ari, and I will never feel like that again. The last time I lost everything, I had B. She taught me to channel my anger, grief, and aggression into grappling. We did it every day, along with mindfulness and meditation. She helped be go from black to white, she helped make me civilized again, fixed me so I could breathe in the world again. Ari, B is the only person who can help me right now, and I can't go to her because if I do, then I lose everything. I have betrayed her and when she finds out, she will cast me out of her life and I will be alone again and I can't live like that again, Ari, I can't! I've already lost you sweetheart, and I can't lose my dragon too." He sobbed, shaking as the trauma became too much for him.

Ari watched him sob like a baby, and it broke her heart. Tears leaped from her eyes as she tried to comprehend what he had told her, what he had done for her over these past months. She realized then that behind that beautiful smile, he had been hurting, tormented by her ordeal. Keeping everything locked up inside while trying to make her and the boys happy. Guilt washed over her as she felt angry with herself.

Did I miss the signs to suggest that he was suffering? I just assumed he wasn't a big talker, and he would tell me if he was unhappy.

She was confused because he had given nothing away. He would arrive at her house with flowers, full of smiles as he kissed her, or he would wait in bed for her to come home so he could make sweet love to her. Mack had never given Ari any reason to question his feelings.

She gasped as something dawned on her. "Oh, God! You made love to me every time you crossed someone off your list. That's why you would get shitty if you couldn't have me. You couldn't cross it off until you kissed my scars and made love to me."

"Yeah," he managed, wiping his tears

"So, all this time, you were making love to me to make yourself feel better about what happened to me?"

"At the start, yes! I knew you wanted me, and I didn't want to hurt you. And I was struggling with what happened to you and how I felt about B. I was confused."

"And now?" Ari asked, tears sliding down her face.

Mack met her gaze, placing his damaged hand on her cheek. "And now I make love to you because I want you and because I can't live without you. I've been so conflicted these past months, Ari, and I know I am a horrible piece of work and that I hurt you. But everything I did and do now is because I love you. I couldn't stand what those monsters did to you, and I don't expect you to give me a second chance. Geez, I don't expect you to want to talk to me again, now that you've seen first-hand the monster I've become. But I want you to know, I am going to see this through and not to make myself feel better, but because I love you and those bastards will pay for what they have done to you!" he said through stifled tears.

Ari looked into Mack's glacier-like eyes, and she could see how damaged his soul was. Tormented by everything that had happened. She understood why he did what he did and although his process and application of everything were all twisted, his heart was always in the right place. Ari also knew that she was the one who kept pushing for a relationship and although he seemed happy to initiate sex, he had been honest with her from the start regarding his feelings for B. It was why Ari hated her so much. She hated the woman that stole her man's heart before she even had a chance with him. Yet, here he sat, beaten and broken from avenging her. His hand resting on her cheek, looking into her eyes and telling her that his heart belonged to her now. Could she honestly be mad at him for everything that he had done, avenging her, lying to her about bruises he collected from working through her list? That made her hate B even more. She looked him in the eyes.

"Mack, I love you so much, but I'm afraid that you're wrong about so many things."

Fear and confusion mingled on Mack's expressive face.

"You are not responsible for what happened to me," Ari continued. "I made a conscious decision as a mature adult to find you, and I'm so glad I did. I have no regrets, Mack, and I do still want you, despite everything that's happened. B isn't the only one who can help. I am right here. But you need to understand that I'm not B."

"I know, sweetheart."

Ari held up a hand, palm out, halting his speech. "No. Mack, listen. Before everything happened, I lived the simple life, so naïve and oblivious to what the world was about. But then I met our son and started looking for you. The reality hit home about how cruel and unforgiving this world is, and it was a life lesson that I needed to learn. Now, I don't care about good and bad or black and white as you and B see it, because I look at the world and do whatever it takes to survive. Mack, I washed evidence off your clothes without knowing what happened, and if the police showed up at my door, I would have given you an alibi, no questions asked. Because I love you and don't want to lose you. Mack, I will do anything to help you and make things right between us!"

Mack stared at Ari in shock as tears rolled down his bruised cheeks. "You still want me after everything I've done?"

Ari nodded and gave him a watery smile. "Of course I do! I love you and I'll always want you! But from now on, we do this together and no more bottling up your feelings or hiding anything from me. You understand me?"

"Promise, sweetheart," he said as he sobbed into her chest, for the first time looking relieved and happy.

"Mack, I need you to do some things for me, too?"

Mack gazed up at her, "Anything."

"I want to tell the boys we're together. I think they already know. They're not stupid. No more lies, no more sneaking and stealing moments together."

"Okay."

"You also have to tell B about us, so that me and the boys can move in with you in Uskiville. I respect that she's your family, but I hate how she controls you, and that ends now."

Mack sat up and stared at Ari. She envisioned the cogs going in his head, thinking of what to say. Ari realized she had to be clear before they examined their relationship. Besides, she didn't fear the dragon in the slightest.

"Ari, I would, sweetheart, but I'm not sure if B will talk to me again when she finds out what I've been up to."

"Then don't tell her!" Ari spat with frustration.

Mack laughed. "Sweetheart, this is B we're talking about. Nothing gets past her and believe me when she finds out, she won't let me stay."

"But it's your home!"

"I know, but B owns the place. Ari, B has rules and for good reason. She's been through a lot, and it's her way of shielding herself and her boys."

"Mack, I don't mean to be rude, but she is a psychopath, a control freak. I don't know what you ever saw in her. She doesn't scare me, and I will be more than happy to talk to her."

Mack shook his head in despair. "Sweetheart, she would have no qualms about ripping your head off. You're not her favorite person either. Let me talk to her, and if by some miracle, she lets us stay, you must try to try to be civil with her. She's my family too, and if you both just gave each other a chance, you'd get on great!"

"Pfft! Fine, have it your way."

Mack let out an enormous sigh. "Anything else?"

Ari, noticing how exhausted he looked and was hesitant about what she was about to ask of him next. "I need to know where you are on the list."

He studied her face. "Just Numbers 17 and 21 left."

Ari pursed her lips. "You've been through the rest?"

"Yeah, sweetheart. I had to."

Ari's eyes narrowed. "Okay, you heal first and then you hurt seventeen, and I mean it, Mackie; you make him feel what it feels like to be a yellow pin."

He nodded. "And then?"

Ari took his hand, looking at him with desperate, tear-filled eyes. "Mack, Number 21 is going to come for us and keep coming unless we stop him. Put an end to all of this, so we can have our happy ever after!" She drew a deep breath and let it out slowly. "I want you to kill Number 21, so he can't do what he did to me to anyone else. He's a red, Mackie and the only one. Promise me you'll do this."

Mack pressed his lips to hers, prizing her mouth open with his tongue, kissing her.

"I promise you, sweetheart. That prick will die by my hands! I'm going to tear him from him to limb with my bare hands if it's the last thing I do."

CHAPTER TWENTY-TWO
Betrayed

"Brother!" Blaze said, embracing the Mauler as he got off his bike at the MC in Sunnyville.

The Mauler gave him a huge grin. "God, I missed you, brother."

"Tell me you have a good reason for dragging me up here," Blaze said.

"I do!" the Mauler said, handing his brother a beer from his six-pack as they sat outside in the sun on a picnic table outside the MC.

"I need your help," the Mauler said, leveling an intense look on Blaze.

"I'm all ears," Blaze said as he sat sipping his beer as the sun shone on him.

"It's about the Irish."

"Aww, not again, brother. Why can't you let sleeping dogs lie? It's been six years, he's gone. Stop this and get on with your life."

"I can't, brother! There's been some developments since I last saw you!"

Blaze leaned forward; interest piqued. "Do tell."

The Mauler described his encounter with Ari before explaining his concerns to his brother. "I don't believe for one second, she had anyone with her. She was too naïve for that. Too prim and proper to be connected to anything or anyone sinister. I think she had inside help that night. I think she had inside help from the boy!"

Blaze looked confused "Nah, Noah would never..."

"I don't know, brother, he's not like us. He has too much of his mother in him."

"Yeah, but he wouldn't betray you."

"I know he did. I can feel it in my bones. That night he tried to send that classy bitch away, stop her from speaking to me and this cock and bull story about her having back up. It doesn't fit brother. And Noah, Zander, and Jimmy won't look me in the eye since that night. I keep finding them huddled up together, whispering. He knows something, and Zander and Jimmy would die for him. I think he's still involved with that Irish piece of shit somehow. They were always close. I just know they're in cahoots."

"Well, what do you want to do about it?"

"I want you to have one of your men follow him. Just tail him for a bit. See what he's up to. Make sure I'm not paranoid. Can you do that for me, brother?" the Mauler asked.

"Of course, I can. I got some guys who Noah won't know. They're pros. I'll call them after my beer, and if anything is amiss with Noah or he's up to something, they'll find out!" Blaze promised.

***

It was a Friday night. The air was warm as the sunset left shades of red in the sky. Noah and Zander were sitting in Zander's favorite spot, looking out over the whole of the Sunnyville valley. It was his quiet spot, somewhere they could hide from the world.

"Something on your mind, Zand?" Noah asked as they sat drinking ice-cold cans of beer.

"Aye!" Zander confirmed, with a troubled look on his face.

"Talk to me, man!"

"That shit that went down with that lassie months ago. I still can't shake it, pal. What your uncle did to that innocent lass turned my stomach, and you know that I'm no' queasy."

"I know, Zand. He's a sick man."

"Tell me about it. I can get behind a lot, but not hurting innocents. It's no' on pal, and I know he's your uncle and all, but every time I look at him, I want to kill him. He's a different kind of evil brother, and I want no part in his sadistic mauling of innocents," Zander finished.

"I know, man, and I'm with you. This can't go on, but we don't have many options right now."

"Aye, we do! Noah, you know I can shoot him between his eyes from a mile off and it would be done."

"No! It's too risky, man. What if you miss?"

"What the fuck! You cheeky prick! When have I ever missed?" Zander spat in shock before continuing, "Now Mack, he fucking misses. But me? No way!"

Noah laughed. "What is it between you and him? This jealousy you've both had for one another is ridiculous. Are all Celts like that?"

Zander laughed, almost choking on his beer. "If you think we're bad, wait until you meet the Welsh. Now they are fiery fucking dragons. There's so much passion in their hearts and fire in their bellies, they fly off the handle at the slightest thing. Don't get me wrong, they love with all of their hearts. But cross them and look out, and that's just the women, brother!" Zander joked.

Noah bellowed. "Noted."

They sat there in silence for a while until Zander broached the subject of Noah's uncle again. "Noah, I love you, pal. You're my best friend. But surely you can see that we're on borrowed time with your uncle. It's only a matter of time before he discovers the truth about us helping Mack and that lassie, and when he does, we're dead."

"I know man. I hate it as much as you do, but we need to be careful. I mean, it was Mack who started all of this. Maybe he should finish it?"

"What do you mean?" Zander asked, looking at him puzzled.

"I say, we tell him what the Mauler did to his lady friend. Explain it's time to stop hiding, so we can work together and put an end to all of this." Noah shrugged.

"And what if he's not interested?"

"We'll just have to explain to him that the Mauler is coming for him, and eventually he will find him and kill him and anyone who's connected to him. We will make him see that it's in his best interests to work with us to end this!" Noah explained.

"Aye, but when push comes to shove, are you capable of watching your uncle die?" Zander asked, looking at his best friend with all seriousness.

"I have to be, Zander. He is a cruel, twisted, and sinister man. No one is safe while he is still alive. Besides, it's kill or be killed these days, man."

Zander could see how hard it was for his best friend. He could see that he was struggling. Deep down, Noah loved his uncle, but he knew what had to be done for his and the club's future.

Zander put his arm around Noah, looking at him with sincerity.

"Well, if we're going to do this, then we do it together. You, me, Jimmy, and Mack, just like the good old days. And when it's over and you're the Prez, you can lead the club into a bright and beautiful future, pal. God knows we need it after these past few years," Zander exclaimed.

Noah let a brief laugh escape. "Yeah man, we do! But between us, I don't want to lead this club anymore. It's tainted with death and destruction. My plan is to put it in the right direction and just stay at the table. I don't want to continue my family legacy, and I don't want that for you. I want us to remain free, simply enjoying the life of a biker."

"What about your dream of running your own business?"

"I'm tired, Zand. I'll set everything up. Then I want Jimmy to run things, not that I'll tell him until it's time."

"Are you sure? This was your dream."

"Yeah man, Uncle Mauler has killed this club for me. Hey, you're not mad that I don't want you to lead, are you?"

Zander laughed. "Fuck no. I never want that kind of responsibility. I'm happy riding and fucking."

Noah cheered. "That's my boy!"

"Right! Come on, this is my moping ground, not yours!" Zander said, pulling Noah from the floor. "I'm sure there are some beautiful skirts waiting for us back at the club. Let's no let Jimmy have all the fun while he waits for us."

"Okay, man, I'm right behind you. I just need to drop Mack a text," he shouted as he watched Zander head back down the overgrown path back to his bike.

Noah took out his phone and searched through the phone book until he found the name Blonde Bombshell. Having to store Mack's number under an alias and message him in code, just in case his uncle went snooping through his phone.

He hit the message icon to send Mack a message:

Hey beautiful!

It's been too long.

I miss you!

We need to hook up!

The old place. Tuesday at 9pm.

Can't wait to see you!

Noah xx

They had only messaged each other a handful of times, so Mack could inform Noah that he was safe, and Noah could update him if the Mauler ever discovered where he lived.

Noah hit send, and it was done. The wheels were in motion to take down the Mauler.

CHAPTER TWENTY-THREE
Cascade of Lies

No sooner than Mack had arrived home in Uskiville, his phone pinged with a message alert. Mack shuddered as he read the cryptic message from Noah. They always text in code just in case the Mauler saw the communication between them. Mack hadn't seen Noah or Zander for years and now he had received a message out of the blue and just as he was preparing himself to square up to the Mauler. Now Noah wanted to meet at their old meeting place in Portland. They hadn't met there since Mack first escaped from the clutches of the Mauler. "What if it was a trap?"

Mack messaged back.

Hey gorgeous!

I'm a little nervous.

It's been so long.

How do I know I can still trust you?

Blondie xx

Mack hit the send button and received a message back almost instantly.

You can always trust me, baby

Our hearts will forever tether us.

I want us to end all this suffering so we can be together.

I want to remove what's standing in the way of our happiness, but I need your help.

Are you in?

Forever yours.

Noah xx

Mack *was* nervous, but he knew he had no choice. He wanted to thank Noah for helping Ari, and he needed his help. At the very least, he needed to tell his plans to kill his uncle, and that had to be done face to face. So, he decided to message Noah back to agree.

Hey Gorgeous!

Okay, I'm in!

My life is in your hands now!

Blondie xx

Mack took a deep breath and headed toward B's office in the hope of catching up with her. It was on his to-do list from Ari. He had plenty to discuss with his dragon and he was hoping to get her permission for the move. Ari was excited at the thought of moving to Uskiville, and he didn't want to let her down. He had to make sure the move was still viable after Dragon found out he had been lying to her about his relationship with Ari. Not to mention his absence over the last few months. Mack had also neglected his management duties. He usually ran the day-to-day stuff while B was at work, but he hadn't worked a day in months. Mack had been so wrapped up in Junior, Ari, and the list, he'd forgotten about his responsibilities in Uskiville. Mack had forgotten about the woman who'd brought him back from the depths of despair. He had forgotten about his person, his dragon. Consumed by guilt, he didn't know what he would say to her. Mack still loved her very much. She was his family, and she would always be his person. But now he loved Ari, and she was his person in ways that B could never be. Mack was determined to make it work with both Ari and B, despite Ari's hatred for B and B's increasing dislike of Ari.

Upon entering B's office, it surprised him to find Frankie sat at her computer, at her desk. Mack would normally do that. It was his job. Frankie was just a bar manager; he had no place at her desk.

"What are you doing at Dragon's desk?" he asked, showing his confusion.

Frankie didn't look up from the laptop. "What's it look like? I'm sorting the books!"

Mack grimaced. "Since when do you do her books? That's my job."

"Since you haven't been here for months and left B to run everything on her own so you could shack up with little miss homewrecker," Frankie growled.

Mack glared at Frankie. "I've been getting to know my son again. I'm sorry if that's been an inconvenience to you all. I haven't seen him for years just in case you forgot."

Frankie rose from his seat to come face to face with his best friend. "And nobody is disputing that Mackie, but you can't expect B to wait for you to come home forever. You're never home and when you are, you're not really here. Your mind is somewhere else."

"I know. I'm here now, though!"

"But for how long? B can't rely on you anymore, and she asked me to help her out while you got yourself sorted. She couldn't coach and also run this place on her own. I mean, you left her high and dry and in peak season. She's been running around like a fucking idiot, Mackie, and she's exhausted. At the very least, you should have called her, but you couldn't be bothered to do that!" Frankie snapped.

"I've had a lot on my plate."

"Oh, I can see that Mackie." He gestured to the cut above Mack's eye. "For fuck's sake! Everyone told her to just get somebody new in, but she's still loyal to you despite you being a selfish prick and using her. You keep letting her down, Mackie, and I'm sick of it. You may be my boss and Prez, but she's like a sister to me and I can't stand the way you're treating her."

"Careful, Frankie, you're dabbling in waters that you know

nothing about! And don't get too comfortable in my shoes. I will be back in them soon."

Frankie laughed, shaking his head as he left the office. "Oh Mackie, you think you can lie and deceive the woman who pulled you off the streets and she'll just let you waltz back in? She has rules, my friend, and you broke them. She knows you broke them."

"I'm not done with you yet, Frankie. I hired you! You answer to me, remember?" Mack shouted after him.

"No Mackie, not any more I don't! You may have hired me, brother, but I work for our best friend. You know, the woman who'd do anything for us! She's like a fucking sister to me and it kills me seeing what you have done to her! And another thing. You're supposed to be our fucking Prez, and where have you been? Fucking some wench! Don't pretend this has been about Junior. It's about you having your cake and eating it. Like it always is, while I've been taking care of both B and club business. Some fucking Prez you turned out to be. I've lost all respect for you, brother. Now if you don't mind, I'm off to meet B for a grapple, since you don't bother anymore!"

Frankie's words fueled Mack with a mix of rage and devastation! He knew he'd been away a while, and he had been a shitty best friend. But he had responsibilities to Junior and Ari. Surely B could have understood that, despite all her flaws. But to replace him by giving his job to Frankie, the man he had hired, and now grappling with him. That was their thing to do together, nobody else's.

Mack sat at his desk sulking. B was his best friend, his dragon, and nobody was going to take her away from him. "When all this is done, when the list is complete and the Mauler's dead, I will have my family altogether, my dragon included," he muttered under his breath as he rested his head on the desk.

He couldn't say how long he had been there when he heard B arrive back from her grapple with Frankie. Rising to his feet, he rubbed his beard and headed into the kitchen.

"Hey!" He gazed at her sweat-soaked, half-naked body. He loved the way she looked after a grapple.

"Hey!" B said, turning around and pinning him in her stare as she ran her eyes up and down Mack's body, pausing at his bruised knuckles and moving on to stop at the cut above his eye.

"Can I talk to you for a minute?" he asked

"I'm listening."

Mack began softly, tentatively. "I just wanted to say that I'm sorry that I haven't been around la—"

"Don't worry about it," B interrupted. "Frankie has me covered. He's going to take on the management role for a while."

"That's unnecessary, Dragon, I'm—"

"Oh, but it is, good boy! I've been busting my ass on my own for a while now, and I get it. You needed time to get your shit together. But it's been months with no phone calls or texts. I'm not paying for a manager who hasn't done a day's work in forever and spends most of his time banging his son's mom."

The words cut through Mack like a knife. "A manager? I thought I was your person. Geez, I go to get my son back, my life back, and you erase me from your family by bringing in Frankie and call me a fecking manager?"

B looked at him with her dragon eyes burning in anger. "What do you want from me, Mack? I gave you a home. I spent years helping you look for your son and I was so happy when you found him. Bloody hell! I'm happy you found Ari to settle down with, even if she is a fucking bunny boiler. I thought, if you're happy, then I'm happy. But I had one bloody rule, and that was for you to be honest with me, and all I've had is a fucking cascade of lies!"

"Dragon, I—"

"Don't fucking 'Dragon' me, Mack. You're a lying prick! You grace us with your presence when you can be bothered. Treating us like we don't matter anymore and expect us to roll out the red carpet. Well, fuck you!"

Shaking her head in disgust, B continued. "You must think I'm fucking stupid. Every time you come home, I see new flesh wounds, cuts, bruises. I don't think you've even realized you have blood seeping through your shirt as we speak."

Mack glanced at his blood-soaked shirt. He must have split his stitches getting up out of the chair.

B shook her head. "We used to tell each other everything, but I don't know who you are anymore, and I don't know what kind of trouble you have gotten yourself into. But I know that all this started with your fuck buddy!"

She went on, unable to contain her resentment toward Ari. "You realize she is going to be the end of us, brother. There's something black about her. It's like she's turned up and brought death and destruction with her. I can feel it. Something bad is coming. It feels like the wheels have been put into motion for something beyond my control and know nothing about. Our world is broken and you either can't see it or refuse to accept it. But I am telling you now, Mackie boy, if anything happens to me or my boys, I am going to fucking end her."

"Hey, come on now!"

"No, Mackie! I told you she would be our undoing. I told you she was fucked up, and you didn't listen. Well, I hope she was worth it! Now, you know the rules and why I have them. I can't have people I don't trust in my life." She whirled about and walked away.

"Dragon, please? Let me explain—"

"Explain what? There is no need for another cascade of lies, and I don't need you to lie about leaving me out in the cold for her! I trusted you! Let you in to my life, made you my family and helped you through your anxiety attacks, your turmoil. Do you know how hard that was for me? I've done nothing but support you, and as soon as you got your perfect little family, you cast me and my boys aside like we didn't matter! You fucking used me, used them, and that makes me so fucking angry!"

In that moment, Mack realized how much he had hurt his best

friend. He had never meant to hurt anyone. On his quest to avenge Ari, he'd hurt the person he loved more than anything in the world. Despite being in love with Ari and wanting to grow old with her, the dragon was his family, and he didn't think for one moment how much this affected her too! He had to make it right.

Taking her hand, he tried to pull her in close to him. "Dragon, I'm sorry!"

B snatched back her hand and moved away from him. "Fuck you, Mack! Do you know what hurt the most?"

Mack looked at her, waiting for an answer.

"You missed Rhys's birthday last week, and after promising him you'd take him out on the bikes, too." Hurt made her voice thick. "He waited in all day for you. Called you a million times, and you left him hanging. Do you know how hard it is to console your son, who thinks his uncle doesn't love him anymore? It's fucking awful. You hurt my baby, and I will never forgive you for that!"

"Oh shit!" he muttered, but B was already walking out of the door.

Her steps faltered as she held the door open. Turning back to him, she said; "Great job fucking up your nephew." Then she left.

Mack stood there with his hand covering his mouth. He couldn't believe the damage he had caused by not being here. B was so strong; he hadn't even considered she needed him too. She was stern and gave nothing away—ever. They didn't talk about emotions or anything like that. But today he saw how hurt she was and there was no coming back from that.

Mack set out to make amends, and his first stop was to see Rhys. He knew where to find him as he walked into the garage to see Rhys adding the finishing touches to his school science project. Mack had always helped him with them, but it was yet another activity he'd let slip.

"Hey, my boy, what are you making?"

Rhys said nothing, clearly ignoring Mack.

"Look, I'm sorry that I haven't been around of late. I've just had a lot on with Ju—"

"Junior, I know!" Rhys said, finishing his sentence for him. "It's okay, Uncle Mack, be with your proper family. Don't worry about us. We're fine."

Mack could tell that Rhys was hurting. He didn't look angry or frustrated. He looked uncomfortably numb, and it broke Mack's heart to see him like that. Mack had been like another father figure to him, and before Mack was reunited with Junior, he would spend most of his time working on projects and spending time with Rhys. Rhys was like a son to him and would tell him everything, and now Mack was wracked with guilt as Rhys looked heartbroken. Mack realized that he had left so much behind when he immersed himself back into Junior's life and instead of finding a balance between home and Ari's he had abandoned his home after becoming intoxicated by Ari's love for him and being a father to Junior.

Mack had received a rude awakening, knowing just how much he had affected B and the boys. Rhys was just a boy; he didn't understand the complexities of falling in love with someone. In his eyes, his uncle and best friend had abandoned him and broke a promise to him on his birthday. It dawned on Mack that he had abandoned his old family for his new one. Casting them aside without a moment's thought to be with Ari and Junior and after everything they had done for him. It disgusted Mack as he approached Rhys, putting his arm around him.

"Come here a minute please, son," he requested, ushering him to sit on the garden wall outside.

"I owe you, your brother, and your mother an apology. I have become so consumed with Junior, Remy, and Ari that I have neglected my family here and I am truly sorry for that, my boy," he explained.

Rhys looked down at the floor. Failing to meet Mack's gaze, he responded, "Don't worry Uncle Mack. We get it. You have found your proper family now. We just got used to having you in our family that we forgot you needed them and not us."

"Hey, hey! What are you talking about? You are my proper family. You, Madoc, and your mother. I love you all so much and I would be nothing without you all." He ran his hand through his hair as he tried to explain. "Look, I've messed up! I missed your birthday, and. that was a shitty thing to do and there is no excuse for it. You are like a son to me, and I let you down. I broke a promise, and I am so sorry, my boy! I am disgusted with myself."

"Forget it, Uncle Mack. You don't have to pretend that you still care," Rhys said as he pushed his arm away to stand up. "If you cared, you wouldn't have left us! You wouldn't upset us like you have and I don't care that you missed my birthday. All I care about is what you've done to my mom. She doesn't even smile anymore. She just works all the time now, and she's always tired and angry. You did that, Uncle Mack. You forgot about her after all that she's done for you, and you don't even stop Ari when she says cruel things to her. Deep down, I know my mom just wants to rip her head off, but she doesn't because she cares too much about you!" he slammed as he headed into the cabin in a fit of rage.

"Rhys..." Mack called after him.

Rhys stopped dead in his tracks. He didn't even turn around as he took a deep breath and sighed. "No Uncle Mack, you've broken her again, and I will never forgive you for that!" he said before running inside and slamming the door behind him.

Mack stood in the silence Rhys left behind and felt destroyed by all that was happening around him. "Maybe I can't come back from this," he whispered as he looked around, and suddenly everything seemed different to him now.

Mack had been out of the loop for so long, everything was changing, and he was no longer on the inside anymore. But there was nothing he could do about that now, as he had to meet Noah and discuss the end game.

CHAPTER TWENTY-FOUR
The Plan

Noah, Zander, and Jimmy waited for Mack to arrive at their old stomping ground. They had hidden their bikes off-road, just like they did when they met up with Mack before.

"Do you think he'll show?" Jimmy asked.

"He fucking better!" slammed the intense Zander.

"He'll show!" Noah said confidently as he tussled his hair into place.

Jimmy's eyes searched the ridge. "And you're sure we weren't followed."

"I'm sure!" Noah said, smirking at his friend's nervous disposition.

"Good, because if your uncle finds out, we're dead," Jimmy said, panicking

"For fuck's sake! What's the matter with you? Grow a fucking pair, will you? We're meeting Mack and getting this done. Do you understand me, Jimmy?" the fiery Scotsman bellowed, shaking his head in disbelief?

"Okay, okay, geez!" Jimmy said.

Rustling in the nearby bushes alarmed them. They drew their guns from their waist bands in anticipation that they may be called upon, safety off, ready to fire! They saw the arm of a\ black leather jacket as they watched someone emerge.

"Shit, I told you someone followed us!" Jimmy cursed with panic and before Noah and Zander could respond, Mack emerged in the clearing. Noah, Zander, and Jimmy breathed an enormous sigh of relief and put their guns away.

"Were you gonna shoot me, you bunch of pricks?" Mack joked as he came closer, and the men embraced each other for the first time in years.

"We've bloody missed you, man," Noah said to Mack

Mack gripped him. "It's been way too long."

"So, I take it your woman found you?" Zander asked.

"Yeah, thanks to you guys, and now I owe you my life and hers! I'll never forget what you've done for me, fellas, even you, you big Scottish prick!" he teased, embracing Zander.

Zander laughed. "I guess some things haven't changed then and dinae worry, I know you're just jealous because I'm a better sniper than you!"

"Feck off!" Mack spat. Mack and Zander had always had a quirky relationship. They were always trying to get one up on each other and even come to blows on the odd occasion. But they loved each other like brothers.

"Hey, love the jacket, man," Jimmy said, admiring Mack's expensive leather jacket with his MC patch on it. Mack had embroidered it with two Gray Wolves, howling at the moon.

"It's my MC patch. A friend came up with it, and I designed it when we set up the club. I got it tattooed on my chest too."

"So, you have your own MC?" Noah asked.

"Yeah, but mine's a legit one. No assault, robbery, or murder. Just making plenty of legit money with financial backing. I'm never going back to pillaging brothers."

Jimmy looked at him, confused. "Hang on! You left with nothing but the clothes on your back and that old bike that Zander sold you."

"I did! But then a fiery fecking dragon found me and provided me with a manager's role and a place to live. Once I got comfortable, I bought a Harley and established my own MC, and now we have bikers from all over the world coming to stay in our log cabins."

Noah grinned. "Nice man!"

"Thanks! Yeah, the dragon saved my life, gave me a purpose again and now that I have Ari and my son, I have some unfinished business with your uncle."

"Whoa! Hang on a minute, so you get driven out of town and land on your feet, while we've all been putting up with shite the last six fucking years? And you didn't think to give us an out? Offer us a place at the table in your MC. Well, that's fucking gratitude for you!" Zander slammed.

"Look, it's not like that. The dragon is very particular about who comes in. I couldn't go making demands like that. Besides, I didn't even realize you would want to. You loved the crack with the Red Pitbull's."

This infuriated Zander. "Oh yeah, we love living from one robbery to the fucking next, risking our lives to feed his uncle's beer and drug addiction. We fucking love how he takes his enemies and innocents and mauls them with that dirty fucking claw of his. Yeah, don't worry about us, you selfish prick. Worry about you and your prick of a dragon."

Mack's hackles went up as he stormed toward Zander. Nobody had ever dared talk that way about his dragon aside from Ari, who he only just about let get away with it. "What the feck did you say, you Scottish prick? Speak ill of my dragon again. I fecking dare you!"

"Hey, hey, that's enough! We came here to talk about putting an end to the Mauler. Now let's get our heads together and devise a plan to end this!" Noah shouted, pushing them apart.

Mack and Zander moved away from each other, and the four men sat at the edge of the ridge, catching up on the years gone by. Noah, Jimmy, and Zander confided in Mack, explaining everything that had happened since his departure. They explained how the Mauler was desperate for revenge, and how he thought that all his Christmases had come early when Ari arrived in Sunnyville.

Mack also filled in some blanks and explained everything about Ari and Junior and his life up north. However, he left out details regarding his dragon. Mentioning her only as the dragon, and not divulging anything about who she was or how important she was to him. Mack made the dragon out to be untouchable and untraceable, explaining his dragon was a formidable force not to be reckoned with.

"So, is this dragon of yours going to help us kill the Mauler?" Noah asked.

"No! My dragon stays clean! Legit! And if you boys need a helping hand after the Mauler's reign of terror is over, it has to stay that way!"

Zander sneered. "So, let me get this straight. You have a formidable dragon who funds your business, your club, and all of your antics, and this dragon could snap you like a twig. Yet you won't ask for his help?"

"That's correct!" Mack said, as a matter of fact and not bothering to correct him on her gender. In Mack's eyes, the less they knew, the better.

"Well, fuck me sideways! What is the point of having a dragon if you cannae get it to breathe fire on your bloody enemies?"

Mack snapped back. "The dragon doesn't do black. Meaning that my dragon is white and legit. No dirty laundry goes the dragon's way, and that's how it stays. So, forget about my bloody dragon and let us decide what we're going to do."

Once again, Noah mediated between the two fiery Celts who spent most of the evening bickering. At one point, they were bickering so loud anyone might have heard them in the distance. Interrupted by rustling in the bushes, they stopped bickering and went to check it out. Nobody was there.

"Geez," a nervous Jimmy said. "What the hell was that?"

Noah shook his head. "It was probably just a bird or wild animal or something. There're loads about. Now let's sort this out!"

"Right! I'm taking that prick down. He's mine, and I know he's your uncle, Noah, but what he done to Ari was a step too far, even for him," Mack snarled

"Agreed man! It gives me plausible deniability if he sees you as the sole threat. We need to agree that we are all in this until the end. Together!" Noah said as he shot a look at the bickering Celts.

"Aye," agreed Zander.

"Agreed," said Mack and Jimmy in the unison.

"And if we do this man, you will have your dragon help us go straight, right? No more robbing or killing?" he stated.

"One hundred percent brother. I got your back. I promise the dragon will help you." Mack confirmed.

"So, we tell the Mauler that you have established contact. We explain to him, you want to meet at the MC as you're pissed about Ari. We take care of the youngsters who we know who we can't trust. Zander will be our smart shooter, we'll make an excuse for him to be away from the club as Mack arrives and don't worry, we'll make it believable, and with Zand in position, he can clip off anyone who poses a threat to you before you take the Mauler down, agreed?" Noah explained.

"Sounds good to me. I can't wait to tear him apart!" Mack seethed.

"Mack, I have to say, man, I'm uneasy about you going up against him alone. I mean, I know that you've packed some muscle on, but the Mauler is an animal. We need a Plan B, just in case," Noah suggested.

"You don't need a Plan B, brother. All you have to do is keep the rest of the pack off my back and I promise you, I will end him. I have been training for this for six years and believe me, I've been grappling with the best," he boasted.

"Well, let's hope the best is good enough, because if it's not, we will have to shoot our way out of there and move in with you and your dragon," Jimmy said.

"Trust me, my friends have been beating the shit out of me for years. Preparing me for moments like this. I'm ready, brothers. I'm going to end it! There's no need for a Plan B or anything," Mack stated.

"And if there is, I will shoot that dirty claw handed bastard right between the eyes!" Zander said.

The men worked out all the finite details before saying their goodbyes. Everything would be in place, ready for the meet to take place, but as Mack walked away, a brief period of doubt entered his mind.

"Hey brothers," he called. "Pack for life, right? No double crossing and I promise you I will welcome you into a life of prosperity and wealth."

Zander approached Mack, looking serious, gripping him by his collar with both hands and staring him right in the eyes. "Listen here, you Irish prick! We wouldn't have risked contacting you if we didn't think it was necessary. The Mauler has got to go! I would do it myself, but that prick won't have none of it," he said, pointing to Noah, who stood there smirking at him.

Zander embraced Mack tight and kissed him on the side of the head. "Look, we may bicker brother, but I got you and you better fucking have me, when all is said and done, because we're brothers to the end and I love ya! Now, go play wi' ya dragon."

Mack laughed. "I wish I could, I wish I could," he said with a smile on his face as he left to head for his bike.

"Right then, let's head back or Uncle Mauler might just decide to maul us, too." Jimmy joked.

CHAPTER TWENTY-FIVE
Betrayal

"Well, you were right, brother!" Blaze hissed down the phone to the Mauler. "My spies just caught them huddled up on the old riding ridge in Portland.

"Son of a bitch," the Mauler spat. "I bet those little fucking turncoats have been helping him all along, and after all I've done for them. Well, no more!"

"There's something else," Blaze informed him. "My little spies heard them mention Mack having a dragon, and it turns out this dragon of his is a woman with a shitload of cash and one hell of a business resume behind her. She owns a huge woodland retreat for traveling bikers and their families. Oh, and brother, she's definitely one for the claw. Tough looking cookie, but she has curves in all the right places. If I were you, I would definitely start there. And if you make sure you secure her assets first, it could be one hell of a windfall for us."

"Oh, really!" he said, allowing a devious look to flash across his face. "Well, it looks like we are going to Uskiville, brother. How soon can you get here?"

"I'll leave shortly,"

"Okay, I'll have everything ready. But brother, come alone. This one is a family affair. We are just two lonely bikers looking for a room," he teased.

Blaze laughed before getting serious again. "What are you going to do about the three stooges?"

"Oh, leave them to me, brother. I have a plan to give them their just desserts. I will fill you in when you get here," he explained, before hanging up.

The Mauler couldn't contain his excitement. He felt like he'd won the lottery. He was glad his instincts hadn't let him down, and he was correct about his nephew and his friends, and now he would finally get everything that he dreamed about. He planned to take Mack's beloved dragon, her empire, and have the pleasure of killing him and the three traitors. The Mauler was ecstatic at the thought and imagined himself doing all manner of sinister things to the dragon as he made Mack watch. He wanted him to suffer for trying to sleep with his old lady all those years ago. As he heard the motorcycles pulling into the club parking lot, he poured himself a drink to celebrate.

"Hm, that'll be my trusty traitors," he said softly as he headed outside with his drink in hand. He watched them park their bikes as he sipped on his whisky. He couldn't help but grin as they approached.

The three men looked at each other.

"What's he grinning aboot?" Zander hissed.

"Who fucking knows? He's probably mauled another pretty girl. You know he likes to get his kicks on the daily these days," Noah spat.

The Mauler called out to the three men. "Boys, boys, boys! It's a beautiful evening, isn't it?"

"If you say so, Uncle!" Noah said, tossing him a false smile.

"Well, before I tell you my good news, tell me about your day, nephew."

Noah shot a glance over at Zander, who nodded. "Well, Uncle, if you're happy now, you're going to go bat shit crazy with excitement when you find out what we've been up to today." Then he explained, ready to initiate the plan to take the Mauler down.

"You don't say... Well, don't keep me in suspense, my boy. I do like a good story, you know," he said as he put his arm around Noah to usher him inside.

Noah fed him the lie of Mack contacting him, suggesting a one-on-one brawl with the Mauler himself. They fed their story with everything that would entice the Mauler into taking the bate.

The Mauler rubbed his chin, grinning. "Well, today just keeps on getting better and better," he gushed. "But I have just one question. There were three of you and one of him, so why didn't you take him down and bring him to me?"

"Because he has a big fucking army that could wipe us oot," Zander lied.

"And a dragon, so I hear!" the Mauler teased. Watching their eyes widen from the information that Blaze had made him privy to.

"A dragon?" Noah questioned, trying to sound convincing.

"Yes," he gloated. "I got some inside knowledge of my own! The dragon is his cash cow, his driving force, and I'm going to take his precious dragon before ending his life," he said, knowing that they would warn Mack. The Mauler wanted Mack to know he was coming for him. It was all a game to him as he stared down the three men.

"So, what's the plan, Uncle? How do you want to play this?" Noah asked.

"What's his conditions?" the Mauler asked.

"Last man standing," Jimmy said.

"You sound nervous, Jimmy," said the Mauler, smelling his fear a mile off.

"N-no, boss, just a lot to process. We haven't seen Mack for years, and now he wants a fight to the death because of some woman."

The Mauler bellowed. "Well, isn't everything over a woman? I want him dead because of a woman, so let's give him what he wants! Set it up. Let the little Irish pissant come and try to take me down."

"You're sure?" Noah asked.

"Nephew, I've never been so sure of anything in my life."

"Well, okay, if, you're sure," Noah said, looking happy and thinking his uncle had taken the bait.

"Do it! Oh, and Noah, when I maul him and he's begging for his life, I want you to finish him."

Noah's jaw dropped. "I thought you'd want to do it yourself..."

"Oh, I'll ruin him, but I think it'll be more sinister if he watches his old friend finish him," the Mauler suggested.

"Whatever you say, Uncle. He's a traitor to the club, right?"

"Absolutely, my boy, and we all know that I can't abide traitors, don't we?"

CHAPTER TWENTY-SIX
Rescue

After meeting with Noah, Mack headed straight to Ari's house. It was late when he got there. Everyone was sound asleep. So, Mack headed to the kitchen to get himself a drink. He was only sitting there for a second when Junior appeared in the doorway.

"Hey son, I'm sorry, I didn't wake you, did I?"

Junior embraced his dad. "No, I couldn't sleep!"

"Something on your mind?"

"Well, Mom told us you two were... you know, um, together."

"Oh, Junior, I'm sorry, son. I wanted to be the one to tell you that," he said, as his blood pressure sky-rocketed. Ari had betrayed him!

"Dad, it's fine and I'm— I mean we're happy for you guys, it's just..."

"What, son? Please tell me. Let's not have any secrets between us, okay?"

Junior gazed at Mack, pursed his lips, and took a deep breath. "Can you just promise me that whatever happens between you and Mom, we will always be together? I don't want to lose you again," he said, embracing his dad again.

Mack held him tight. "Oh, my boy, I will never let that happen again, I promise!"

Junior pulled away. "Thanks Dad."

Mack smiled back and tussled his hair. "I love you, son."

"I love you too, Dad. Oh, yeah, Mom says we're moving up to your place in Uskiville, and I can't wait! I love aunt B, and it's so peaceful up there. You're my hero Dad, and I can't wait to be a real family, living all in one place."

Mack let out a nervous laugh. "Me too, my boy. Now off to bed. You have school in the morning."

Mack smiled at Junior as he left the room, though inside, he was raging with Ari for filling Junior's fragile head with everything, when he wanted to be the one to discuss it with him. He hadn't even sorted things with B yet.

Mack sat, thinking to himself. "Some team. She just went off and did whatever the hell she wanted. What happens if B tells me to leave? She has every right to. What will we tell Junior then? He'll be devastated to learn B and I have fallen out, might even blame himself." He stroked his beard thoughtfully. *Maybe her plan is to make B the bad bitch here.* "Not on my watch!"

Mack couldn't face going up to bed with her now; he was so furious with her, and he didn't want to fall out with her again. He knew exactly what to do to make himself feel better as he grabbed his keys off the counter and slipped out the back door.

As Mack headed to his penultimate destination, fueled with rage, he knew Ari was jealous of B and how insecure she was. But Ari was damaging his family, and he had to stop her, make her see it couldn't be about her, Junior, and Remy all the time. B and the boys were his family too, and she would have to learn that.

Mack reached the club in the early hours, engulfed with rage. Just like he had been with the last MC, he stepped foot in. He saw three bikers outside the club, and he thought the club looked quite quiet. Mack had been so clinical for most of his pin board missions, but once again he was led by rage. Seething, he approached the men who were sitting outside the bar smoking cigarettes.

"Hey, I'm looking for the Prez," he stated.

"I'm the Prez! Who the fuck are you and what are you doing outside my club?" said a tall, greasy looking viper of a man.

Mack didn't answer, punching him in the jaw and sending him hurdling to the ground. The two other men lunged at Mack, punching him as Mack attempted to land punches of his own. Mack became like a man possessed, unleashing himself onto one man while the other landed blows to his ribs. Mack hardly flinched as he sent another guy crashing to the ground and turning to strike the man who had been trying to break his ribs. Mack gripped his head and head-butted him, breaking his nose with one swift blow. The Prez was on his knees, trying to decide whether his jaw was broken, when Mack grasped at his greasy hair and flung him back down to the ground. Mack, now possessed as if someone else had taken control of him, kicked the man repeatedly in the face, ribs, and wherever he thought would inflict the most pain.

"You attacked the woman I love when all she did was come to you for information, you fecking bastard," he bellowed as he continued to kick the Prez.

He had become lost in his anger again and hadn't realized that the two men who he'd beaten had gone to raise the alarm, bringing out half a dozen bikers baying for his blood. The first one tackled Mack to the ground while two others dragged away their now unconscious Prez.

Mack didn't have a chance to compose himself as the other four men beat him. As he felt the blows to his body, he realized he was in trouble. He realized how foolish it had been to turn up to an MC in the black of night on his own and expect to walk away in one piece. Mack tried to fight back, but the four huge bikers became relentless as they rained down blows to his head, chest, and legs. Helpless, Mack knew there was no way out now, as he felt the searing pain from a boot to the face. Mack had reached the point of no return, drifting in and out of consciousness, when he heard a shotgun going off, snapping him back to consciousness as the bikers backed away from him with caution.

Wiping the blood from his eyes, Mack lifted his head to see who he was up against next, when he heard a familiar voice calling out to him.

"Up you get, Mackie boy," Frankie said as he bundled him up to his feet in one big swoop, guarded by Mack's entire MC.

"I'd say we're even now men, you hear me?" Frankie said as he stood pointing his double-barreled shot gun at them, while Mack's pack bundled him into the back seat of the truck and put his bike in the trailer on the back.

Sounds of disgruntled voices echoed in the air, and before long, Frankie had returned to his truck, speeding away, while checking his rear-view mirror to ensure that they weren't being followed.

Mack's pack dealt with his wounds, shooting Frankie a meaningful look as they eyed up his old injuries.

"Where are we going? And how did you know where to find me?" Mack asked.

Frankie glared at him. "Well, first we are taking you back to Ari's because if B sees you like this, you're fucking done, you stupid piece of shit. She's not stupid, Mackie boy. She saw the state of you when you stopped by, and she knew you were in trouble again.

"My dragon sent you?" Mack asked.

"Yeah, dick wad! She's had me tail you today and you're so fucking lucky that she did. She thought you might need saving. You forget, she knows you better than you know yourself. She knows you've been lying, and if she saw what I saw tonight, I think she'd kill you herself. Now you're lucky that you're our Prez and we're in your pack. You're lucky that we can forgive you for being nothing but a lying worthless piece of shit and hurting our family. And the reason that you're lucky is that you're going to fucking tell me everything that's going on so I can fix the family that you broke. God, you're supposed to be the Prez, not me! You're the one who should be laying down the law and keeping us in line, not the other way around."

"Frankie..." Mack tried to interrupt.

Frankie ignored him. "Mackie, you may be the Prez but the only reason I'm not slitting your throat right now is because our best fucking friend is back home worried sick about you. And while we both know she'd never admit that I can see that beneath that rock hard exterior, her heart is fucking broken. Rhys is right. You've broken her again, Mackie, and that, my friend, is unacceptable."

"You're right. I'm sorry, Frankie, I never meant to hurt anyone, especially my dragon." Mack coughed and winced in pain.

"I'm not fucking interested in your apologies, Mackie. You've gone rogue, and you'll have to face the music in church when this is done Prez. As your best friend and VP, I have watched you for months, neglecting your responsibilities and shitting on the one person in the world who would do anything for you. I've watched as she's gone into herself again, just as she did when I first arrived. Now tell me everything brother or I swear to God, I will not be held responsible for what I do if you don't, and I don't give a damn about club rules when it comes to her."

"Okay," he said as he explained everything from start to finish, including his plan to end the Mauler.

Frankie listened. His eyes glowering as he seethed in silence, fixated on the road ahead as he followed the signs for Portland.

"B cannot find out about the Mauler. We get in, you kill him, then it's done. You hear me?" Frankie commanded, as if he was delivering a briefing to his fellow marines like he had back in the day.

Mack looked confused. "What? You'll help me?"

"Geez, Mackie, You're the fucking Prez. Had you just come to me and told me, brought it to the table? We could have cleared this the right way, but you had to be the hero, didn't you? If you had just trusted me, trusted the club..." Frankie trailed off, letting out an enormous sigh of disappointment.

Mack looked at Frankie and put his swollen hand on his shoulder. "I'm so sorry Frankie and I know I need to make it right with the club I just couldn't turn you black, too. I knew what needed to be done, and I couldn't risk Dragon finding out and kicking us both out of her life. She can't lose both of us. When she kicks me out, she's going to need you and that's why I'm doing this alone."

Frankie shouted, looking like he wanted to kill Mack. "The hell you are! Listen to me, you Irish fuckwit! We had a deal that as your best friend and VP, I get to call you out on your shit. Now, listen, B needs you too, and you won't survive two minutes with your kamikaze attitude."

Mack said nothing as he stared down at his broken body. Frankie shook his head at him, white knuckling the steering wheel. "What happened to you, man? We were brothers, I respected you. Passed on my knowledge so you could become a better Prez and you did. You became so clinical, so efficient. I thought I taught you better than to be sloppy."

Mack, now feeling disappointed with himself, turned away from Frankie. "You did and I appreciate it. It's just Ari pissed me off tonight and I was just so angry, I lost the plot!"

"Yeah, and looking at you, it's not the first time."

Mack sighed. "I'm afraid not."

"Look, I may be out of line here, but what do you see in her, brother? She's led you down a path of no return. Look at the state of you. The day you hired me you told me to look after B at all costs. You made me fucking promise and now that's what I'm doing! God, B took you in, cleaned you up, made you white and this is how you repay her? By beating up club Presidents and avenging your fuck buddy.

"Tread carefully Frankie. She's not a fuck buddy. I love her!" Mack growled, wincing as he tried to sit up.

"You're full of shit, Prez! You have only ever loved one woman, and she is at home pretending she doesn't care that she's lost her best friend. This home-wrecker of yours is a flash in the pan and she's going to get you killed."

"I'm warning you Frankie. Stop bad-mouthing her. And you're wrong, I do love her, and after I kill the Mauler. I'm going to fix everything and move Ari and her boys up to Uskiville to live."

Frankie laughed. "You have got to be kidding me! Geez, she's got you fucked in the head, hasn't she? How is B supposed to feel about this? Do you just expect her to welcome you back with open arms? Because I'm telling you now, I won't let her get hurt by your drama anymore. She can and will always come before the club in my eyes. I don't care about club rules when it comes to her and there was a time, she came first in your life too."

"That's not what I want," Mack shouted in frustration. "I just want us all to become a family, and I think we can once all this is over."

Frankie looked at Mack in disbelief.

"I think you've taken one too many bumps to the head, Mackie, and let me tell you, if you bring Ari up to Uskiville, you'll lose B forever, and God knows what that'll do to both of you. I mean, you're tethered for crying out loud. The bond between you is sickening, but you don't deserve to have her in your life anymore!"

"I have to win her back, Frankie. I have to try!" Mack said, feeling desperate and emotional. He couldn't take anymore! He needed to put an end to the chaos that had ruptured the fabric of his life. He wanted normality back in his life, and that had to start with his best friend. It had to start with his dragon.

Frankie looked at his desperate best friend, letting out a tremendous sigh.

"And the club? Are you willing to make amends for your actions? The club maybe in its infancy Mackie but people look up to you. We were just starting to get off the ground with it too. Finally built a team, B came up with the cut name and design. It was almost established, and you fucked it before we had a chance to do something."

"I want it all back Frankie. Dragon and the club. I'm sorry brother, I'll make things right and earn your trust again. I just need to put an end to this shite, once and for all."

"Well, we better get to work if we're going to fix everything. Tell me what you need, Prez."

As they headed back to Ari's, they spent the rest of the journey discussing Mack's next move. Frankie suggested Mack take a few days to recover at Ari's, so B wouldn't see his current state. They were on their way there when Mack sent her a message letting her know he would be home soon. He was still angry with her, but he knew she would worry if she didn't hear from him.

Hey sweetheart,

I'm on my way back to you.

Just one more to go now, princess.

Then we're free!

Love Mack xx

Ari responded in an instant. It was as if she had been waiting for his text.

I thought I heard you come home earlier.

But you were gone by the time I came downstairs.

I've left you a surprise on the counter.

Can you bring it back to bed with you?

I don't want the boys to see it!

I really hope you like it!

Love Ari xxx

Mack smiled at the text. He was finding it difficult to remain mad at her. She was always leaving him little gifts to find, like whisky or art equipment, with notes of endearment attached to them. She was sweet like that. Ari brought out his creative side, and when he was around her, with the love and passion running wild and free throughout his body, he created some of his best work. He smiled as he replied, much to Frankie's distaste, who glared at him as he watched his phone light up.

Thank you! Whatever it is, I will love it.

I think it's high time I started spoiling you now, princess.

And when this is over, I promise you I will spend the rest of my days spoiling you.

See you soon.

Love Mack xxx

An hour later, at 3:27 a.m., they arrived at Ari's with Frankie helping him through the door and sitting at the dining table before pouring them a drink. Mack sipped his whisky, appreciating its taste as it soothed his throat. He sat there trying to collect himself when he saw the color drain from Frankie's face after putting his glass in the sink.

"What?"

Frankie stared at the countertop saying nothing!

Mack, a little confused, hauled himself up to his feet and staggered to the countertop to see whatever it was for himself. He gasped as he looked down and saw the white stick. Frankie looked at him in disbelief at first, but when he saw Mack's face, he could see it wasn't the gift he was hoping for and grabbed the bottle of whiskey from the table.

"Congratulations, Daddy!" he mumbled as he put the bottle in Mack's hands, encouraging him to drink.

Mack took a huge glug of whisky before putting it down on the counter. His fingers trembling as he tried to pick up the gift that Ari had left him, He stared at it, along with a note that read, "Congratulations, Mack! I'm as surprised as I'm sure you are, but we have been blessed with another child to call our own."

Tears trailed down his cheeks, and he dropped to his knees and sobbed. Frankie couldn't tell if he was happy, angry, or devastated. His best friend had been pushed to his limits already, and now Ari was pregnant. Frankie couldn't understand why she would choose to tell him before he matched up with the Mauler. He had enough to deal with without adding a pregnancy to the mix. Frankie dropped to his knees to comfort his best friend. He was furious with Ari and hated her for breaking his family. To him, she was a home wrecker and now she had trapped Mack, leaving him with no way out. He held his best friend while he sobbed.

"I got you, brother! Don't worry, we'll figure this out," he told him as Mack now held onto him.

Ari appeared in the kitchen doorway, gasping at the sight of the man she loved.

"What the hell have you done to him? I bet this was that psychotic dragon, wasn't it?" she said, screaming at Frankie in a fit of rage.

Frankie saw red. Fists clenched and looking demonic, he flew to within an inch of Ari's face. "How fucking dare, you! Don't you mean you? You stupid bitch!" he snapped. "As if he doesn't have enough on his plate. Are you that much of a fucking bunny boiler? You couldn't wait until after he dealt with the Mauler before telling him? What do you think this is going to do to him now?"

Ari stepped back, regarding the inconsolable Mack, still sobbing. Then she looked back at Frankie. "I thought he'd be happy."

Frankie gritted his teeth, "Yeah, he looks it, darling! Great job! Tell me something, how can you love a man and inflict so much pain on him? You've come into his life like a fucking wrecking ball, destroying his family, his friendships, and his fucking health. B got him to a good place, and he was happy, but you just had to fuck with things, didn't you?"

"I've not done anything of the sort. I didn't tell him to do this!"

"You didn't stop him, though, did you? Geez, we would have welcomed you with open arms, but all you've done is cause chaos, death, and destruction. Mackie almost died tonight avenging you, for Christ's sake and if it wasn't for B sending me to follow him, then he would be. You've turned him back into a murderous criminal for your own gains and now you've trapped him with a baby. You disgust me, you horrible, selfish wench," he roared.

"I—I..." Ari tried.

"Save it you, harlot! I won't fall for that naïve pretty girl look. You've broken two of my best friends already. You are poisonous! When will it end?"

"Get out of my house!" Ari cried. She didn't know what else to say to the green-eyed monster that Frankie had become as he glared at her with his terrifying demeanor.

"I'm not going anywhere until I know my best friend is alright!"

"Stop! Please!" Mack said with a look of exhaustion.

"Frankie, I need to talk to Ari. Head off home now. I'll be fine!" he said as he stifled the last of his tears and propped himself up against the same counter he'd dropped from.

"Are you sure, Mackie? I don't want to leave you like this. Why don't you let me take you home? We'll explain everything to the B and hope that she is forgiving when she sees what that wench has done to you."

"Screw you! He is home!" Ari snapped.

"No! His actual home where people don't ruin his life," Frankie spat.

"Hey, stop it, the two of you, please?" Mack pleaded as he looked at Frankie. "Frankie, I need to stay here. Give Dragon a big kiss from me and tell her I'm sorry for everything. Tell her I'm sorry and I promise to make everything right again. Please, Frankie, will you do that for me?"

Frankie placed a hand on Mack's shoulder. "No problem, man, I'll check in with you tomorrow," he said, eye-balling Ari, and slamming the door on the way out.

Ensuring Frankie had left, Mack turned to Ari. "How the hell did this happen?"

"I don't know. It wasn't intentional, I swear!" she explained.

"And I'm just supposed to believe you? How can I, Ari? You do what you want, manipulating every situation to get what you want. Just be honest with me!"

"Mack, I promise you, I didn't do this to trap you!"

"It doesn't matter anymore! None of it does!"

"Don't be like that, Mack, please?"

Mack could only stare at her for a few seconds. "Sweetheart, you're like a hurricane. You've swept through my life, turning it upside down and every time I try to catch my breath, something else sweeps me back again. Tell me, why is loving you so damn hard? I feel like it's killing me!"

Ari began to cry.

"Please Ari, no more fecking tears!"

Ari fought hard to keep them back, wiping her face with her sleeve. "So, we're over?"

He released a heavy sigh. "Ari, if only things were that simple. I fecking love you so much it hurts. A few years down the line and I would be the happiest man on the planet receiving this news. But here I am, sitting on your kitchen floor, covered in blood after I lost my shit tonight, because of you, Ari."

"What did I do?" she asked, looking perplexed by Mack's comments.

"Why did you tell Junior about us without telling me? Why did you tell him we were moving to Uskiville when you know I haven't sorted things with Dragon? You backed me into a corner, pressured me, and what if she doesn't want us there? Are you going to pin that shit on her, making her the enemy again because you're jealous of her? You said we would do this together, but you just went and did everything that suited you, suffocating me. Not to mention, I am going to be a father again and I might not even get to meet this one, let alone be a father to it."

"Don't say that!"

"Why not? It's true!" Mack snapped. "I have to face the most dangerous man that I have ever met, so we can live and be together. But after tonight, I'm not sure if I'm up to the task anymore. There's one person I know that could tear him apart and would do it for me in a heartbeat. Yet, I can't ask her! My dragon would go black for me just as I have done for you Ari, but after she saved me, she would disown me for putting her through all this. I need my dragon Ari and I can't have her and for the first time in a long time, I'm scared."

"Call her, Mack, please? If she can put an end to this, let her."

Running his hands through his hair. "No! I can't! I have to do this on my own, and I'm tired Ari, so fecking tired of the despair and destruction. I don't know myself anymore and as much as I love you and I'm grateful to you for giving me my son back, there's a tiny part of me that wishes I never laid eyes on you."

Ari stared at him as if he'd stabbed her through the heart with a rusty blade as Mack continued. "I was good, Ari. B made me good, and now, I'm bad and as black as they come. I want to be white again, Ari, because I'm terrified of the man that I've become for you."

Ari sat on the floor in front of him. She gripped his bruised chin and looked him dead in the eyes. He could tell that she was angry.

"Now you listen to me, asshole. Do you think I wanted this? I never even got a parking ticket before this and now look at me, destroying evidence and worrying if my dysfunctional excuse of a boyfriend still loves me. Sitting here, night after night, wondering if you're coming home. Lying to our son about you. I never asked you to avenge me or take the law into your own hands. You did that with your fucked up way of thinking. Now, you tell me, why is it so easy for me to love you? Especially when I know that a part of you loves a woman that I despise." She let go of Mack's chin and shook her head in disbelief.

Mack had never seen her looking so angry, and he was aware of how hard it was for her. It was hard on them both.

Ari and Mack sat in silence once again, neither of them speaking, not looking at each other. Ari reached up to retrieve the bottle of whisky, unscrewing the cap, and attempting to take a sip. Mack snatched the bottle from her, putting the lid back on it.

"Hey, no! Don't do that! I don't want our baby to come out addicted to scotch."

"What do you care? You're ending things with me, anyway."

"Jesus! I never said that, Ari," he explained, feeling bone-tired now. "I was just trying to make you understand how I was feeling. I still love you, sweetheart. I'm just head fucked at the minute, that's all."

"So, you're not breaking up with me?"

"Jesus! No! Sweetheart, I'm just trying my hardest to process everything."

"What about what you said to Frankie about making things right with the dragon?"

"Yes. I am going to make it right with her, and you're going to accept it. My dragon is my family, Ari, and her boys are like sons to me. If you think for one second that I'm giving them up for you, then we have a problem. My dragon and the boys haven't come out unscathed in this mess of ours, and it's not fair. I've hurt them, we've both hurt them, and they did nothing to us. Dragon has done nothing to you besides exist. Yes, she's fierce and advised me to stay away from you for a bit. But looking at the state of us now, Ari, she had a God damn point. I don't regret us one bit, but baby, you have to accept my family if you want to be with me. Please tell me you understand that.

Ari glared at him.

"For feck's sake, Ari, you want to live in a home that she owns, on her land, that she worked hard for. If you love me and want this to work, you're going to have to put a lid on your jealousy and be civil to her. Ari, she doesn't know that I still have feelings for her. It's not her fault. I was honest with you from the start with all this and let me assure you, you won't win if you make an enemy out of her, I promise you that!"

"I know," Ari said, sulking. "She just infuriates me with her perfectness. It's always her way or the highway."

"Ari, the dragon is far from perfect. She's more fecked up than the two of us put together and that's saying something. Can you please just promise me you'll try when we go up there this weekend?"

"Fine, I'll try. But for you. Not for her," she said, pouting.

"Thank you," he said, letting out a gigantic sigh of relief and putting his head back against the cabinet so he could rest his eyes.

Ari could see that he was drained.

"Come on Mack, it's been one hell of a night. Let's get you to bed."

CHAPTER TWENTY-SEVEN
Beginning of the End

Mack woke the next morning to a text from Noah explaining that they set the showdown for the following morning at 9 a.m., leaving Mack no time to recover from his injuries sustained the night before. Noah also explained that the Mauler knew about his dragon and had planned to make her his when he was done with That fueled Mack's rage; he was growing tired of all the threats and drama in his life. He replied to Noah's message, agreeing to the meet before heading into the bathroom.

Staring back at himself in the mirror, he could see that he had aged over the last few months. Everything had become too much for him, but he knew it would end tomorrow. Splashing his sore face with water, he began cleaning himself up before heading into the bedroom to get dressed. Mack grimaced as he struggled to put on his socks, only to find Ari rush to his aid.

"Here, let me," she said, placing a hand on his chest as she slid down onto her knees to put them on for him.

Mack's cheeks flushed with embarrassment. "Thank you, sweetheart!"

"You should get back in to bed."

"I'm okay. Boys at school?"

"Yes. I've taken a few days off and I can't even take advantage of you in the state you're in."

Mack gave her half a smile as he put his fingers to her chin so she could look at him. "Ari, I need you to do something for me."

The cheeky smile that she had worn as she teased him moments ago had faded as she gave him her complete attention.

"Anything?"

"Once I've left tomorrow, you need to head to Dragon's cabin. Take Junior and you don't stop until you arrive on Dragon's driveway. Remy will be fine at his dad's, but you and Junior can't be alone. I need to know that you'll be safe while I'm gone."

"And where will you be?"

He stared into her eyes, "I'll be taking down Number 21."

"Mack, you can't, not in the state you're in."

Mack pulled her in to him, kissing her temple as she held him tight. He could tell that she was terrified.

"I have to do this, sweetheart. It's the only way that we all survive this."

"At least wait until you're healed. You can't move without being in agony."

"I can't wait, Ari!"

Ari pulled away from his embrace. "Why not?"

Mack sighed, shaking his head in disbelief.

"Number 21 now knows I have a dragon, and he wants her for himself, and if I don't leave tomorrow, he will move in on Uskiville, and B doesn't deserve that."

"Then tell her, explain to her what's at stake."

"I can't and I won't, Ari! I've done enough damage. Dragon cannot find out about this. I need you to go up there tomorrow and wait until I get back. Just tell her I went fishing with Frankie to make amends with him. She'll believe that."

Ari shook her head in despair. "What if something goes wrong?"

Mack chuckled at the thought.

"My dragon will protect you. Ari, she's a force to be reckoned with. She can keep you safe. It's instinct for her. Hell, if the Mauler turned up, and it was one-on-one, Dragon would destroy him. But if he turns up with his pack or his psychotic brother, you get in her Humvee, and you get as far away as possible, and Frankie, Zander, or Noah will find you. Do you understand?"

Ari was silent, numb at the realization that Mack would be fighting for his life tomorrow, all their lives, and it rocked her to her core.

"Ari. Tell me you understand!" he shouted, snapping her out of her trance.

"I do," she murmured.

Mack saw how scared she was. He was scared, too. Facing his worst nightmare would never be easy, but he could hardly walk, let alone fight. But Mack knew what he had to do. He held Ari tight. He didn't want to let go. He was on the brink of either getting his life back together again or losing everything, including his life, and the thought terrified him. Mack had done everything he could to avenge Ari. He had fought and killed for her and now he knew he might have to die for her, and he wouldn't have it any other way.

"I love you, Ari, and no matter what happens to me tomorrow, I promise the Mauler will die."

She kissed him, forcing her tongue deep into his mouth, drawing back and gazing into his eyes, before pulling out of his embrace.

"No, Mack, you promise me he will die, and you will come home! Promise me! I can't bring our children up without you!"

Mack took her head in his hands again and nodded in agreement.

"Promise!" he whispered and kissed her on the lips.

"Now, why don't we do something special tonight? Order in, play some board games with Junior, watch a movie. Anything you like?"

"Sure."

"Come on. Let me make us a cup of tea. Tea makes everything better." he said, wincing as he stood.

Mack spent the day making all the arrangements for his meeting with the Mauler the next day. He had spoken to everyone, and everything was ready for the meet. The only person he hadn't talked to was B. She hadn't returned his calls or messages. He knew she was mad at him, but he was desperate to hear her voice, just in case he never had the chance to talk to her again. He wanted to apologize for going black and for betraying her. Also, he wanted to tell her how much he loved her, even though he was in love with Ari and wanted to be with her. He wanted to explain that he would always love her, too.

That evening, just as he had suggested, they had a family board game night, except for Remy, who was staying at his dad's for the weekend. He watched in awe of Junior and Ari as they giggled their way through the evening, and he noticed how Ari would glance at him with a nervous expression as she soldiered on, despite everything. The evening drew to a close, and they packed up everything ready for bed with. Junior, who was beaming after enjoying the luxury of having his parents to himself that evening.

Turning to Mack and Ari, he said, "This has been the best night ever, and I can't wait until we move to Uskiville, so every day can be like this."

Mack felt a lump in his throat and tried his best to stop himself from choking up as it filled him with emotion. The thought of never seeing his son again was tearing him up inside.

"Come here," he said as he took hold of his son, embracing him tight. "I love you, my boy! You're the best thing that's happened to me, and I am so proud of the young man that you've become."

Mack embraced Junior, glancing at Ari, trying to hide her tears. Unable to cope, she slipped out of the room so Junior wouldn't notice her crying.

"I love you, Dad. Oh, and when we move to Uskiville, can you teach me how to ride a motorcycle like you did with Rhys? He told me all about it, and it sounds so cool."

Mack grinned. "Sure, son. I'd like that. Now off to bed."

With Junior in bed, Mack locked up and headed upstairs to find

Ari sobbing into her pillow, trying hard to muffle the sounds of her sobs.

"Hey, hey, come here, it's alright sweetheart," he said as he took hold of her and stroked her head. "Please don't cry, my love. I hate seeing you so upset," he said as he wiped away her tears.

Ari gazed up at Mack, "You promised me you would come back yet you just said your last goodbyes to our son. You can't do this to us, Mack. It will destroy us. You must kill Number 21 tomorrow."

"I'm sorry, sweetheart. I got caught up in emotion. I will end him tomorrow, and we *will* get on with our lives. Ari, I will not break my promise to you!"

Ari nodded in agreement and, still sobbing, buried herself against his chest and was asleep within minutes. Mack gently rolled her onto her side so he could get some air and headed out onto the bedroom's balcony. He no longer winced as he moved now. A lot of the pain that he'd felt had subsided. But he still felt weak, which made him doubt himself, and doubt was dangerous to him. B had taught him to never doubt himself again when she took him in. She had built up his confidence and made him into a formidable fighter with Frankie's help, but now he didn't feel formidable. He needed a pep talk, and he needed it from B.

Mack then drew in a huge, deep breath, filling his lungs with the night's cold air. Breathing out, he retrieved his phone from his pocket and tried B one last time. The phone rang three times before cutting off. She was hanging up on him. Mack pursed his lips and tried again, getting the same response, but this time he waited for the voicemail.

"My beautiful Dragon. I'm so sorry that I've ruined everything! I'm sorry that I betrayed you, hurt you and the boys. You mean the world to me, and I know you're hurting. I'm so sorry and so scared of losing you forever. Please, please talk to me, Dragon. I'm desperate to hear your voice. I love you and the boys so much."

He ended the call and waited, praying for her to call. Five minutes went by, and the phone still hadn't rung. He stared out at the starlit skies, and it reminded him of being sitting on B's back porch drinking shots of whisky and laughing the night away with her. Those days were long gone now. His heart was hurting for her. It was like he was grieving for a lost loved one, and he hated it. He was about to head inside when his phone vibrated in his pocket. He reached in to grab it and low and behold, it was B. His heart raced as his fumbling fingers struggled to hit the answer button.

"Dragon!"

"Hey," she said in a low voice.

Mack's heart pounded nearly out of his chest. "Thank you for answering. It's such a relief to hear your voice. The thought of you not talking to me again scared me."

"I wasn't sure that I would. I'm still not! But I know something's up as Frankie is acting like a fucking idiot and you're gushing like a little sissy boy in voicemail messages."

"Dragon, I have so much to tell you, and you're going to hate me. Tomorrow, I have to do something and I'm doubting myself. Now I'm not giving you details over the phone as I want to explain in person, and I know I don't deserve to be your best friend right now. But Dragon, I need your advice, and I need you to tell me I can do this!"

The Dragon fell silent, and Mack thought for a second that she might have hung up, until an enormous sigh echoed in his ears.

"Mackie, you can do anything that you put your mind to, and you're the fiercest son of a bitch, I know. So, whatever it is, just do it! You don't need my advice or approval. You never have! Now I don't know what you've gotten yourself into and I will probably hate you for it, but if you need my help, just ask and I'll be there."

Mack took a deep breath. "Oh, Dragon, if only I could! But I started this, so I'll finish it. Besides, you—"

"Wouldn't understand?"

"Yeah."

"How did we get here, Mackie? When did we stop trusting each other? Look. Whatever it is, I know you and I know you can do what needs to be done. I just hope that it's something you can come back from, for your sake."

Mack looked up at the black sky, which resonated with him as it matched his soul. He knew it and B knew it. Mack took another deep breath in. This was so hard for him. He wished he could tell her everything, but he was so scared that he would lose her forever, so he stood there in silence.

Mack tried to steady his voice, wishing she was there to hold him like she had done so many times before. "I'm sorry, Dragon, I've ruined everything, and I don't know if I'll have the chance to make it up to you."

"Why doubt yourself?" she asked, voice still low. It was like she could hear his thoughts. B always had been able to read him like a book.

"Uh," he said, trying to remove the lump in his throat, "because I can't do this without my dragon by my side, and I won't have you near this."

Mack had done so much without her these past months, but that was small stuff compared to going up against the man of his nightmares. Number 21, the man who hurt the woman he loved, who wanted his dragon, and Mack wasn't sure if he could do what needed to be done.

"What the fuck have I told you about self- doubt?" she asked, her voice seething with frustration.

"That it could kill me."

"Exactly. So, stop being a stupid prick, get your shit together, and sort your fucking life out! Put this to bed Mackie, or I will!"

"Dragon, I'm scared!"

"Mackie, you have proved these last few months that you no longer need me to wipe your ass for you. Now man up, otherwise, this will end you. And let me tell you something, boyoh, I'm the only person who gets to do that, for all the shit that you've put me through. Now do I have to come down there to choke the self-doubt out of you, or can I go back fucking the chiseled hottie who's lying naked in my hotel room?"

Mack let out a laugh. "Fuck no! The last time I stopped you from getting laid, you choked me out cold."

"And I am going to do it again if he's asleep when I get back in there. We're only on round three and I can see he's tiring."

"Geez, Dragon, you're going to kill someone one day."

"Well, at least they'll die happy, good boy!" She chortled in her strong Welsh Valleys accent.

"God, I've fucking missed you, Dragon!"

B went quiet again for a second.

"Mackie, all joking aside, when we meet up again, you know that the conversation will be a lot different."

Mack nodded in agreement, as if he was standing right in front of her.

"Does it have to be?"

"Black and white, Mackie boy. Black and white."

"It's one slip, Dragon, I promise. I'll never hurt you again! Give me one more chance, please?"

"Good night! You Irish prick!"

Mack sighed. "Good night, Dragon, I love you!"

"Fuck off, you sissy!"

Mack bellowed. He loved her quirky sense of humor. He was about to hang up when she spoke again.

"I love you too, Mackie boy, and never forget it!" she said before hanging up.

Mack stared down at the phone in shock. His dragon had shown no genuine emotion before tonight. Dragon always turned everything into one big joke. She was an emotional cripple, yet tonight she said the three words he longed to hear. Of course, he knew it wasn't meant in the way he had previously wanted it to. It was more like a brotherly, sisterly, best friend kind of I love you. But that was huge to him. He beamed with pride. It had just taken him six years to drag one honest emotion out of her crippled mind and tonight, when he needed it more than ever, she told him what she was feeling. But most of all, those three words gave him hope he might not lose his dragon after all. Yes, things would be different, but maybe she would allow him to stay in her life. She hadn't answered his question after all.

B's pep talk gave Mack his confidence. She always knew what to say to him and at the right time. She was special like that, and now his self-doubt had all but gone. He was ready now, ready to fight, and he was ready to put an end to the man who had caused his family so much pain. Mack told himself that the Mauler would die tomorrow, and he would die by his hands.

CHAPTER TWENTY-EIGHT
Relentless Mack

Ari woke up the next morning, scared to open her eyes. It was the day she had dreaded. Not knowing whether the love of her life would meet his maker that day was just too much for her. But within seconds, her mind wandered somewhere unexpected as she felt Mack's lips sink into her right breast. She opened her eyes to be met with his, but something was different. His eyes weren't tired and dull looking anymore. They were on fire, like a burning sun. Smiling at her, he sucked on her mouth and began to seduce her, much like he had previously when he crossed a Prez off his list. Ari moaned with pleasure. She wasn't sure what had come over him as he felt his lips on her clitoris, enticing her sex with his tongue. His long and delicate strokes arousing her, sending shock waves through her body as she became wet for him.

"Oh Ari, sweetheart. You don't know how much I need you right now," he groaned as he licked his way up her body until he faced her.

Ari moaned as his pulsating erection glided to meet her entrance, her body tingling as she waited for him to enter her. Mack's eyes glazed over as he entered her, gasping as he filled her. Ari, soaked by his touch, moaned into his mouth as he made passionate love to her, ravishing her body as he lusted after her. Ari knew he had to have her, and she was happy for him to take her as he plowed her into the mattress. She had missed hearing his rugged breaths as he worked to please her, but she wanted him to conserve his energy for later, when he would need it more.

"Mack," she panted, interrupting his stride. "Let me ride you, baby, please?"

Mack slowed down and rolled her on top of him, holding onto her backside to keep himself inside her. Ari rose to ride him, placing her hands on his firm but bruised chest, and bounced on his hard cock. She watched him grin with pleasure, riding him as he filled her with quick succession and knowing he needed it hard and fast by the way he tried to take her beforehand. Mack growled. struggling to cope with the tempo yet, Ari felt him encourage the pace by holding onto her hips and assisting her, almost lifting her up and down onto himself.

"Oh Mack," she moaned, feeling him pulsate through her entire body.

Mack groaned again, now looking desperate to take her as he sat up to meet her gaze. Sliding his legs over the side of the bed, he picked her up, wrapping his legs around his waist. He walked toward the wall, pinning her up against it, entering her again and placing her arms above her head.

"Oh, God," she cried as he took her against the bedroom wall, pumping her as fast as lightning. Mack was taking her like a man possessed, and Ari had never seen him like this before, but she loved it and wanted more.

"Oh, baby, I want to make you scream," he growled as he let his raging erection pleasure her G spot.

Mack glided through her with the passion of a lion taking his lioness. Grasping her backside, he penetrated her as hard and as fast as he could, making Ari scream as she took him in, in all his glory, convulsing and exploding into yet another orgasm. Ari, trembling and dripping with sweat, was done. However, the wild and wonderful Mack was just warming up. He had never been a one and done guy, so he continued to take her until he came hard against the wall, unleashing himself inside her. Dripping with sweat himself, he carried her to the bed, laying her down and kissed her.

Ari moaned again. "Oh, thank you Mackie, that was sensational!"

Mack gazed at her with a devilish look in his eyes, eyes on fire as he beamed at her. "Oh sweetheart, I'm not done with you yet."

Turning her over, he pulled her hips toward him, teasing her soaking wet entrance with the tip of his manhood. Ari couldn't believe how hard he'd become again so soon.

"I know you like this position, baby, so let's see if I can please you again, shall we?" he teased.

His Irish accent and thick, gravelly voice drove Ari mad, making her wet again with pleasure. "Oh, Mackie, please..."

"Okay, my queen, anything to please you," he said as he filled her with his sex.

Ari clenched around him as he penetrated her. "Christ, Mackie, you're so big."

Mack panted as he thrusted inside her, slipping in and out of her, slow and hard. "Oh, sweetheart, you're like silk around my cock."

"Oh God, Mackie, it's so good."

"Oh, you like that, baby, don't you? I can feel how wet you are for me, and I love it!" he said as he lost himself inside her, delivering sharp blows to her G spot.

Ari gasped. "I don't know how much I can take."

"Sweetheart, my hard cock is about to rock you to your core. I am going to take you like never before."

Ari writhed with excitement as Mack increased his pace, delivering hard blows with his throbbing cock, and growling as he made her take it. He penetrated her so hard it hurt, but she didn't want him to stop as her sex begged for more.

Feeling him stiffen, Mack gnarled in excitement. "Oh, yes!"

As Ari begged for more, Mack, gripped her hips, digging into her skin, making her yelp. "Yes, Mackie. More, please."

"Take it, Ari! I need to give you everything I have."

"Oh, God!" she cried as she came, clamping down around every inch of him as he rode her. She had felt nothing like it. She bucked and writhed, trying to compose herself, to allow him to finish as he struggled to keep hold of her trembling body.

Taking her like it was his last time. Clamping down hard on her hips and thrusting rapidly, he growled at her. "I'm coming, I'm coming. Take it please..." he begged as she felt him release, erupting into a long and glorious climax.

Once he finished, Mack turned her over and flooded her mouth with kisses. "Oh baby, promise me I can take you like that forever?"

"God, Mack! That was incredible!" she enthused. "You can do that to me again whenever you like."

Mack giggled like a schoolgirl, looking pleased with himself.

"Why don't we do that again when I get back later?"

Ari, a little confused by his change of demeanor since last night, couldn't help but ask him, "Okay, what's going on? Last night you were bleak and miserable, resigned to meet your maker, and this morning, well, you're like an invincible God. I'm not complaining. But why the three-sixty?"

Mack kissed her nipples, making Ari moan as they hardened for him.

"I had to rid myself of self-doubt baby, and I have. And now I know everything is going to be alright."

"Yeah?"

"Yeah, baby. Today I'm going to finish that sick mother fucker and we will have our happy ever after, I promise."

Ari smiled. "Good, because the quiet countryside and white picket fence are calling out to me."

"And you shall have it, my queen."

"Queen? Have I been promoted?"

Mack's lips curled into a huge smile. "Well, you did just let me screw you into oblivion. I think you've earned it."

"Oh, Mackie, you are so romantic," she teased.

"Oh, baby, I am going to show you just how romantic I can be when I get you moved into my cabin!"

Ari couldn't get over the change in him. "Who on earth did I wake up next to this morning? Because he has to stay!" she demanded with a huge grin on her face.

She liked the playful, sexy, and confident Mack even more than the serious and sullen one that she had fallen in love with. *I wonder if he was like this before I came along.*

Mack chuckled and spent the half an hour being playful and whispering sweet nothings into her ear. Ari was so happy that she forgot what Mack had to do that morning.

A short while later, after enjoying a steamy romp in the shower, Mack's phone rang. It was Frankie. Mack finished his conversation, chucked on his clean clothes, and brushed his teeth, before returning to the bedroom.

"Show time," he said with a glint of humor in his voice and a devious sparkle in his eye.

Anxiety swamped Ari as she realized where he was going. "Don't go, Mack, please. There has to be another way."

Mack got down on his knees in front of her, smiling and putting the palm of his soft hands to her cheek. "I promise you I will be home in time for dinner. Now, wake Junior and head up to Dragon's. Tell her I'll catch up with her soon, okay?" he instructed, before kissing her soft lips and squeezed her hand as he got up to leave, only to have her squeeze his in return.

Ari followed him with her eyes. "Back before supper!"

Releasing himself from her grip. "I Promise!"

Ari sat for a moment trying to collect herself. She had just experienced a side to Mack that she didn't know existed and wanted to get to know it more. She prayed he would come back to her. Prayed that he would put an end to their suffering.

Taking a deep breath, Ari rose from her bed. "Right, Ari, put on your big girl pants and get yourself to Uskiville."

CHAPTER TWENTY-NINE
Meat Hooks

The Mauler was singing as he roamed around his club at five a.m. that morning. It was the earliest that he had ever risen from his pit. He was sober for the first time in years, wanting to relish in his successes, when he took everything away from Mack.

He woke everyone up early, much to the confusion of Noah, Zander, and Jimmy, who had informed him that Mack wouldn't arrive until 10 a.m. They were even more confused by the arrival of Blaze, who was dressed like a combat soldier ready for war.

"What the fuck is he doing here?" Zander asked Noah.

"I don't know, man, but I don't like it one bit," Noah whispered as his Uncle Blaze came to greet him.

"Noah, I hear today's the day you make your uncles proud?" he stated with a sinister look in his eyes.

"Yes, sir, it is! I'll do anything for the good of the club!" Noah said.

"I know, my boy! Listen, your uncle is waiting for you three in his office. He says something about a special mission for you all. He's beaming with pride for you, son, so let's all head in and see what he's got for you?"

"Of course!" Noah said.

The three men approached the office door and looked at Blaze for approval.

"Well, go on. You know he doesn't like to be kept waiting," Blaze said, bundling them into the room.

Upon entry, the Mauler stood at his desk cleaning his claw, ready to use on Mack. He turned to them, grinning like a Cheshire cat.

"Morning, boys! I have a special job for you today," he said.

"Anything. Say the words and it's done," Noah said.

"In good time, nephew. But first I want to you to tell me something. I want you to tell me why you helped the Irish prick get away six years ago. I want you to look me in the eye and tell me why you're helping that Irish prick and why you are trying to set me up to meet my demise."

"Uncle, I..." Noah began.

"Don't fuck with me, boy. I know the truth. It's been staring me in the face for a while now, but I have proof and I know you and the Scottish prick helped him get away years ago."

Zander glared at Noah as the Mauler grinned with delight.

"I had you followed to the ridge when you met with the Irish. They've been watching and listening for a while. But I want to know why. Why would you betray your own flesh and blood?" he demanded.

Noah took a deep breath and stared his uncle down.

"You have to ask? You're a bully, a sadistic fuck, who gets off on torturing innocent people. It sickens me, watching you run this club into the ground. Grandad would turn in his grave seeing you right now, you sick piece of shit!"

The Mauler sneered. "Oh, don't sugar-coat it, boy, and as for your grandfather, where do you think I got this claw from? I found it in his stuff a few years ago." He dragged one finger along its length in a loving gesture. "It called out to me. It needed to be used. I have done your grandfather proud, boy. It's you who's the disappointment here."

Noah threw him a look of surprise as he tussled his hair in shock.

The Mauler continued, winking at the two youngsters in the room's corner to signaling to them to grab Noah. Pinning his head down on the table. "But don't worry, I'll soon put you right."

Zander and Jimmy attempted to spring to his defense, only to be met with the barrel of Blaze's shotgun.

"If you lay a hair on his head, I'll kill you, you sick prick," Zander said to the Mauler.

"Now, now, Zander, we both know that you're better at long-range shots and even you're not quick enough to beat the barrel of a shotgun. But don't worry, you're next," he promised, before looking at Jimmy. "And Jimmy, sweet and loyal to the end Jimmy. You should put your loyalties in the right place. You could have been an outstanding leader one day, but now we'll never know."

Turning to the youngster, the Mauler crowed. "Take his shirt off."

Noah tried to fend them off with no success.

"Hold still, boy!" he commanded as he gripped his curls, pushing his head down onto the table.

With two youngsters now holding him still, the Mauler grinned as he tore through the skin on Noah's back with his claw. Not once, not twice, but three times, listening to Noah wail.

Zander, now raging, that his best friend had been mauled, attempted to disarm Blaze, only to be smacked in the face with the butt of Blaze's gun, busting his nose wide open.

"Bring the Scottish dickhead to me. I'm looking forward to this one," the Mauler said as he kicked a whimpering Noah to the floor.

Blaze pushed his gun into Zander's back, urging him to move into Noah's place for his mauling. Zander looked down at Noah's mauled back. He wanted to take Blaze and the Mauler out, and he could, but he couldn't risk the three youngsters putting a bullet in his friends; he had to bide his time, to pick his moment.

Zander then dropped to his knees and put his hands in the air as he allowed the youngsters to remove his shirt. The Mauler pushed him down on the table. "Now, let's see if the rumors are true. Is it true you don't feel pain, boy? Or are you every bit as fucked as me?"

The Mauler took his claw and penetrated Zander's skin, digging in deep as he ripped through his muscular lats. Zander gritted his teeth; he didn't cry out like Noah had. He didn't want to give the Mauler the satisfaction, instead taking deep breaths, trying not to think of the pain that seared through him.

The ringing of Noah's phone stopped the Mauler from administering his second stroke.

Blaze insisted one youngster retrieve the phone from Noah's pocket. *Blonde Bombshell* popped up on the screen.

"Well, well, I wonder if this could be our favorite Irish." The Mauler regarded Noah with one eyebrow raised.

Noah didn't respond, just looked away, telling the Mauler everything he needed to know.

"Answer it and if you try to warn him, Jimmy here will take one in the back of the head," the Mauler said.

Noah nodded in agreement and answered the call, placing it on speaker phone.

"Hey man," he said trying to act as normal as he could with his back slashed open.

"Hey, we're about forty-minutes out. We left early to make sure everything was ready," Mack said.

Noah glanced at the Mauler then looked at Jimmy, shaking his head.

"All good on this end, ready and waiting. Are you ready for this?"

"I was born ready, brother! I'm taking my life back from that sick cunt, and he'll rue the day he ever laid a hand on my family."

"I hope so, man," Noah said, grinning at his uncle.

"Right, well, I'll see you soon, then. Not long until we're all free now, brother."

"I can't wait, man. See you soon," he said then hung up.

"Shit!" Blaze cursed. "Let's get out of here, brother. We can't risk them catching us on the road if we are going to take his dragon."

The Mauler looked at Noah, rubbing his chin.

"Okay, hang the treacherous traitors up. Let the Irish prick find them. Let them see his face when they tell him we have gone to take his dragon and everything else that he loves. The youngsters can hold him for a while so we can get up there." Looking at the youngsters, he warned them. "But don't lay a finger on the Irish. He's mine."

"If your intel is right, brother, it's dead there in off season. We'll stroll right into the dragon's den and take her, and by the time the Irish prick gets home, I will have ruined his precious dragon more than I ruined his woman. After all, it's her he really loves, according to your little spies."

Noah looked at his uncle, confused, and the Mauler laughed as he realized he knew something that his nephew didn't.

"Oh, you didn't know the dragon was a woman. Oh, yeah! Your Irish friend has been living the sweet life. The boys at his bar informed my little spies all about how he's in love with her. Fine ass bitch too, looking at the pictures I have of her. A little feisty, and rumor has it she can make grown men cry." His smile was pure evil. "Oh yeah, I'm looking forward to breaking that bitch in."

Noah looked at Jimmy and Zander, who looked at him in astonishment. Mack said his dragon was invincible, not some hard face woman that could handle herself, and now the Mauler and Blaze were going to have their way with her two.

As the brothers readied themselves for their trip to Uskiville, Noah, Jimmy and Zander were bound and hung up by their wrists on the Mauler's meat hooks that hung from the ceiling. It took the youngsters and Blaze to heave the pulley that Zander hung from, with Zander laughing and taunting them as they did so. Noah and Jimmy, being a lot smaller and lighter, were then winched up on theirs.

The Mauler and blaze were heading out, when the Mauler turned on his heels, "Oh and boys, I look forward to reacquainting you all with the claw when you reach the dragon's den later. If you can make the trip to your current state nephew. But don't worry if you can't, we'll be reunited soon enough."

The Mauler departed, leaving the three men hanging from the rafters. They listened for the bikes' engines to roar off into the distance before they began thrashing around, attempting to free themselves from their shackles. Noah was struggling the most after sustaining the worst of it from his psychopathic uncle. Zander was flawless, clinical even, as he raised his legs and placing them over the beam parallel to him. From there, he could work on freeing his hands, putting his ex-military skills to good use. You would never have thought the Mauler had mauled him, as the tough Scot didn't display any signs of trauma other than the blood that dripped down his back.

After freeing himself, Zander slipped down to the floor like a silent assassin, then he released his brothers with the same elegance. He told Jimmy to cauterize Noah's wounds while he took care of the youngsters.

Noah searched around for his phone to call Mack, but the Mauler must have taken it. He would have to wait for Mack to arrive to warn him, as he was the only one that Mack trusted with his number. Jimmy cauterized Noah's wounds as best he could with a heated poker from by the fire, its embers still hot from the early hours.

Gunshots sounded from the bar, and Noah and Jimmy rushed out of the back. Sneaking into the bar with his gun in hand, Noah witnessed Zander choking one of the traitorous youngsters to death and as he glanced around, he saw the others lying dead, murdered by the Scot's hands. The Scot was scary when he was baying for blood, and these youngsters had betrayed him. Though Noah supposed they weren't exactly youngsters anymore either, with the youngest of Zander's victims being in his early thirties. It was just a reference that the Mauler used for fresh meat. When Zander finished with his last prey, they headed back to the office so Jimmy could at least seal his wounds too before Mack arrived.

Mack, Frankie, and his four men arrived a short while later and made their way into the club after seeing that all the bikes were gone besides Noah's, Zander's, and Jimmy's, which had been trashed by the youngsters. Upon entering the bar, they saw the carnage that Zander had left behind, fearing the worst as the smell of burned flesh engulfed them. They strategically made their way toward the Mauler's office, with Frankie leading the charge as if it was a mission that had come from the marine corps, and Mack having flashbacks of his time spent here all those years ago. Mack signaled to Frankie to cover him as he entered the office, only to lower his weapon at the site of Zander being burned with a hot poker, and not even flinching in pain.

"What the feck happened here?" Mack asked as Frankie and the rest of the Gray Wolves looked on, a little disturbed by Zander's apparent lack of pain receptors.

Noah rushed toward his brother, wincing in pain. "Mack, we gotta leave now. The Mauler's been watching us the whole time. He left half an hour ago, and he's going to kill your dragon."

Mack's face filled with dread, losing all its color, as Frankie put a hand on his shoulder, "Don't worry brother, he'll not find her. She flew out to the UK this morning. I didn't tell you because she asked me not to. I think she knew you had enough on your plate.

"Oh, God! Ari and Junior are heading there." he cried as he pulled out his phone and hitting the call button.

"Come on, pick up," he demanded.

The voicemail kicked in. "Hi this is Ari, please leave a message..."

Mack waited for the beep. "Ari, if you get this, don't go to B's. It's a setup, baby. The Mauler is heading there. Get the hell out of there. I'm on my way!" he said in a panic and ran out onto his bike.

"Shit!" Noah said, as they all chased after him.

Zander, Jimmy, and Noah dived on the back of the Gray Wolves' bikes, and they all sped up the highway to save Ari and Junior. It would be a race against time.

Mack sped up the highway, trying to intercept the Mauler and Blaze before they got to Ari and Junior. Many terrible thoughts tried to etch themselves into Mack's mind, but he fought to keep them out. He had to be clever, clinical this time, and there was no room for error if he wanted to save his family.

CHAPTER THIRTY
Double Take

Ari and Junior arrived in Uskiville, excited to be there. They parked at reception to let B know they had arrived, only to discover a sign on the door saying, "Closed for two weeks."

Ari wasn't surprised. Mack told her the retreat closed for two weeks in off-season. It was their time to relax after a busy year. Not to worry, she thought as she headed over to B's cabin.

B's Humvee was in the drive, but there was nobody home. So, Ari and Junior headed to the bar to see if she was there. Mack warned her it would be quiet, but it was eerily like a ghost town. As they headed toward the bar, they were relieved to see two motorbikes parked outside.

"Thank the lord," Ari said. "I was beginning to think we were the only ones here."

Upon arrival Ari pushed the big bar doors open with Junior in toe, acknowledging the bartender, who she had seen many times before, standing behind the bar.

Greeting him with a smile. "Hello again."

Only the bar manager didn't greet her with his usual warm welcome. He just looked at her, alarm on his face and paralyzed with fear.

"Are you alright?" Ari asked, looking at him and feeling a little concerned.

The bartender's eyes darted across the room and Ari followed his eyes, gasping at the monstrous figure standing before them. It was Number 21, the Mauler, the man who haunted her family.

As he stood in front of her wearing the same sadistic smile, he wore the night he tortured her. "Well, hello again, darlin'. How lovely to see you."

Ari, in a state of terror, gasped, bundling Junior behind the bar, pushing the bartender aside to escape.

The Mauler let out a laugh, "Oh, you can run..." he bellowed and as Ari got behind the bar, his face appeared in front of them again. "But you can't hide!"

Ari backed into a space behind the bar, confused how he got around so fast to meet her. She let her eyes dart around the room for another exit, only to be met by him again, and that's when she realized there were two of them. Twice the trouble, twice the evil.

"There's two of you?" she cried, before bellowing with everything she could muster as she gripped Junior's arm.

"Stay the fuck away from us!"

"Now there's no need for hostilities," the Mauler teased.

"I just want to introduce you to my twin brother." he said, turning to his twin. "Blaze, this is the only woman to escape my clutches alive.

Blaze subjected her to a minacious glare. "Pleasure to meet you."

Ari froze in fear. She knew the trouble they were in as the Mauler stepped toward her. "See, I came up here to find myself a dragon, but you two will do just nicely until I find her." A malevolent smile slithered over his face.

"Leave my mother alone!" Junior demanded. "My dad will be here soon, and he will kill you if you lay one finger on us."

The Mauler glared at him. "Oh, I'm counting on your daddy coming, Junior, but I will be the one doing the killing, son. See, your daddy betrayed me back when you were a boy and now, he needs to pay the price." He approached the bar, urging the terrified bartender to pour him another drink.

Ari and Junior were trapped behind the bar and Ari wondered what happened for the fight to reach Uskiville instead of Sunnyville. Knowing she had to bide some time for her and Junior, she engaged the Mauler.

"Where's Mack? I thought the meet was taking place at your club."

The Mauler glared at her as he sat sipping his drink, resting his gun on the bar in front of him. "It was, but Mack broke the rules and didn't play fair. He turned my family against me so, I thought I'd come up here and mess with his."

"The dragon will rip you apart if she finds you on her property. She isn't a fan of psychopaths," Ari snapped.

"Well now, it appears she's not here right now, but I am looking forward to meeting her." He shrugged. "I'm going to leave my mark on her as I did with you, only I'll go all the way with her, seen as she is far more beautiful than you." he teased.

"That's a matter of opinion," Ari spat. Even in the height of immense danger, she still allowed her blood to boil at the mention of B.

The Mauler's eyebrows shot upward. "Oh, do I detect a hint of jealousy? But now, why wouldn't you be? From what I hear, he's in love with her, always has been, and can you blame him? This dragon of his has it all. She has the looks, money, power, and control. What do you offer? Nothing but a train wreck of a body and a huge jealous streak," he spat.

The words rang altogether too true with Ari, making her feel insignificant. "Screw you!"

"Touched a nerve, have I? Look, I'll tell you what I'm going to do. I'm going to offer you a deal. If you take me to the dragon, I will let you and your son walk away." He looked to his brother to reinforce his lies.

Blaze chipped in with a glint of humor in his eyes. "Yeah! All we need is the dragon. We aren't interested in damaged goods. Fresh meat is what we're after, and look at it this way, your love rival will be out of your way forever."

Ari didn't want to give up the dragon, but she knew she and Junior had a better chance of survival if they were out in the open. They could grab someone's attention or try to escape, or at least bide some more time, hoping Mack would arrive soon.

She glared at the two men, but inside she was terrified. Two sadistic psychopaths from the same gene pool were too much for Ari. Trying to maintain her composure, she stood tall, displaying all five feet and two inches of her.

"Okay, deal," she said, knowing Madoc and Remy would be at their dad's and remembering what Mack told her about his fierce dragon. Ari hoped B could save them if things went sideways.

"Mom, no! You can't!" Junior cried

"Junior, Aunt B can look after herself. You're my priority, and she will destroy these two, anyway."

The Mauler beamed, getting up from his bar stool. "Good choice! We'll let the boy go as soon as we reach the dragon's cabin. I know it's around here somewhere, so you just lead the way."

Taking a firm grasp on Junior's shoulder and pointing his gun at Ari, the Mauler led them outside. He stood next to his bike as they waited for Blaze to follow them out.

Gunshots cascaded through the air, making Ari and Junior cower with fear. She hoped that it was Blaze who had met his demise, only to be disappointed as he emerged from the bar.

Running his fingers through his hair, he laughed maniacally. "Had to tip the bartender," he said.

The Mauler chuckled with him as they headed up the path with Ari taking them the long way around to B's cabin, praying she wasn't there. Mack said she could handle herself, but Ari thought that the two psychopaths would be too much for even the mighty Dragon to handle. Ari could tell how desperate they were for her. They wanted her and wouldn't stop until they had her.

The ostentatious cabin still showed no signs of life as they approached the front door. "We're here. Now a deal is a deal. Let Junior go!" Ari demanded.

"The boy can leave when we have the dragon and not before. Now be a good girl and knock on the door," the Mauler said, waving his gun at her.

Ari headed up the steps to B's cabin and knocked on the door. She prayed B would answer, to save Junior, if nothing else. She knew they wouldn't let him go, and she just hoped Mack or B would appear soon.

After knocking several times, there was no answer. Where could she be? Her Humvee was there, and if she wasn't home, surely, she would have driven it to her destination.

"Well, isn't that convenient?" Blaze said, "You knew she wasn't home, didn't you, you sly bitch," he said, grabbing her by her wrist.

"No, no. I didn't," she insisted. "B goes nowhere without her Humvee; she must be around here somewhere."

"Well, I suggest you call her and find out where she is," the Mauler sneered as he threw a cell phone at her.

"I can't. I don't have her number."

The Mauler became inpatient as he spat through gritted teeth. "If you're lying, then I'll put a bullet in the boy's head."

Ari's stomach churned in fear. She could see Junior trembling. He was terrified. "I'm not, I promise! She can't be far. Look! There's a key under the mat. We can wait for her."

The Mauler looked at his brother, who shrugged his shoulders before going to retrieve the key. He opened the door, and the Mauler bundled Ari and Junior inside.

"So, this is how the other half lives," the Mauler said as he threw Junior onto the huge plush sofa. He swept his gaze around the room, admiring his surroundings.

"I guess so," Blaze returned. "Get us a drink, wench!" he ordered, looking at Ari.

Ari went to the kitchen cupboard and retrieved two glasses,

pouring whisky in both, as Blaze watched. She was inches from the knife block but had to resist the urge to pick one up as she couldn't risk Junior's safety. So instead, she picked up the glasses and carried them across the room and placing them on the coffee table.

The Mauler took the glasses, handing one to his brother. "To revenge and slaying a dragon, brother," he said as he clinked his glass against his brother's.

Ari couldn't help but scoff.

"Something funny?" the Mauler asked.

"It's premature, isn't it? You haven't achieved your aim yet?"

The Maulers' eyes turned cold, sinister looking, and he stared at Ari as if she'd just burst his balloon. Placing his glass on the table, he rose to his feet. "I've had just about enough of your lip, woman. Maybe it's time I finished what I started a few months ago."

Ari was terrified, wishing that she'd kept her mouth shut and not poked the bear.

"Blaze, watch the boy and call me if his daddy arrives. Damaged goods and I have unfinished business," he said.

Ari froze with fear as Junior leaped in front of her. "Get away from her you—"

"Hush boy!" the Mauler interrupted as he backhanded him, sending him to the floor with a thud.

Ari screamed as Junior lay there, barely conscious.

"Watch him," the Mauler growled to his brother as he picked up a terrified Ari and threw her over his shoulder.

Ari tried desperately to free herself from his grasp, screaming as the Mauler headed toward the bedroom. He was going to finish what he had started back in Sunnyville.

The sound of motorcycles roared through the cabin, rattling the walls. Blaze peered out the window to discover Mack and five other bikers, including Noah, Zander, and Jimmy, pulled up outside.

"There here!" Blaze shouted

"I can see that!" the Mauler growled. "Get the boy. It's show time!"

CHAPTER THIRTY-ONE
Daddy's Home

Mack got off his bike and roared, "Mauler, outside now! We end this today."

The Mauler who had now placed Ari in front of him like a human shield emerged from B's cabin with a gun to her head. "Well, well, look who decided to show up. Took your time! Your harpy and I have been reacquainting like old times."

Mack, with a gun pointed at the Mauler's head, armed with his new Gray Wolves Pack, stood composed as his face grew into his usual possessed and stark stare.

"Mackie!" Ari cried, relieved to see him.

"It's okay, sweetheart. That prick is going to die today," Mack said, before turning his attention back to the Mauler. "Now where's my son, you sick son of a bitch?"

"Oh, he's taking a nap. But don't worry, Uncle Blaze is looking after him."

Mack's eyes grew wide, his jaw clenched, pushing the veins out of the side of his head. "If you've harmed one hair on my boy's head. I swear to God..."

"You'll what?" the Mauler snarled. "I have the upper hand here, pissant! It's good to see that you've put some meat on that scrawny ass body of yours. But that won't be enough to match me and my claw, boy!"

"Well, why don't you let Ari and Junior go and we'll find out, shall we?" Mack challenged.

"As tempting as that is, I'm not fucking stupid. Your new MC versus two of us? No, I'll tell you what you're going to do. You are going to fetch me your dragon so I can tame her and keep her as my own," he demanded. "You bring her to me, and I will let these two go."

Mack's blood boiled, as a demonic and possessed feeling settled over him, the same feeling he had every time he had his prey in his sights. "You're never getting my dragon, Mauler!"

"Listen, boy, we can do this the easy way or the hard way. But either way, I'm taking the dragon, and you're going to die."

"Okay, let's make a deal. You let them go, and you get me. One on one, right here, right fucking now. The boys will wait at the end of the road. Whoever emerges alive at the end of the road takes the dragon," Mack offered.

"And what is stopping them from blowing me away when I emerge triumphant?"

"My word! I'm the Prez of the Gray Wolves. They are bound by code. If you emerge triumphant, Frankie will deliver the dragon to you. He is bound by my command." Mack glanced at Frankie for a nod of agreement.

The Mauler stood thinking it over, but Mack became impatient.

"What's the matter? Scared you're going to lose? I don't fancy your odds either, mind. How long have you waited to make me bleed? Are you really going to pass this opportunity by?"

Unable to resist the offer, the Mauler shouted to his brother. "Blaze, wake the boy. We're doing this!"

Back inside, Blaze began jostling Junior awake and slapping his face until Junior came to.

"Come on, boy! Daddy's home," he said as he dragged Junior to his feet and onto the front porch.

Junior saw his dad and attempted to flee. "Dad," he cried, trying to break free from Blaze's firm hand.

"It's okay, son. This will be over soon," Mack said.

Blaze set both Ari and Junior down in front of him, holding a shotgun to Junior's head.

Mack glared at the Mauler. "Let them go before we do this. Your war is with me, old man."

"They can stay where they are and watch you die. Besides, I might need them to ensure my freedom once I'm done with you," the Mauler teased.

"Then my pack don't leave this driveway." Mack glanced at Zander, thinking that he might need his sniper skills.

Zander nodded, understanding what Mack was asking of him. Zander would have to execute it at the right moment to ensure Junior and Ari's safety.

"Are we doing this or what?" Mack shouted.

The Mauler gave his gun to Blaze, lifting his shirt to show that he was now unarmed.

"And your boot," Noah snapped, knowing that his uncle concealed his extra weapon there.

The Mauler sneered at Noah in disgust before retrieving the weapon and tossing it away. Mack carried out the same execution and the pair squared up on B's drive, with his Wolves circling them like a pack of wolves circling their prey. Zander didn't move, though, nor did he have his eye on the fight. He leaned against B's Humvee with a clear view of Blaze. The moment Blaze flinched; he would take his shot.

Mack and the Mauler danced around, bobbing, and weaving to avoid being struck. Mack landed the first punch, catching the Mauler across the jaw, sending him stumbling back. The Wolves cheered him on as the Mauler spat out the blood that had collected in his mouth.

"You've grown strong, pissant, but now it's high time I end you!" the Mauler crowed.

"I'm not a scared little boy anymore, old man," Mack growled as he flung himself at the Mauler, sending them both crashing to the ground.

As they grappled along the hard concrete, the Mauler who was much bigger than Mack, appeared to have the advantage as he climbed on Mack, raining down blows on Mack's face, splitting his head open along his hair line.

"Dad!" Junior cried in fear as he watched the Mauler get the better of Mack.

"Get out of there, Mackie," Frankie bellowed, encouraging his best friend to free himself from the Mauler's mighty wrath.

The Mauler's grin burned into Mack's retinas as the older man barbarically beat him around the head and Mack continued to move, trying to find an opening to sweep the Mauler and gain the higher ground. He knew he couldn't stay underneath, and when the Mauler got complacent by raising both of his arms to beat down on Mack, Mack swept the Mauler over and landed on top of him. Just as he did when he grappled with Frankie and B.

Mack was strong in this position now, as he unleashed himself on the Mauler with fierce blows of his own. The Mauler gasped in shock at the unexpected turn of events.

Blood flung and splattered everywhere as Mack spread the Mauler's nose across his face. The Mauler's eyes filled with fear as he realized he was in trouble, looking at his brother for help. Blaze gasped when his brother looked up at him helplessly as Mack became lost in his rage. He raised his shotgun as Ari and Junior cheered Mack on, unknowing of Blaze's intentions, then took aim at Mack's head.

BANG!

Blaze dropped his shotgun, clutching his shoulder, where Zander had shot him. It was the cleanest shot he could manage with Ari and Junior close by.

Ari and Junior panicked and ran free, straight to the Wolves circling the fight with Jimmy, wrapping his arms around them to comfort them.

Zander headed up onto the porch in search for Blaze but found only blood smears. In the mere seconds it had taken Zander to cross the driveway and run up the steps to the front porch, Blaze had slipped away somehow. Zander followed the trails of blood, hoping they would lead him to Blaze, so he could finish the job. He called out to Noah to help him look, as Mack continued to dominate over the Mauler.

Mack had been mostly oblivious to the sound of the gun; he was already lost in his destruction of the Mauler.

Muffled, choking sounds echoed in the open air surrounding them as the Mauler gasped for breath. His arms dropped as his eyes bulged out of his head, pupils fixed and dilated until he didn't make a sound anymore. Mack looked down at him and became still as the realization hit him. The Mauler was dead!

Mack stood up over the Mauler's dead corpse, wiping his bloody nose with the back of his hand as relief washed over him. The Mauler's reign of terror was over, and Mack and his family were finally free. Turning to face his family, he could see Ari and Junior sobbing, so he opened his arms to welcome their embrace. Junior was first to reach his dad, crying in relief, and Ari soon followed. Mack held them, wrapping his arms around them, and squeezing them tight. He had never felt so frightened in his life as he did tonight.

"It's over!" he told them as they sobbed.

Zander and Noah returned a short while after, having found no trace of Blaze. His bike was still outside the bar, so they trashed it to limit his chances of escape, and Frankie took the rest of the pack to hunt him down. They knew the area better than anyone as Mack took his family inside and Noah, Zander, and Jimmy took care of the Mauler's body. They returned a short while later to a cleaned-up Mack with no signs of a struggle outside, either. Mack had already gotten Ari to clean him up, and he'd showered, while Junior had power washed B's porch and drive. Mack sent Ari and Junior into his cabin so he could debrief the men following their mission.

After he ushered them into the living room, Mack guided them toward the coffee table. Sitting on the table before them was a bottle of Welsh whisky with four glasses and Mack poured himself a glass before handing one to each of them.

"Thank you, brothers. I will never forget the day you saved me and my family," he said as he raised a glass to them and knocked back his shot.

The others downed theirs in one too, with Zander picking up the bottle. "Oh my God, I knew the Welsh made Welsh cakes, but I didn't know they made whisky. If I did, I would've been drinking it years ago. It's fucking beautiful. How did you get your hands on this?"

"It's from the dragon's hometown. She has a case imported every month," Mack explained.

"Well, I'm fucking stealing this one, then." Zander sat down on the sofa studying the bottle, before turning to Mack. "So, your dragon is Welsh, then?"

"Well, yes. Isn't that where dragons are from? I mean, they have a big fecking dragon on their flag, after all."

"Hm, have you fucked her yet?"

"No! I'm with Ari."

"So, you're with Ari, but you love the dragon?" Zander said, looking a little confused.

Mack let out an enormous sigh. "It's complicated."

"Well, explain it to us, then. If we're going to join forces, we need to know what's happening. No lies, just the truth, Mack," Noah said.

Mack glanced at the front door to make sure they were alone and retrieving a picture of her from the fireplace, tossing it to Zander.

"I fell in love with Dragon the moment I laid eyes on her. She's fiery and scary and makes me want to explode whenever she looks at me. I've been in love with her forever, but she's not interested in me like that. She's not interested in anyone like that."

"And?" Noah asked.

Mack huffed. "So now I'm in love with Ari. Not like I am with my dragon is all. Geez, when she takes a man to bed, she brings him to his knees. Dragon has her way with her prey and once she's done, she leaves, because she's incapable of getting close to anyone. She's cut herself off from emotions and feelings. The only love she ever shows is for her little Scottish boys. She worships those kids of hers!"

An enormous grin flashed across Zander's face. "Whoa, she likes the Scots, then. Sounds like a girl after my own heart."

Mack laughed and said, "Well, she's just as fucking crazy as you and if she ever finds out what happened here today, I'm finished and so will you all be. We need to keep what happened here to ourselves."

"Well, you don't have to worry about us, man," Noah stated. "This shit's going to the grave with us."

"Good, and I'll keep things quiet at this end," Mack said.

"Okay, so what happens now?" Jimmy chirped in.

"I promised you I'd help you start fresh, and I will. So, try these on," he said, handing them each a new cut, with a moon and two howling Gray Wolves on the patch.

Mack smiled as he watched the men try them on. He took the bottle of whisky from Zander and poured another round. "Welcome to the Gray Wolves, gentlemen."

"So, we'll run the southern pack and you run the northern pack, agreed?" Noah said, as he admired his new jacket.

"Yeah, and I'll arrange a meeting with my dragon once I smooth things over with her. I'm going to need some time, though, fellas, as the dragon and Ari don't get on."

"Jesus Christ, is there anything uncomplicated about your life?" Jimmy asked.

"I guess not." Mack joked.

"Well, if you ever want to send the dragon south, I'll happily oblige, she's beautiful," Zander joked as he gawked at her picture.

"Fuck off," Mack said.

"How no? You'll be helping me with my bucket list."

"If you ever go near my dragon, I will tear you apart, you Scottish prick," Mack said, with a tone of seriousness in his rasp.

"Fuck you then, ya greedy Irish piece of shit. I'll have myself a dragon one day, wait and see!" Zander snarled.

The men continued drinking and catching up into the evening, locking up B's cabin and heading to Mack's, where Ari and Junior waited for them. They loved to hear them reminisce about the good old days, and Mack and his pack could relive them through a new alliance. Mack even gave his new Wolves twenty-five grand that he had saved up to get them up and running again, to make their club their own. He didn't care about giving his savings away, he had everything he wanted there in Uskiville and this was the start of a new future as the Founder and head President of the Gray Wolves MC.

The southern chapter stayed the night before heading home, where they would continue the search for Blaze. Two weeks later, there was no sign of him. Noah and his crew had even gone to his club, but it was deserted. Shut down. He'd been and gone, but the question was where?

The MC was desperate to tie up the loose ends connected to the Mauler as Frankie searched with his pack of Wolves. But Blaze was nowhere to be found. Mack warned his brothers to remain vigilant and keep a watchful eye on the dragon, as he knew Blaze would keep her in his sights.

CHAPTER THIRTY-TWO
The Beginning of the End

Mack moved Ari and the boys into his cabin without seeking B's approval first. He didn't want to wait any longer, desperate to start his new life with his family in Uskiville. Mack left a message on her voicemail explaining that Ari and the boys had moved in, and he knew that she'd be mad about it, but he didn't care anymore. He was determined to be happy with Ari, and as B wasn't returning his calls or texts, he planned to just deal with the consequences when she arrived home.

Killing the Mauler had empowered Mack. He found a new confidence in himself as the one true Prez of the Gray Wolves and having two MCs made him feel invincible enough to believe that he could tame his dragon. She would have to get used to his new family, and Ari would have to learn to play nice with his dragon if she was going to be his queen. Having spent the last two weeks acting like newlyweds in their first home together, they had almost forgotten about B's return. Their lives had settled into contentedness as there had been four weeks without drama, with Junior being the only exception. He didn't like the idea of lying to his aunt B. He had grown fond of her, and the thought of her return was making him anxious.

Ari agreed to try her very best and make amends for her jealousy toward B, accepting that she would be a permanent figure in their lives. She did own everything, after all. Mack decided he would do something special for B's arrival back home, despite her lack of communication with him of late. They hadn't spoken since the night before his battle with the Mauler, providing him with the pep talk that took away his self-doubt and convinced him he could kill the sadistic monster.

Now settled back in Uskiville, Mack found a and new normal, but he still felt unfulfilled because he was missing his dragon. He was a little hurt that she didn't inform him she was leaving the country. Frankie had informed him she had taken the impromptu trip back home as she couldn't face him if he was going to be beaten, broken, and bruised again because she hated seeing him in pain. Also, she didn't want to be around if the police turned up to arrest him after going back to black. Frankie explained to Mack that she needed plausible deniability to ensure the safety of her business, coaching career, and her boys. She explained to Frankie, if Mack wanted to risk everything for Ari without having the decency to provide her with an honest explanation, then she would not be around when the law caught up to him. She would be done with him too if that happened in her absence.

Mack could understand why she was angry with him. He'd cut her out of his life while getting to know Ari, and Ari had been so rude to her every time she visited Uskiville. But Mack was determined to make things right and show her he was done with black and ready to move forward with her and his new family.

On the day B was due to fly home, Mack went shopping, filling her fridge with groceries, and spending all day cooking her favorite meal of pulled pork, loaded fries with chocolate pudding and custard for dessert. He even ordered a case of her favorite wine, placing a couple of bottles in her fridge, thinking that she would need a glass or two upon her return. Frankie set out around five o'clock to pick her up, leaving Ari to set the table and Mack to make the last-minute preparations for the dish. The boys had already eaten and were back at Mack's playing video games. Tonight, was just for the adults, and Mack was so excited to reconnect with his dragon. He couldn't wait to catch up like the good old days. To Mack, his dragon was the last piece of the puzzle, the last thing to cross off his list so he and Ari could live happily ever after.

Frankie returned an hour later, bundling through the door with B's luggage. Mack rubbed his hands together. "She's here," he said to Ari as he rushed to the door.

Standing in the doorway, Mack popped his head past Frankie, who was entering the cabin, only to find that B wasn't with him. Glaring at Frankie, he asked, "Where is she?"

"She dropped me off with her case. She's off to Sal's bar," Frankie said, looking exacerbated.

"Did you tell her I was looking forward to seeing her, that I cooked her favorite meal, fetched her favorite wine and everything?"

Frankie nodded. "Yeah man, I did. But she said that she hadn't gotten laid in a month, and it was the first thing on her to do list."

Mack raged. "What?"

"Look, Mack. B said that she wasn't in the mood to play happy families tonight and she told you that things would be different when she got back. She's still pissed, Mackie, and you can hardly blame her."

Mack dropped his head in despair, plonking himself at the table, feeling devastated.

"She's not going to see past me going black, is she?" he asked sadly.

Frankie came and sat beside him, reaching for the bottle of chilled white wine, and poured Mack and himself an enormous glass.

"You know what she's like, Mackie boy. She has to process shit in her own way. You broke her trust, took her control away, and left her hanging for months. She gave up on you returning home. So, you're gonna have to give her time to get used to you being around again."

"And what if she doesn't trust me again?"

Frankie sighed, "We'll just have to hope that she does, but truth be told Mackie boy, deep down you knew this was only going to end one way with her. You betrayed her, man, broke her. Me, I can forgive, but you know B can't. She's incapable of that.

Mack clenched his jaw. "No! I haven't come through everything just to fall at the last hurdle. I'm going to Sal's, and I am going to drag her out of there if I have to. This shit needs to end."

Frankie grabbed him, "No, Mackie boy! Keep a clear head. If you do this now, you'll lose her forever. For Christ's sake, let her relieve her stress and then she'll be home. You know she's never gone for long. She fucks and runs, remember?"

"But it's too dangerous for her to be doing that now. Blaze is out there, and why the hell is she at Sal's? It's too close to home. The press will have a field day if they find her entangled with some random hookup."

"And that's why I sent along Bamfa to be her wingman tonight. He's desperate for a shag as his now ex-wife hasn't put out since having their fourth kid. He'll look after her and escort her back soon," Frankie insisted.

Mack snapped as he paced up and down the kitchen. "She knows the rules, Frankie. We agreed she's not to do this on her own."

"I know, that's why I told her *you* insisted Bamfa go with her tonight, because you were worried about her. See, I'm trying to help you. Now sit down and drink your fucking wine while we wait."

Mack sat down in his chair, tapping the table.

"What a selfish bitch! I'm going to give her a piece of my mind when she gets home. Upsetting my Mackie like this. He's slaved all day for her," Ari declared.

"What did you call her?" Frankie said as he rose from his chair, looking infuriated.

"Oh shit! Frankie, she didn't mean that," Mack said as Ari stepped back in shock, scared by Frankie's reaction.

"Yes, she fucking did. Say it again," he told her. "Slag my best friend out again, wench, and see what happens."

"Hey, hey! Come on, settle the feck down and that's an order from your fecking Prez," Mack bellowed.

Frankie looked at Mack in disgust. "You need to put her back in her box if you want any chance of a future with B. Now I'm going to get some fucking air," he said as he stormed out, slamming the door as he left.

"Seriously?" Mack said, glaring at Ari. "I know you're trying to help sweetheart, but please watch your mouth around the people who worship the dragon. She means a lot to everyone around here and you can't go slagging her, even if you are pissed at her. She's their muse, Ari. They will fight to the death for her as I did for you. So please, no more aggravating them. Things are hard enough as it is."

Ari dropped onto the sofa in a sulk. "What, so she never gets called out for being a bitch? That's ridiculous."

Mack didn't care to comment on it, as he sat drinking B's wine instead. Of course, he thought Ari was right, as he sat there thinking maybe it was high time someone started calling B out on her crap. He had just finished the bottle when a half-cut B entered through the front door.

Mack, half-drunk and fueled with rage, couldn't look at her. "Nice of you to fucking join us," he spat. "Don't worry, your food is fucking stone cold, and I only slaved over it all afternoon."

"I didn't fucking ask you to cook it, good boy," B spat back as she pulled the second bottle of wine out of the fridge and began drinking it straight from the bottle.

"You're a selfish bitch, Dragon. We have been waiting all night for you and you stroll in half cut and after fucking driving."

B laughed. "Sorry, I didn't realize I had a curfew and Mummy, and Daddy would wait up to tell me off. Am I grounded now? Are you going to take my allowance?"

"Stop being pathetic," he hissed.

"Honestly, Mackie, I don't know what you're so pissed about. It's not like I've done anything different from what we've always done."

"Well, a call would have sufficed. Seriously, Dragon, I just don't get why you do it to yourself. You could have anyone and be happy. Yet, you go around putting yourself in danger by fucking random guys. You're going to get yourself hurt."

"Funny, you didn't see a problem with it before she arrived. We enjoyed new people on the regular before her," B snapped, pointing at Ari sat in the room's corner, trying her best to keep out of it.

"Well, maybe I've grown up."

"Fuck you, Mackie! You haven't grown up. You're the same selfish twat you've always been. You went back to black, and like I said the conversation would be different when I saw you next."

"Dragon..."

"No, Mackie. Don't give me your bullshit. You chose to go black for her, so, I'm done with you! What did you think? You could make me a meal, butter me up and we'd all play happy families? You're taking the piss! Not to mention moving her into my bloody property. Who the fuck do you think you are? You may be Prez of your Wolves good boy, but this is my land, my fucking livelihood, and my fucking rules. Now if you don't mind, I want to go to bed, and do me a favor and take the trash out when you leave," she said glaring at Ari."

"Hey, hey, don't be like that," Mack said, softening as he realized how she felt.

"Sorry good boy, but we're done!" she said, before guzzling a third of the wine out of her bottle and strolled out of the kitchen toward the back porch. "I wish you had just stepped up and became the man I know you're capable of being? You worked so hard to become white and it looked so good on you and now you're as black as her soul and all you bloody do is throw your cascade of lies at me," B said, glaring at Ari, conveying her contempt for the woman who tore her family apart. "Good luck with your new family good boy. You're gonna need it,"

"Dragon, you've got this all wrong."

Guzzling yet more wine, she looked at the two of them in disgust. "No, I haven't good boy. You forget, I know you inside out and back to bloody front. Now, I know you've gone and gotten yourself into deep shit and despite the lies, I know enough to know that you can't be here anymore jeopardizing me and my children's future. Now you've made your bed, so go fucking lie in it."

Mack's heart shattered in two. He loved Ari, but B was still his world. His family. And now she didn't want him in Uskiville anymore. "Dragon, no. I want to fix this. Please give me a chance to make this right. I'll do anything,"

"Then do us all a favor and fuck off back to Portland and take your home-wrecking, poisonous bitch with you!" she finished, launching the now finished bottle of wine into the kitchen area, smashing it to pieces.

Mack approached her with caution as he tried to calm her. "Dragon, come on. Please"

He knew once her eyes burned like wildfire, the dragon fire in her belly would become too much for her to handle, and it worried him that she might do something stupid. Normally, that wouldn't be a problem, as it was directed at other people. But this time B directed her rage at him and Ari, and that was dangerous.

"Don't fucking call me Dragon anymore. You lost that right the day you started seeing her and lying to me. I get that she's the mother of your son. I get you feel fucking guilty about what happened to her. But you're lying to yourself too. Telling yourself you have feelings for her when all it is, is guilt."

"I do have feelings for her, Dragon. I love her," he confessed.

B laughed maniacally. "Bull shit! You're trying to fit a square peg into a round hole. It doesn't fucking work! I've seen you look at hookers with more sincerity than you do her, so what the fuck am I missing? What's the big secret? What are you not telling me? What have you been lying to me about for months?" she asked?

Mack went white. He couldn't tell her the truth now. She was already on the warpath. He dreaded the thought of what she would do if she knew what had really happened these past few months.

"See, there it is again, the face of guilt and shame. It's getting to you, Mackie boy, isn't it? This cascade of lies again. Lying to the one person who gave a shit about you when everyone else left you," she said, trying to provoke him.

"I'm not lying. It's all in your head, Dragon. I've just fallen in love with her, that's all."

"Don't you fucking dare try to play mind games with me, Mackie. I know you better than you know yourself. No get out the fuck out before I choke the both of you!"

Before Mack could retaliate, Ari fired at B from across the room.

"Mack may fear you, but you don't scare me! I've been beaten and broken by bigger and stronger people than you'll ever be. Who do you think you are, speaking to him like that? You're nothing but a controlling psychopath, trying to keep him wrapped around your little finger. He can't even breathe without your permission and the way you exercise control, the way you see the world, is just fucking fucked up. You're pathetic, Dragon."

"Ari, stop!" Mack bellowed, but she continued.

"You need help, Dragon, with your fucking whiter than white superhero complex. Who do you think you are? I get that you're jealous of Mack having his proper family, a family who doesn't try to control him and hurt his feelings," she sneered, drunk on the rage that fueled her.

"Ari, shut the fuck up," Mack demanded, fearing what would come next.

"No Mack, this bitch needs to know we're in love and she can either get with the program or leave!"

Until that point, B glowered at her with a sinister grin, as if she was allowing Ari to unravel so she could get the truth. Ari was no good. To B, she was the angel of death who flew into town, bringing everything to its knees until she got her claws into what she wanted. But to suggest that B could leave her own home, to leave what she had built from scratch, to threaten her and her children's livelihood, well, that just wasn't happening. She could have Mack; B knew now that he was lost to the devil in disguise. But everything else, well, that was hers. She had poured her blood, sweat, and tears into Uskiville and nobody was going to take it away from her.

B laughed maniacally as if she had lost the plot. Mack knew she had been pushed too far beyond her limits. Something inside her had snapped as he watched her sneer in delight. Her eyes grew wide like a predator with its prey in its grasp, like a dragon ready to unleash the force that rose from the depths of her soul. Mack watched in slow motion as B threw herself at Ari and he knew he wouldn't be able to stop her. She was too strong for him, and the adrenaline that no doubt coursed through her veins now was no match for him. He tried to hurry as he watched his best friend launch herself at the mother of his unborn child. He saw the fear in Ari's eyes as she looked at him pleading for help, but he wasn't quick enough, and he was terrified; B was going to kill her.

B fast approached Ari as she tried to scramble across the room, but B was way too quick for her, grabbing her and pinning her against the bookshelf, sending books crashing to the floor. Her eyes were like wildfire as her hands traveled toward Ari's throat as Mack tried to pull her away, screaming at her to stop, but B couldn't hear him anymore. She was lost to the anger and fire that roared inside of her. Ari had threatened her livelihood, her children and everything that she held dear, and B would not let her take that away from her.

Mack managed to create some breathing space between her and Ari, forcing B's hands away.

"Stop! Please don't do this. She hasn't got a clue what she's saying, sweetheart," Mack pleaded as he took hold of B's head in his hands.

"Please, please, don't do this," he cried, and for a split second, B softened.

That was, until Ari made a run for the front door, making B snap again. She head-butted Mack in the nose to break free of his tender grasp and hurdled over the sofa with her long legs. B, now sober as a judge as Ari came within her grasp.

She had her now.

"Whack!" B hit the ground with a thud. The wind was well knocked out of her fiery sails. Trying to catch her breath, she wondered what had hit her. Had she been shot? She struggled for breath.

Opening her eyes, B found Frankie on top of her, panting and looking at her in relief. She looked confused as her eyes focused on Mack, caressing Ari's tear ridden face, with blood dripping from his nose. B inhaled slow and even breaths as she sat on the floor, seething at Frankie for stopping her.

"Christ! I've lost you too?"

Frankie looked at her, confused. "No, B," he said, pulling her into his chest. "I couldn't give a fuck about her; she's got her claws into him and that's fucking it. I just didn't want to bury a body for you. I would. I would do anything for you, but you were on the edge of turning black then, and you would have never recovered from it. Please, don't let some jealous little home-wrecker turn you into something you're not like she has done to Mackie. She's not fucking worth it, and neither is he."

B nodded. "Thank you, Frankie. What would I do without you in my life?" she said as she hugged him back.

A broken Mack wiped the blood from his nose as he watched Frankie embrace his dragon. Her words cut through him like a knife to the heart. B was *his* dragon, not Frankie's.

Frankie glimpsed at Mack's distraught face. "I think you both should leave Uskiville. This is not fucking working."

"And you," B said pointing to Ari, "I know exactly who you are and what trouble you bring, and let it be said, the day that something happens because of you and your actions, is the day that I will happily go black. I promise you I won't stop until I end all the destruction that your dirty little cascade of lies has brought upon my family. Now get the fuck out of my cabin!"

Ari was in tears. "You've got me all wrong, B."

"No! I've got you all right! Now leave or I promise you it will take more than this pair to stop me from tearing you apart if you don't."

Frankie shot Mack a look. "Get her out of here brother."

Mack's jaw dropped as he wiped the blood off his nose and nodded in agreement. He knew Ari had pushed B beyond her limits; nobody had dared challenge her like that before, it was reckless and as much as he loved her, he was furious with her as he led her out of B's cabin, only to stop in his tracks after Frankie called out to him.

"Oh, and Mackie, let me be clear. My loyalties lie with Bs. You've made your choice, and I won't follow you into the darkness anymore," Frankie said.

Mack pursed his lips and nodded in agreement; he knew what tonight had meant. He knew that he'd made a choice and he knew that he'd lost B forever.

As Mack stepped onto the front porch and into the cold dead of night, Ari turned to him, pulling him close to her. "We're free baby, you're free! I know I wanted to stay here, but we can set up somewhere else and grow old together."

Mack pushed her away in disbelief. "Is there something fecking wrong with you?"

Ari stood in shock. "I don't understand. You're free! You don't have to bow down to her rules anymore, you don't have to feel anything for her anymore. She's cut you loose, and her spell over you is broken. I thought you'd be happy. I mean, it's a shame that we have to leave here, especially after we've just settled in, but..."

"Is that what you think's been happening here? Let me tell you something. That's my *family* in there, and you just made me fecking choose between them and you. You gave me no choice and just because you are jealous of my dragon. I thought I'd finally gotten through to you, but you're just as selfish as you always were."

"No Mack, I—"

"Yes, you fecking are!" he said through gritted teeth. "I have been nothing but honest with you since the start. I told you I will always love her. She is my family, she will always be my family and as angry as she is, she would never make me choose. That's why Frankie asked me to leave, because he knows the alternative is me having to choose to never see her again."

"Mack. I'm sorry! I did it because I was angry, and I hate seeing what she does to you! I love you, and you said you loved me, so let's build a future together. A future free of her control," Ari pleaded.

Mack stared at her in frustration. "You just don't get it, do you? She doesn't control me. I chose her because I love her. Maybe not like I love you, but in my own way. She is my family and the only one I had when the world tore me apart. Yes, she has a fecked up way of looking at things, but that's how she safeguards herself, and tonight you threatened all of that."

Ari narrowed her eyes with a confused look on her face.

"Ari, you told her to leave her own fecking home, and you have no idea how hard she fought for that. I told you to stop, but you kept pushing her buttons. Geez, I could have handled it, but it's you that took the control away from me, and it's you that controls me, not Dragon, You! And you've never bothered getting to know who she really is because you are so busy feeling threatened by her!" He slammed his hands down onto the porch railing.

Ari was once again lost for words. He turned to look at her, and she saw the devastation in his eyes. Mack was broken!

Rubbing his hand across his tired brow, he said to her: "Ari, I'm in love with you and I want to be with you, but you broke my family tonight in a fit of rage. I know you were trying to stick up for me, but you almost turned my dragon black, and she can never be black. You frightened her, brought out the worst in her and for your own gains. Tonight, I saw the side of you that the dragon has tried to warn me about since the day she met you. I had no choice but to betray her tonight, to save your life and stop her from doing something that would haunt us all for the rest of our lives. I betrayed her for you. and now I am without the family that brought me in out of the cold. So, you better fecking love me the way you say you do, otherwise, every-thing has been for nothing." A feeling of dejection washed over him.

Ari studied Mack's distraught face, realizing that she had made a terrible mistake by gunning for B tonight. She knew she should have let Mack handle it, but she had been fueled by the jealousy that had built up inside her since the day they'd met. Ari's penny drop moment allowed her to understand that as much as Mack was in love with her, he needed B. He needed his dragon to protect him from the cold like she always had. She could do that for him in ways that Ari couldn't, and Ari knew she wasn't strong enough for that. Mack and B looked after one another, tethered in ways beyond Ari's comprehension, and she knew if she wanted to be with Mack, then she had to accept that and fix things.

After all Mack had done for her, avenging her, making everyone that hurt her pay. Ari realized how right B was. Ari had, in fact, brought death and destruction into his life. Yes, she had brought Junior, but Junior and Mack had a right to be together. They were family, but so was B.

Ari approached Mack, taking his hand. "I'm sorry, Mack, I am a terrible person. My insecurities took over, and I just kept thinking that I would lose you to her. I will make it right, I promise."

"I think we might be past that," he said as he held her close. "Ari, I've lied to her multiple times, and I had never lied to her before meeting you. But lying to her became so easy as one lie fed into another as I tried desperately to keep her from learning the truth. She asked me to be honest and truthful. She asked me to stay white. They were her only requests when she took me in off the streets and that was easy until I met you. Then, with every touch and taste of you, I wanted more! But that meant lying to and hurting my best friend in the entire world. It meant going black and no matter what you do now, my dragon will never trust me again. She will never see me as the same man because all she'll see now are the lies, the deceit, and the black. So, I'm sorry, sweetheart, but this is something that can't be fixed," he choked out as he broke down and sobbed.

Ari felt awful, thinking she had ruined everything, but she was determined to fix things. But for now, she needed to get Mack home. She thought seeing Junior's would make him feel better, and he had his son and a family who loved him for who he was. Taking his hand, she led him down the steps, only to be met with Remy. He was frantic, panting and crying.

"Mom, Mack, Junior's gone!" he spluttered as he tried to get his breath back and choke back the tears.

"What! What do you mean gone, son?" Mack said

"He snuck into B's and heard her say that we had to leave, and he was upset. He said that everywhere he goes, trouble follows, and he won't cause anyone any more trouble again. I tried to chase him, but I lost him in the woods. I think he might do something stupid."

"Oh, no! Mack, we have to find him!" Ari cried.

Mack reached out and grabbed the wall to support himself, terrified. He had only just gotten his son back, and now he faced losing again. He became frantic as he tried to think of what to do.

"Right, son! You go back inside in case he comes in, and we'll go look for him."

"No! I wanna help, he's my brother, and I know him a damn sight better than you!" he hollered.

"Remy, no. Mack's right, it's dark and we can't risk losing you, too. Please, we need you here in case he comes back," Ari suggested.

After a moment of internal battle, Remy agreed, and he watched Mack head for B's.

"Where are you going?" Ari quizzed. "Remy said that he headed for the woods."

"Yeah, and there's only one person who is going to find him out there in the black of night and she's in there," Mack said as he continued up the steps.

"What about the police?"

"He's been gone five minutes, Ari; they'll not do feck all yet, and I'm not waiting around. My dragon will find him," he said as he burst into B's cabin.

B and Frankie were sitting by the fire drinking whisky when Mack came in. They looked at him in disbelief at first, until B saw the look on his face. She knew that look; he was scared.

She jumped up to her feet, throwing whisky everywhere. "What's happened?"

Mack clung to her, putting his forehead on hers. He was shaking, so B embraced him as Ari looked on with the same scared impression on her face.

"What happened?" B asked Ari.

"Junior overheard you telling us to leave, and he took off into the woods. Remy thinks he's blaming himself for us not getting along," Ari said through her tears.

B turned to Mack. "Listen, Mackie! We'll find him, but you need to help me, okay? Besides, I have a good idea where he might be going."

Ari jerked backward a step and cast a quizzing stare at B.

"He's followed me up the valley before. It's just a hunch, but I have a feeling that's where he'll be. Now, come on," B said, taking Mack's hand and dragging him out the door.

CHAPTER THIRTY-THREE
The Hunt for Junior

Frankie retrieved some torches from the garage. Then B headed up the path after Junior, sending Ari and Mack up and along another path parallel to where she was. She directed Frankie to drive around to the other side of the valley just in case she was wrong, and Junior slipped passed her, Mack, and Ari. B knew the woods better than anyone after spending most of her time there, escaping from her hectic life. She loved the calm and as she headed deep into the dark woods; she found a sense of peace. She knew where Junior was going. It was where she would go if she was desperate and lonely.

It didn't take B long to reach the top of the valley. She had made the trip a thousand times. It was her sanctuary. There was a small cliff edge where she liked to sit, and it was where Junior had followed her previously. After reaching the branch-covered path, B pushed her way through the sea of branches and made her way to the cliff's edge. Coming into the clearing, she discovered Junior, his head hanging low as he sat with his legs dangling over the cliff edge, looking down over the valley. B gulped at the thought of going near the cliff edge with a hundred-foot drop. It made her feel queasy. She preferred to enjoy the view away from the edge.

Moving closer to Junior and being careful not to startle him, she called out to him.

"Hey, Boyoh," she said as she sat herself down about three feet from the edge.

"Hey, Aunt B," he said sniffling

"I thought I'd find you here."

"I like it here! It's quiet," he said as he wiped his tears.

"Yeah, it's beautiful here at night. I love how the stars light up the sky. Rhys and Madoc come here often with a telescope to stargaze. You should join them sometime."

Junior raised his head to meet her gaze, tears rushing down his face. "How can I if you're making us leave?"

"Look mate, I apologize for what you heard at the cabin. I was angry..."

"It's okay. Aunt B! I know this is all my fault. Trouble follows me wherever I go. First my mom, then Ari, then...."

B stopped him in his tracks. "You think this is your fault? Junior, no, my lovely, none of what's happened is your doing," she said as she moved closer to him and trying not to look over the cliff edge.

"But you don't understand, when you were away—"

B stopped him again. "Junior, your mom's passing wasn't your fault. She chose her path, as did Ari to find your dad, and as for what you saw and heard earlier, that was definitely not your fault, mate. You have been handed some shitty cards, that's all, but I promise you, that's all going to change. I'm sorry you had to witness me and your parents falling out tonight. I'm ashamed of my actions, and you should have never had to witness any of it. Please forgive me?"

"Does that mean we don't have to leave? Because I like it here, I love hanging out with Madoc and Rhys, and I love living at Dad's too."

B regarded the young boy's sad face. Riddled with guilt, she knew she couldn't send them away after what Junior had been through, despite what she thought of his mother and father.

"No mate, I will sort things with your mom and dad, I promise."

Junior dived into her arms and sobbed. "Thank you, Aunt B, I love you!" he cried.

B held him there, stroking his head until he was ready to pull away.

Once he calmed down, he turned to her. "Aunt B, why did you all fall out tonight?"

B stared out over the Valley, portraying herself as the wicked woman, she explained to him. "Junior, if you can choose to be anything, you should always choose to be kind and honest. I try to live by that my lovely. When I met your dad, it was all that I asked of him, and of late I have had my doubts about how honest he and your mother have been with me. Now I love your dad, but I guess tonight, I became a little confused between what was true and what was a lie, and that's my fault mate, not your mom or dad's. I lashed out at your parents. It was cruel and I don't deserve to call your dad my best friend. Junior, I don't get close to people often. I find it hard, but when I do, I love them with all my heart and sometimes that makes me do crazy things."

"So, you just want the truth, and we can all return to normal?"

B smirked and nodded. "The truth is all that I've ever asked for, my lovely boy."

Junior fidgeted with his shirt button, tugging on it. "Aunt B, I want to be honest too and there's something I need to tell you. See, I have been lying to you too!"

B studied his face, trying to gage what Junior meant. "Oh."

Junior's eyes shifted to the black skies, unable to look at her. "Something happened when you were away, something bad…"

B's eyes widened. She knew Mack and Ari had lied to her, but she never thought they would involve Junior. "It's okay my lovely, I won't get mad, you can tell me."

Junior nodded. "The night you went to Wales, Mom and I were…"

"Junior!!" Mack cried as he emerged from the clearing, with Ari in tow.

Embracing him, Mack pulled him away from the edge while Ari

checked him over. "Are you alright, son?"

"I'm fine!" he said, a little embarrassed.

"You scared the living daylights out of me, son. Please, promise me you'll never do anything like that again. I lost you once, I can't lose you again," Mack cried.

"I'm sorry, Dad, but Aunt B kept me safe, and you don't have to worry about leaving anymore. Aunt B promised we can stay, and all be a family."

Ari and Mack appeared thunderstruck as they met B's despondent gaze, and with a nod of her head she started back down the hill. "It's true! You can stay, and I won't get in your way."

Mack chased after her, taking her by the wrist. "Dragon, wait please."

B turned to him, aware that Junior was watching and listening to everything. She knew how fragile he was, so she did her best to conceal all the hurt in her heart and forced a smile. "It's fine, Mackie boy, be with your family. That boy of yours blames himself for everything that's happened in his life. You need to show him that none of this is his fault. Teach him like I taught you. He has the same delicate heart as you, and you need to help him heal. So, get him home, okay?"

Mack knew it was all for Junior's benefit. He knew how good B was at faking her happiness. She had done it in front of her own kids daily until she'd fallen out with Mack. But he didn't call her out on it, as he could see that she was trying for Junior's sake. They headed back down the hill, following a path that brought them outside B's garden. B stopped by her back door.

"Why don't you come to our place for some tea," Ari suggested, trying to make an effort.

B looked at Ari. "Thanks, but I'm going to turn in. All that hill walking has caught up with me," she said, smiling at Junior and nudging his chin with her soft fist.

Junior swayed as he looked at the ground. "Sorry, Aunt B."

B smiled at him. "No problem, my lovely boy. Just make sure you don't hog that spot too much, okay?"

"Sure."

B strolled up the steps toward her back door, glancing over her shoulder to Junior after remembering that he'd been about to tell her something.

"Junior, what were you going to say on top of the ridge about something bad happening here while I was in Wales?"

Mack and Ari froze and stared at Junior. Junior looked at his parents before stepping forward to talk to B. Mack took Ari's hand and squeezed tight.

"Aunt B, you just want truth and honesty, right?"

"Always," she said, smiling at him.

"But what if that truth does more damage than the lie?"

B reached out to grasp his hand. "My boy, a cascade of lies is never a good thing to conceal. Eventually, all the lies will burst into your life and destroy everything you love. That's why the truth is so important to me. It keeps me honest, and it keeps me safe."

Junior looked at his aunt and cleared his throat. Taking a deep breath, he stared at his father's distraught face. "Then I need to tell you something, Aunt B."

"Okay, get it off your chest, my lovely, and I promise I won't get mad."

Junior looked at his mother, who wore the same distraught expression as his father, before turning his attention to B.

He took a deep breath and began; "Aunt B, when you were in Wales..." he said as he looked at his father, who was now staring at the floor. "My dad..." he struggled.

"It's okay, buddy, if it's too hard just now, then we can talk in the morning."

"No! I need to get this off my chest. It's hurting me."

"It's okay, son, go ahead. I don't want you suffering anymore," Mack said softly.

Junior's face softened as he nodded. "Aunt B, when you were in Wales, my dad—my dad, and I raided your cabin for all of your

British sweets and chocolate. I'm sorry, I know it was wrong, but it was just amazing, and the British stuff is just the best. I'm so sorry, Aunt B," he cried, hugging her.

Mack and Ari looked flabbergasted as B held the sobbing Junior. B's eyes narrowed as she shook her head in confusion. This wasn't what she had expected Junior to tell her. She looked at Mack, who was looking back at her rather sheepishly.

"Is this true?"

Mack pursed his lips, staring at her as if he didn't know what to say, "Uh, yeah, we had a rummage and pigged out, and the poor boy has been terrified you were going to kick him out ever since."

"Um, okay," B said as she looked down at Junior, who was trying to wipe his tears. "Is this really what you thought was so bad that you couldn't tell me?"

Junior looked at his dad and back at B. "Yes, Aunt B, it's true! I'm nothing but a horrible liar!"

"Hey, come here. Don't be daft! You, boyoh, are an amazing and kind-hearted boy who has to stop putting the world on his shoulders. It's too big for me and I'm twice your size. And you can eat all the chocolate and sweets you bloody well want from my cabin. You don't even need to ask, okay?"

Junior laughed at his aunt as he wiped his tears with his sleeve. "Okay."

"But Junior, you need to promise me something. Promise me, whenever you feel anxious or sad again, you come to one of us, okay? Bottling everything up is like building a ticking time bomb in your soul, and if you keep adding to it, you'll just explode, my boy. So, no more, okay? No matter how horrible you think it is."

"Okay Aunt B, no more bottling things up, no more lies. Just truth and honesty. We promise, right Dad?" he said, looking at his dad to ensure that Mack knew what he was getting at.

Mack approached Junior, kissing him on the head. "Promise! Now say good night to Aunt B. She'll turn back into a dragon if she doesn't get into bed before sunrise."

Junior laughed as he wished everyone good night, and Ari led him inside so Mack could talk to B.

"Thank you for finding him and letting us stay and thank you for not killing Ari. I know I don't deserve to stay here. I know I went black, and I know you will never forgive me. But you're my family dragon, my best friend and as much as I love Ari, I just don't work without you!"

B didn't even look at him, she couldn't. She just couldn't cope with the pain and the lies.

Mack turned her toward him, once again placing his forehead on hers, just as they did whenever they needed each other.

"I don't want to move on with my life without you in it. I'm so sorry, Dragon, and I'll spend the rest of my life trying to make this up to you. Please, just give me one more chance. Let me show you I can be white again?"

B moved away; she was still hurting, "Mackie, I don't know if I can ever trust you again. You broke me just like the last man in my life did, and I promised myself I would never hurt like that again. All I did was try to help you, and you hurt me. Now I will always love you and I will be as nice as I can, for Junior's sake, but I can't let you waltz back into my life and break me again. I just can't. You're black now, and I'm white!"

Mack's voice trembled. "Please Dragon, I beg you!"

"Go to your family Mackie, they need you now." she said as she headed back up the steps to her back door.

Mack called out to her. "You are my family too, Dragon, so tell me what you need me to do to make this right."

"I don't need anyone or anything anymore, Mackie," she said as she let out a tremendous sigh and walked inside, closing the door behind her.

Ari, studying them from the porch, watched how the man she loved crumbled to the ground in tears. She raced to his aid as he sobbed into her chest as if he was grieving at the loss of a loved one, and all she could do was hold him while he cried.

CHAPTER THIRTY-FOUR
Loss & Starting Over

The next morning, Ari headed out onto the back porch to get some air, exhausted after being up all night trying to console Mack. Ari was wracked with guilt about her part in Mack and B's falling out, and she was desperate to fix things, but she didn't know how.

If only I had acted better toward B instead of letting jealousy get the better of me.

Walking across the lawn behind the two cabins, feeling the soft blades of grass tickle her feet, Ari basked in the beauty that surrounded her home. Yet she felt ugly for her outburst the night before. She wanted to make things right in Uskiville. But how? She wanted to talk to B to see if she could change her mind. B had to be feeling hurt too, Ari thought, as she sat herself down on the grass at the foot of the hill that they ventured up the night before. She loved to watch the tree branches sway in the light breeze as the smell of the cut grass wafted up her nose. Ari found a pleasant spot to lie down. She just needed to collect herself as she rested her head on the grass and closing her eyes so she could bask in the morning's ambience for a second. Inhaling and exhaling, taking nice and even breaths, Ari felt at peace.

"Uh hum," she heard, as someone cleared their throat.

Ari opened her eyes to find B looking at her as if she was a mental patient, and Ari, feeling startled, bolted upright. She hadn't realized she was blocking B's path. B had just returned from the cliff edge looking disheveled. Ari noticed the big, dark, puffy circles around B's normally beautiful and bright eyes, and she wore the same clothes she'd had on the night before.

Did she go back up the hill and stay all night?

"You're blocking my path," B said to her, interrupting Ari's thoughts.

Ari scurried out of the way to let B pass, and as she watched B walk away, Ari couldn't help but open her mouth. "He's still yours, you know."

B stopped dead in her tracks and replied, "Ari, he's yours, so look after him or I will end you."

"You still care about him, right?" she blurted, trying to stop the words from escaping her mouth but losing control of her vocalizations.

B, who had continued toward her cabin, stopped again, this time doing a complete three-sixty to confront her, and she looked unimpressed as she opened her mouth. "What do you want from me, Ari?"

"Nothing. I want to apologize."

B tilted her head with a glint of amusement. "I think we're a little past that lovely girl!"

"We don't have to be. Look, I know I fucked up. From the moment I laid eyes on you, I was jealous of you. Jealous of your beauty, your strength, and your 'I don't take no shit' attitude. Then I met Mack, and something happened. I wanted him, but there you were in all your glory, tethered to him, and I hated you for it."

B's eyes narrowed and her brow furrowed. "Bloody hell, Ari! How many times do I have to explain that Mack and I are best friends? Nothing more! God, he's not even my type. Not to mention he's like a brother to me."

"I know, I know, but I couldn't even have a conversation with him without him mentioning you twenty times. He worships you, B, and I tried to change that, and I'm sorry."

"Is that's why you were an absolute bitch when you came to visit?"

"Yes, and I'm not proud of it, B. See, when Mack and I got together, he looked past all of my scars and trauma. He looked past the nightmares and how damaged I was. He made me feel like a beautiful woman again, and I fell for him hard."

To Ari's surprise, B sat on the grass next to her, and Ari assumed it was to listen to what she had to say, so she continued.

"B, he tried to push me away, he told me you suggested he get to know Junior better first, and instead of seeing you as his best friend offering him some advice, I saw you as a threat, as someone trying to come between us."

B shook her head, amused by Ari's words. "Ari, I didn't say that to Mack because I had something against you. I thought you were a lovely woman to start with."

"You did?" Ari said, surprised at B having a sensitive side.

"Yeah, it's just I knew that both you and Junior were fragile, and Mack hadn't long sorted himself out either. I just thought that Mack and Junior's relationship was more important."

B began playing with the blades of grass in front of her before continuing. "Ari, I've been there, where I have been so hurt and broken that it affected my children. I watched how my sons struggled through my divorce and our family home was ripped apart by a new woman entering their father's life. I didn't want you and the boys to suffer like I had. I didn't want Mack to suffer either. You had all suffered for so long. I simply tried to offer some tried and tested advice to my best friend, that's all."

Ari rubbed the back of her neck. "Shit! I got you all wrong."

"You got a lot of things wrong about me Ari, because like everyone else, you just assumed you knew my character. I'm not stupid Ari, I know people think I'm just a fucking crazy psychopath. But I was broken a long time ago, broken beyond repair, and that's why I see the world the way I do. It's why I have rules. They keep me from falling apart. Mack knows that, and he understands why we can't be friends anymore."

Ari bit her lip before speaking. "You know, he told me how you see the world B, and while I can't understand it, I respect why you do it. The human heart is precious, and I understand why you feel the need to protect yours by keeping it locked away in the depths of that fiery dragon body of yours. But you need to know, you don't have to be like that with Mack, because he loves you. B, right now his heart is breaking over you, and I can't fix it. Please give him one more chance."

B huffed. "It's too late Ari, I'm sorry. Too much has happened. There's been too many lies!"

"B, he's still white. I promise you that."

B looked at her, raising an eyebrow. "You know about that?"

"The black and white thing? Yeah. Mack told me one day, after I was being a bitch toward you for like the thousandth time. He was trying to make me see how wrong I was about you, but I wouldn't believe him."

B tried to hide her embarrassment by looking away, as Ari brought her back to her attention. Tears washed away Ari's foundation as she thought of Mack. "Look B, you think he went black, but you need to understand he did everything to save me. B, if you knew all the beautiful things, he has done for me and Junior these past months, you would know that his heart is still pure and white."

B stood and walked away, shaking her head, as if she had heard enough and Ari pushed once more, trying not to wake the beast lying dormant inside B.

"Look, you were right! It was my fault he went black, and I made so many mistakes, but please don't punish the man I love for something I did. Hate me forever, not him, because he's in there grieving about losing his best friend and has been all night."

"Here," B said, returning to her and handing her a tissue. "You know, getting upset and sitting cross legged on the ground isn't good for the baby."

Ari's hand covered her mouth as her eyes shot open. "You know about that?" she asked, as she wiped her tears and uncrossed her legs.

B cracked up. "Of course, I do. I'm a fucking dragon. We can sense that a mile off."

Ari giggled as B continued. "You know I fucking hate being called that. I know I'm fiery and Welsh, but he has always made me out to be like some crazy triad grand master. I'll have people after me next, like in the movies."

Ari's face crinkled in nervous laughter at B, who did not know how true that actually was.

"No offence, B, but they would take one look at you and run. You're scary when you're mad. I thought I was done for last night."

"Me too," B said with a casual shrug. "But next time, full disclosure on the whole pregnancy thing. It scared the shit out of me when Frankie told me last night. I would never have forgiven myself if I'd hurt you and the baby. I just felt so threatened by you, Ari, and when I feel threatened, the dragon comes out."

"Well, how about we keep that bitch locked up from now on?"

B laughed. "Oh, believe me, I've tried."

"Well, maybe you need a friend to help you."

"Ari…"

"I didn't mean Mack. I meant someone of the same species, with a vagina perhaps." Ari smiled at her.

"Oh, you mean like a gal pal or BFF. Ha-ha, I don't think I meet the criteria for that. I don't click with women; in case you haven't noticed."

"You know, there's a first time for everything. Besides, you'll have to learn soon. What if I end up having a girl? She'll need someone cool to help her out when her mother is being unreasonable."

B smiled. "You know Blethen is a fantastic name."

"Blethen? I like it! Where did you hear that, and what does it mean?"

B erupted in laughter. "Blethen is my name Ari, and it means wolf cub."

"Oh! I just thought your name was Bailey or Brittany or something like that. But Blethen, I love it!"

B smiled at her, looking heartbroken. "You wanna know something? Mackie and I have propped each other up for so long, I feel like I've lost part of me, and I'm in mourning. The worst thing is, I've been there before, and I hate it! It's why I see the world like I do. It's why I cut people out of my life when they hurt me, because it's the only way that I can stop myself from falling apart. This might sound fucked up to you, but it keeps me from crumbling, Ari. But I miss my best friend," she said, looking away, getting angry with herself for displaying signs of weakness.

"He misses you too, B. Please go to him. This is torturing you both, and if you make up with him, I promise to never interfere with your friendship again."

B stood up and offered a hand to Ari, pulling her to her feet with a gentle tug on her hand. "Lead the way Ari. I have to make things right!"

CHAPTER THIRTY-FIVE
New Beginnings

Ari headed inside to find Mack on the sofa with his head in his hands.

She kneeled in front of him. "Hey, Mack, how are you feeling?"

Mack shook his head as he kept it buried in his hands.

"Please Mackie, I hate seeing you like this."

"I'm broken baby. I broke my dragon, and now we're both broken forever."

Ari glanced up at B standing in the doorway, urging her to talk to him. Ari stood, kissing Mack on the head, before making way for B. "I'll make some tea," she said on her way out of the room.

B strolled into the room and stood before Mack. She didn't do feelings or all the mushy stuff that most women did, so she spoke to him in the only way she knew how.

"You know, you look like a complete sissy when you do that."

Mack, who clearly hadn't realized she was there, shot up in his seat, his jaw gaping as he gawked at her in disbelief.

"Hey," she said, smiling as she stuffed her hands in her pockets.

"Dragon," he whispered

B hovered toward the sofa. "Can I sit down?"

"Yeah."

She sat next to him. She was unsure what to say at first as he studied her in silence.

"We've balls upped this best friend thing. Who would have thought that one of us would fall in love, leaving the other behind?" she said softly.

"Dragon, I—"

"No, let me finish, Mackie, please?"

Mack nodded in agreement.

"You meeting someone, falling in love, and having a baby? That's a lot for a best friend to take, especially when that friend has missed her best friend so much. But I want you to know that I'm happy for you."

"Thank you, Dragon. You don't know what that means to me."

"Mackie, all I've ever wanted is for you to be happy, and you've grown so much. I mean, shit, you even called me irresponsible last night, and what I'm trying to say is I'm proud of you, settling down, I mean. And Ari is okay too, I guess."

Mack grinned but remained still, as if he was contemplating what to say or do. B looked at him, waiting for him to say something, but he grabbed her, hugging her tight. B closed her eyes, exhaling in relief at his warm embrace as she hugged him back.

"I missed you, Dragon."

"I missed you too, Mackie, but promise me, no more lies," she said as she sat there holding her best friend as his tears soaked her shoulder.

"Promise. I'll never ever hurt you again."

Ari peered in from the kitchen, grinning from ear to ear. She was so happy that Mack and B were whole again, and B didn't seem so bad when she got to know her a little more. All the jealousy dissipated as she witnessed how much Mack and B needed each other. So, she carried on making tea while they reacquainted themselves with each other.

Upon entering the room with a tray of tea and biscuits, Ari placed it on the table.

"Here you go. I made some British tea."

"Thank you," B said as she brought it to her lips. "Hmm, that's a valiant effort in the art of tea making Ari. I commend you, but please never do it again." She tried her best to be nice.

"What's wrong with it?" Ari asked. "I make good tea."

Mack laughed at the look of disgust on B's face. "It can't be that bad, Dragon."

B looked at him in amusement. "Try it."

Mack glanced at Ari, smiling back at him with encouragement as he took a sip.

"Geez, I'm glad I only drank coffee at your place," he choked out amid laughter.

B laughed hysterically as she picked up the mugs of terrible tea, and even Ari chuckled at herself.

"Right, I'll make it! And from now on, you leave the tea making to us Brits. It's what we do best," she said, making her way to the kitchen.

Mack watched B leave before gazing back at Ari.

"Come here, you." He held out his hand to her. "Thank you, sweetheart! I don't know how you got my dragon here, but I'm so happy that you did."

Ari took his hand in hers. "I just listened to her. And Mackie? You were right, and I was so bleeding wrong. B was just trying to help, and when she told me about the breakdown of her relationship, I could tell she just wanted what was best for us."

"She told you about that?"

"Yes, she told me how hard, things were and how it hurt her and the boys. I get it now Mack, I get the dysfunctional behavior, the overprotectiveness. I get the Black and White. I see how broken she is and why you feel the need to protect her. Mackie, the way she sees the world now is heartbreaking."

Mack gazed at her, stunned by her words.

"What is it?" she asked

"Ari, I've never been told that story. I just assumed her ex-husband hurt her. B's never spoken about it before."

Ari stared at Mack, confused, "Well, maybe it's a woman thing?"

He rubbed his chin, appearing astonished. "Maybe, or maybe you've cracked the stone that encases her heart. Ari, this is huge, baby."

Ari, feeling even more proud of herself, looked at Mack with sincerity in her eyes. "We have to help her, Mackie, even if she hates us for it. Nobody should live how she does, it's dark and dangerous. I saw the expression in her eyes today and it wasn't psychotic dragon fire red. Her eyes were desolate, almost desperate looking, and I felt so sorry for her. We have to help her open up her heart again."

"Oh sweetheart, you're suggesting that we try to tame the dragon and I'm not sure that's possible," he said, as he rubbed her cheek, smiling at her.

"Well, I tamed you, didn't I?" she teased.

Mack burst out laughing. "Tamed me? No, with B I was tame. You did the opposite. You wound me up and let me go, baby. You made me dance in your hurricane of crazy, and it damn near destroyed me."

"Yes, but look at the man that you've become. When I met you, you were as dysfunctional as B is. It's no wonder you are both tethered. You've spoken in the same tongue for years. I forced you to open your heart, and maybe I can do the same for her."

A grin spread over his face. "Darling, I'm so proud of you! You are finally seeing the wood from the trees. This is what I've been trying to tell you. Can you see now she's no threat to our relationship anymore? I don't look at her how I look at you. It's only you!"

Ari nodded. "Thank you, Mackie. Thank you for fighting for me, thank you for loving me, giving me my family, our white picket fence, and my happy ending. I love you!"

A sense of contentment filled her as he covered her mouth with his, massaging her tongue with his, sending ripples of pleasure down Ari's spine.

"Ari, it's me that should thank you, sweetheart. You broke me from the spell I was under. I was blind, and you forced me to see. I was hurt, and you healed me. You gave me everything, baby, and I want to spend the rest of my life giving everything to you."

"And what about B?"

Mack ran his fingers through his hair. "I suggest we concentrate on ourselves for a little while. Maybe concentrate on growing baby Alexander and let the dragon get used to having you around. She may be broken, but that makes her more dangerous than ever, and if you play with fire baby, you're going to get burned. Let's have our happy ending now, like we planned, and leave my dragon to find her own path."

"Okay Mack, whatever you want. But Alexander?"

"Yeah! I want to name him after Zander. As much as we fight and he's a pain in the ass, he saved yours and Junior's life and truth be told, I've always loved the name,"

"I like it. He saved me too, you know, but what if we have a girl? And if you say Dragon, I'll castrate you!"

Mack laughed. "No baby. We'll call her Alexandra Blethen. It's clear we owe B and that Scottish prick, and they'll like this!"

"If that's what you want,"

"I do. This is our happy ending, baby and it's all I've wanted since the day we met!"

Baby Alexandra Blethen was born on the twelfth of December, weighing a healthy 7lb 8oz, and everyone was besotted with her. Mack showed her off as he crowned her as the first Gray Wolves man-cub and predicted that when she was older, she would be every bit as formidable as the two people they had named her after. Ari and Mack were in love with her, and Junior and Remy became over-protective big brothers, eyeballing anyone who went near her.

B had become the proud aunt they had hoped she would be, taking every opportunity to cwtch up with the beautiful blond-haired, blue-eyed baby. Mack and Ari witnessed the walls surrounding her heart crack a little every time she held her

Goddaughter. B even became a house maid to them of sorts as they would come to her cabin every day for their meals, and she would have all the children stay at her cabin to give Mack and Ari some much needed alone time. With B's help, Mack and Ari got their happily ever after in Uskiville. They were in love, had a beautiful family and a dragon who would die for them.

Epilogue

Six months had passed by since Noah had seen his old friend and Prez. He rode into Uskiville solo, much to the distaste of Zander, Jimmy, and Stevie the roadie, who left him on the outskirts of town. Noah wanted to confront Mack alone regarding breaking his promise to help his club.

He arrived at Uskiville late in the afternoon, enjoying the cool breeze in his face as he rode through the quaint town. Upon arrival to the retreat, he wasn't sure where to go, so he rode around the perimeter, until he saw Mack emerge from the on-site bar and pulled up alongside him.

"Mother fucker!" he shouted as he climbed off his bike, tossing his helmet on the grass to embrace his dear friend.

"Hey, hey, it's grand to see you, Prez! What are you doing here?" Mack asked, looking surprised to see him.

"We're in financial trouble, and I know you said to wait, but we just can't anymore. I have to meet the dragon, Mack, and as a show of good faith, I came into town alone to protect her identity.".

"I appreciate that, Noah, especially as I know the Scottish prick, would love a taste of her."

297

Noah snorted. "Yeah, he hasn't shut up about her since seeing that picture of her in your cabin before we left last time."

Mack grimaced. "I swear, Noah, if he goes near her, our alliance is over."

"Calm down, Prez. He's not going near her. Why do you think I left him on the outskirts of town? They'll head back until I'm ready to ride out again."

Mack's face softened. "Right, okay. Let's get you set up at her cabin. Mine's a mess since Ari and the kids moved in and the baby arrived. No more wandering around my cabin in my undies!" he joked. "But don't worry, the dragon will look after you, besides we all practically live at hers and she's the best cook, believe it or not!"

Arriving at B's, they walked up the steps to her big cabin and Noah remembered how nice it was as he approached the porch, recalling the events of that dark night.

Upon entry, a fine breeze flurried throughout the cabin. B must have been feeling the heat, as most of the windows were open. It was quiet, but there were noises echoing from the back garden, so the fellas headed toward them. Mack led Noah through the double doors at the back of the cabin to find four teenagers splashing about the pool with baby Alexandra asleep in her pram. Ari and B were lying on sun loungers catching the sun, both in bikinis looking sun kissed. They were too busy talking to notice Mack and Noah's arrival.

Noah glanced at B, almost salivating, as he failed to take his eyes off her. "That's your dragon?"

"Yeah, and don't even fecking think about it, small fry. Besides, I've seen her almost kill men your size in the bedroom," he joked, before interrupting the two women. "What are you two gassing about now?"

"Oh, hey, honey! I didn't know you were home." Ari beamed as she darted off the sun lounger to kiss him.

"Will you sort this bloody woman of yours out?" B slammed. "She's doing it again, and I promise you, I will lose my shit if I come home from work tomorrow night to find another man at my door!"

Mack's eyes narrowed, and his brow furrowed as he looked at Ari.

"Don't you look at me like that MacIntyre Kelly! She needs a good man, and she won't find one hooking up with random guys for casual sex!"

B gave Ari a look that could kill. "Oh! Keep your bloody noise down! I don't want my boys thinking their mother's a slag, and who I sleep with and what I do with my body is bloody nothing to do with you!"

"Well, I think it's reckless!" Ari said in a matter-of-fact tone.

"I don't give a toss what you think, my lovely. Now do me a favor and stay out of my business. And Mackie, I'm fucking warning you, if she tries to set me up with one more fucking bloke, I am taking it out on you! So put her back in her box and make her stay there!" B said with a hint of frustration in her voice.

"Jesus, why do I get the shit? Ari, I've told you. You can't come along trying to change her. This past year, you've driven her bat shit crazy, and I get it in the neck because she won't hit a woman. Have you not learned anything after she broke my nose and almost killed you last time?"

Ari grinned. "Nope!"

"Well, you should, because she just takes it out on me. So, if you love me, for the love of God, leave her be," Mack said in exasperation!

Ari glanced over her shoulder at B. "It's only because I love you like a sister, and I want you to be as happy as Mack and I."

B shook her head before turning and looking Noah up and down, watching him squirm as she eye-balled him. "So, who's the pretty boy?"

Noah's eyes lit up; he found her brassiness charming. Trying not to drool over her, he extended his arm to shake her hand. "Noah! Mack's oldest and dearest friend. Pleased to meet you, ma'am."

B raised an eyebrow and shot a look at Mack. "If that's true, then why did I have to pull him off the streets when his life was torn apart and why have I not met you before?"

B was still annoyed his friends hadn't been there for him when he needed them. Not to mention that they hadn't visited Uskiville once in the time that B had known Mack. B didn't trust, and this past year she had seen a lot of change with Mack's new family. She liked Ari in small doses and loved baby Blethen and the boys who got on great with her boys. But everything was changing for B, and she didn't like it.

"B, Noah is one of the guys that saved Ari's life when she came looking for me! He couldn't come beforehand because his uncle would have killed him! So, give him a break, please?"

B nodded. "Fair enough!" she said, before walking toward the cabin. She turned, looking back at Mack, "I take it he's staying with me then?"

"Is that okay?" he asked like a frightened puppy, making Noah's jaw drop in shock at the fact that his Prez seemed scared of a curvy blonde.

"Well, we can't leave him out in the cold, can we? Besides, with that pretty little face, he won't last two minutes," she said, sounding a little humorous. "Come on, pretty boy! Let's get you sorted!"

Noah looked at Mack, a little shocked, before following B with his knapsack strapped to his back. She showed him to one of her many spare rooms and let him get settled in. Once he emerged from his room after his shower, he entered the open living space to find B cooking with Mack hovering over her shoulder. They were both bickering over the spices B was adding to her dish and Ari was lying on the sofa with her feet up, oblivious to it all, reading a magazine. The kids were nowhere to be seen!

Noah approached Ari. "Geez, anyone would think those two were a couple the way they act."

Ari didn't look up from her magazine. "Honestly, they bicker like brother and sister. It's constant, and it drives me mad. But I learned early on, I had to accept it because they wouldn't be without each other! I think Mack suffocates her a little, though."

Noah turned to study them. "Well, he certainly listens to her! I've never known him to be so compliant with a woman."

"It's anything for the quiet life with Mack, besides she's...his dragon!"

"I just can't believe that beautiful woman is his fearless dragon."

Ari smirked. "Don't let her blonde hair and perfect figure fool you, Noah. That woman is more dangerous than you can ever imagine and talk about unpredictable!"

Noah looked at her and looked back at Ari, whose eyes widened and nodded. "You'll see her before the weekend's out. Mark my words!" she said before delving back into her magazine.

"And what about you?" he pressed. "Setting her up on dates she doesn't want to go on. A little dangerous, isn't it?"

"B doesn't do anything she doesn't want to, and I'm just trying to make her see she should want to settle down! She won't look beautiful forever. besides, she won't hit a woman."

Noah shook his head at her. "Ari, you need to stop meddling and let her live her life. If she doesn't want to settle down and wants to fuck the whole of Uskiville, that's up to her. It's her life, not yours! Zander is just the same! He's not interested in settling down, he doesn't do feelings or that mushy crap, he likes to fuck and that's it, and there's nothing wrong with B being the same."

"Noah, I'm just trying to stop her from being so dysfunctional and help her be more human. I absolutely love snuggling up to Mack at the end of a long day. It's serendipitous, and she could have that too if she just gave someone a chance."

Noah ruffled his hair, almost defensive of B now. "Well, maybe that's not for B! I take it she's tried, given the fact that she's had two kids. With the same guy?"

"Yes, she was married for years until her husband had an affair and she divorced him, but that was years ago!"

Noah gave Ari a cheesy grin. "Well, if I'd been with one person for years and became single again, I would be fucking everything that moved. As Zander says, 'variety is the spice of life pal.'" He fell silent, leaving her to her magazine as he went to catch up with Mack and B.

After dinner, everyone cleared their plates and headed onto B's deck with a bottle of the good stuff. Noah enjoyed getting to know B and soon realized that she was quite funny and had an extremely quirky side to her! They all spent the entire evening drinking and sharing anecdotes, and Noah couldn't believe how calm things were at the woodland retreat.

Ari and Mack were so wrapped up in each other, but Noah would often catch Mack studying B. That was, until Mack noticed him doing so. Noah simply smirked as if to say, "I see what you're doing mate and it's a dangerous game you're playing!" But Mack didn't seem to care, and B was oblivious to it as she chatted away to her boys.

Noah found himself enjoying B's company. They had a lot in common. They had similar ideologies about business, and B even gave him some advice and offered to help him get his bar out of trouble, with a little encouragement by Mack.

At nearly midnight, the women retreated for the night, leaving Mack and Noah to it. They drank and reminisced about past times until Noah plucked up the courage to question Mack about B.

Grinning at Mack, he asked. "So, what's the deal with you and B, now that you've kissed and made up?"

Mack raised an eyebrow and sat back in his chair. "What do you mean?"

"Cut the crap. I see the way you look at her and both women are totally oblivious!"

Mack sighed and took another sip of his whisky. "And that's the way it's gonna stay!"

Noah could see the hurt in Mack's eyes at the mention of B. It was as if he was nursing his broken heart. "Sorry, Mack."

Mack pressed his lips together and shook his head. "Don't be. Only I can be besotted with two women. I love Ari, and B and I will never be, so I have to live with that."

"I bet it's difficult, though, man."

"Nope. You know my dragon is a big deal around here. I mean big!" Mack continued, changing the subject. "She's a high school soccer coach who makes some serious money. She also sold a string of gyms for a ridiculous profit, before she left the UK, so let me tell you, brother, she is one hell of a businesswoman.

"I can see that, Mack."

"Her only downfall is that she sees the world in black and white, hence why I am glad that you came here alone. She doesn't agree with my old life, as she is white, and people like you and I are black."

"Have you ever told her how you feel, Mack?"

Mack laughed. "Uh, yeah! A few months after we met. She had just gifted me with the keys to my cabin and I told her. I couldn't keep it in any longer!" he said, shaking his head and pouring himself another glass.

"What did she say?"

"She told me she didn't feel the same, and I needed to can it if I wanted to be in business with her. It fucking destroyed me! I thought I had a shot with her, but she doesn't want anyone. She's spent the last six years oblivious to me not getting over her. I honestly think she's switched off, so she can't feel anything. She's numb when it comes to relationships and whenever she goes out to get laid, a little piece of me fucking dies. But she can never know I'm in love with her because it would destroy us!"

"Shit! Man! I'm sorry! Does Ari know any of this?"

Mack wiped a stray tear from his eye. "She knows I was in love with her, and she knows B's not interested in me, and that's enough for her! I was honest from the start. Ari knows I love her and would never hurt her! So, this is my cross to bear, Noah. Some things just aren't meant to be!"

"And here's me thinking you have the whole world in your hands!"

"Oh, I'm a lucky guy. I have everything that I need in life right here on this idyllic little plot of ours, and I'll never ruin it or hurt either of my girls."

"That's a little messed up, but I understand. But what's the deal with keeping her hidden? I get Blaze is still out there, but we've got your back."

"I've still got plenty of enemies from Ari's list and as far as everyone external is concerned, she's just a soccer coach. See, this town is like the town that land forgot, and it's only known for B's success as a coach! So as long as everyone sees her as a coach, that's all that matters. She can't be seen mixing with criminals. Her coaching career would be compromised, and I won't do that to her." He shrugged. "So, when anyone asks me about the business, I just tell them it's funded by my dragon. It puts the fear of God into them, keeping them away and it keeps her safe! She hates it, of course. She thinks I'm paranoid. but she knows nothing about Ari and the list. We told her you saved Ari from your uncle and took over the business after he died of a heart attack."

"But Mack, you're painting a target on her back. Your enemies know, if they want to get to you, they need to find the dragon. What happens if they turn up one day and find that it's B?"

Mack looked serious for a moment. "Then they'd better fucking pray for mercy because she is the scariest mother fucker I have ever encountered. Yes, she looks all sweet and innocent, but believe me when I tell you. Get on the wrong side of her and she will tear you apart. See, when someone is emotionally dysfunctional like B, only seeing black and white, they have no fear, and that my brother makes her dangerous!"

"I hear you, man! You know, she reminds me of Zander, like a lot! They share the same cold outlook on life."

Mack shrugged. "Yeah, I suppose so!"

Noah snorted. "Mack, she is literally a female version of him!"

"Feck off!

"What? She is!"

"No! My dragon is classy! Besides, as cold as she is, she has a big fecking heart. She idolizes her boys and everything she does is for them, and I mean everything. Let me tell you something. If B accepts you, you're lucky, because then she will fight to the death for you! She is a complex and powerful woman!"

"So, she is a real dragon?" Noah joked.

"Absolutely. You'll get a glimpse of that part of her in the morning when you join us for a grapple."

Noah looked confused. "I'm not grappling with a woman; I'll bloody kill her!"

Mack regarded him with amusement. "We'll see, my friend. We'll see!"

The next morning, B was already at the gym when Mack and Noah arrived. She was finishing up a weightlifting session with Frankie.

Mack greeted them with a look of amusement on his face. "Hey! You ready?"

"Yeah, just getting a shake!" B shouted over as she dived in the fridge to retrieve one before heading to the mats!

They paired off, with Mack grappling with Noah first and B with Frankie. They did five-minute rounds, and all took turns to grapple with each other. It was the last round and B was paired up with Noah. Noah didn't like the idea of grappling with a woman because he thought he would hurt her!

B glowered at him with a twinkle in her eye. "Come on then, pretty boy! Let's be having you!"

A flash of concern flashed over Noah's face. "I don't want to hurt you, so if we do this, promise me you'll tap as soon as things get rough?"

B looked at Frankie and Mack, who were trying not to kill themselves laughing. B raised an eyebrow and couldn't help but curve her lips into a smile.

"Okay, let's go!" she said and offered him a fist bump to start the grapple.

Noah responded and both Frankie and Mack watched how B

instantly arm dragged him, placing him in a perfect choke hold, so he had no choice to tap.

Gasping for air, Noah stared at Mack and Frankie, who were hysterical at the sight of Noah's face and Noah requested a rematch. They started again, only this time, B had him in an arm bar.

"Again!" Noah demanded, only to be schooled by B round after round, and after about the fifth submission, he conceded. Sitting back on his heels, grinning, and shaking his head, he beamed at B.

"Geez! You are a dragon!"

B laughed. "Well, I am Welsh!"

Noah stared at her. "You know, my VP would love to put his mark on you!"

Only to see Mack's face turn from laughter to an evil snarl. "Over my dead body!"

THE END

Printed in Great Britain
by Amazon